THE WINGS
OF PEGASUS

THE DRAGONRIDERS OF PERN®

The author respectfully suggests that books in the Pern series be read in the order in which they were published. Which is:

Dragonflight	*The Renegades of Pern*
Dragonquest	
The White Dragon	*Dragonsong*
Moreta: Dragonlady of Pern	*Dragonsinger*
Nerilka's Story	*Dragondrums*
Dragonsdawn	

THE ATLAS OF PERN by Karen Wynn Fonstadt and THE DRAGONLOVER'S GUIDE TO PERN by Jody-Lynn Nye with Ann McCaffrey both provide additional interesting information as companion texts to the main novels.

THE WINGS OF PEGASUS

TO RIDE PEGASUS
PEGASUS IN FLIGHT

ANNE MCCAFFREY

Published by arrangement with
Del Ray/Ballantine Books
201 East 50th Street
New York, New York 10022

Printed in the United States of America

CONTENTS

CONTENTS

TO RIDE PEGASUS

This Book is
respectfully dedicated to
Betty Ballantine,
a woman of many talents.

CONTENTS

CONTENTS

PART ONE

TO RIDE
PEGASUS

PART ONE

TO RIDE
PEGASUS

The slick pavement, oily with rain and motor lubricants that had dripped from the hundreds of ill-repaired vehicles utilizing the major north-south artery into Jerhattan, caused the accident. Henry Darrow had not been exceeding the speed limit when he passed the old two-seater. But he had a date with destiny. And kept it on time.

Had there been no rain that day, or had the lane been closed as scheduled for resurfacing, or had the old two-seater maintained the minimum speed in the left-hand lane, Henry Darrow would not have been exasperated enough to pass, would not have skidded on the slick paving, would not have crashed into the guard rail, would not have fractured his skull so that a bone fragment pressed against the brain pan; had the accident occurred even half a mile further up the arterial road, Henry Darrow would not have been sent to the one hospital in the area equipped with a special electroencephalograph.

As things came to pass, this was how his accident was to occur: exactly how. In fact, he had jotted down the exact time in his astral notebook: 10:02:50 post meridian. He had also reminded himself that day not to take the arterial route back into Jerhattan but he had not foreseen one slight delay at the gasoline station which caused him to change his mind and take the fateful route, forgetful of his own prognostication.

Of course, since it was a major turning for him as well as millions of other people, he could never have avoided the accident. Which is why his subconscious—or so it is maintained—prevented him from remembering his forecast at the critical moment.

Henry Darrow was therefore injured, seriously, with minor

fractures in the left leg as well as the depressed fragment of skull bone. Had Henry been fully conscious during surgery, he would have assured the surgeons that, despite the severity of the wound, he would live. They would have been dubious. Henry Darrow *knew* when he was going to die—from myocardial infarction, some fifteen years, four months, and nine days in the future.

He couldn't tell them since the cranial pressure affected his speech center and he was mercifully unaware of his surroundings. Brain surgery can be a harrowing experience.

The operation was technically successful and Henry was assigned a bed in the intensive care ward, cardiac and encephalographic monitors keeping close track of his vital systems. The Southside General Hospital boasted the very latest technology, including one of the ultra-sensitive electroencephalographs, familiarly known as "Gooseggs." The Goosegg equipment was developed during the Apollo flights in the 70s, to monitor the effects of the mysterious "lights," which periodically afflicted the astronauts, and to record any suspected damage by cosmic radiation to the brain tissue. The ultra sensitive equipment was primarily used now in hospitals to detect brain damage to newborn infants suffering oxygen starvation during birth, or, as in Henry Darrow's case, brain injuries where similar oxygen deprivation, bleeding, and pressure must be ascertained.

The intensive care nurse on duty when Darrow regained his sense after surgery was, as Destiny preordained, Molly Mahony, a rather plain girl who good-naturedly bore a lot of teasing from her colleagues for her avowed dedication to nursing. She was invariably assigned the critical cases because she had a knack of pulling them through the crises.

"Dr. Scherman, would you look at the print-out on Mr. Darrow's EEG?" she said when the resident checked in at her station. "The alphas are unusually strong for a man as critically injured as he, aren't they?"

Scherman looked obediently at the graphs, nodded sagely and then gave her a wink. "He been conscious at all? Giving you a line?"

Molly shook her head, very serious though she knew he was teasing her. Scherman always did. "He's not regained consciousness, Dr. Scherman. I'm to notify Dr. Wahlman when he does. But should I give him a ring about these readings?"

"Ah, don't bother, Molly. That one's lucky he can print anything out on the Goosegg. You'd've thought he'd've known better."

"Better? About what? He was an accident casualty, wasn't he?"

"Better about going out at all. He's Henry Darrow, the astrologer. Christ, it costs a fortune to consult him about your future." Scherman snorted. "And he couldn't cast his own properly."

Scherman left after a cursory glance at the other i.c. patients. Molly Mahony looked with renewed interest at the brain injury. She knew of Henry Darrow, though she wouldn't have admitted it to many. No more than she would have admitted to anyone that she felt she had the gift of healing. Unlike her grandmother who'd had no medical background and ran into problems with her "healing hands," Molly had professional cachet and knew best how and when to apply her "whammy."

Having a unique talent, Molly was keenly interested in all the paranormal manifestations. In her lexicon, the astrologist merely used the signs of the zodiac to focus a precognitive gift, one fortunately more scientifically based than tea-leaf reading or card-telling. Just as the nursing profession allowed her to focus her healing talent on a scientific basis. So she knew of Henry Darrow and now tiptoed, like an awed sycophant, to the bedside and stared down at a face she hadn't noticed before.

His face had character even in lax-jawed abnormal coma. The eye-sockets were black and blue pits, and here and there a trace of blood had escaped the emergency clean-up. It was unfair of her to look at him in such a condition. She laid the back of her hand gently against his cheek, not liking the color of his skin. She flicked back the sheet, took a fold of the pectoral skin, and gave it a brutal twist. Well, at least he had reactions. She patted the sheet into place and stroked his cheek again.

The cardiograph pulsed slow but regular, though there were traces in the reading that spelled the beginnings of arteriosclerosis. No more than would be apparent in any reading of a forty-two-year-old heart which had lived well and hard.

Now she placed strong, slender fingers on his temples, pressing lightly, trying to "feel" where the real injury was. Not that which the surgeons had corrected when they removed the splinter and released the pressure on the brain. But the psychic injury, the essential blow to the vitalities of the man, which had been shocked

by the proximity of death, by the exigency of the operation—that
ultimate violation of personal integrity.

So often in her reading of case histories, she'd seen the simple
term "heart failure," or the more complex medical annotation of
heart stoppage for a variety of physically inexplicable and unnecessary reasons. Shock, they would term it for lack of better explanation, "the patient died of shock." Fright, Molly called it. When a
patient of hers retreated from reality in this sort of fright, Molly
would draw that violated integrity back again with her Talent.

The response to her healing touch on Henry Darrow's brow was
different and puzzling. The cardiogram etched bolder, stronger
peaks and the Goosegg made frantic passes on all four recording
bands.

Henry Darrow's eyelids flickered, opened, and a faint smile
crossed his lips.

"What the hell hit me?" he asked.

"You hit you," Molly replied, "on the center post of your car
when you crashed into the guard rails, Mr. Darrow. Head ache?"

"Christ yes!" He moaned and tried to reach upward.

"Don't. You've suffered a severe concussion, head lacerations,
your left leg is fractured . . ."

There was mischief in the clear green eyes that met Molly's.
"You're not supposed to tell me such things, are you?"

Molly smiled. "You know anyhow. And you really ought to pay
more attention to your own predictions, Mr. Darrow."

The Goosegg chattered crazily and Molly whirled to see what
was happening. But Henry Darrow was grabbing her arm, his eyes
widening with bewildered surprise and incredulity.

"You're a Gemini. What's your name? You're going to marry
me."

L ove at first sight is a rare enough incident, particularly in a
hospital setting, despite what the romances say. But far rarer
was the scientific accident that proved a long suspected truth. For
what had registered on the Goosegg's chart was indisputable proof
that the parapsychic talent exists. Henry Darrow had a precognitive experience when he looked at Molly Mahony as a person, not
just the nurse in attendance, and "knew" she would be his wife.

They did marry, as soon as his leg was out of the cast. Marriage was not the only thing Henry foresaw for Molly: he knew, too, her date of death, a fact he never disclosed to her. Talents, he learned very shortly, had to discount such precogs in their own lives if they were to operate efficiently for others. Molly was treasured, loved and cherished all the days of her life by her husband because he knew how little of her time he would enjoy.

The significance of the Goosegg's remarkable activity did not immediately impinge on Henry's awareness. To Molly Mahony belongs all the credit, therefore, for lifting the parapsychic function from the realm of chicanery to science.

For starters, Molly was fascinated with the unusual strength and pattern of Henry's EEG charts. She couldn't dismiss, as Dr. Scherman had, the variations. In her favor was a natural inclination to place Henry Darrow's mind into an exceptional category. Added to that, she knew Henry'd had the precognition of their marriage at the precise moment the Goosegg went wild. At the very first opportunity she tried an empiric experiment. She attached the electrodes to her own skull the next time she had occasion to exert her own ability in the intensive care ward. A similar variation occurred in her reading; not as intense as Henry's, but significant. She took several more of herself, and copied those portions of Henry's records which showed this curious excitation.

She was rather surprised that Dr. Wahlman, Henry's surgeon, did not cancel the Goosegg monitoring when Henry appeared to have recovered from the worst of the concussion. She wondered if Wahlman was as interested in the EEG variation as she was.

Henry had two more precognitive incidents before she felt she could approach Dr. Wahlman with her private conclusions.

"For my own information, Dr. Wahlman, what is the significance of this activity in an EEG?"

"Well, now," said Wahlman, taking the graphs diffidently and studying them in a manner which told Molly that he hadn't a clue. "To be frank, Mahony, I don't know. This particular sort of printout usually occurs just prior to death. And Darrow's very much alive." The surgeon looked towards Henry's closed door with some irritation. Henry had insisted on pursuing his avocation of charting horoscopes, had even imported his computer, embarking on a cerebral activity which apparently had no deleterious effects on his rapid recovery but did not strike Wahlman as exactly the sort of occupation suitable to a man recovering from a near-fatal head injury.

"And these?" Molly showed him her own graphs.

"Whose are these? A terminal reading? No, couldn't be. The alpha's too intense. What are you up to, Mahony?"

"I'm not certain, doctor, but I do know that when Mr. Darrow is . . . hardest at work, that's when this sort of variation occurs."

"Jasus help us, the damned Goosegg's queer for astrology?"

Molly smiled and apologized for bothering the surgeon with anomalies.

"Mahony, if you weren't the best post-operative nurse we have, I'd tell you to bug off. But if you have any idea, any unreasonable idea, why that kind of reading occurs, would you please let me in on the secret?"

She let Henry in first.

"The moment you woke up after your accident and asked was I Gemini and then said I was going to marry you, was that a precog?"

"Fact, my love—fact!"

"No, Henry, stop that now. Later. Answer me. Was your precognitive faculty at work?"

"Violently." The modified bandage on his head gave him a slightly rakish look but he stopped caressing her, responding to her serious mood.

"And, for instance, when Mrs. Rellahan was here, you told me that you had an intense prevision . . ."

"Hmmmm." Henry's mouth tightened slightly with dislike.

"This is what the Goosegg printed out. See, here the rapid needle, strong strokes, the length of the pattern . . . And, in these . . ."

"That's not my pattern, too, is it? Quite a difference."

"No, that's my brain waves. And this is what happens when I'm healing."

Henry looked slowly up at Molly, an incredulous joy brightening his eyes, a light suffusing his face that rewarded Molly for her efforts and intuition.

"Molly, my own heart's darling, do you know what we have here?"

The world in general remained skeptical. Fortunately Henry Darrow cared very little for the world's thoughts but he was able to produce proof to a powerful, wealthy few that the parapsychic faculty existed in certain individuals and could be manifested at will.

A whole new line of research was instigated by those private persons and concerns which had long hoped for scientific recognition of the paranormal abilities.

"I've always had a presentiment of Destiny, of being on the threshold of some vast important breakthrough," Henry told Molly during the early hectic days shortly before they formed the first Parapsychic Center. "Most megalomaniacs do, too, and your psychotic paranoids like Nero, Napoleon, Hitler and Kyudu. That's why I had that team of psychiatrists examine my mental health with fine Freudian tongs. Nonetheless it's a prejudicial admission. D'you know, I've been afraid to forecast my own future too far in advance now? Some details are unwise for any man to know . . ." He looked with unfocused eyes at the blank wall in front of them for a moment before he smiled reassuringly at her. "I've been a dilettante up till now and my critics can say either that I gained my wits in that accident, or lost the few I had, but *that* event was the threshold of my . . . of our destiny."

"Damn the torpedoes and full steam ahead," Molly replied, gesturing theatrically.

"And torpedoes there will be," Henry agreed grimly.

"I thought you said you didn't see far in advance . . ."

"For myself, I meant. Not for what we must do." He was silent again for a moment. "God, it's going to be fun."

Molly looked at the amusement in his eyes, the anticipatory gleam of malice. "For whom?" she asked.

His eyes sparkled as he turned his gaze back to her.

"For us," he said, hugging her affectionately, "for all of us," and he meant the newly recruited Talents. "We may perceive the outcome, but half the fun, most of the fun in life, is getting there. And I've got just enough time."

As soon as he was sufficiently recovered to argue with his surgeons (and because Molly assured Wahlman that Henry couldn't get around *her* vigilance), he was allowed to go back to work full time. Not, as previously, in his capacity as a dilettante astrologer, but as the manager, organizer, fund-raiser, and recruiter par excellence for the Parapsychic Center.

"Mary-Molly luv, it's going to be accomplished in steps, this establishment of the Talented in the scheme of things. Not society, mind you, for we're the original nonconformists," and he tapped his forehead just below the pink flesh of the newly healed head wound. "And Society will never permit us to integrate. That's okay!" He consigned Society to insignificance with a flick of his fingers. "The Talented form their own society and that's as it should be: birds of a feather. No, not birds. Winged horses! Ha! Yes, indeed. Pegasus . . . the poetic winged horse of flights of fancy. A bloody good symbol for us. You'd see a lot from the back of a winged horse . . ."

"Yes, an airplane has blind spots. Where would you put a saddle?" Molly had her practical side.

He laughed and hugged her. Henry's frequent demonstrations of affection were a source of great delight to Molly, whose own strength was in tactile contacts.

"Don't know. Lord, how would you bridle a winged horse?"

"With the heart?"

"Indubitably!" The notion pleased him. "Yes, with the heart and the head because Pegasus is too strong a steed to control or subdue by any ordinary method."

"You couldn't break our sort of Pegasus anyhow," Molly said firmly. "Wouldn't want to even when he flies so high . . ." She burrowed into Henry's arms, suddenly frightened by the analogy.

"Yes, luv. When you ride the winged horse, you can't dismount. Anymore than you can suppress the Talent you've been given. We'll find our bridle, I think, with time and training and more practice at riding.

"That Goosegg was the really important break. Now we can prove parapsychic powers exist and who has them. We can discredit the charlatans and clowns who've given the rest of us a bad name. The real Talents will be registered with the Center, and we'll have graphs to prove they've had valid Incidents. The Center will supply them with the specialized jobs that utilize their Talents. From just a sampling of validly Talented people we've already attracted, I can think of hundreds of top jobs."

"Even Titter Beyley and Charity McGillicuddy?" Molly

Mahony Darrow's eyes danced with mischief because Titter drank
continuously and Charity pursued an old profession diligently.

"Takes a thief to catch a thief and Titter's been stealing for years
to support his habit. Remember that Charity's heart of gold beats
in a true telepath's breast."

"Size 42-C."

"Molly!"

"Go on with our future, Henry."

"I want Watson Claire as our PR man because I know damned
well he's a receiving telepath: he must be to handle clients the way
he does. He's got a positive genius for presenting *the* campaign a
client'll buy. Claire's the sort of person we've got to enlist, for his
sake as well as ours. Ours, because we've got the biggest goddamn
public relations program on our hands, and the public can make or
break us. His sake, because he's not happy pushing products he
despises."

Molly nodded sympathetically.

"We get an intensive information program going and that will
help recruiting. Then we've got to start rescue operations for those
hidden Talents and especially those poor misfits in institutions because they heard voices . . . which they did . . . or they imag-
ined impossible things, which they didn't. Or their empathy with
the world around them was too great to be endured and they abandoned reality. And we've got to figure out the best way to train
these Talents once we've got them verified.

"*Then* we've got to get exactly the right place to live in."

"To live? But this apartment is . . ."

"Okay for us, for the time being. But not for the rest of us. No,
now don't worry, Molly luv. I know where we're going."

Molly regarded him steadily for a second. "But you don't know
exactly how we'll get there, is that it?"

Henry laughed, nodding.

"That's the challenge, luv."

"And then what's on the agenda? I'd better know the worst."

Henry chuckled to give himself time to evade. "Then comes one
of the harder jobs . . ."

Molly's eyes grew round. "You've outlined a lifetime's work and
then tell me one of the harder jobs . . ."

"Will be to establish professional immunity for the Talents so
we don't get sued out of our eyeball sockets because we said some-

thing would happen which didn't because we said it would. Oh, we'll get it sooner or later, but I'd rather sooner than later when you consider the money that'll be tied up in suits. But that won't be my headache."

"It won't be?"

"I can't live forever, luv."

She clung to him and he gave her only a quick embrace.

"I'll live long enough, Mary-Molly luv, and so will you." He put her away from him then, for he had to keep his desire in check with the pressures of his destiny.

N ow, gentlemen, the subject all wired up to the electroencephalograph, familiarly known as the Goosegg, is a telekinetic Talent. That means, gentlemen, that he can move objects without any other agency than his mind. Ralph, would you be good enough to demonstrate?"

Ralph, who used to be known as Rat Wilson, was not the most prepossessing of individuals, being skinny to the point of emaciation, with a rodent-like face and a mouth that remained slightly open due to untended tonsils and adenoids; but his rather large grey eyes were dancing with mischief and interest. That he had perfected his art in the variety of correctional institutions which had attempted to remold him to society's requirements was irrelevant—now.

He sat under the electrode net of the Goosegg at one end of a large hall, a camcorder throwing a picture of the print-out on the big screen above him. Forty-seven scientists and businessmen were seated around the room, in the center of which sat a table with a variety of objects: a hammer, nails and a plank of wood; a coffee tray with an urn, cups, cream and sugar; a guitar; and a training set of waldoes, limp and grotesque without hands to fill the gloves.

Henry Darrow walked to the other end of the room, as far from both Ralph and the table as possible.

There was a significant silence in the room, with the audience casting glances from table to Ralph to Henry. Suddenly a cup rattled, rose, was joined to a saucer and aligned itself under the spout of the urn which was tapped almost simultaneously to pour coffee into the cup. Belatedly, a spoon clattered into the saucer.

"Who takes it black?" asked Ralph as cup and saucer veered to the nearest watcher.

"I do," said one cool businessman, lifting his hand.

"Hang on to it then, mac," replied Ralph. "Got it?"

"Hey!" The man closed his fingers around the lip of the saucer but when Ralph released it, he was unprepared and the black coffee sloshed over the saucer rim onto his hand.

There was a slight wave of amusement, shattered by the crash of a hammer driving a nail into a block of wood.

"I'll make the next one white. Who's for it?"

A second cup was delivered to its receiver as the hammer drove the nail smartly into the wood. At the same time, the waldoes jerked alive and began to assemble the objects in the tray. The guitar twanged with a bawdy ballad.

With cups sailing around the room, the crack of the hammer to the tempo of the song, the industry of the waldoes leaving everyone gaping, Henry returned to the stage, taking a pointer and starting the sales pitch.

"As you will notice, if you can take your eyes from the flying saucers, Ralph's use of his Talent results in the hard variations of the alpha waves, here and here. The beta fluctuation is rapid, deep. Note the difference at the beginning of the graph before Ralph started. Notice the increase as he stepped up the output of the parapsychic faculty. Has anyone any doubts about the authenticity of this demonstration? Will you accept this print-out as valid, and that the graph represents Ralph's paranormal ability?"

"Stop him!"

Henry signalled to Ralph and coffee cups crashed to the floor. The hammer bounced and fell to the table and the waldoes went limp to a discordant twang on the guitar.

"For chrissake," and the man on whom a cup of coffee had fallen sprang to his feet, wiping at soaked pants and dancing from the hot bath. Instantly the cup righted itself and incredibly refilled with the just-emptied coffee.

"Sorry about that, mac, but someone said stop!"

The abrupt surcease of the parapsychic was recorded on the graph, as was the minor activity of mopping up the spill.

"Hey, my pants are dry!"

"Are there any other questions?" asked Henry, winking surreptitiously to the grinning Ralph.

"Yes," and a heavy set man towards the rear of the room stood slowly to his feet. "Coffee vending machines handle this sort of service, an idiot can drive a nail; granted a waldo is used for delicate sterile operations, any rock musician plays electric guitar . . . not all at once, admittedly, but how would someone like Ralph be employed? And incidentally, I know his background."

"You might say," Henry said with a smile, "that Ralph is a real product of his background of reform school and correctional institution. That's how he acquired his Talent. Society wasn't ready for Ralph or his Talent. We are.

"We've demonstrated here that Ralph can do a variety of things simultaneously; tasks requiring multiple action such as assembling coffee implements and teleporting them to the proper destination, as well as exercises requiring a certain strength and/or precision.

"However, Ralph has a limited range. We've duplicated today's fun and games over a distance of half a mile, but not further with any precision or strength. Ralph is not a superman. That's the first point I wish to impress on you. He has a Talent but it's a finite one, suitable for certain, rather limited use. He would be a profitable investment for someone like yourself, Mr. Gregory, for precision assembly under vacuum, sterile or radiation conditions.

"I don't say that Ralph is a totally reformed character at all," and Henry grinned at Ralph, "but he is now able to purchase legally the things he used to heist. He is subject, and he knows it, to the mental examination of a strong telepath. He also thoroughly enjoys his present occupation."

"You bet, mac." And the scathing look Ralph bent on the audience left no doubts that the little man delighted in disconcerting the men of distinction, rank and position.

"If you can't cure'em, recruit'em," Henry added.

"Are you implying, Mr. Darrow, that half the population of jails and mental institutions are peopled by your misunderstood parapsychics?"

"Not at all. I admit we're testing many so-called misfits to see if thwarted or yes, misunderstood, paranormal Talents are not partly responsible for their maladjustment. But that does not mean they are all graduates of institutions.

"Talent, gentlemen, can include something as simple as being a born mechanic. We've all known or heard of the guy who just listens to the sound of an engine and knows what's wrong with it.

Or the plumber who can dowse the exact location of a break in water pipes. Or the pyromaniac who "knows" when and where a fire will break out and has so often been accused of starting it; the woman whose hands ease a fever or soothe a pain, the worker who knows instinctively what the boss needs, the person who can always find what's been mislaid or lost. These are everyday, but *valid*, evidences of the parapsychic Talent. These are the people we want to include in our Centers—not just the more dramatic mind-readers and clairvoyants. The Talented are rarely supermen and women, just people who operate on a different wavelength. Employ them in the proper capacity and utilize their Talents to your advantage."

"Besides money, what do you want from us, Darrow?"

"Doctor Abbey, isn't it? From you and your colleagues all over the world, I want the public admission that Talent has left the tearoom and entered the laboratory. We have scientific evidence that the parapsychic faculty exists and can be used, at will, with predictable result. Science, gentlemen, by definition, is any skill that reflects a precise application of principles. The principle in Ralph's case is moving objects without artificial aid."

"I might buy the teleportation, Darrow," replied Doctor Abbey, slightly contemptuous, "but go back to the tearoom a minute. Give me an example of the science behind precognition."

"I knew you'd ask that, Doctor Abbey. And I predict that you will receive a favorable answer to your latest inquiry into the problem—" Henry raised his hand to suppress Abbey's exclamation, "I'm discreet enough, Doctor Abbey—into the problem you're investigating with Doctors Schwarz, Vosogin and Clasmire. That, Doctor Abbey, is predictable, scientific and accurate enough—since your correspondence with the three men is a closely guarded secret—to be convincing. Right?

From the stunned expression on Dr. Abbey's face as he sank into his chair, Darrow knew he was right and Abbey was convinced.

"Now," Henry asked the audience in general, "all of you have had problems which I believe some of our Talents can solve. What am I offered?"

Why, after fourteen years and nine rent increases—which I didn't protest by the way—will you not renew my lease?"

"Mister Darrow, I've been told that your lease is not renewable and that's what I've been told to tell you."

"How come the 'Mister Darrow,' Frank? Now look, I've paid my rent right on the button for fourteen years. I've had no more than legitimate redecorating, why am I not able to renew my lease?"

Henry knew the problem, had foreseen this situation, but he was human enough to like to see people squirm. Particularly, if it might let in a little wisdom and understanding of Talent.

Frank Hummel looked very uncomfortable.

"C'mon, Frank. You know. Don't try to kid *me* you don't."

Frank looked up with a miserable expression in his eyes. "And that's it, Hank. That's just it. You do know. You know too goddamned much and the other tenants are scared."

Henry threw back his head and roared with laughter. "No one's conscience is clear? My God, Frank, do they really think I *know* or care, for that matter, about their petty intrigues and affairs?" Then he saw he'd offended Frank and wished he were a telepath, not a precog. "Frank, I 'see' no more than I did when I used astrology to focus my Talent. No one was afraid of me when I was just a stargazer."

Frank did squirm at Henry's choice of phrase because that's how the man thought of Henry.

"I can't read minds," Henry went on, "and come to that, Frank, I don't really know what's going on under my nose. My Talent is not for individuals: it's for mass futures. Oh, yes, important individuals who will affect the lives of millions. But not if Mrs. Walters in 4-C is going to have a baby . . . not unless I have cast her individual horoscope . . . and she's too scared of her husband to come to me for that." Henry sighed for even that piece of common sense insight was now being misconstrued by the apprehensive real estate agent. "Look, everyone in the building knows Walters's opinion of me, and how scared she is of him. That takes no Talent at all, Frank. And it takes no Talent either to know that Walters is probably one of the prime instigators in getting me evicted."

"You're not being evicted, Mr. Darrow."

"Oh no?"

"No! It's just that your lease is not being renewed."

"How much of an extension can I have to find new quarters? You know how tight the housing situation is in Jerhattan."

Frank looked everywhere but at Henry.

"Frank . . . Frank? Frank, look at me," and reluctantly, hesitantly, the man obeyed. "Frank, you've known me for fourteen years. Why, suddenly, are you afraid of me?" Henry knew the answer but he wanted Frank to admit it. One man, one Frank Hummel, wouldn't change the struggle of the Talented for acceptance but it might change one other mind now, three next week. Every ally was valuable. And to have allies one had to admit to enemies.

"It's just that . . . that . . . hell, you're *not* a star-gazer anymore, Mister Darrow. You're for real." The apprehension in Frank Hummel's face was equally real.

"Frank, thank you. This isn't easy for you and I will make it less easy but I want you to remember fourteen years of a very pleasant relationship. I knew you'd be here today. I knew it four months ago when Molly and I had that series of graffiti painted on the door and the so-called burglary attempts. I've a lease on new quarters. We're moving tomorrow."

Frank already had too much to think about. "You mean, you *knew?* Already? But I just got the orders yesterday and you *told* me that you didn't see individual . . . and you're—"

"I'm not lying about what I can see, Frank, but I'd certainly better see what affects myself, or a fine star-gazer I'd be. Right?"

Hummel was slowly backing out of the apartment, less and less convinced. Once again Henry wished he were a telepath—or at least empathic—and could know what was running through Frank's mind and counter it.

"Do me one favor, Frank," Henry said. "On the 18th of next month, in the fourth race at Belmont, bet every credit you've been saving on a horse named Mibimi. Only don't place your bet until the last minute before the race. Will you do that for me? And then when Mibimi wins, remember Talent is useful."

Frank had retreated to the elevator and Henry wondered if the confused man had taken in his tip. He didn't often give them but for a friend you can do a favor . . . if it'll cement his friendship.

Henry shrugged as he closed the door. The scene just played in his living room had been repeated over and over, with acknowledged Talents as reluctant dramatis personae.

Just another of those paradoxes which assailed them from all sides now that Talent was respectable. By removing the onus of haphazard performance, by having Talents registered with the Center, they could contract for premium wages. But suddenly the Talents were also elevated into the genus "pariah," found themselves untouchables, unwelcome and feared, all through misunderstandings.

Watson Claire was mounting a massive soft-sell public information program, abetted by his contacts in the media profession who were delighted at something newsworthy. Judiciously applied blackmail kept the worst newsmongers at bay. But it would take time, Claire said (and Henry understood), for the program to seep down to the level where it was most required . . . in the housing developments which were now ousting anyone suspected of possessing Talent.

Well, the immense warehouse Henry had leased in the dock area would suffice until he'd figured out how to appeal to George Henner. That financial wizard had an accounting to make and Henry was vastly amused by recent findings. It was going to be fun watching Henner's reactions.

He picked up the comunit to call the warehouse: the shielding had been in place a week ago so there had been just the finishing of the living quarters. Maybe he should have used telekinetics to move his furnishings? No, that would be a bad scene, however personally satisfying it might be. Some things even Talents had better do the usual way.

My name is Henry Darrow, Commissioner Mailer. This is my wife, Molly; Barbara Holland is our finder, and Jerry comes along to lug the Goosegg. I believe this is your list of most wanteds?"

"Just what is this?" The Commissioner for Law Enforcement and Order had risen in indignation from his paper-free desk. "My appointment was with James Marshall, not you, Darrow."

"I know. Jim got it for us because you've refused to see . . ."

"A bunch of tearoom crackpots!"

"Well, we're here and you're going to listen . . ."

"Not if I have any say . . ." The Commissioner was fumbling

with his desk set and swore when the telltale lights did not wink
on at his touch.

"It won't work, Commissioner Mailer," Henry told him. "I forgot to mention that Jerry's telekinetic and keeps closing the
switches as soon as you press. Sorry. You're incommunicado until
you listen. And watch. Barbara, if you would, please? Here's the
list. Just sit here. Ready, Molly?"

The Commissioner's raging did him no good since his office was
soundproofed. He continued to fumble futilely with his comunit,
unable to believe that it wouldn't function because some nonde-
script young man stared at it. He didn't notice that Molly was
quietly placing the electrode net on Barbara's head. The girl adjusted it into the scalped spots in her hair and nodded to Henry.

"I gather these are in order of preference?" Henry asked the
Commissioner. Henry perched on the desk, unperturbed by the
Commissioner's belligerence and profanity.

"Preference? What'n'hell are you talking about, Darrow? Get
your circus out of here. This is a law enforcement and order . . ."

"Neither of which you are able to maintain with the current
restrictions on your men," said Henry, interrupting with such a
forceful tone that the Commissioner's sputtering died and he
stared at Darrow in amazement. Few people had addressed the
LEO man in that tone of voice. "That's why I'm here, to render
assistance you can't get from any other agency. Now sit down,
shut up, and listen. Who do you want us to find for you first?"

"Find?"

"Find!"

The two men locked eyes and there was a quality in Henry's that
wrought a sudden change in the Commissioner.

"All right," Mailer said in a tight hard voice, "find me the man
they call Joe Blow."

"The Joy Pill man?"

"That's him."

Henry flicked out the second IBM card and handed it to Barbara
Holland.

"Enough for you, Babs?"

The girl studied the sketch drawn by police artists from verbal
descriptions of victims of the elusive Joe Blow. She read the notations on his most frequented locations, his general modus ope-
randi. Then she looked up at Henry with a grin.

"This isn't a really fair test, Henry," she said.

"Ha!" exclaimed the Commissioner, an unholy delight in his eyes.

"No," said Barbara, "because I've encountered him so it's easy to track him down." She closed her eyes, clasping the card between her hands. The needles on the Goosegg began to whip across the graph paper. Her smile widened and she opened her eyes. "He's on the corner of 4th Avenue New East and 197th Street. He's wearing a long blue duty mac, with waterproofed shoulders, and a long blond wig. No moustaches today. He's carrying nothing illegal but he has a great deal of money on him and some folded papers."

The Commissioner was fumbling with his comunit. "For God's sake release it or whatever. I've got to get . . ."

"Why?" asked Barbara. "You want him with dust or acid or the Brown Joy, don't you?"

"I want him in any way."

"Can you charge him?"

"I've only got to get him . . ."

Suddenly the comunit came alive on every previously pressed band, but the Commissioner got it sorted out and had a squad vehicle dispatched to the coordinates, to apprehend a man answering Barbara's description. Then he turned back, smiling sourly at the four people. "We'll see what we'll see. If such a man is there, we'll have him in three minutes. My people are quick and efficient."

"So are mine," said Henry and looked expectantly at Barbara, who nodded.

"What's that all about?" demanded the Commissioner.

"I'm keeping track of him," Barbara replied, and suddenly the third band began to show activity.

"That is the Goosegg at work, Commissioner Mailer," said Henry.

"Are you reading my mind?" Mailer looked alarmed and angrier.

"Not at all," Henry replied. "I'm not a telepath. I'm a tea leaf reader on a grandiose scale . . ."

The Commissioner pursed his lips to hear his own description of Henry Darrow thrown back at him.

"All right, then, tell me now if my men'll succeed?"

"Barbara can tell you better than I. I don't deal generally with individuals. My specialty is mass movement. But Barbara can find Joe Blow for you now and any time you want to check on his whereabouts . . ."

"They have him," Barbara said, and held out her hand for another card.

The Commissioner stared at her suspiciously.

"Oh, let's let his men tell him, Babs."

She shrugged and settled back in her chair. Then brightened and smiled sweetly at Mailer. "You left your pipe in your ski jacket, Commissioner, the blue one which you don't usually wear. If you call home right now, you'll find your wife there. And remind her the coat is under your red dressing robe in the first closet."

Mailer regarded her with narrowed eyes. "I thought you said you weren't a mind reader."

"I never said that," Barbara replied, then pointed to Henry. "He did. And I can only get impressions of lost articles. You did lose the pipe and were just now thinking where had you put it. And the only reason I know about your wife is because you say you can never find her when you need her." Barbara kept her face very straight but Henry knew her to be possessed of a sense of devilment, very much in evidence under that air of innocent helpfulness.

This "finding" was making far more impression on the Commissioner than her location of Joe Blow.

The comunit buzzed.

"They picked up a man, answering that description. What do they do with him? He's demanding rights."

Mailer was unprepared for only one moment. "Search him. There's been a local robbery and a man answering his description was seen nearby. You're supposed to find a wad of credits and papers. Invoke citizen search prerogative."

"He's carrying roughly 8000 credits, sir," said Barbara.

"The heist was 8000."

There was a second long tense silence.

"He's got it, sir."

"Book him!"

The fleeting expressions on Mailer's face now told of intense mental conflict. He was a man to whom a miracle had been offered and he was too scared to accept it.

"Barbara is parapsychic, Commissioner. We brought Goosegg to prove to you on a scientific basis as reliable as ballistics, without a tea leaf in sight, that her mind generates a specific type of electrical impulse when she uses her parapsychic Talent. She can't read your mind except when you, or anyone, are worrying about something lost, strayed or stolen . . ."

"Stolen—" The Commissioner pounced on the word.

"If you mean that hijacked shipment of crowd gas, Commissioner," said Barbara, "it's in a warehouse, with a southside feel. It's very dark inside, which hampers me: I can't see in shadows. I can make out some white air-freight containers, they've a plastic feel, rather than wood or steel. There's a geometric design in dark paint in the lower left hand side." She frowned and the Goosegg chattered rapidly for a moment and then toned down to a mild, normal swing. "I'm sorry. There simply isn't enough light there."

The Commissioner snorted but her information had obviously given him something to work on. "South side . . . air freight . . . white . . ." His fist slapped down an end key. "Jack . . . what air freight companies use white containers with geometric designs in lower left hand . . . Oh, they do. Now, what air freight companies use southside depots . . . Oh. Hmmm. Well, check your contacts like right now." He turned a cold dispassionate look on Barbara. "You can't be more specific?"

Barbara gave Henry a quick glance before answering. "I've already narrowed the search to a small section of the city with as many specifics as I can see. There can't be *that* many warehouses for air freight! I've done more than you've been able to, Mr. Mailer."

"Now, just a minute, young lady . . ."

"You've had more than a minute, Commissioner, and my time is valuable." Barbara was on her feet, the electrode net in her hand. "We're wasting time with this one, Henry. And I don't like him. Miserable vibes from him, just miserable!"

She left the room. Molly quietly began to pack up the Goosegg while the Commissioner stared first at the open door and then at Henry.

"She operates more efficiently with an occasional word or two of thanks, Mailer. Most people do." Henry gathered Molly into the curve of his arm, motioned courteously to Jerry to take the Goosegg and wishing Mailer a pleasant good-day, left.

"Hey, just a minute . . ."

Henry turned at the door. "As Babs said, Mailer, you've had more than a minute and our time is valuable."

Does Charity have to be sedated again, Gus?" Henry asked the Center's physician. "We've got her a temporary contract to find out the troublemaker in the Arrow Shirt Company."

Gus ducked his head, his face twisted into a grimace, wanting to say no and having to say yes. He leaned against the now flagged door to Charity McGillicuddy's two roomed accommodation on the living floor of the Center's warehouse building.

"Even with the shielding we've got, Hank, it's not enough privacy for the empaths and telepaths. Not enough physical distance. No way to get out and away from ourselves, if you get what I mean. We're sort of all crammed into this warren despite the conveniences and amenities. You might say, it's too much of a good thing . . . to close a buddy-buddy act. Like an overdose of euphorics. Everyone's high here on sheer good fellowship. And it's much too much for Charity."

Henry looked towards the corridor window with the projection of sunlight on the grass, a huge spreading beech tree, russet against an autumnally blue sky. Though it was so realistic that the leaves moved gently and the angle of sunlight altered slowly, Henry knew it to be only a projection and his mind would not accept the fantasy that deluded millions of warren dwellers.

"Talent requires certain realities not obtainable in this age," Gus went on. "And one of the most important is physical freedom and elbow room." He snorted, aware of the impossibility of fulfilling that requirement in Jerhattan's overcrowded boundaries.

"We've been offered that old game preserve in . . ."

"Too goddamned far to commute and most of us gotta." Molnar was head neurologist at the Midtown Hospital Center although he spent more time as the Center's physician.

"Okay," Henry said, "I'll do what I can."

"Henry?" Gus eyed his friend suspiciously. "What are you up to now?"

"Me? Nothing." Then Henry Darrow assumed a crouched stance and rubbed his hands together, chuckling evilly. "But Destiny . . . haha HA! I know when we twain shall meet. Soon!"

Gus rolled his eyes heavenward to deal with Henry Darrow in this whimsical mood.

"Oh, don't worry, Gus," Henry said in a normal voice. "I usually call 'em, you know."

Gus nodded sourly.

"Content yourself," Henry continued, "with the enticing thoughts of dissecting my brain when I die, and trying to figure out just how I do it."

"Ha!"

You can't subpoena Barbara Holland, not on those grounds, Commissioner Mailer," Henry Darrow said. "But you can hire her services from the Center . . ."

"What Center?" demanded Mailer, looking scornfully around the minuscule space that served as Henry's office.

"The Center we'll shortly acquire with the wages you'll be paying Talents like Barbara, and Titter Beyley and Gil Gracie and . . ."

"Titter Beyley?" The Commissioner hovered on the verge of apoplexy.

"Yes, Titter. He drank to stop finding things. Alcohol affects the parapsychic faculty, sometimes it inhibits, as in Titter's case; sometimes it sharpens."

"Now, just a minute, Darrow . . ."

"My minutes are valuable, Mailer. I only have so many. You want things and people found: Barbara has that faculty and so does Titter Beyley. Actually Titter's much better for inanimate objects than Barbara. He doesn't like people. And the day you find out he's been drunk on duty, *then* complain."

And you mean to stand there, young man, and tell me that I'm going to get shot at Saturday? Again!" Governor Lawson tipped his chair back and roared with laughter: an exercise he broke off abruptly to glare with an intensity akin to hatred at Darrow and the wraith-like Steve Hawkins. "So what else is new?"

"The predictive Incident says that a .38 slug will penetrate the right ventricle." Steve's voice shook slightly. Henry wondered if he'd made a mistake in bringing Steve, who was very new to his gifts and the Center's staff. "The man will approach from the left . . ."

"What does it matter where he comes from?" The Governor said, sharply, hostilely. "Oh, I don't disbelieve you, Darrow. Or you, Hawkins. I've heard too much about you people to be skeptical anymore. But, if I don't appear . . ."

"You have to appear," Henry replied. "We ran the alternates through a probability computation and find that your appearance at that Forum Meeting must take place to sway a currently uncommitted 8% of the popular vote to your party. Without that 8%, you fail to receive the critical majority and if you fail, the Laborites can obtain the plurality they need to effect a counter-measure that would have disastrous consequences on the economy."

Governor Lawson began a chuckle, his belly shaking first before the amusement was shunted up the rotund abdomen to the chest and finally became audible in the head cavity. Finally Lawson's lips parted to emit a rich, juicy laugh.

"So, that's the way it'll be, huh?"

"Yes, if your eloquence doesn't falter with foreknowledge."

"Huh? How's that?"

"You have been given a prescience of the immediate future. Such knowledge could, in itself, alter the circumstances of the future. We do not always have either the personnel or the foresight to modify the future. In your case, we make an exception. A Laborite Majority is not a good thing for the Talented."

Governor Lawson nodded in appreciation of that expediency.

"Your man will intercept the bullet?"

Henry nodded.

"And the nut will be put away? That's better than leaving him free for another shot. Good! How many political figures does your group protect?"

"Those who need it. And we'd appreciate a kindly word for the Center when Steve diverts that bullet."

Lawson nodded agreement. "Those who need protection? Or those whom you need, Darrow? No, don't answer that one. Answer this . . . will I win this election?"

Henry smiled slowly. "You know the answer to that one, Governor, but the *fun* lies in making certain you've played the game right."

"How far do you guys play fun and games?"
"Just far enough!"

Now, Mr. Rambley, what seems to be your problem?"
"Not my problem, Mr. Darrow. Yours!" The Internal Revenue Department man smiled a thin smug smile and began to pull IBM cards from his neat fake-pig case.
"Really?"
"We have here WT forms from the Department of Law Enforcement and Order, from Johns Hopkins, Bethel General, Midtown, from Dupont, Merck Pharmaceuticals . . . need I go on?"
"Just as you please."
"These salary chits represent the earnings of Barbara Holland, Titter Beyley, Charity McGillicuddy, Gil Gracie, Frank Negelsco, Augustus Molnar . . ." Again the IRD representative regarded Henry Darrow with a cute expression on his fleshless face. "I could continue . . ."
"Just as you please. I give every government official the courtesy due his office." Henry inclined his head toward Mr. Rambley who, for the first time since he'd minced into Henry's tiny lair, looked nonplussed. "After all, some of my best people are employed by the government."
With an irritated sigh, Rambley closed the stack of cards and tapped them in an admonitory fashion on the desk.
"Come now, Mr. Darrow. These people," and he brandished the cards, "earn tremendous salaries and yet there is no record of a single tax deduction, no returns . . ."
"They donate their salaries *in toto* to the Parapsychic Center. They lease their services contractually to the various employers. The Parapsychic Center files a corporate form to cover them. Under Corporation Law . . ."
"No one in their right minds would . . ." Rambley bounced on the end of his chair with indignation and disbelief.
"I never said any of the parapsychic Talents were in a right mind. In fact," Henry went on with gentle amusement, "there is every reason to believe that the core of the parapsychic is, if anywhere, in the left hand part of the brain."
"Mr. Darrow," Mr. Rambley was on his feet. "You did say that you gave government officials the courtesy due their office?"

"Yes, didn't I? Consequently, you're wasting time, your government's and mine, Mr. Rambley. The individuals represented by those neatly slotted cards do donate their total income to the Parapsychic Center. Our accountant will be glad to show you the appropriate records and contractual agreements . . ."

"But . . . but I *know* that that Titter Beyley creature is driving a four passenger 350 horsepower vehicle!" Such an incongruity shocked Mr. Rambley.

"Yes, Titter's always wanted to drive a big one. The car belongs to the Center. You can check the registration papers."

"And that . . . that Charity McGillicuddy has a blue ranch mink coat."

"Indeed she has. She requisitioned it from Stores about four months ago."

"She requisitioned . . . from Stores?"

"She has a position to maintain now and her appearance is of great concern to the LEO office. Think how embarrassing it would be for someone employed by the LEO Commission to be arrested for wearing stolen furs. Of course, Charity says that now she can buy 'em instead of 'lifting' 'em, half the fun's gone. But it gives her a great moral boost to wear blue ranch mink in the LEO Block. We try to keep our workers happy."

Rambley had stared at Henry Darrow through this ingenuous explanation but his indignation rose with every gently spoken word.

"This won't be the last you'll hear from me, Mr. Darrow. You do not mock the Internal Revenue Department, Mr. Darrow." He slammed the file cards into his case, hands trembling with outraged dignity. "You'll hear from us."

"That's fine by me. Just call ahead for an appointment. Only consider the fact that Senators Maxwell, Abrahams, Montello and Gratz approved our corporate structure."

Rambley's eyes widened.

"And the presidential advisor, Mr. Killiney, acted as our financial assistant. Don't you have *his* card in that file?"

Rambley exited, reduced to mutterings.

Do you often trick your way into a private home, Mr. Darrow?"

"When I've been unable to secure an appointment any other way, yes, Mr. Henner." Henry smiled pleasantly, trying not to glance with obvious envy at the spaciousness of the magnificently furnished living room. Such accommodation was almost archaic.

George Henner appeared more amused than irritated by Henry Darrow's impertinence as he leaned back in his Italian brocade armchair.

"If it's money for your palm-reading, table-tilting crystal-gazing tricks, forget it."

"On the contrary, sir. I've affirmation that I can ask you to join our happy band." Henry smiled at the surprise in Henner's yellowed eyes.

"Join you?" Henner burst out laughing. His head went back showing a veritable gold field of fillings in his upper teeth. "By God, Darrow, you've made my day! If you can't lick 'em, recruit 'em?"

"Actually," Henry went on smoothly, seating himself and crossing his legs, counterfeiting an ease he didn't feel. He noted the flicker of irritation in Henner's face but the financier had a reputation of letting a man have enough rope to hang himself. "Actually, Mr. Henner, your abilities in the financial world are as solidly derived from the parapsychic as my own. Incidentally, you're the crystal ball reader . . . although I see you've got a modern computer for stock market print-out instead of the old glass case."

Henner gave an amused grunt but said nothing, his silence a subtle prod to keep Henry talking.

"You're known," Henry continued obediently, because that was the way the interview ought to proceed, "to have a genius, a second sight into what stocks are going to rise, which will fall, what bond issues will pay the keenest long-term profit. And I can prove that you're parapsychic."

Henner cocked his head slightly to one side, his amusement deepening, as he tacitly encouraged Henry to produce his proof. Darrow spread the graph out on the table. "I know you've followed the newsmedia coverage on us, so you're familiar with this sort of graph. What you may not immediately appreciate is the fact that this is your graph."

Henner became immobile with attention.

"When you had your last routine physical a month ago, your physician employed a Goosegg. He didn't realize that it wasn't his own office model so he's blameless. You did, however, experience what we call an Incident and it is recorded on this graph, here and here. I believe the Incident was in connection with the Allied Metals and Mining merger in which you managed quite a 'killing.' "

"You don't read thought from an EEG graph, Darrow."

"Hardly. But you placed a phone call directly you were through your physical to your office and within the next few hours the merger was announced . . . but not before you had acquired a tidy pile of Allied stock. Are my *facts* correct?"

Henner nodded slowly, his eyes, narrowed to intense slits, watching Henry Darrow's face.

"That's proof," Henry said, rustling the graph paper, "that you're parapsychic, Mr. Henner."

The silence which ensued, designed to make Darrow exceedingly uncomfortable, did not. For a long space, Henry returned George Henner's stare, then folded his arms and gazed around the beautiful room. Finally he turned back to Henner and smiled.

"Blackmail?" asked Henner.

Darrow shook his head.

"No. You'd be far too clever for that. No, I'd hazard the guess that you want to borrow my Talent, as you call it, to make your fortunes? That would still be essentially blackmail, wouldn't it, Darrow?"

Henry pursed his lips a little, expressing dubiety.

"Well, then what is it you want from me? It's something."

"Actually, it's the twelve acre tract of land on the Palisades."

Once again Henry wished he were a telepath to read the emotions swiftly passing through George Henner's mind. He had startled the financier, he had touched the most vulnerable point of the shrewd man's life: his intense love, and need for, the beautiful estate of Beechwoods. It had been in Henner's family for a hundred and forty years, was a showplace which few saw. And Henner's need of Beechwoods was as great and for the same reasons as Henry Darrow's."

"How could you know?" demanded Henner in a hoarse whisper.

"That the State intends to confiscate all privately held lands within a hundred mile radius of the Jerhattan city limits? I know because it is as important to me as it is to you to know these things."

Henner was on his feet, pacing to release the energy of his anger. In a barely audible monotone he inventively assigned destinations to the State en masse, the needs of the unhoused, unwashed multitudes in general and those particular officials who had failed to keep Henner's ancestral home inviolate.

"If, however, the property is already owned by a religious, medical, educational or charitable institution which will accommodate a sufficient number of our ever-expanding population, they cannot confiscate your property even under the terms of Section 91, Paragraph 12 of the Housing Act of 1998."

"This is 1997, man. That Act isn't passed yet. I can still defeat it."

"No. It will be passed."

Henner tried to stare that knowledge out of Henry's mind.

"And you know the inevitability, Mr. Henner. None of your contacts can hold out any hope of defeating that measure, nor of defending your Beechwoods?"

"And it's your table-tilting tea-leaf readers who'll infest my home?"

"Your physical condition is poor, Mr. Henner, and your nerves damned near the breaking point. The solitude and privacy of this house and its grounds are vital to your life. It would be to any parapsychic mind forced to tune in on the emotional chaos that haunts the very air we breathe. You know you've been living on borrowed time for the past year. You know what alternative dwelling accommodations will do to you."

"Do you happen to know," asked Henner casually for he'd got control of himself again, "the exact date of my death?"

"As I know the exact time of mine, Mr. Henner. You will die of a heart attack, the aorta will be closed by a globule of the arteriosclerotic matter coating your veins, at nine-twenty-one PM, exactly one year, nine months and fourteen days from now."

A gleam of challenge livened the deadly intent of Henner's gaze. "And if I don't?"

"If you don't, then revoke the grant of Beechwoods to the Center. In the meantime, you'll have secured your last days in the ancestral home, which is your prime concern at the moment."

"I could have a heart transplant . . ." Henner was clearly enjoying this.

"Not with a diseased liver and the condition of your arteries."

"And that's your prophecy, Darrow?"

"A medical certainty," Henry said. "I've toyed with the notion of a transplant myself since my death will also occur from myocardial infarction on a certain May twelfth, at ten-fifty-two PM. But by May twelfth of that year, I intend to have accomplished the major part of what needs to be done to establish a viable, self-sufficient Parapsychic Center in North America . . ."

"On the Beechwoods estate?"

"On the Beechwoods estate. By May twelfth, I shall be grateful for the peace and tranquillity of my grave."

Henner's eyes flicked from Darrow's to some inner middle distance, the harsh cynical lines of the financier's face softened.

" 'Ease after war, death after life does greatly please'?" The words were softly spoken but there was no quarter in the hard look Henner then turned on Henry Darrow.

"In your scheming where does this house end up?"

"As an integral part of the Center."

Henner's expression was ironic. "And my money? I've no next of kin."

Darrow laughed. "You keep harping on your money, Mr. Henner. We don't *need* your money. Check our books on that. But only the Center can offer one of its own members what his money hasn't been able to secure for him."

For a long time Henner gazed out the French windows that gave on the flagged terrace, toward the sweep of magnificent lawn and the superb beech trees. When Henner finally turned back to Henry, his hand was extended. The two men shook three times in the ancient custom of binding a bargain.

"Answer me one thing, Darrow! Did you foresee winning?"

"I knew that we would eventually secure Beechwoods, Mr. Henner," he said, permitting regret to tinge his voice. "But I wanted your cooperation."

"Cooperation? You goddamn well know I had no choice!"

"Didn't you?"

Gcorge Henner had wandered into the Graph room just as the first of the three Incidents was recorded. He had the habit of appearing in the various departments, taking what he called a perverse interest in the eventual eviction of the Center from Beechwoods. In point of fact, Henner had admitted to Molly Darrow that the Center had given him something to live for. He'd been feeling much better since Henry'd conned him out of Beechwoods. Despite his professed intention of harassing Henry, George Henner's passing suggestions were usually solid advice. And despite his crotchety and often irascible manner, the Talents became fond of him.

"Got a strong Incident," Ben Avedon, the duty officer, told Henry on the intercom just as George Henner wandered into the Graph room. "Patsy Tucker."

In moments, Henry and Molly arrived in time for Patsy's phone call of such details as she'd "seen."

"I'm on the water again," she said, breathless in an attempt to verbalize before details escaped her. "And there're boats. Four. Sun's at a late afternoon angle, on my left so I must be looking north. There's land beyond the boats, pines, a bluff. And oil on the water. I can see it all rainbowy. The oil scares me. It's going to ignite, and then the water's covered with flames and the boats are eaten up and . . . oh, it's going to be wicked, Ben. Can you locate? Have I given you enough? I can't remember anymore and the flames cover any details."

"It is a sooner?"

"Awful soon. Today. I'm sure of it. But it's morning, and I saw late afternoon . . . is there time enough?"

"Sure. Plenty of time. I'm feeding the computer with the data right now. Old didactic will pin the place down, Pat. But have you a notion about the size of the boats involved?"

"Oh, yes, of course. How stupid of me. I forget you haven't seen. One's small, a pleasure craft . . . a power boat . . . no sails. That's the one that goes on fire. Two long low boats . . . I guess they'd be tankers. And a higher boat . . . I mean, one higher above the water . . . And they're all much too close together. That's the problem because they'll all catch fire."

"A pleasure boat, two tankers and a freighter in the late afternoon. That's fine, Pat. And the pines and bluff and being close together indicate channel of some description. Now . . . think hard again, Pat. Did you see any markings on the boats, funnel markings, ensigns, names?"

After a silence Pat mournfully admitted "seeing" nothing because the fire and smoke occluded.

"Get one of the pyros on it," Henry told Ben. "Patsy, Henry here. That's a good job, lass. Now take it easy. We'll buzz you back with confirmation. Grand work, Pat." Henry disconnected her line, shaking his head, knowing how worried the girl would be until she heard they'd prevented the collision. If only there'd been markings to speed up identification, and then if the participants could be dissuaded from arriving on the previewed scene. . . . He moved deliberately to the computer panel and began tapping out queries. "Undoubtedly a seaway. Could be Sheepshead Bay area, East River . . . no, not there. Or one of the canals . . ."

"St. Lawrence, with tankers *and* freighters . . ." suggested Ben.

"Or the Great Lakes . . ." said Molly.

Before there'd been a print-out on possible locations or what traffic was already in the St. Lawrence Seaway, a second graph began to chatter.

"Right on time," said Ben. "Here's Terry, our local friendly reliable pyro."

"How come you don't *know*, Hank?" George Henner asked, settling himself on a stool in the corner.

"Not enough people involved, George, and too close a range for me. That's Patsy's specialty—cliff-hangers. Besides, don't you agree that the good executive makes all the long-range decisions and leaves the picayune nitty-gritty details to keep his staff occupied?"

George grinned but he said nothing more, listening as intently as the others to Terry Cle's verbalization of his "sight." The broad outline correlated with Patsy's although he "saw" the event from a different perspective. He had sufficient detail on one tanker and the small craft to result in exact IDs for both from Ship Registration. And there was a tanker of the Iricoil Line proceeding down the Seaway en route for Toronto, ETA 7:48 PM at that port. The small craft, the Aitch Bee, was registered to an A. Frascati, and was at that moment moored in a small boat basin on the American side of the Seaway.

Probability figures the cost of the collision and fire at several millions and a thirty-six hour tie-up of Seaway traffic, plus delayed cargoes which would complicate schedules and routines for ninety-two companies, involving work-loss of some eighteen thousand people.

"Okay, Ben, get out the usual warning format. See if Iricoil will listen to us."

"And if Iricoil doesn't want to believe?"

"We get after this Frascati. In fact, he'd be easier to bully than Iricoil but we've got to warn them, too."

Iricoil was suspicious and uncooperative and, in phrases just short of insult, refused to consider diverting the tanker. Its supplies were urgently required in Toronto by late evening. Frascati was not at his home nor in his business office. Urgent messages were left for the man to contact the Center before taking out his pleasure craft. Henry was dialing the Seaway Authority Control when George cut the connection.

"I've got an idea, Hank," George said. "I've watched this routine so often and seen you insulted, ignored, and calumniated. No one trusts the altruist anymore, whether he's Talented or not. You've warned Iricoil, tried to do them a favor. They aren't buying. Well, like the puppy who leaves too many messages, let's rub their nose in it."

"You mean, let the accident occur?"

"More or less. Considering what's involved in terms of credit and work-loss, and considering that I have shares in four of the companies to be affected by the snarl-up, will you play it my way, this once?"

Henry began to relax. "What have you in mind, George?"

"You did leave timed messages at Iricoil and for Frascati, didn't you?"

Ben Avedon tapped the computer panel. "All time-sealed, George."

"Fine. Now, issue a fax warning to Seaway Authority. Then give me a few comlines to work from and Molly to help me. Irenee was telling me about their new oil-pollutant at Dupont. This would be good PR for him. Always like to oblige friends. Which reminds me, you get on to Jim Lawson . . . our revered Governor owes you a favor or two for that bullet Steve stopped. And ask him for a few more VTOLs and a couple of frogmen."

"Why?"

"*You* don't know?"

Henry grinned. "Would you believe an educated guess?"
Henner chuckled. "My, my, how the mighty have fallen . . .
Guessing!"
"Run the show your way, George."
"Yes, let a pro show you how, Henry Darrow. You're too
damned soft. You talk too much. Action speaks louder than a hun-
dred of your Talented words."

At exactly 16:32 hours of a bright spring afternoon, an Iricoil
tanker proceeding down the St. Lawrence Seaway fouled its
propellor on a tangle of steel cables, origin unknown. The tanker
drifted athwart the current as a United Line freighter entered the
narrow channel from the opposite direction. A second tanker, also
United Line, making speed enough to reach Toronto port by dark,
cruised into the danger zone, although it was apparent that the
Iricoil boat was in distress. Both United Line ships continued, evidently hoping to pass the injured vessel, one on the port, the other
on the starboard. Likely they would have succeeded but the Aitch
Bee, also impatient to reach port, came bucketing down the
searoute. It swung rather close to the distressed vessel. As Frascati
ever after maintained, he wanted to see if he could be of any assistance in getting a message ashore: a ridiculous alibi since the
tanker was well equipped by radio and ship-shore telephone. Frascati's propellor became fouled on the same villain cable. The
freighter began to pass the disabled pair and her wash slammed the
small craft into the Iricoil tanker. The United Line tanker was
broadside of the Iricoil when her bow swung out. Tanker #2
swung to starboard to avoid a collision and her stern banged into
Iricoil, splitting a seam in the aft oil hold just as the small craft was
ground between the two bigger hulls. Its galley fires caught old
grease and spread in the cabin as the yacht's gasoline tank was
breached. Oil pouring from the Iricoil vessel would shortly ignite
from that flame.

At this point the hovering rescue copters intervened as newsmedia cameras recorded the event from every angle. Foam quickly
doused the yacht fire, the oil-pollution material gobbled up the
split petroleum and kinetics held back additional oil loss by pressure until the teleports could get the conveniently handy plates
into position. Other kinetics and the frogmen worked loose the

steel cable and it was hoisted out of the way. "Captain" Frascati
and the two crew members (his sons) of the damaged yacht were
lifted up and another team of kinetics kept the little ship floating
until the belatedly arriving coast guard cutter could tow it into
port.

The Seaway was not blocked since all four vessels were cleared
out of the narrow channel before others made the passage. There
was no loss of life and no long-term pollution of the water. The
Parapsychic teams were volubly and embarrassingly thanked for
preventing a major disaster, and by cocktail time everyone was
pleased by the denouement, especially Patsy Tucker and Terry
Cle.

The congratulatory euphoria lasted twelve hours, at which point
the Seaway Authority began to realize that matters had come to
near-disaster in an unprecedented way.

"What was the meaning of sending us only a fax to announce a
major disaster?" the Seaway Commissioner demanded in such sten-
torian tones that George Henner need not have listened in on the
second comunit in Henry's office.

"You were informed by fax as usual," Henry replied in a mild
tone of voice.

"By fax! When countless millions of credits were at stake? And
blockage of the most important waterway in North America? And
do you realize that we have only just balanced the sealife ecology in
that strip of waterway? That oil . . ."

"You were informed . . ."

"Well, I'm informing you that you're in for a suit of criminal
negligence . . ."

"Negligence of what, Commissioner? You were informed nine
hours and thirty-eight minutes prior to the accident by this ex-
officio group, which is not a government sponsored or accredited
agency. We act for and in the public interest. But we are under-
staffed and overworked. You could have queried this office for more
particulars, although all we had were included in that fax. Your
Authority could have held back any one of the four vessels involved, thus preventing the . . ."

"Are you accusing the Seaway Authority of negligence?"

Henry held the receiver away from his ear, shook his head, and
replied in his mildest manner, "Forewarned is forearmed, sir." He
caught George Henner giving the high sign of approval.

"You'll hear from us, Darrow. You people can't get away with irresponsible behavior like this."

The connection was rudely and noisily broken.

"Did you figure a lawsuit in your calculations, George?" asked Henry.

Henner rubbed his hands together in glee. "*If* they sue, we'd win."

Henry couldn't exactly share in Henner's gleeful anticipation. The precog knew of the multitude of lawsuits which would be served on Talents in the next decades and the sheer cost of inspired defense made him shudder. The money would be available but it was credit that could be used to better advantage in training and identifying Talent, not defending against misunderstanding and greed. By late afternoon, Henry's premonitions of immediate disaster were borne out by additional suits of negligence which arrived from United Line, Iricoil Tankers and A. Frascati.

"Let me handle this," George Henner told Henry and his hastily convened executive staff. "I don't need any crystal ball or anerodic graph needle to tell me how to manage this sort of crap."

Before he had Henry's voiced approval, he was on the wires to the major media networks, chatting familiarly with presidents and commissioners. By the time the films of the Parapsychic Center's assistance had been widely aired, with a few choice comments on how the Center operated to forestall major disasters, the threatened legal action against the Talents was withdrawn. Suits were entered against the Seaway for criminal negligence. Then the Center, on George Henner's advice ("Make 'em pay for it, when they don't listen to you."), sent bills for the rescue operations to Frascati, United Line and Iricoil Tankers.

"And from now on, Henry," George said, "don't ever follow up your faxed warnings with personal phone calls. Don't be the supplicant, damn it. Be the prelate!"

Henry watched with inner amusement as George Henner paced up and down the floor, his eyes flashing, even his stride firm and aggressive so that Henry could see traces of the strengths which had amassed George Henner his considerable fortune and which had overwhelmed less determined adversaries in the business world.

"There's no point in you bruising your larynx with persuasion. You've proved your worth over and over again and this Seaway

bollix ought to make a validated Parapsychic warning worth the
paper it's printed on, even at the dreadful price of paper these
days."

"A sound argument, George, and I appreciate your help . . ."

George stopped midstride, glaring at Henry through narrowed
lids.

"Yes, I am helping you, aren't I? Shouldn't do that, should I?"

"My friendly enemy," replied Henry with a laugh.

"Ha! Tell me that when my executors snatch the rug of Beechwoods from under your telepathetic feet . . ."

"And we need you, George," Henry raised his voice to over-
whelm Henner's snide remarks. "If I can convince a skeptic like
you, I'm well away to swaying John Q. Public to my side. He's
more variable than you, and he will be the hardest to win over."

John Q. Public, however, quixotically decided the Seaway Authority had been foolish to ignore the Parapsychic warning. Criticism was heaped on the Seaway from every quarter. Later the
Authority was somewhat exonerated of primary guilt since the
Court felt that good judgment on the part of any one of the other
three skippers would have prevented the accident and no costs
were awarded the claimants. The official records cited and credited
the Parapsychic Center with averting a major calamity, and loss of
life and property. All Transport Authorities were severely enjoined to heed any warnings from the Center which involved public transport.

For the next few weeks all precogs of traffic problems, possible
fire, storm or spring floods throughout the world were instantly
acted upon. The Center was beseiged with anxious calls about
whether Mr. S could undertake that long distance flight, or Mrs. J
could safely make her annual pilgrimage from Florida to Wiscon-
sin, and if there had been any precog about the transfer of cyanide
cylinders to the authorized Atlantic Trench dump. Thousands of
hopeful people applied for the simple tests which would indicate if
they possessed some useful Talent.

"It's an ill wind that blows no good," Henry remarked to Molly
after another hectic day answering urgent calls and dealing with
anxious queries.

"I suppose so," she said, sinking wearily into the armchair of
their private suite in the main house. "But I wish we had more
Gooseggs or a surer way of spotting the live ones."

"Any today?" Henry fixed Molly a stiff drink.

"Yes," and she brightened as if she'd temporarily forgotten the event. "One very strong receiving telepath out of forty-five aspirants." She accepted the drink, turning the glass in her hand as if the amber liquid held some other answer. "Henry, they come in so hopeful . . . and some of them leave so angry and disappointed. As if *we* ought to be able to find what doesn't exist . . ."

"Not your fault, love. Everyone wants to be, in some way, unique, and can't realize that being unique is a responsibility as well as a privilege. You can't cure that. How strong's the telepath?"

Molly brightened. "I think he's very strong, but he's been blocking thoughts, the way they all do. Out of fear. He may need a lot of training."

"No, not too much," Henry said easily, pulling his chair close to Molly and clasping her free hand. "Young fellow, isn't he? Welsh extraction, Welsh name. Right?"

"I just sent the report in . . ." Molly began, startled, and stopped mid-sentence, arrested by Henry's knowing look. "Not another one, Henry?"

"They do seem to appear right on schedule," Henry grinned at her but there was a shadow in his eyes. "Right on schedule. One day I'll be wrong."

"Don't, Henry." She clasped his hand tightly, reassuringly, knowing the strain of his unfortunate infallibility, knowing that some of the events he foresaw he'd rather not have seen. "And, he is, as you predicted, Welsh," she went on in a light voice, "by name, Daffyd op Owen. Very likeable chap. He's important?"

Henry nodded. "He won't need more than some basic pointers and a few quiet weeks here to wash the 'noise' out of his mind and learn to project as well as receive."

"Well, that's one on the plus side of the ledger." She rotated her shoulders to ease the day's strains but Henry's disclosure about young op Owen made her feel much better about her labors.

"When is he moving in?"

"Don't you know?" she asked in a bantering fashion.

"What I know I wish I didn't. What I'd give anything to know, I have to wait and see."

She smiled at him lovingly. "You mean, if we retain Beechwoods?" When he nodded, she chided him gently. "How often have you been wrong in the merest detail?"

"It's not how often I'm right, Molly luv, it's will I be wrong *this* time, this once? This important, crucial, critical once? Such a terrible gift, luv. Terrible when your knowledge means the loss of a friend . . ."

"Henry, your recognition, the very challenge of the Center," and her arm gesture encompassed all of Beechwoods, "have kept George Henner alive . . . and kicking." She peered into Henry's face, reassuring him by touch, word and look. "He's determined to do you out of Beechwoods, if only by a minute. That determination alone has strengthened his hold on life. I've seen his medical reports, Henry, I know." She leaned back in her chair. "You've done him quite a favor and he knows it. I shouldn't be surprised if he hasn't left the Center Beechwoods anyway."

"He hasn't. He showed me the will."

Molly opened her mouth to say something then thought better of it.

"All right," Henry went on, catching her look of mischief, "so he could write a second one in secret . . . No, we've a wager on and . . ."

"I know what you mean, hoping to win the wager loses a friend."

"I can see horizons wider than mortality but I cannot always see the sparrow fall."

S o young op Owen will be your successor?" George Henner was in a very testy mood that morning.

"Yes, but of course, not for some time yet . . ."

"You've got it all foreseen, have you?"

"Certainly the basic problems . . ."

"Ha! I thought you'd already solved the basic problems . . ."

"By no means, my friend," and Henry's laugh was mirthless. "I've had the easy part. No, really. The establishment of the Center —and others in time in strategic parts of the globe . . . is only the first bit: scarcely the worst.

"Once we'd elevated parapsychic Talents to a demonstrable, scientific basis, it was only a question of some decent organizational effort to make us self-sufficient and independent. We did dodge the governmental attempt to take control because we operate more efficiently as a private agency and because you could imagine the tax payers' shrieks about funding tea-leaf readers. Funding was no real problem once we could prove Talent. Training, now . . . that is a long term program. We've got to develop more efficient techniques in recognizing and training Talent and that takes Talented personnel. Getting industry and the government to accept our workers was child's play with what we can offer." Then Henry sighed. "The suspicions of the general public can't be totally allayed but with the help of a discreet PR program, people can become accustomed to the Talented.

"No, George, some of our biggest problems are yet to be solved. The knottiest one is establishing legal protection for Talent. Without that, all we've carefully built could be wiped away in legal fees, damages and law suits . . . particularly against the precogs. Oh, I see that we'll get professional immunity sooner or later. I'm greedy. I want it sooner. And that's why a telepath like Dai op Owen is required as Director. He's more sensitive to the immediate situation. By God, the times I've wished I were a telepath . . ."

George snorted.

"It's easier for a man who can delve into thoughts, not the future. That's assured."

"Ha!" Light flittered from George Henner's sunken eyes. "Not yet. You've three days, four hours and five minutes to go."

"No," Henry replied gently, "no, old friend, *you've* three days, four hours and five minutes to go. And I shall miss you."

"Ha to that as well! See any new signs of decay?" George jerked his head this way and that.

Henry shook his head slowly. "I will miss you, you old bastard."

"Will you? Will you when I defy your prediction and you and your Talents are thrown out into the mass noise again?"

Henry summoned a laugh. "Then why haven't you died long ago?"

George glared at him. "I intend to make you sweat, Henry Darrow. Sweat. Bleed. Die a little."

"And you wonder I want a telepath as a Director?" He gripped George firmly by the shoulder and gave him an affectionate shake. "Play the enemy if it pleases you: if the choler makes the blood continue to run in your veins. You're more our friend than enemy. And I know it."

"Ha! You are nervous. You're worried that you're wrong. That this time you're wrong! I'll prove you wrong if it's the last thing I do."

Henry cocked his head at George, grinning ironically. "You may at that, you old bastard. I've never claimed infallibility, George. And you've heard me state time and again that foreknowledge of the future can alter it . . ."

"Cop out! Rationalization!" Henner shook with triumph. "You're admitting defeat! Ha!"

"Have I made your day, George? Fair enough! I've got to go placate that tax man again. See you later."

"Don't waste your time with him. He's stupid. No way they can tax the Talents with the structure *I* helped you build. And don't miss the party! The Death Party!"

"Christ, Hank," Gus Molnar complained to Darrow, "he's had me checking him over on the hour all day! And then that gaggle of 'impartial physician witnesses' check on me." Molnar ran his hand nervously through his long fair hair, his eyes restless with anxiety and irritation. "And suddenly he won't let Molly out of his sight. Said her healing hands would turn the trick. Give him the minute he needs. Goddamn old bastard!"

"Cool it, Gus. It's what he needed to keep him alive." Henry chuckled and straightened his tunic jacket, poked at his softly tied scarf.

Gus made a disgusted noise in his throat. "You're so damned sure?"

"Not at all. Unfortunately."

"Unfortunately? With the future of the Center at stake on one man's heart beat?"

"I've seen that we do get the property. I regret that it has to be validated by the death of an old and valued friend. I could almost wish that he does live past the appointed minute . . ."

"Minute . . ." Molnar corrected him. "Bastard's got a huge alarm clock rigged, to the Greenwich-mean-time minute!"

"C'mon, Gus. Let's go to the wake and cheer the corpse on!"

"My God, Darrow, how do you do it?"

The Death Party was assembling, reluctantly, in the vault-roofed lounge of the Beechwoods mansion. George had invited a select few to be "in at the death."

Indeed, as he said himself, he had outlasted most of his contemporaries and those three represented today were more enemies than friends. George quipped that business enemies had a reputation of being in at the death. He was dressed in his Vietnam campaign battle dress, remarking that he'd cheated Him then as a twenty-year-old, so it behooved him to keep the appointment now suitably attired. Most of those present were Talents or connected with the Center. Young Daffyd op Owen was present. So were LEO Commissioner Mailer, trying hard not to look uncomfortable, Governor Lawson, several Senators, representatives from four charitable organizations (probably benefiting under the will, Henry decided when he saw the guest list), and the four physicians who'd been chosen at random from the AMA directory by George and flown into Jerhattan for the event. That was George's way of solving any medical question. With a touch of ghoulish humor, George had decreed—not that he didn't trust the Talents implicitly, but one had to protect oneself—that the autopsy would be performed on his corpse immediately after death had been assumed.

The party consequently generated little joviality despite the abundance of liquor and exotic foods on the sideboard. George ate sparingly, drank slowly. Anything he consumed these days, he complained, tasted sour or flat or insipid and caused heartburn.

Conversations were conducted in sepulchral tones and languished easily. The occasional laugh was quickly suppressed. Only Henry Darrow contrived to look at ease though Molly knew, by the way he rubbed his thumb and index finger together constantly, that he was in a highly nervous condition. She didn't dare touch him since she was not a whit less distraught herself, and would only double Henry's tension. The person who was suffering most was young Daffyd op Owen. She had become very fond of the sensitive young man and wished that he didn't have to be present. He'd not had time to learn to shield himself, certainly not in such an emotionally loaded situation as this. Daffyd was visibly sweating, yet gamely trying to simulate proper party behavior as he chatted with another young Talent, a precog named Mara Channing.

As the appointed time drew nearer, any semblance of normality dwindled: efforts to keep party talk going faltered. Everyone had one eye on the clock and the other on George Henner.

"You're supposed to be happy," George Henner complained when the current silence remained unbroken for sixty-four seconds. "My death means you're all safely ensconced here." His scowl was ambiguous. Then he pointed a finger at Henry. "So tell me, Hank, if you lose the wager, where will you go? I . . ." and he laughed hollowly, "or my executors expect you to vacate the premises . . . immediately."

"And we will. I've assembled every telekinetic we've got . . . and a flock of physical muscle men. We can clear the premises in an hour, I'm told. You will grant us that much time?"

Henner grunted, then brightly asked where the new Center would be located.

"I've a site upstate seventy miles: woods, a small lake, very pastoral. The disadvantage being the distance to commute. You know what copter traffic is like over the City and the Talents are contracted to be at work on time . . . no matter what."

Henner's chair had been wired to monitor his life-systems, and the results were broadcast on a screen visible anywhere in the room. George glanced up at it incuriously.

"All systems still go?" he asked, swinging around to the nearest medical man who, startled, nodded. "Three minutes and counting, Henry?"

"George, may I remind you that this excitement is bad for you?" Henry said.

"Excitement bad for me? Goddamn you, Darrow, it's kept me alive months past the estimate those jokers gave me. You've kept me alive, damn your eyes."

"Damn 'em?" Henry laughed. "That was the point, George, and you've admitted it before impartial witnesses, too."

Henner pursed his thin, bloodless lips, glaring at various people in the room, unsatisfied with his present victim's reactions and unable to vent his feelings on anyone better suited than Henry. His restless, probing glance fell briefly on Molly.

"Having to leave here will put your program back, won't it?"

Henry shrugged. "For this decade, perhaps yes. The new location will be too far for prospective Talents in the subbie class to come for the test. We can have mobile units . . . once we have the personnel. Trouble is the units have to be especially constructed . . ."

"Yes, yes, you've told me all that." George flounced around in his chair, seeking a new or comfortable position as well as another victim. But he returned to Henry. "You'll be sorry you've kept me alive. In exactly two minutes and four seconds . . ."

"No, George, I won't ever be sorry for your life. Only sorry for your death."

"I can believe that!"

"Indeed you can!" cried Molly, unable to bear George's taunting acrimony.

"Molly . . ." George's voice entreated her and she instinctively stepped toward him, her hands outstretched to give the comfort which had often eased him. But he leaned away, suddenly suspicious even of her. Her hands flew to her mouth as the rebuff wounded her. But his reaction broke Henry's tight control.

"Damn it, George, she only wants to help."

"Help me? Live? Or die?"

Molly began to cry, turning towards the wall. But Henry took her in his arms, for once the comforter.

"Molly didn't deserve that from you, George. The wager was with me!"

"He didn't mean it that way, Henry," said young op Owen, the words bursting from his lips, as if he'd been holding back for some time the desire to speak out.

Henner nodded, his face flushed with what Dai op Owen afterwards said was remorse. But the monitors began flashing warning signals.

"Hell, Molly," George began in a choked voice, "I don't distrust *you.*" Then the death alarm went off. "Ha! The appointed minute . . . And I'm alive! You're wrong, Henry Darrow. You and all your tea-leaf, table-tipping crystal-gazing . . ."

At precisely 9:00:30, George Henner's heart gave a massive contraction and stopped. Cameras on the dead man recorded that his hand raised slightly, towards Henry and Molly before the dead body collapsed.

Accustomed as they were to the death processes, the physicians in attendance were held motionless by the dramatic circumstances. Gus Molnar reacted first, hand moving towards the adrenalin syringe.

"No!" cried Dai op Owen, stepping forward, his hand outstretched. "He wants to die. He doesn't want to win the wager."

"My God," cried one of the physicians, pointing to the screen.

"Look at the Goosegg. It's gone wild. The mind's still alive . . .
No. Consciousness has gone. But God, look at the graph."

"Let him go. He wants to go," Daffyd op Owen was saying.

Molnar looked first towards Henry whose face was expressionless, then at the other physicians staring at the monitor readings.

"That means the brain's dead, doesn't it?" asked LEO Commissioner Mailer, pointing to the Goosegg graph now scribing
straight lifeless lines.

Two of the medical men nodded.

"Then he's dead," said Mailer, glancing towards the Governor
who nodded accord. "I'd say you won the bet, Darrow."

"The wager said 'minute', I trust, not second?" asked one of the
Senators.

"He shouldn't've excited himself like that," a doctor muttered.
"This party was a mistake. Of course we weren't consulted on that.
But it set up circumstances which would obviously result in over-
stimulation, certain death for a man in Henner's condition."

"Or, there's the voodoo element in this," another physician said
without rancor. "Tell a victim often enough that he'll be dead at
such and such a time and the subconscious takes over and kills the
man."

"Not in this instance," said Gus Molnar, loudly and belligerently. "And there's ample medical substantiation, including your
own remarks," he added, pointing at the voodoo adherent, "that
the stimulation provided by the original bet kept George Henner
alive long past his own medical men's estimate. The bet did not
cause his death, it caused his life."

No one ventured to refute that statement.

"I believe," spoke up one of the attorneys present, "that the autopsy was to be performed immediately?"

As if on cue, two men appeared from the hallway, wheeling a
stretcher. Silently they approached, their passage unimpeded as
guests stepped aside hastily. The body was laid on the stretcher in
silence. But, as the men took their positions to leave, Molly broke
from Henry's embrace. With gentle fingers, she closed the dead
man's eyes. The tears streamed down her face as she kissed George
on the forehead. The stretcher glided out of the room. No one
spoke until the last sound of footsteps in the hall was gone.

"Mr. Darrow," said the attorney, his voice sounding abnormally
loud after the requiem silence, "I was enjoined by Mr. Henner to

make a few announcements at this time usually reserved until several days hence. I was to tell you that this was one wager he didn't wish to win and hoped he wouldn't: no matter what indication he gave to the contrary. He said that you were sportsman enough, Mr. Darrow, to appreciate the fact that he had to try to win." The attorney turned to the physician who had brought up the voodoo insinuation. "He also ordered me to counteract any attempt to bring charges resulting from a misinterpretation of today's sad occasion. He empowered me to say that he had implicit trust in the integrity of all members of the Parapsychic Center. We," and he gestured towards his colleagues, "are to be the executors of Mr. Henner's estate, the bulk of which, excluding a few behests and excluding these grounds now the irrevocable property of the North American Center for Parapsychic Talents, is to go into a Trust Fund, providing legal assistance to anyone registered with the Center who may be imprisoned or charged with damages or lawsuits following the professional use of their Talent, until such time as specific laws are promulgated to give the Talents professional immunity." The lawyer gave Henry a wry grin. "He said, and I quote, 'If you ride a winged horse, you'd better have a wide net when you fall. And that takes money!'

"He also said that after he was dead," and the lawyer faltered, embarrassed by the inadvertent rhyme, "he said the party was to begin. That this was to be considered a joyous occasion . . ."

"He *was* glad," Daffyd op Owen said, and his rather homely face lit with happiness. "That was so astonishing. His mind, the thoughts were happy, so happy at the moment of death. He was happy. I tell you. *I know* he was glad!"

"Thank God!" was Henry Darrow's fervent prayer. He raised his untouched drink. "A toast, ladies and gentlemen." Glasses obediently were lifted. "To those who ride the winged horse!"

One after another the glasses followed Henry's into the fireplace of Beechwoods to preserve the tribute to George Henner's memory.

PART TWO

A
WOMANLY
TALENT

I f you were one whit less honorable, Daffyd op Owen," exclaimed Joel Andres heatedly, "you and your whole Center could go . . . go fly a kinetic kite."

The passionate senator was one of those restlessly energetic men who gave the appearance of continuous motion even in rare moments of stasis. Joel Andres was rigid now—with aggravation. The object of his frustration, Daffyd op Owen, Director of the East American Parapsychological Research and Training Center, was his antithesis, physically and emotionally. Both men, however, had the same indefinable strength and purposefulness, qualities which set them apart from lesser men.

"I can't win support for my Bill," Andres continued, trying another tack and pacing the thick-piled green carpeting of op Owen's office, "if you consistently play into Mansfield Zeusman's hands with this irrational compulsion to tell everything you know. If only on the grounds that what you 'know' is not generally acceptable as reliable 'knowledge.'

"And don't tell me that familiarity breeds contempt, Dave. The unTalented are never going to be contemptuous of the psychic abilities, they're going to continue being scared stiff. It's human nature to fear—and distrust—what is different. Surely," and Andres flung his arms wide, "you've studied enough behavioral psychology to understand that basic fact."

"My Talent permits me to look below the surface rationalizations and uncover the . . ."

"But you can*not* read the minds of every single one of the men who must vote on this Bill, Dave. Nor can you alter their thinking. Not with your thinking and your ethics!" Joel was almost derisive as he pointed a nicotined finger accusingly at his friend. "And don't give me that wheeze about lawmakers being intelligent, thoughtful men!"

Op Owen smiled tolerantly at his friend, unaffected by the younger man's histrionics. "Not even when Senator Zeusman steals a march on us with that so apt quotation from Pope?"

Andres made a startled noise of exasperation, then caught the look in the other's eyes and laughed.

"Yeah, he sure caught me flatfooted there." He deepened his voice somewhat to mimic the affected bass of Mansfield Zeusman:

> " 'Who sees with equal eye, as God of all,
> A hero perish or a sparrow fall . . .'

"What a rallying cry that is! Why didn't *I* think of it first? Mind you," and Andres was deadly serious again, "that quote is pure genius . . . for the opposition. Spikes our pitch in a dozen places. The irony is that it would be just as powerful for us if we'd only thought of it first. Dave, won't you reconsider," Joel asked, leaning across the table to the telepath, "eliminating the precogs from the Bill? That's what's hanging it up now in Committee. I'm sure I could get it put on . . ."

"The precogs need the legal protection most of all," op Owen replied with unusual vehemence, a momentary flash of alarm crossing his face.

"I know, I know," and Andres tossed a hand ceilingward in resignation. "But that's the facet of the parapsychic that scares—and fascinates—people most."

"And that is exactly why I insist we be as candid as possible on all phases of the extrasensory perception Talents. Then people will become as used to them as to 'finders,' 'ports' and 'paths.' Henry Darrow was so right about that."

Joel Andres whirled back to the desk, gripping the edges fiercely. "The prophet Darrow notwithstanding, you don't tell suspicious, frightened people everything. They automatically assume you're holding something back because *they* would. *No* one dares to be so honest anymore. Therefore they are sure that what you're with-holding is far worse than what you've readily admitted." He caught the adamant gleam in Daffyd's eye and unexpectedly capit-ulated. "All right. All *right*. But I insist that we continue to emphasize what the *other* Talents are already able to do . . . *in their narrow specialized ways.* Once people can stomach the idea that there *are* limits on individual psionic Talents, that all Talents are not mind readers cum weight throwers cum fire dowsers cum crystal-ball-seers, all rolled up into one frightening package, they'll start treating them as you want Talents treated: as professional specialists, trained in one area of a varied profession and entitled to professional immunity in that area *if* they are licensed and registered with the Centers. *Don't*," and the hand went up again as Daffyd tried to interrupt, "tell them you're experimenting to find out how to broaden every Talented mind. *Don't* ask for the whole piece of bread with jam on it, Dave! You won't get it, but you will get protection for your people in the practice of their speciality, even your precogs. I'll bear down heavily on the scientific corroboration of authentic foresights," and Andres began to pace a tight rectangle in front of op Owen's desk, his dark head down, his gestures incisive, "the use of computers to correlate details and estimate reliability of data, the fact that sometimes three and four precogs come up with the same incident, seen from different angles. And most importantly—that the Center never issues an official warning unless the computer agrees that sufficient data coincides between Incident and reality . . ."

"Please emphasize that we admit to human fallibility and use computers to limit *human* error."

Joel frowned at op Owen's droll interjection. "Then I'll show how the foresight prevented or averted the worst of the Incidents. That Monterey Quake is a heaven-sent example. No heroes perished, even if a few sparrows did fall from gas discharges."

"I thought it was the meddling with the sparrow's fall that perturbs Senator Zeusman," Daffyd remarked wryly. "For want of that seed, the grain won't sprout . . ."

"Hmmm, yes, it does! 'What will be, will be,' " and Andres mimicked Zeusman's voice again.

"Since he initiated Pope," said op Owen, "I'd reply 'Whatever is, is right.' "

"You want me to turn Papist now, huh?" Joel grinned wickedly.

Daffyd chuckled as he continued, "Pope also advises, 'Be candid where we can but vindicate the ways of God to man!' "

The gently delivered quote had an instant effect on the senator, comparable to touching a match to a one-second fuse. Midway to explosion, Andres snapped his mouth shut, sighed extravagantly and rolled his slightly yellowed eyes heavenwards.

"You are the most difficult man to help, Daffyd op Owen!"

"That's only because I'm aware how carefully we must move in the promulgation of this Bill, Joel. I don't want it backfiring at the wrong time, when some of the basic research now in progress becomes demonstrable. The Talents can't be hamstrung by obsolete statutes imperfectly realized on a scrabbling compromise basis."

"Dave, you want to run before you can walk?"

"No, but trouble has been foreseen."

"Darrow again, huh? Or are you hoist on your own petard?" Joel waggled a finger triumphantly. "Trouble stemming from current non-protection. Go cast up a precog *after* the Bill is passed."

"Ah-ha" and Daffyd mimicked Joel now, "but we don't see the Bill passing!"

That rendered Andres speechless.

"And we are hoist on our own petard," the telepath continued with a hint of sorrowful resignation in his voice, "because all our preventive methods *are* affecting the future, unfortunately, much as Senator Zeusman presented the syndrome in his Sparrow's Fall peroration. That was such a masterful speech," op Owen said with rueful envy. "Valid, too, for as surely as the Center issues a warning, allowing people a chance to avert or prevent tragedy, they have already prejudiced the events from happening as they were foreseen. That's the paradox. Yet how, *how* can an ethical man stand aside and let a hero perish, or even a sparrow fall, when he *knows* that he can prevent unnecessary or premature loss."

"The Monterey Quake could *not* have been prevented," Joel reminded him, then blinked in amazement. "You're not holding out on *me*, are you? You haven't found a kinetic strong enough to hold the earth's surface together?"

Dave's laughter was a spontaneous outburst of delight at his friend's discomposure.

"No, no. At least . . . not yet," he said just to watch the outraged expression on Andres's mobile face.

There were few people with whom Daffyd op Owen could relax or indulge in his flights of humor and hyperbole. "Seriously, Joel, the Monterey Quake is a spectacular Incident and a prime example of the concerted use of Talent, minimizing the loss of life or property. We have never had so many precogs stimulated in their separate affinities. And it's the most concrete example of why precogs need legal protection. Do you realize that the Western Center was deluged with damage suits for the tsunami that followed?"

"*That* was predictable."

"But *we* issued no warnings. And it's against such irrational attitudes that precogs need legal protection more than any other Talent. Theirs is stimulated by mental perceptions as erratic as a smell in the morning air, a glance at a photo, the sound of a name. In a sense, precog is tremendously unreliable because it cannot be used as consciously as telepathy, teleportation and telekinesis. And to protect the Talent as well as the Center, we insist on computer corroboration when details are coherently specific. We never issue a public warning until the computer admits reliability . . . and we get damned because we have 'heard' and not spoken. Of course, a number of our precogs have become absorbed into business where peculiar affinities place them. For instance," and Daffyd held up a tape-file, "this young man, who's applying for progeny approval, is a fire-conscious. But he's one reason this city has such low fire-insurance rates: his Talent prevents them—a blessing indirectly passed on to every resident . . ."

"Hmmm, but scarcely spectacular enough to register with the average egocentric Joe Citizen," said Andres sourly. He was restless with Daffyd's earnest review of facts he knew well. "However, every little bit helps, Dave, and the public moves a lot faster pro bona pocketbook."

"True, exactly true, and they get rather nasty when we try to save them money and will not understand that a legitimate forewarning automatically alters the future, even to the point of preventing the foreseen Incident which will have cost old publican money, or time, or effort he *then* feels was unnecessary."

"And there we are, right back at square one," said Joel in flat disgust. "That is what Mansfield calls 'meddling' and what makes him fight this Bill with every ounce of his outraged moralistic, neo-religious, mock-ethical fibre. Remember, he's backed by the transport lobbies, and every time one of your precogs hits that jolly little brotherhood, causing delays, hurried inspections, the whole jazz—you got a number-one headache. Because, when the predictions don't happen as predicted, Transport swears your meddling is superstitious interference, uncalled for, unnecessary and nothing would have happened anyway."

Daffyd sighed wearily. "How many times have we found bombs? Fuel leaks? Averted hijacks? Metal fatigue . . . mechanical justifications?"

"Doesn't signify, Dave, not if it touches the pocketbook of the Transport Companies. Remember, every precog implies fault: human or mechanical, since the Companies will not recognize Providence as a force. And human or mechanical, the public loses faith in the Company thus stigmatized. When Company profits are hit, Company gets mad, sues the precog for defamation of character, interference, et cetera."

"Then we are to allow the traveling public to fry in their own juice or be spread across the fields because a precog has seen a crash but doesn't want to offend a Company? For want of a screw the nail was lost!" op Owen's usually soothing voice was rough with asperity. "Damn it, Joel, we have to preserve impartiality, and warn anyone or anything that is touched by the precognitive Talent, or we do usurp the position of the Almighty by withholding that evidence. I don't care if the transportation companies then decide to disregard the warning—that's their problem. But I want my people protected when, in good faith and based on computer-accepted detail, they issue that warning. We have no ax to grind, commercially, thanks to the Darrow endowment and member support, but we must continue to be impartial."

"I hope your altruism is not going to be your downfall," said Joel, his manner unusually grave.

"There's been no warning that it will," Daffyd replied. A hint of irritation in his voice.

"You're too honest to be up against us crook politicians," Joel said, grinning, then glanced at his watch. "Wup. Gotta go."

"You push yourself too hard, Joel. You don't look well."

"A bit liverish, that's all, and no snooping."

"Not without permission and you know it."

"Hah! Among friends, I don't trust telepaths. Say, how's the recruiting program?" Joel asked as he swooped up his travel cape and case.

"We get hopefuls every week," the director replied as he escorted the senator to the elevator. "Sometimes we even catch a few young ones, before they learn to suppress a perfectly normal ability."

"That's another phrase you should delete around Zeusman," Joel said. "He will not buy your premise that every mind has psionic Talent."

"But, Joel, *that* is scientifically valid. We know that those who possess Talent have strong, healthy twenty-first chromosome pairs. It is certainly admissible evidence that when the twenty-first is blurred or damaged to any degree, brain function is inhibited. And, with the Downs's Syndrome, you have mental retardation."

"Don't beleaguer me," Joel said with widened eyes of innocence, "I believe!" He laid a hand on his heart. "I couldn't doubt—not after that 'finder' located my brother in the mine shaft before he bled to death. If we could only subject Mansfield Zeusman to such an experience, he wouldn't be so skeptical. Can't one of your pet Talents do something about that? I thought they always keep an eye on controversial men to prevent assassination and stuff."

Op Owen gave a snort. "Would Senator Zeusman honor a precog foreseeing his own demise?"

"Hmmm. Probably not. Say, you're not funded on the Government Research Program, are you?"

"No, thank God. The Henner Bequest was reserved for that. Why?"

"Hmmm. Just that Zeusman is extending this argument against the Bill to all 'specious'—as he terms it—forms of research, government funded. And spring is appropriations time, you know."

"Fortunately, we've never had that kind of pressure."

"Talented of you," Joel said with a grin.

Behind him the elevator door slid open and a young woman, obviously in a hurry, ran out, right into the muscular frame of the young Senator.

She blurted out an apology, flushing with embarrassment as Andres reached out to steady her. Then her eyes opened wider as she saw op Owen and one hand flew to her mouth. "I'm awfully sorry, sir."

Just as Daffyd recognized Ruth Horvath, he also identified the combined emotions of shame at her precipitous arrival into a distinguished champion of the Talented, regret for her impulsiveness in coming to the Tower at this hour, and the underlying hope and apprehension that had compelled her to come. Instinctively, Daffyd touched her with soothing reassurances: but Joel Andres's amiable and admiring glance was the tonic the pretty woman needed.

"No harm done, I assure you, Miss . . . ?"

"*Mrs.* Horvath . . . Senator Andres," Daffyd said and watched Joel's expression change from delighted interest to flattering chagrin.

"I do apologize, Senator," Ruth repeated, her cheeks blushstained again.

"And I apologize for being in the wrong place at the wrong time and . . ." an extravagant sigh ". . . too late." He bowed deeply to Ruth, reluctantly stepping aside to let her pass.

Instead she fumbled with the elevator button.

"I'm on my lunch break," she said with a stammer. "I've got to get back."

The panel slid open and Andres stepped in beside her, one finger jamming the "hold" button.

"Me, too," he said, grinning down at her.

"Your file is on my desk right now, Ruth," Daffyd said, suddenly comprehending the reason for her visit and her hesitancy in mentioning the subject in Andres's presence. "I'll call you tomorrow."

Her face lit up, her eyes became eager and, as she glanced away, Daffyd thought he saw the shine of tears.

"Take care of yourself, Joel. You're working too hard."

"A pleasure, I assure you." Joel's laugh was cut off by the closing door.

Daffyd op Owen stood looking at the indicator panel for a few moments before he turned slowly back to his isolated tower office. He had much to think about. Not that he would deflect one centimeter from his course of action. Only his firm beliefs sustained him for it didn't require precog, only intelligent extrapolation— which some uninformed people insisted was the essence of precog —to determine the difficulties still faced by the Talented all over the world. The Bill was so vital a forward step, raising the Talents from the onerous category of "mental chiropractors," (Senator Zeusman's phrase, though chiropractic treatment had long been an accredited branch of medicine), to a creditable position among professional abilities. Mansfield Zeusman had already stalled the Bill in Committee for months, was capable of stalling it through the summer, and keeping it off the agenda next year. The senator was hoping to find some discrediting Incident that would forever banish hope of legal protection for the Talented.

The sheer genius of that Pope quotation was a measure of their opponent's worth, op Owen mused as he turned to the mass of administrative files awaiting him. The pity of it was that the quote would have been much more applicable to the Talent side of the argument. Come to think of it, much of Pope's "Essay on Man" was to the point.

Other pertinent lines came easily out of mental storage. Not much that Daffyd op Owen had once seen could elude his recall . . . a blessing as well as a handicap.

> With too much knowledge for the Skeptic side,
> With too much weakness for the Stoic's pride,
> He hangs between, in doubt to act or rest:
> In doubt to deem himself a God or Beast:
> In doubt his mind or body to prefer
> Born but to die and reas'ning but to err . . .

"Enough!" and op Owen roused from introspection to direction. He flipped open the nearest tape case and slapped it into the playback. It seemed somehow meet that it was the Horvaths' progeny application. Were op Owen a superstitious man he could have accounted it a good omen: a favorable auspice for the work he and his fellow directors around the world were inaugurating. Breed like to like, strengthen strong genetic Talent traits and develop, not the super race of omniscient, omnipotent superpeople Zeusman basically feared, but people trained and conditioned from childhood to use their Talents for the benefit of man. And, by such service, force the World to recognize the treasure that can be unlocked in the unused, untapped portion of the human brain.

A flaming, shattering precog caught Lajos Horvath at the moment when REM sleep was over and his unconscious mind was rousing from that phase of rest.

His groan of anguish awakened his wife instantly. With the reflex of training, Ruth flipped the recorder and pulled the retractable electrode Goosegg net to his head, expertly clamping the metal discs on the circles of his scalp that had been permanently depilated.

Blinking her eyes to see the reading in the dawn-dim room, Ruth watched the definite pattern of an Incident emerge. Center was already picking it up for authentication. The Incident lasted a scant eleven seconds before the brain waves settled back to a calm reading. She lay back, going through the discipline that would relax her and prevent her from imposing her haste-urgency reaction on Lajos. As soon as he roused, she must be composed enough to question him for a verbal report.

She achieved the proper repose quickly, suppressing the thrill of satisfaction at her success. She was no longer as troubled by flashes of envy that Lajos possessed a valid Talent while hers was so nebulous as to elude identification. Now it was enough for her to know that, by the exercise of the deep empathy which existed between them, by her womanliness, she made his development more certain. Lajos needed her as a buffer, a source of solace from the sharp edges of Talent. Even the strongest personality could succumb to the Cassandra complex that destroyed the sanity of the unwary precog. Why was it, Ruth mused in a quiet inner voice, that tragedy has such a vicious way of reaching out of the mists of the future: like a falling man, blindly grabbing at anything to restore balance and avert his fall?

Again the needle rushed across the graph, a slight *whoosh* barely audible in the quiet room. Ruth glanced over to make sure the Incident was being beamed to the Center and noticed the smile on her husband's face. A smile? A happy premonition? She forced herself to relax, unaccountably assailed by a raving curiosity. Lajos so rarely had happy foresights, and fleetingly she regretted that he was a precog.

Lajos stirred restlessly. He was waking now. She turned on the voice recorder and leaned towards him.

"What is it? What do you see?" she asked in the soft persuasive voice the Center had taught her to use at these times. Her ability to stimulate his verbal accounts was highly praised, for it was sometimes difficult for the precog to articulate the semi-real into sufficient detail for preventive or supportive action.

"Flames!" Lajos groaned. "Must it always be flames?" He sat bolt upright in bed then, his brown eyes wide as he stared straight ahead at the retinal image of his premonitory vision. The electrodes were jerked from his skull, retracting with a metallic clink into the case. "The ship's burning, exploding. Throwing flaming debris across the harbor into the suburbs. Damp it! Deflect! Shield those passengers. Watch out! The propellant will spray. It's exploding. Contain it!"

"Markings on the liner?" a gentle but insistent voice whispered from the intercom.

Lajos shook his head, blinking furiously in an attempt to hold the fading sight. "It's awash with flame. I think I see an eight, a four, a three—or is it another eight? It's a Reynarder. It must be. They're the only ones who use that class."

"Which class?" the inexorable whisper wanted to know.

Suddenly Lajos sagged, panting with shock, cold sweat breaking out on his forehead. He lay back exhausted.

"It's gone," he moaned. "It's gone."

"You had a second one," Ruth said. "What was that about?"

Lajos's brows drew together in a half frown as he brushed his straight black hair out of his face. He kept it overlong to hide the depilated circles where the electrodes fit. His lips curved in a half-sided smile. "Something good?" he asked hopefully.

Ruth suppressed her sigh. Lajos rarely detailed the felicitous ones.

"Incident validated, a strong reading, Lajos," the intercom voice said. "Report in as soon as you're able."

"They'll check it out, won't they?" Lajos asked needlessly.

"Action already initiated."

Lajos lay so still that Ruth knew it was not passive quiescence but rigid strain. Another thorn in the Talented's side was the harsh realization that their warnings were often disregarded and they were forced to see their predictions come horribly true. Ruth wiped the sweat from Lajos's forehead and began to massage his neck and shoulders. After a moment he grinned weakly up at her.

"What a way to start the day, huh?"

"At least you ended on a happy note. Maybe that means they'll prevent?"

"If they can correlate enough data, in enough time," he said gloomily. "*And* Reynarder bothers to listen!" He flopped onto his stomach, pounding the mattress with impotent fists.

Ruth transferred her attention to his muscular back. She loved the line of him, the broad double plateau of his shoulder blades with the small mounds of hard muscle, the graceful curve that swept down to the narrow waist, the hollow of his spine, the Grecian beauty of his buttocks. She quickly suppressed a flare of desire. This was not the time to intrude sex on his personal anguish. And she knew that her intense sexual hunger for him stemmed from a yearning for the child of his seed. A daughter, tall and fair, with Lajos's dimples in her cheek. A son, strongbacked and arrogant, with thick black straight hair.

This hunger for his child was so primal, it paralyzed the sophistication overlaid by education and social reflexes. Nowadays a woman was expected to assume more than the ancient duties required of her. Nowadays, and Ruth smiled to herself, the sophists called those womanly talents, Maintenance, Repair and Replacement, instead of housekeeping, cooking, nursing and having babies, but the titles didn't alter the duties nor curb the resurgent desires. And, when you got down to it, men still explored new ground, even if it were alien lands, and defended their homes and families. You could call Lajos's precog a kind of an early-warning defense system. Well, then, she'd added the chore of being Cerebral-Recording Secretary to Maintenance and Repair but they'd better let her Replace soon or. . . .

She concentrated on more soothing thoughts, using her latent empathy to ease his remorse. When he began to take deep long breaths, she knew he was conquering the aftermath of the Incident, dispelling its destructive despondency. He had done everything he could. He could *not* change the course of every fated life. Some events had to come to their dire conclusions, for out of present tragedy so often rose future triumph; the result of sorrowful recriminations was often the catalyst of progress. A specious rationale in the Silver-lined Cloud Approach but true enough to save the sanity of the Talented.

It was a bitter thing, Ruth understood, to be Talented: bitter and wonderful. But it was worse to have evidence of Talent and never know what it was. Nonsense, she told herself sternly, discarding these reflections, you can't be what you can't be.

"Ahh, you've got the right spot," Lajos said gratefully and she doubled her efforts across the heavy shoulder muscles.

And yet, when she anticipated his desires and needs, sometimes the words from his mouth, she wondered just how she had tapped that need; just what might awaken the occluded Talent within her.

The Center believed that psionic abilities were latent human characteristics: their absence due to malfunction of the necessary brain synapses or, even more basically, underdevelopment due to a protein lack in the gene. When chromosomes in the twenty-first pair were damaged or blurred, no Talent was detected. There was no aberration in Ruth's chromosomes, and although she tested as Talented, her ability was unidentifiable. She had never been able to stimulate an Incident involving any of the known abilities. She'd met Lajos during the testing: they'd been approached by the Eastern American Center after finishing their secondary schooling and had qualified for the six-months' training designed to stimulate latent Talent. Their genetic history had been taped back to the fourth generation. They had endured hours of cerebral recording on the Goosegg under a variety of stimuli. Ruth was finally labeled "indeterminate"; Lajos showed strong precog tendencies.

Ruth still secretly hoped that her Talent would develop. She'd been assured that this was a possibility: they cited her high empathy rating, her ability to anticipate attitudes and actions of those nearest and dearest to her. True, she might be no more than a receptive telempath, one unable to broadcast but receptive. Ruth therefore alternated between hope and despair: being a practical creature, she dwelt mostly on the pessimistic side of the pendulum, refusing to believe anything but the most conclusive evidence. This attitude was reinforced during Lajos's worst Incidents, when she wanted no part of the cruel gift.

Lajos Horvath was one of several thousand Talented people, licensed and registered with the Center; devoted to its precepts and ideals, contributing all of his salary to it. The Center was not paternalistic, nor did it require any recompense. But the Talented preferred to live together, if possible, on or near the Center's grounds at Beechwoods, among their peers: reassured and reinforced. As the Center "policed" its own members, it also protected them.

Ruth had no specific objections to their situation: she had willingly taken the course orienting unTalented partners to their gifted spouses. She would have undergone a far more arduous requirement, so deep was her love of Lajos. But lately, obedience to E.A.C. had begun to gall Ruth and it was not due to any fault of the Center's. She recognized that.

The muted buzz of the intercom roused both of them. Lajos propped himself up on his elbows, his profile towards her so that she observed the thin bitter line of his mouth and knew that he was steeling himself.

"Lajos," it was Daffyd op Owen, "you were correct. A class 7 Reynarder had a propellant leak at Buffalo jetport."

Something in the director's slow deep voice told them that Lajos's information had not averted.

"And?" Lajos's question was a firm demand for the truth.

"We had to compute the variable details with the possible airports near water, flights landing or departing on the Reynarder line. We got only one other personal precog involving the Incident but your data alone—particularly the registry—was sufficient. The loss would have been catastrophic without your warning. Teleports on the Rescue Squad deflected most of the flaming wreckage into the Lake before it could land in the suburbs. Kinetics managed to shield the passenger deck until the propellant could be foamed. The passengers and crew suffered massive heat prostration but all will live. Ruth, does he need a tranquilizer?"

"No!" the negative exploded from Lajos's lips.

"Good lad!" op Owen's voice was warm with approval. "We've authenticated the Incident. It averted a major tragedy: one more pound of evidence on our side of the scales for the Bill. And the passengers and jetport personnel *know* who gave the warning."

Lajos went limp with relief as the Director signed off with expressions of gratitude. Lajos half-turned his face and Ruth didn't know for a moment whether to comfort him or not. She waited. Finally he gave a long shuddering sigh and relaxed, one hand slipping over the side of the bed, fingers limp, the veins in his forearm bulging, blue under his unusually fair skin.

"Then what I saw—didn't happen, Ruth. The jet didn't turn into a flaming hull, exploding all over the suburbs. So what did I see? Which didn't happen because I saw it? Because my seeing it was sufficient to alter the future?" He shook his head, his beard stubble rasping against the tightly drawn bedsheet, but his voice was no longer hoarse with recrimination; it was calm: his philosophy was asserting itself.

Ruth felt the muscles in her shoulders unknot and only then realized how tense she had become, waiting for his reaction.

" 'A paradox, a paradox, a most ingenious paradox,' " she chanted lightly, stroking his back with her fingertips. "My darling pirate," and she kissed his cheek.

Lajos bounced out of bed and stretched, his sleep-pants falling off his narrow hips. He grabbed them back up, not out of modesty but to keep from tripping over them on the way to the bathroom.

"Maybe the good precog you had . . . it followed a bare sixty seconds after the first, you know," Ruth remarked later as she served his breakfast, "was the realization that you had averted."

Lajos considered that, then shook his head. "No. The two were definitely non-related."

"Why is it," Ruth asked with mock shrewishness, "that you can detail the horrors but not the happies?"

He didn't know and began to eat heartily, his appetite indicative of restored equilibrium.

"Got to run, honey. Be a busy day. And that's no precog. It's a sure thing." He grinned then kissed her soundly. "Annual review of contracts, and Zeusman notwithstanding, the Firm handles the government's insurances in this city."

Ruth would have to hurry as well. She disliked being late although her job was not essential. She fitted filaments to fractional feeders, an intricate, delicate operation which required deft hands even with waldo-aids, and a certain tenacious patience with micro-movements. Her employers never objected to her occasional delays as they employed teleports and telekinetics for the transportation of delicate equipment and to assemble by remote control the "hot" components of instrumentation to be used in the Jupiter probes. Ruth did not need to work, for Lajos was highly paid, but she preferred to keep busy until their request for progeny was approved. She wanted so to be a full-time mother.

There was unlikely to be a problem in receiving approval—eventually—but anyone was liable to pick up a dose of accidental radiation that could blur or damage chromosomes. They knew their genetic patterns were sound and they had completed the three years' probation to establish the compatibility and stability of their marriage. For the last six months they had undergone continual egg and sperm cell check for possible aberrations. It was time-consuming, but who wanted a handicapped child? It had taken years to weed out the psychedelic damages that had resulted in the freaks of the late Seventies and early Eighties. There were still occasional mutants as a result of the heavy Solar Winds in the first decade of the twenty-first century. It was only common sense to check every variable.

But Ruth found it hard to be patient. She asked for very little of what her heritage had once seemed to offer. She didn't mind being an unidentifiable Talent, she had adjusted to it. She didn't really mind the often worrisome role of a passive observer to the mental

agonies of Lajos's perceptions: she loved him and she helped him.
She did mind the growing sense of futility. Nowadays, with shelter
and food assured one, with the excitement of space explorations to
capture the imagination, with leisure to develop interests and hob-
bies, everyone had the opportunity to use their full capabilities, yet
she was constantly frustrated. If only she could be a full woman to
Lajos, not just caring for him, but raising his children, preferably
his Talented children! She would do everything in her power to
make sure they would succeed where she had failed.

On his firm's table of organization, Lajos Horvath was listed as a
"Contract Analyst and Underwriter" of the Eastern Headquarters
of the Insurance Company. Conservative in so many areas, the
insurance field had been one of the first major industries to see the
advantages of staff 'precogs'; particularly one such as Lajos whose
accuracy in fire-hazard control had been established beyond question.

Most of his precognitive Incidents dealt with flaming substances,
as other precogs seemed to have reliable affinities for water, autos,
metals or certain types of personalities. There was a friendly debate within the Center whether "finders" were precogs or clairvoyants, but they had affinity for "lost items," organic and inor-
ganic. There were four in Lajos' Firm, and they represented huge
annual savings for their employers.

Once Lajos's precogs would have been ascribed to astuteness or
hunches or shrewd extrapolations. Indeed, he himself was perfectly willing to put the vaguer apprehensions under that general-
ity. But training and sensitivity had sharpened many "hunches"
into definitive perceptions: Check the cellar of that building for
dangerous refuse, the janitor is lazy and has not discarded all possible combustibles. The wiring in that attic is frayed and the owners
tend to overload their circuits with heavy-draw appliances. Sometimes the Incident was sustained: This building will be vandalized,
fire is involved. The police were then requested to keep that building under surveillance. The surveillance was sufficient to prevent
the breaking and entering which Lajos had predicted, but the
Company had long ago learned not to protest the measures suggested by their perceptives. Insurers are accustomed to statistics,
and Talents saved them too much in claims. Sometimes, as that
morning, Lajos would experience a general alarm, touched off by
the imminence of a violent fire, or a sudden flaring of fire-danger

resulting from a vehicular crash. There were days when nothing activated his Talent. And days, of which this was one, when everything seemed to smell vaguely of smoke or be wreathed in ghostly flames. He had to censor half a dozen false impressions by checking them against the small office Goosegg. He had learned to differentiate the valid precogs: that was why he was licensed and registered by the Center.

He finished the pile of contracts, noting those about which he experienced twinge-hesitations that indicated a future review would be wise. On his way home, he suddenly felt a lightness of spirit, an ebullience quite unaccountable after his strenuous day. He didn't try to analyze it, too delighted with the relief to want to question the source. But, as he opened his door, Ruth raced into his arms.

"We've been approved as parents," she cried, clasping him tightly to her in an excess of elation. "Director op Owen himself called me just a few minutes ago. *You* ought to have been home when he called."

"Which proves that op Owen is no precog," Lajos said with a chuckle as he pressed her soft slenderness to him. He buried his lips into the curve of her neck. "That's an anodyne for this morning."

"Why for this morning?" she asked, pulling back and searching his face with worried eyes.

"Oh, it's all right, sweetie, but he knew I'd hear all the details. Reynarder Inc. was warned the instant my Incident identified the ship but they refused to issue a blanket halt on all outgoing and incoming vessels with those numerals. Reynarder's money is back of the Transport Lobby and they support Zeusman, you know. They *can't* admit that Incidents, backed by cerebral variations, computer-sorted, validated by the Center are NOT superstitious nonsense. But a lot of people check out their flights nowadays with a licensed precog."

"Then I say that companies like Reynarder deserve what they get!"

"Hey, we can afford not to be petty. And besides, I want to talk about us: about our child. What'll we have first? Boy or girl?"

Ruth stiffened in his arms and pulled back to look her husband straight in the eye.

"Do we have to specify? Does it have to be predetermined?" she asked in a small voice, aware even as the words popped out that she sounded resentful. "Oh, I don't mean it that way. It's just that when you predetermine, it takes away all the mystery that's left to motherhood."

"Ruthie," and Lajos's tender teasing voice thrilled her. "You're a real recessive. O.K., we'll just let nature take its course."

"Can't we eat first?"

Lajos threw back his head and laughed boyishly at her deliberate coquetry. He hugged her until he heard her ribs crack and her dinner sizzling.

It was a magical night. Ruth responded to lovemaking with an ardor that astounded her husband: a surrender that left him breathless and not a little awed: as if, sloughing off the onus of contraceptive interference, she could allow herself to be touched to the depths of her being.

If the quality of their loving had anything to do with the final product, their child ought to be a perfect human, Lajos thought as they finally fell asleep in each other's arms. There was no guarantee that conception occurred that night. In fact, Lajos hoped that it hadn't if Ruth would react like this until she did conceive.

Shortly, however, it was apparent that conception had occurred. Ruth developed a luminous beauty that touched everything around her with harmony. Jerry Frames, the Center's resident physician, with a healing talent, privately told op Owen that the foetus was female and that Ruth was healthy enough to experience no problems.

The girl weighed seven pounds and three ounces at birth and was immediately christened the Little Princess by the nursery staff in the Center's hospital. Her parents called her Dorotea and were utterly besotted with her miniature perfection, her pink-and-gold beauty. They were oblivious to the curious stares and whispered comments of the staff. It was Ruth, preternaturally sensitive to anything regarding her daughter, who began to notice the surreptitious glances, the cluster of people constantly near her daughter's crib.

"You're hiding something from me," she told Jerry Frames accusingly. "There's something wrong with Dorotea."

"There's not a thing wrong with her, Ruth," Jerry replied sharply and thrust the baby's chart at her. "You've enough pediatrics to read the medical notations. Go ahead."

Ruth scanned the sheets quickly, then reread word and graph, checking the laboratory reports of body function, the cerebral and cardiac readings, even the nourishment intake and eliminations. There was definitely nothing abnormal about Dorotea. Even her chromosome mapping was XX/healthy/normal. Reassured, Ruth passed the clipboard back, and smiling confidently, continued to nurse her child.

Frames later said that he'd had a moment of pure panic because he couldn't remember how much genetic training Ruth had had or might remember. Op Owen assured him that his instinctive impulse had been the only possible course under the circumstances.

"It's exceedingly fortunate though, Jerry," the director said, his eyes active with speculation, "that they are already under the Center's protection. That child must have every safeguard we can provide. I want equipment installed in her nursery, tuned to her pattern day and night. If what we suspect is correct, it may manifest itself in her first six months. Can you imagine the strides we can make in formulating an early childhood program with such a superb example?"

"A pure case of doing what comes naturally."

"Nothing must interfere with the child's development."

"I still don't see why we've kept it from the parents. Are you stepping down from your 'know-all, tell-all' pedestal after all?"

Op Owen returned the physician's sardonic look.

"I'm not a precog, but I felt a strong reluctance to inform Lajos."

"Why? He'd be walking nine feet tall to think he produced such a Talented child."

"Haven't we changed sides, Jerry?"

"It's one thing to withhold information from the unwashed public, but another to clam up on one of the gang."

"We don't know positively that Dorotea Horvath is . . ."

"Come off it, Dave. Cecily King is a strong TP and she *heard* that child protest birth. Oh, I know that some of 'em can cry out in the womb but this was no physical cry or it would have been audible to the rest of the delivery room personnel. Is your stumbling block Ruth Horvath?"

Op Owen nodded slowly.

"Well, that makes a little more sense, although I'd say she'd welcome her daughter's Talent. A kind of vindication that she's never been identified. Unless you call the transmission of strong genetic traits a Talent."

Op Owen shook his head, his lips pursed in thought. "She has wanted a child desperately. As a mother wants a child: not as a Talented person wants evidence of succession." He spoke slowly, the words dragged out of his mouth as if he were sorting the thoughts. "Lajos says that although Ruth is a great help and very understanding, sometimes his Incidents bother her more than she admits. Let's just let things take their course. We'll keep an eye on them."

"What they don't know won't hurt them, huh?" Frames sighed. "Wish you'd let that attitude spill over into other areas, Dave."

Op Owen regarded the doctor intently. "I can conceivably bend a little privately, for the benefit of those under my care, but I cannot as easily rationalize the broader issue which I cannot oversee or control."

"All right, Dave, but I feel, and Joel Andres feels, that private reactions are a strong basis for predicting public ones. You're reluctant to tell Ruth Horvath, a girl conditioned and trained to accept Talent, that her child shows exceedingly strong telepathic Talent. You willingly want to broadcast information that even frightens me, and I'm Talented, to a public that is in no way conditioned to accept a fragment of that knowledge. The two attitudes cannot be reconciled."

"The ethical position of the Talented must never be questioned."

"Dave," and there was entreaty in Jerry Frame's voice and manner, "*you* are unable to be unethical. The withholding of prejudicial knowledge is not unethical, it's plain good ol' common sense. Which you are sensibly applying to Ruth Horvath's case. How many times I have considered telling a patient he's bought it and how few times have I actually come clean. Very few people can stand the whole, complete, unvarnished truth."

"I hang between, in doubt to act or rest," op Owen said, resigned as well as frustrated.

"What's that?"

"I apologize, Jerry. Your point is well taken. I've erred—on the side of the angels, I hope—but this attitude of mine towards Ruth Horvath *is* a curious vacillation from my tendency to be forthright. Yet I know that there is a reason to be slightly devious."

"Then you'll ease back on this all-open-and-above-board routine?"

"Yes, I'll ease back as you put it."

"Still," and Jerry frowned slightly, "it isn't as if they won't find out soon enough." He meant the Horvaths.

"They need time to get used to the idea." Op Owen was thinking about humanity.

Where on earth did she get those blue eyes?" Lajos asked as he sat entranced by his three-month-old daughter's attempts to capture her toes. She flopped over, gurgling cheerfully to herself.

"Heavens, it's possible," Ruth replied, beaming fatuously as she caught her daughter's eye. "I may be grey-eyed, and you brown, but we both have ancesters with blue eyes—four generations back."

"I always said you were recessive, hon."

"Humph. I don't mind in the least, not if it produces a blue-eyed blonde daughter with dimples. And I've got her, haven't I, love? You're all mine."

"Except for the twenty-three chromosomes from me."

Dorotea twisted her head backwards over her shoulder and burbled moistly at her mother.

"Love at first bite," Lajos said in a mutter of mock surliness. "There's a conspiracy of females against this poor lone male."

Dorotea impartially gurgled at him, her eyes bright and wide and happy.

"You never had it so good," said Ruth.

And Lajos privately admitted the truth of that. Ruth was so enthralled with her daughter, their apartment had a noticeable atmosphere of benevolence. He was more relaxed than ever, and despite an increase in Incidents, extending beyond his usual affinity, he suffered less from the depressions and exhaustions that were the inevitable postlude.

The day Dorotea's Talent blossomed, Daffyd op Owen was reviewing the records obtained overtly and covertly from the Horvath apartment. He'd had Lester Welch, his electronic chief, rig a buried web in Ruth's mattress, in case the baby instinctively contacted her mother first. However, Lester had pointed out the slight variation in Ruth's readings. It was more as if the needle had snagged itself on an imperfection in the graph paper. There was no such variation on the baby's recordings. Welch had been about to discredit the occurrences until he checked them against Lajos's and discovered that the minute variations in Ruth's chart always occurred exactly at the onset of Lajos' Incidents.

"She might well be a latent 'receiver,'" op Owen said to Welch, "only now beginning to develop from continued proximity to her husband and the advent of the child. I can't present another explanation."

"That'd be nice, Dave. Ruth's a good little person: cheerful, intelligent and crazy for her husband and child. Just the sort of well-balanced, understanding parent to have for a . . ."

Lester was abruptly staring at op Owen's retreating back. The man had leaped to his feet and raced down the hall to the recording room. Lester Welch was not Talented, although his electronic engineering was often sheer inventive genius, but op Owen didn't react like that without good cause. When Welch reached the doorway, he saw that Charlie Moorfield, the day engineer, was hunched over the console, unconscious, but op Owen's attention was for a graph.

"Take a close look at Dorotea's graph," op Owen said, grinning fit to pop his jaw, and then he passed his associate on his way out.

Common sense told op Owen that, despite the urgency of the summons, there could be no danger threatening the baby. Yet he could not disregard that call. What could have happened, he wondered as he ran down the front steps. Suddenly he noticed that there seemed to be a mass exodus from all parts of the building. And everyone was headed in the same direction. As abruptly as the call had been issued, it ceased. People slowed down, stopped, looked around, grinning foolishly.

"What was that?" "Who called?" "Wot hoppened?"

"It's all right," op Owen found himself reassuring them. "A new technique improperly shielded," he said to the telepaths. And grinned at his own dissembling as he continued towards the Horvaths' apartment.

There was a crowd in the hall before their apartment. Op Owen politely pushed his way through the disturbed residents. Dorotea, her baby face still tear-streaked, was held high in her mother's arms, cooing and chortling at the smiling faces around her. Op

Owen's arrival signaled the crowd's discreet dispersal and shortly, he was alone with the mortified mother.

"I'm so embarassed, sir," Ruth said, jiggling her baby as she walked nervously up and down her living room. "I fell asleep with the tape recorder blaring away. And I just . . . didn't hear Dorotea wake up . . . I've never done such a thing before and we've never permitted her to cry long . . ."

"No one is remotely suggesting that you mistreat Dorotea." Op Owen smiled as the baby flirted delightfully with him. "In fact a little honest frustration is very useful. It certainly placed her Talent."

"Ooooooooh," and Ruth collapsed on the sofa, staring wide-eyed at Daffyd op Owen as she absorbed the implication, which she had been too preoccupied with calming Dorotea to see.

"She broadcast a *very* loud signal. I shouldn't be at all surprised if every Talent in the city heard her."

No sooner were the words out of his mouth than Lajos charged through the door.

"What happened to her? How did she get hurt? My head is splitting!" Lajos snatched Dorotea from her mother's lap to examine her firsthand. She began to whimper, catching his anxiety.

"Only her feelings were hurt," Ruth replied, suddenly very calm. Op Owen noticed that with approval: she was dampening her own distress to soothe the others. "I'd fallen asleep with the tape recorder blasting away and just didn't hear her when she woke up hungry and all damp." She took her daughter back, rocking her until the baby began to beam again. "She was hurt because she felt she was being ignored, isn't that right, sweetie?"

"Well, good god!" Lajos sank onto the couch, mopping his forehead. "I never heard anything like it before. Sir," and he turned to op Owen, "look, this can't . . . I mean, can this sort of thing happen every time my daughter's upset?"

"Oh, I'm sure she's likely to protest many assumed indignities, Lajos. Babies have to suffer some frustrations to grow. We'll just move you all to a shielded apartment and dampen down that lovely loud young voice."

"You're not surprised about Dorotea at all," Ruth said, regarding op Owen with round, suspicious eyes. "So that's why everyone was so excited about her in the nursery."

"Well, yes," the Director agreed slowly. "She was heard by the TP nurse at birth."

"But I thought psionic Talents don't usually show up until adolescence . . ."

"Conscious Talent," op Owen said, correcting her.

Ruth looked down at the drooling baby in her arms. A strained look crossed her pretty face. "But I want Dorotea to have a normal, happy childhood!"

"And she won't because she's Talented? Is that it, my dear?" Op Owen knew, sadly, that his instinct about not telling Ruth at once had been all too well-founded. "Except for this ability, which might as well be drawing freehand, she *is* a normal, healthy child, totally unaware that she is in any way remarkable . . ."

"But I know you'll want to test her, and all that, with stimuli . . ." Ruth's distress was so acute that she couldn't go on.

"Ruth!" Lajos bent to comfort her, surprised by her reaction. She clutched her daughter tightly to her.

"My dear Ruth!" op Owen said gently, "testing and stimuli are for people who come to us after they have subverted and suppressed their Talents. We know what Dorotea is already, a very strong telepath. And we've been 'testing' her, as you call it, already. As for stimuli, I assure you," and there was nothing forced in op Owen's chuckle, "*she's* applying the only stimuli . . . to us."

Lajos laughed, brushing his hair back from his forehead as he remembered his frantic homeward flight. Beneath his arm, he could feel Ruth relaxing. A slight smile touched her lips.

"Dorotea will have an unusual opportunity, my dear. One denied you and Lajos, and myself, and so many other potential Talents. She has the chance to grow up in her Talent, learning to use it as naturally as she learns to walk and talk. We will all help her to understand it . . . as much as we do ourselves," he added with a wry smile. "To be candid, Ruth, we are in much the same position as your daughter. We are all learning to act in a publicly acceptable fashion with this new facet of human evolution. Psionic Talents are in their infancy, too, you know.

"You might even extend the analogy a little to include the Andres Bill, which we hope will afford all Talents professional status and legal protection. We, in effect, must prove to the public, our parent-body, if you wish, that we are not 'bad,' 'naughty' or 'capricious' children. Dorotea has already contributed something to that end," and op Owen caught himself before he explained his own revelation. "Dorotea needs love and reassurance, discipline and understanding. She'll pick that up from you, Ruth, with your warmth and sweetness. I want her, possibly more than you do, to have a normal, happy childhood so that she will be a normal, happy adult."

He rose, smiling at the baby's infectious gaiety.

"See, she knows how pleased we are with her right now, the little rascal."

Op Owen left, assuring them new quarters within the week. Ruth was so quiet and thoughtful that Lajos remained home the rest of the day. He found the revelation of Dorotea's Talent as much a shock as Ruth apparently did. However, by morning, he was consumed with a paternal pride and, in the succeeding days, discovered an overweening tendency to maunder on about his daughter's prowess. By the time they moved to the larger, shielded apartment, he was accustomed to the notion and, since Dorotea made no more frantic summonses, succeeded in ignoring it. Until he noticed the gradual change in Ruth. At first, it was no more than a sudden frown, quickly erased, or a nervous look towards the baby's room if she slept longer than usual. Then he caught Ruth looking at her child with that wary expression he had once privately called 'the Freak Look,' which unTalented people occasionally directed at him when they discovered his affiliation with the Center.

"You've got to stop that, honey," he blurted out. "You've got to keep thinking . . . strongly . . . that Dorotea is just like other kids. Or you'll prejudice her. Which is the one thing we have to avoid."

Ruth vehemently denied the accusation but she turned so white around the lips that Lajos gathered her quickly into his arms.

"Ah, sweetie, she hasn't changed just because we've found out she's Talented. But she *is* perceptive and she can sense your feelings towards her. You start suppressing that 'freak-feeling' right now. You think positively that she's our beautiful baby girl, sweet and loving, kind and thoughtful. She'll have that opinion of herself and it won't matter that she's a strong TP as well. She'll merely consider that part of the whole bit. It's when she senses criticism and restraint and hypocrisy that we'll be in trouble. I had to get used to it, too, Ruthie. Say," and he tilted her chin up and grinned down at her reassuringly, "why don't we get a little help from op Owen? Talk this over with him. He can put a block on if you need one."

The very suggestion that she couldn't love and understand her own child made Ruth indignant. She'd had years of parent training. She understood every phase of early childhood development. She adored Dorotea and she certainly wouldn't do a thing that might jeopardize her daughter's happiness. They both felt better after such a candid discussion and the problem was shelved.

S ir, I thought you ought to see the Horvath charts," Lester Welch told op Owen. "A variation keeps appearing in Ruth Horvath's. See?" And Welch unrolled the paper, pointing here and there to the almost imperceptible alteration in Ruth's normal pattern. "See, here and here, it's a couple of microseconds longer and broader. It begins to broaden minutely until it hits this frame which has remained constant. Now, compare her time-sequence to Lajos's . . . and remember we're picking up her pattern anywhere in the new apartment just as we pick up his from the office."

Op Owen saw the correlation immediately.

"He's finished no precog in six weeks?"

Welch contented himself with a nod as op Owen studied the graphs.

"If I didn't think it was impossible, I'd say Ruth was suppressing him. But how?"

"Don't you mean why?"

"That, too, of course, but 'how' is the bigger question."

"If you mean the type of pattern, Dave, I can't give you that. There isn't enough to identify it as a known variation."

"That wasn't exactly what I meant, although I would like a magnification of this to study. Can you put on a more sensitive gauge, or a faster needle, to lengthen the stroke?"

"Hmmm." Welch considered the suggestion. "I'll rig up something, I guess."

Op Owen chuckled. "One of the comforting things about you, Les, is your unfailing rise to the challenge. I don't believe you know what failure is."

Welch regarded his superior with some surprise. "Failure is an inability to consider what is not presently known. Like Ruth Horvath's variation?" Then he added, "Or Senator Zeusman's strategy?"

Op Owen dismissed that with a wave of his hand and continued to scan the Horvaths' readings. "Dorotea's first Incident rocked him, didn't it?"

"Yes, it shows up in his sleep pattern as unusual restlessness the first nights, but see, he's calming down by the third."

"It's from that date that his precogs begin to dwindle."

"By God, you're right. I thought he'd be too stable for a deviation like that."

"Yes, he's been too consistent a precog. I think I'll call him in and drop a few leading questions to see what reaction I get." Op Owen initiated the call then and there.

There's nothing wrong with Dorotea, is there, sir?" Lajos asked as soon as he entered the office.

"Good heavens, no," Daffyd op Owen said, gesturing Lajos to a chair.

"It's about my drop in Incidents, then, isn't it?"

Op Owen eyed his young colleague for a moment, savoring the peripheral emotions the man was generating. It took no Talent to recognize the defensive nervousness in Lajos's attitude.

"Not exactly. There are always periods of rest for precogs, caused by any number of valid reasons, including the absence of fires. However, your graphs show an onset of Incidents, broken off just as they begin."

"Once or twice in the office, I've felt as if something was preventing me . . ."

"Preventing you . . . ?" Op Owen prompted Lajos gently as he had broken off, startled by his own phrasing.

"Yes, sir," Lajos went on slowly, "it's as if something's preventing me from previewing. Sort of like . . . glancing into a strange room and having the door slammed in your face."

"Aptly put. Could you suggest why . . . or perhaps what . . . is preventing you?"

"You think it's a psychological suppression, don't you?"

"That's my first thought."

Indignation and disbelief were Lajos's instant reactions.
"Why would I want to suppress suddenly?"
"Something you yourself don't *want* to see. Precog is not the
easiest of Talents, Lajos," op Owen replied. "Often the precog
imposes his own block, as a relief from the psychological pressures."
"If you think there's a chance that I'm developing the Cassandra
complex . . ." Lajos was heatedly provoked now.
"No, that follows an entirely different pattern."
"Dorotea's preventing me?"
"If this occurred only in your home environment, we'd have to
seriously consider the possibility. But it's improbable for a variety
of reasons: the prime one being that her room is shielded to protect
her from overtones of your precogs as much as to protect us from
her blatant calls."
"Ruth?" Lajos's hushed question had the power of a shout. "She
is Talented after all. But why suppress me? She loves me. I know
she does. She's always helped with Incidents. It made her feel a
part . . ." Lajos stared at op Owen. Then shook his head, violently
disagreeing with the natural conclusion. "No! I don't see why suppressing me would . . . do her any good."
"Has something else upset her? The suppression starts not long
after Dorotea's first Incident."
Lajos covered his eyes, groaning deeply. He collected himself
almost immediately and, looking up at op Owen, recounted Ruth's
curious uncertainty about Dorotea.
"Yes, I see now what has possibly happened. She's made you her
whipping boy."
"Now wait a minute, sir. Ruth's not petty or vindictive."
"I'm not for a moment implying that she is, Lajos. Let us both
try to see her conflicts. She's had to make so many adjustments.
She had such hopes when she entered the training program. I remember her cheerfulness and vivacity so well. It was difficult to
have to disillusion her. You two married and she has exhibited skill
in assisting you. But even the most generous soul experiences
twinges of envy. She looked forward to maternity as an outlet for
her natural inclination and the assuagement of her failures. Suddenly she finds herself with the extraordinary daughter who makes
even the Director of the Center jump at her whim." Lajos weakly
returned op Owen's smile. "I thought at the time she was very

much distressed at the thought of relinquishing any of Dorotea's care to our impersonal toils. I don't believe we entirely relieved her fear that the Center will usurp her role in her daughter's upbringing. Can you see why she may be *indirectly* punishing you for circumstances that threaten her happiness?"

"Yes, I can." Lajos's admission was dejected.

"Now, it's not as bad as that," op Owen said firmly. "In fact, stop feeling guilty and look at the very positive side—Ruth actually has been able to suppress your strong Talent."

"And that's positive?"

"Yes. The underlying problem is Ruth's lack of Talent. We now can prove conclusively that she has one. She has demonstrated it superbly. Severe frustration often breaks down blocks. And she's had that."

"Of course." Lajos's face began to light up. "Whoa. You said she doesn't know she's doing it?"

"I've proof for her. And the further proof will be the renewal of your precogs. I'll have a talk with her and straighten this out today."

He made the call as Lajos left. There was more to the problem of Ruth Horvath than touched the little family. *If you don't tell all you know, how much is enough?* op Owen wondered.

A ll right, I'm forced to believe you," Ruth said, her defensiveness waning under op Owen's gentle redirection, because she also could not deny the evidence of the graphs: of that remarkable, infinitesimal variation that had to be an Incident.

Daffyd op Owen felt himself begin to relax with her admission. He had known it would be a stormy confrontation: one reason why he had not delayed it. Ruth had been appalled by the knowledge that she had subconsciously blocked Lajos. She finally admitted that Dorotea scared her: that she had lost all joy in her daughter and was terrified of predisposing the child towards her.

"Yes, I have to believe you," she repeated, not bothering to stifle resentment, "but it's a pretty poor excuse of a Talent," she added bitterly, "if all I can do is block my husband's, and not even know I'm doing that."

"On the contrary," op Owen replied with a laugh, "it's exactly the one you need the most . . . applied properly."

Ruth glared at him, waiting pointedly for an explanation. "You've a strong moral code, Ruth. You would not permit yourself to act against your daughter, though her Talent frightened you. But you will have to waive that most laudable principle. Until Dorotea has developed sufficient discretion to handle her mental gift, you are going to *have* to block it."

Ruth blinked in surprise and then her eyes brightened, her mouth formed an "O" of astonishment as she began to understand. "Of course. Of course, I understand." Tears of relief welled in her eyes. "Oh, of course."

Op Owen smiled at her. "Yes, Dorotea cannot be permitted to dip into any mind she chooses. You must restrict her by your ability to block. You won't need much pressure to dissuade her from broadcasting or eavesdropping."

"But won't Dorotea resent it? I mean, she'll feel me doing it, won't she?"

"All children require limits. Want them. As long as those limits are consistent and reasonable, a child as aware as Dorotea of her parents' approval and affection won't resist. In any event, by the time she could, or would, we shall have been able to instill discretion *and* your moral code. Right now, Ruth, you have all that's required to keep Dorotea from becoming a nuisance and a brat."

Ruth instantly reacted with indignation to his calculated insult and then laughed as she recognized the bait. She left his office considerably reassured, once again at harmony with her situation.

Op Owen envied her that carefree assurance. He still didn't know what to call what she'd done. Yes, she had suppressed Lajos's precog over the last six weeks, but in the four months prior to that Lajos's abilities had increased in strength and efficiency and, except for duration and width, by a similar application of psionic effort on Ruth's part. What did her Talent actually affect? And would it, as he had so blithely assured her, be able to "block" Dorotea?

Well, if she thinks she can, she will. At least she is no longer afraid of her precocious child, he thought. He swung his chair round, gazing out at the peaceful view of the grounds of Beechwoods, seeing the city beyond with its spires, towers and living blocks.

Was I right in my analogy that Talent is in its infancy, and the public is the parent? With the duty to block the undisciplined child? The Talents are more disciplined that the average citizen we often have to search out and rebuke, protect and cherish. It would be catastrophic for the parent to fear the child. How much of the whole truth would reassure, as it had Ruth?

Those who truly understand psionic powers need no explanation. Those who need explanation will never understand.

T wo mornings later, while reviewing contracts covering institutions holding government research grants, Lajos experienced one of his strongest Incidents. So powerful was the flame-fear that it was all he could do to pull the Goosegg recording web to his skull and depress the key that would relay the reading back to the Center.

"Flames!" he said, gasping; his mind reeled with the panoramic intense preview.

"Where?" he was prompted.

"A sheet, in front of a huge window, overlooking . . . the grounds. Rhododendrons. Red ones. The clock in the church tower . . . nearly twelve. Too much heat! The converter is flawed. It'll blow. There are so many people watching. They don't belong there." Lajos was abstractedly curious at the sound of indignation in his voice. "They caused the fire. Meddling. I know *him!*" Lajos struggled to get a clear picture of that face.

"You don't like him. Who is he?"

"Ahhh . . . the flames. Obscuring everything." Lajos fell back in his chair, shaken and sweating.

"Can you make it to the Center? I'll send transport," the duty officer said.

By the time Lajos reached the computer room in the Center, the system was already chuckling away at the details, locating which laboratories had scheduled visitors in the a.m.: laboratories using heat converters. The church clock tower suggested a college so that data was added as well as the planting of red rhododendrons.

Op Owen greeted Lajos with a grin of approval. "That was the most intense pattern you've ever projected. Have you any idea why that premonition should affect you so?"

"None, sir," Lajos replied, taking the seat op Owen indicated. He was still shaken.

"The man you knew: he was someone you obviously dislike. Do you have the impression that you've met him personally?"

"No. I recognized his face, that's all. Then the flames leaped up." "We don't have much time," and op Owen's eyes glanced towards the wall clock, registering quarter to eleven. "Your precog came at 10:12. Unfortunately this appears to be appropriation time and every lab in the country is having its share of visitations. I want to play back your answer, Lajos. I was struck by two things and if you can pinpoint them also, we'll have the 'where' at least."

"Anything." Lajos could see the vivid overprint of the flames in his mind and tried to see beyond their obscuring curtain. "And one day, figure out why I have a pyro affinity."

"Keeps insurance rates low, Horvath," Welch said drily as he rewound the tape. "Don't knock small favors."

L ajos listened as objectively as he could, appalled at the odd wooden quality of his voice, the fear when he mentioned the flames.

"I've got it, sir," he said. "The converter, the lab, the church tower. Knowing that the people didn't belong there. Wherever it is, is familiar to *me*."

"Charlie," Welch spoke over his shoulder to the programmer, "add Horvath's place and travel card."

Almost immediately a print-out appeared.

"Sir, it's North East University. Checks out, clock in church tower, visible from research laboratory which uses a heat converter."

"Any visitors scheduled today?"

"No report on that yet, sir, but they do have a government funded research project in neo-protein and subcellular engineering."

"Check the university direct," Welch said after a nod from op Owen.

"Only limit it to a request about visitors," op Owen added. "There was something else I want to check first."

"Excuse me, sir," Charles broke in as op Owen lifted his desk phone. "Several parties are expected during the course of the day. Dr. Rizor wishes to speak to you."

"When your office puts in a guarded call, Daffyd op Owen, I'm curious. Come clean."

"Henry, we are not alarmists . . ."

"Precisely. So . . . ?"

"We've had a valid Incident that appears placed at North East. Several of the details have not coincided, however. We are fallible, you know."

Rizor's snort was derogatory. "What's the rest of the precog?"

"It centers around the heat converter in the lab building opposite the church tower."

"And? God, it's like pulling nails from you, Dave."

"The heat converter may be faulty. The precog was that it will blow due to a sudden hot lab fire, just before noon, while visitors are on the premises."

"I'd hate for something to happen there now, Dave. We're on the verge of a breakthrough in the neo-proteins. Running tests that are awfully good. But no visitors are expected there."

"Then a variable has already altered the precog."

"That's too glib a dismissal, Dave. Why would a lab fire stimulate your precog? I didn't think they usually worked out of their own area."

"Our precog recognized one of the visitors."

Welch signaled urgently to op Owen.

"Look, Dave," Rizor was saying, "I'm taking no chances. I'll have that converter checked and the building cleared. That'll alter circumstances, too. Besides I don't want visitors in that building until we complete the program. A breakthrough will warrant government funding all next year. I appreciate your calling, Dave. Let me know when I can help again."

Welch was practically apoplectic before op Owen hung up.

"Washington sent in an urgent personal precog for Mansfield Zeusman!"

"That's who I saw," Lajos cried, jumping to his feet.

"Get Senator Zeusman's office on the phone, Charlie, and don't indicate the origin," op Owen said.

"Dave," and Les Welch had a peculiar expression on his long face, "he's the last person to warn. One, he won't believe you. Two, he's our principal antagonist. Let that damned hero perish."

"Les, you have a dry sense of misplaced humor."

"I'm practical as all hell, too," Welch added.

"Can you tell me if Senator Zeusman is expected in the office this morning?" Charlie's voice carried clearly in the tense silence. "Oh, I see. Can you tell me where he plans to be in the morning hours? But surely, he left an itinerary? Thank you." Charlie's voice was wooden and his face expressionless. "He is not in the office. The assistant is a very rude, uncouth bumptious twit."

"If he's not in the office," op Owen said, "he's college hopping— him and that Research Appropriations Committee of his. He's the sly kind is Zeusman, loves to arrive unannounced."

"He could be on his way to North East then," Lajos said.

Op Owen told Charlie to get Rizor back on the line.

"Sir," Charlie reported, concerned, "Dr. Rizor has left his office. Is there a message?"

Op Owen picked up an extension phone. "Miss Galt? Daffyd op Owen here. We have reason to believe that Senator Mansfield Zeusman will pay an unscheduled visit to your campus before noon. Will you please inform Dr. Rizor immediately? Good. Thank you. I can be reached at the Center on a priority call basis. Yes, the situation could be considered critical."

Lajos felt himself unwind a trifle but his apprehension did not completely abate. He smiled weakly at op Owen.

"Paradox time."

"How so, lad?"

"Dr. Rizor believes. He is already altering the circumstances I foresaw. We may have undone ourselves!"

Op Owen's eyes flashed. "At the risk of Zeusman's life, and that of how many others you saw in the precog?"

"No, sir, I didn't mean it that way," Lajos replied, stung by op Owen's scorn. "I mean, that fire can't happen now because Rizor will prevent Zeusman from entering the lab."

"I'd still prefer to see that sparrow fall!" Welch's mutter was clearly audible.

Op Owen swung his chair in idle half-arcs but his eyes remained on his dissident engineer.

"I am not in the least tempted, gentlemen," he said in his usual easy voice. "We are not God. Nor are we trying to replace God. The psionic arts are preventive, not miraculous. We are fallible, and because of that fallibility we have to be scrupulously impartial, and try to help any man our senses touch, whoever he may be, whenever we can. Lajos is right. We have already . . ."

"Sir," Charlie's interruption was apologetic but determined, "two more danger precogs involving Mansfield Zeusman. One from Delta and one in Quebec. Neither could get through to Zeusman and are applying to us."

Op Owen looked as if he might be swearing silently. He glanced up at the clock, its hands inexorably halfway past eleven.

"We haven't altered the future enough," Lajos said with a groan.

"Charlie, alert all rescue teams in the North East area," op Owen said, his words crisp but calm. "I'll try for Rizor. Les, get Lajos a sedative. Henry, I'm glad I could reach you . . ."

"Don't worry about a thing," Dr. Rizor replied cheerily. "I've a crew checking the converter and the building is completely off limits. What's this Miss Galt says about Zeusman paying us an unexpected visit?"

"Evidence points in that direction, and we've new precogs of danger for him."

"Look, we're all set here, Dave," Rizor told him in an easy drawl. "No one can pass the gate without checking through my office and . . . Oh, no! *No!*"

The connection went dead. Op Owen looked around at the others.

"That's known as locking the barn when the horse is gone," said Welch in a flat voice. "Lay you two to one and no previewing, Rizor just discovered that Zeusman uses a heli-jet for these jaunts of his."

"Charlie, get me through to one of the mobile rescue team trucks."

"Sir, they're converging on the campus. Only they've been delayed at the gate," Charlie said in a quiet sad voice after a moment of urgent cross-wire phoning.

Welch scratched his head, smoothing his hair back over his ears, trying not to stare at op Owen's expressionless face. Lajos wondered how the Director could sit so calmly, but suddenly, not the tranquilizer but an inner natural composure settled Lajos's tensions.

"Sir," he said to op Owen, "I think it came out all right."

Everyone glanced up at the clock which now ticked over to high noon. The secondhand moved foward again, and again, the sweepsecond duly circumscribing its segments of time. The phone's buzz startled everyone. Op Owen depressed Receive and Broadcast.

"I want to speak to the Director of this so-called Center," a bass voice demanded authoritatively.

"Op Owen speaking, Senator Zeusman."

"Well, didn't expect to get *you.*"

"You asked to speak to the Director; I am he." Op Owen hadn't switched on his visual.

The composed answer appeared to confound the Senator briefly. He had not activated the screen at his end either.

"You've outsmarted yourself, Owen, with this morning's exhibition of crystal-balling. I thought you'd have better sense than to set one up and try to fool me into believing in your psionic arts bunk." The senator's voice was rich with ridicule and self-satisfaction. "Heat converter's blowing, indeed! They're constructed not to blow. Safest, most economical way of heating large institutional buildings. A *scientific* way, I might add."

"I tell you, Senator," Rizor interrupted, "there *is* a flaw in the bleed-off of that converter. My engineers reported it."

"Get off the extension, Rizor. I'll settle your hash later. Applying for funds to run a research program which you arbitrarily interrupt at a vital stage on the say-so of crackpots and witch doctors? Your university is unfit to handle any further public monies over which I have any control." Zeusman was almost snarling.

"I won't get off the extension, Zeusman. This is my college, in what is reputedly still a free country, and I don't regret in any way having listened to Dr. op Owen. There was a flaw which would have exploded under conditions foreseen . . ."

"Don't defend Owen, Rizor," Zeusman said. "His meddling costs his defenders too damned much. How's Joel Andres feeling these days, Owen? How's his amyloidosis progressing? Just remember when you predict his death that the research your scheme interrupted here might have saved his life."

There was a loud clack as Zeusman broke the connection.

"Dave?" Rizor sounded defeated.

"I'm still here," op Owen replied. "What's this about Joel Andres?"

"You've had nothing? I thought you always kept a check on important men . . . like Zeusman." The name was grated out.

"Nothing's been reported on Joel. Precog is highly unpredictable, as you've just witnessed."

"That damned converter *was* faulty," Rizor was angry now and defiant. "It would have blown in the next overload. You saved Zeusman—and you've also saved other people."

"And Joel? Is it true about his liver?"

"So I understand," Rizor said in a heavy voice, "And our research was for a neo-protein to replace the faulty endogenous protein and restore a normal metabolism. Don't worry. The experiments can be reinitiated."

"With Zeusman withholding funds?"

"There are other sources of funds and I intend to use your so-called 'meddling' to advantage. Damn it, the converter would have blown!" Rizor was muttering as he ended the call.

Lajos was utterly spent when he returned to his apartment. Ruth took one look at his face and fixed him a stiff drink. He took it down, and with a weary smile flopped onto the bed.

"Dorotea asleep?" he asked hopefully. He was too disturbed not to generate emotional imbalance and too tired to suppress it.

"Fast asleep. Good for a couple of hours, honey," Ruth replied, her strong fingers already at work on his tense muscles. She did not question his depression and weariness. Slowly she felt him relax as her massage and the stiff drink combined to bring surcease.

He woke in time for dinner and seemed in control again, laughing at Dorotea's antics, playing with her on the floor until her bedtime. Only when the baby was safely asleep in her shielded room did he tell Ruth all that had happened.

"Oh, no, not Mr. Andres," she said when he finished. Lajos didn't notice her quick flush as she recalled her one personal encounter with the magnetic Senator Andres. He'd been . . . so kind to her and she'd been so embarrassed.

"How could I guess that he'd be involved? It was the flames. And how could I know that Zeusman would be saved at Andres's expense?"

"Why, you couldn't, darling," Ruth cried, alarmed at his self-castigation. "You couldn't! You mustn't blame yourself. You saved lots of lives today! Lots!"

Lajos groaned, miserable. "But why, Ruthie . . . *why* does it have to ricochet off Andres? If Rizor hadn't ordered the converter off, the experiment would have been concluded. All they had to do was keep visitors out."

"No, that's not quite true," Ruth told him in stern contradiction. "You said yourself that the heat-converter proved to be flawed.

That flaw would not have been discovered without your precog. It would have exploded during the next lab fire. Who knows who might have been killed then?"

"But Andres is the one who needed the neo-protein!"

"They'll come up with a neo-protein somewhere else, then," Ruth said, very positively to distract Lajos. "They've made so many strides in organ replacement . . ."

"Except livers! That neo-protein was supposed to correct some kind of abnormal protein growth . . . faulty endogenous protein metabolism . . . that's what's killing Senator Andres . . . stuff is cramming into his liver and spleen, enlarging them and there's no known way to clear the amyloids. And when the liver doesn't work, that's it, honey. Ticket out!"

Ruth went on stroking Lajos' forehead gently, knowing that he must find his own way out of this. He burrowed his face into her neck, entreating the comfort that she never denied him. Later her mind returned to the terrible paradox, the tragic linkage of circumstance and the sorrow of the well-intentioned Good Samaritan.

God gives man stewardship of his gifts and the free will to use or deny them. Why must it be, that a man acting in good faith, finds himself reviled?

As sleep finally claimed her in the early morning hours, she wondered if she ought now to use her Talent to prevent Lajos from precogs like this. No, she drowsily realized, she had no right to take negative action. One must always think positively. One is one's brother's keeper, not his warder!

I rather expected a call from you, Dave," Joel Andres said, his grin on the vidscreen slightly waving from atmospheric disturbance. "And that's no precog. No indeed," he rattled on, without permitting op Owen to speak. "The good senator from that great midwestern state called especially to warn me that I'm the next sparrow to fall because my pet witch doctor read the wrong crystal ball. Hey, that rhymes. Now, I don't believe that for a moment, Dave, on account of I don't think that that stupid mock-protein goop would have been jelled or curdled or what have you, in time to save my misspent life anyhow." The words were lightly said but there was an edge to Andres's voice that ruined the jovial effect.

"How long, Joel?"

"Probably long enough to get that Bill out of Committee, Dave, and I'll count the time well spent. Zeusman can't put down the mass of evidence in favor of psionics, the tremendous saving of loss of life already effected by validated precogs. By the way, Welch told me that the precog came in at 10:12. Do you know the time when Zeusman gave his pilot orders to fly to North East?"

"10:12?"

"Right, man. And that's in the record! Right in his flight log and a friend of mine impounded it because the pilot isn't so contemptuous of the circumstances as Zeusman. That pilot was scared silly by the coincidence. And don't think I'm not going to ram that down Zeusman's double-chins."

"He'll never admit our warning saved his life, Joel," Daffyd said.

"Hell, he doesn't have to admit it. The facts prove it. But I must say, Dave, you made one mistake." Joel's chuckle was rich.

"Had I known what I know now, I do believe that this once, I'd've sat back and twiddled my thumbs."

"Ha! *I* don't believe that for a minute . . . no, maybe you would have," and the lawmaker's voice rippled with amusement. "If this has buckled your altruistic armor, it's worth it. Worth dying for, because there's nothing trickier to tie down than an honest man gone bad! Now let me go to work."

"Joel, let me know . . ."

"Hang loose, man. Don't rob me of my cool. Not now!"

The senator signed off but Daffyd op Owen sat staring moodily at the wall opposite his desk, unable for the first time in his life to divert his train of thought. His mind writhed in recrimination as bitter as an ancient inquisitional penance.

"Dave?" Welch's brisk voice broke through his introspection. "There's an anomaly on . . . Oh, I'll come back later. . . ."

"No, Lester, come in."

Welch gave his friend a speculative look but he unrolled the graphs without comment.

"Ruth Horvath!" Op Owen was surprised, almost irritated that she should be the subject of the intrusion.

"Couple of things. Here . . . on the baby's chart . . . Incident after Incident . . . compare it with Ruth's. No pattern. Not even an inky hiccup. I thought you said she could block that baby."

Curious now, op Owen scanned the charts. "What's this?" he asked, pointing to a sustained emphatic variation.

"That's the anomaly. Happened last night. It's a spontaneous variation. All her others have been triggered, usually by Lajos. And, if you'll look at the peaks and valleys in last night's records, you'll see that the pattern is kinetic."

"That's too tight for a true kinetic touch."

"Well, it's not TP, it's not 'finding' and what'n'hell would she be trying to do, fast asleep? 'Finding' is a conscious application, anyway. No, this is a kinetic pattern."

"For what reason? Against what?"

"Who knows? The point is, while she has stopped suppressing her husband, she hasn't started blocking her daughter. And that's going to be serious. I mean, we don't need a teething telepath broadcasting discomfort."

"Teething?"

"I forget you're not a parent," Welch said with tolerant condescension, "to *small* babies, that is."

Op Owen was engrossed in the patterns and it was obvious that Ruth was not responding and seemed unable to use a conscious block. And that was too bad. He frowned at the unusual kinetic display of the previous night.

"She's got it. She used it."

"Not consciously."

"I hate to resort to therapeutic interference. It might jeopardize her ever using it consciously."

"It's therapy for Ruth, or that baby'll tyrannize both parents. And that's bad. A kid that strong has got to have limits, right now, before she can develop precocious resistance."

Op Owen examined the charts one last time, shaking his head as he noticed the telepathic patterns on Dorotea's chart, saw the impingement on the mother's and no block.

"These could be legitimate calls . . ."

"Don't evade, Dave. I know you hate interfering with Talent; that it should be spontaneous. Admit Ruth Horvath is one of those who cannot use Talent consciously. Meddle a little!"

Op Owen rose, his face drawn. "I'll drop over to see them today. Let's hope she responds well to hypnosis."

"She does. I looked up her training record."

Two days later Welch came back in triumph, trailing two sheets of graphing tissue like victory streamers.

"You did it, Boss. Look, pass blocked, time and again, with a minimum of effort on Ruth's part. But damn it, she's not a pure kinetic. What could she be moving with such an infinitesimal touch? How does she apply the block?"

"Unconsciously," op Owen replied with a sly grin. "However, it may be because that touch is so delicate, she can't do it consciously. I didn't *look* very deeply. But so many kinds of Talent are fairly heavy-handed, violent. Like using awls in place of microneedles." He winced a little, remembering how his mental touch had uncovered Ruth's pitiful lack of self-confidence in her Talent. All her Incidents occurred without her awareness, deep in the subconscious levels of her mind into which Daffyd saw no need to trespass. She was a nice womanly person: her surface thoughts revolving around her husband, her daughter: all her anxieties were needless guilts over minor details. It was, therefore, relatively easy to block her notions that she would inadvertently harm Dorotea, or try to suppress Lajos. It was easy to erase conscious knowledge of her Talent, replacing it with a feeling of accomplishment and well-being: the post-hypnotic command to respond to Dorotea's telepathic demands and channel them firmly into speech centers. He also displaced her reluctance to have other Talented children because she felt inadequate. Ruth must have great resources of self-assurance. He planted them.

Now op Owen turned to Welch. "Ask Jerry Frames how soon Ruth Horvath can bear another child. I'd like her first two fairly close together before she gets cold feet."

"Cold feet he calls it!" was Welch's parting crack.

I'm sorry, Daffyd," the Washington precog said, "I've stared at Joel Andres's picture for hours. I've read his House speeches, I've read his memoirs. I've sat in his outer office until the Senate police asked to have a word with me. Then *he* came in, and recognized me, of course. And gave me a scarf to hold." Mara Helm paused. "As a memento, he said. But I don't see it."

"You've had no stimulation about him at all?"

"Nothing dire."

"What do you mean, nothing dire?"

"That's what I mean and all I mean, Dai. Nothing conclusive, in that his life concludes. And, as you know, my accuracy is unfortunately high."

"I don't understand this, Mara."

"No more do I when I hear the gossip around town."

"Which is?"

"That Senator Andres is spending his last moments helping a minority group that not only has predicted his imminent demise but destroyed his one chance of a cure." Her voice held no inflection as she uttered these quick sentences, but her dislike of imparting the gossip was obvious to her listener. Mara cleared her throat suddenly. "I do have a precog though," she added, mildly amused.

"A good one, if I recognize that tone of voice. I could stand some pleasant tidings."

"I'll be seeing you shortly," and she laughed mischievously. "In the flesh, I mean. Here!"

"In Washington?" Daffyd op Owen was startled. He rarely left the Center and, at this moment, he had no desire under heaven to set foot in Washington.

Two weeks later, Daffyd op Owen, in a swivet of anxiety which no perception could dispel, disembarked from the heli-jet on the Senate landing pad. Mara Helm and Joel Andres were waiting for him. Daffyd had no eyes for anyone but the senator who strode forward, grinning broadly, eagerly grasping the telepath's hand, forgetting in the excess of his welcome that Daffyd avoided casual physical contacts.

However, op Owen wanted more than anything to touch-sense his friend. And was reassured by the vigorous sensation he felt equally strong through mind and body. He might disbelieve the evidence of his eyes as he stared at Andres's clear pupils, the healthy tanned skin with no trace of the yellow, indicative of liver disorder. Op Owen could not deny the feeling of health and energy that coursed to him in that hearty handclasp.

"What happened?" he asked hoarsely.

"Who knows?" Joel replied. "The medics called it a spontaneous remission. Said my body had started manufacturing the right enzymes again. Something to do with a shift in the RNA messenger proteins or some rot like that. Anyhow, no more amyloids in the perivascular spaces—if that makes any sense to you—the old liver and spleen are back to normal size and I can *feel* that. So, friend, *I* no longer need that neo-protein research that Zeusman scrapped."

Mara Helm remained aside, smiling benevolently at the two men, until they finally remembered her presence.

"Dai, see?" and she laid a finger fleetingly on his sleeve. "You're here as predicted!"

"Did you bring the graphs and records I asked for?" Joel inquired.

"Here they are," and Daffyd handed the neat package over.

"Good," and the senator's expression was maliciously gleeful. "We're going to hoist Senator Mansfield Zeusman today on *his* petard. However," and black anger surged across Andres's face, "I beg your indulgence, Daffyd. Certain—what would you call them, Mara—security measures?"

Mara's lips twitched but there was an answering indignant sparkle in her eyes.

"A shielded cage?" Daffyd asked.

"Yeah," and the sound was more of a growl than an affirmative. "Don't think I didn't protest that insulting . . ."

"In fact," Mara said, "he ranted and screamed at the top of his voice. All Washington heard. I elected to keep you company in the gilt-wired gold-fish bowl," and she gave op Owen a flirtatious wink.

"You'll have an advantage over me," Andres said. "You can switch off the sound of Zeusman's voice."

"Who? Me?" Daffyd asked and the three entered the Senate Building laughing.

Op Owen was not surprised at Mansfield Zeusman's insulting treatment. He expected little else. Although the senator had initiated the investigation of all the Centers, he had never personally entered one. Obviously Zeusman was among those who believed that any telepath could read every mind: he would be unlikely to believe that telepaths performed their services much as a surgeon does an exploratory operation in the hope of uncovering a patient's malignant disease. Zeusman also decried the psychiatric sciences, so his attitude was at least consistently narrow-minded.

"One more thing," Andres said as he held open the door into the shielded room, "you're here at the Committee's request, not Zeusman's, or mine. They may want to question you. Please, Dave, don't tell *all* you know?"

"I'll be a verbal miser, I promise."

"That'll be our saving," Andres replied. He obviously distrusted op Owen's sudden meek compliance.

"Doesn't Joel look wonderful?" whispered Mara as they seated themselves.

"Yes," Daffyd replied and then shut his lips. Even that interchange, broadcast into the chamber beyond, drew every eye to them. Op Owen crossed his legs, clasped his hands and composed himself outwardly.

Zeusman was not as large a man as op Owen thought he'd be. Nor was he a small man in stature which might have explained the aggressive, suspicious personality. He resembled a professor more than a senator, except for the elaborate gesticulations which were decidedly oratorical. And he was expatiating at length now with many gestures, pointedly ignoring Andres who took his place at the conference table.

The other five members of the Committee nodded towards Andres as if they welcomed his arrival. Their smiles faded as they turned back to the speaker. It was apparent to Daffyd that Zeusman's audience was heartily bored with him and had heard the same arguments frequently.

"These Experts claim . . ." and Zeusman paused to permit his listeners to absorb the vitriol he injected into that label, "that even the advertisement of that precognitive word changes events. Now that's a cowardly evasion of the consequences of their pernicious meddling."

"We've been through that argument from stem to stern before, Mansfield," the lanky bald man with a hawk nose said. Op Owen identified him as Lambert Gould McNabb, the senior Senator from New England. "You called this extraordinary session because you claim you have real evidence prejudicial to this Bill."

Zeusman glared at McNabb, McNabb calmly tamped down his pipe, relit it, pinched his nose between thumb and forefinger, blowing against the pressure to relieve his eardrums, sniffed once or twice, put the pipe back in his mouth and turned an expectant face towards Zeusman.

"Well, Mansfield, either hang 'em or cut 'em down."

"I have your attention, Senator McNabb?"

"At the moment."

"My contention has always been that protection for these meddlers is against common sense, ethics, and all the laws of man and God. They usurp the position of the Almighty by deciding who's to live and who's to die."

"To the point, Mansfield," McNabb said.

"Senator McNabb, will you desist from interrupting me?"

"Senator Zeusman, I will—if you will desist from jawing."

Zeusman looked around for support from the other five members of the Committee and found none.

"On the 14th of June, I left my offices in this building for the purpose of visiting several of the universities requesting the renewal of Research Funds. As you know, it is my custom to arrive unannounced. Therefore, it was not until we were airborne that I gave my pilot his directions."

"What time was that?" asked Andres quickly.

"The time is irrelevant."

"No, it isn't. I repeat, at what time did you give your pilot his flight directions?"

"I fail to see what bearing . . . ."

"I have a transcript of the pilot's log, from the files of the Senate Airwing," Andres said and passed the copy over to McNabb.

"Ten twelve, Daylight Saving Time, the record says," McNabb said in a drawl, his eyes twinkling as he casually flipped the record across the table to the others.

Zeusman watched, frowning bleakly.

"I have here," Joel went on before Zeusman could grab the floor, "authenticated graph readings of four precognitive Incidents: one from Eastern American Center, the Washington Bureau, Delta Center and Quebec. The period, allowing for time zones, in which these precogs occurred is between 10:12 and 10:16. Excuse the interruption, Zeusman, but I'm trying to keep things chronological."

Zeusman awarded Andres a vicious smile and then a keener look. Op Owen wondered if Zeusman was only now aware of Andres's improved health.

"Ahem. When my heli-jet landed at North East University, I and my party were physically restrained by Dr. Henry Rizor, the Research Dean and members of his staff, from conducting our in-

vestigation of their project on the specious grounds that a precog
had been issued, predicting a flaming death for me and my party,
due to a faulty heat converter which was supposed to explode.
Well, gentlemen, I fathomed this little trap immediately."

"Whoa, whoa, Mansfield," Robert Teague said, tapping the material now in front of him. "The precog reports I have here . . .
by God, I'm getting so I don't need an expert to translate them for
me anymore . . . indicate that's exactly what was to have happened. At . . . ah, shortly before noon. When did you arrive at
North East?"

"Quarter to twelve."

"Then you'd've been in the building around twelve. I'd say you
owed these precogs your life."

"My life? Don't be ridiculous!"

"I'm not. You are," Teague replied with considerable exasperation.

"I'm no fool, Bob. I know when I'm being had, in spite of all the
forged records going. The whole business was rigged. Heat converters don't blow."

"Right, so how could one be rigged to blow at precisely twelve
noon at North East when no one, including yourself, knew when
or where you were going that morning until 10:12?"

"A flaw was discovered when the heat converter was dismantled:
air bubble in the steel tank," Joel Andres said, passing another
affadavit to Teague. "The main chamber has been replaced. It
could have blown, through that air bubble flaw, under just such
circumstances of overload as predicted."

"But it didn't!" Zeusman said in a roar.

"No, because it had been turned off to prevent such an occur-
rence."

"Exactly. The whole thing was a hoax. Ten-twelve, twelve noon,
whatever. *And,*" Zeusman rattled the words out so loud and so fast
that no one could interrupt him, "in turning off that so-called
faulty converter, the experiment then in progress, paid for by government funds, was ruined just before what was certain to be a
successful conclusion of a highly delicate, valuable project. I've
papers of my own to present"—he dramatically flung stapled
sheets to the table—"depositions from the various qualified, highly
trained, highly reputable scientists in charge of the neo-protein
research. And here is where these . . . these meddling godlets

overreach themselves. That neo-protein research, so rudely interrupted on the brink of success would have produced, by *scientific* methods—accurate, repeatable, proven—a substance that would prevent certain all-too-common and terribly painful deaths due to liver failure. Prevent an agonizing death facing a certain member of this august Committee. And, if these precogs are so omniscient, so benign, so altruistic, so wise, why—I ask you, *why*, did they not foresee the effects of their own meddling on their avowed champion?"

Op Owen's altruism and benignity hit an all-time low and he found himself obsessed with an intense desire to turn kinetic and clog Zeusman's windpipe permanently.

"Ah ha," crowed Joel Andres, leaping to his feet, "why should they foresee my demise, my dear colleague? Due to liver failure? How interesting! Of course, you have a paper to prove it, Senator, such as my death certificate?"

"Easy, Joel," said McNabb, squinting at Andres keenly, "Anyone can see you're healthy as a hog, though I must admit you had been looking a bit jaundiced. You look great now, though."

"But I had a report that he was dying of liver failure," Zeusman said.

"Got that authenticated?" Teague asked sarcastically.

"Easy, Bob. We know Mansfield's been doing the job he was elected to do, protect his constituents and this country. That used to be as easy to do," McNabb paused to drag on his pipe, "as finding decent substitute tobacco. But Mansfield *proved* that was bad for most of us."

"We're discussing experts, not tobacco," Zeusman reminded him.

"No, we're discussing progress, on a level some of us find as hard to take as giving up tobacco. However, it was proved that tobacco was unhealthy. These people have proved that their Centers protect health and property, and they go about it scientifically. Everything I've heard today," and McNabb jerked his pipe stem at Zeusman as the latter started to interrupt, "*proves* conclusively to me that you've been putting the wrong eggs in the right basket. That precog was for *your* health and well-being, Mansfield, which these people are pledged to protect: you didn't have to take the warning . . ."

"I was forced . . ."

"Lots of us were forced to stop smoking, too," McNabb said, grinning. "This artificial stuff still doesn't taste right but I *know* it's better for me.

"Most important of all, Mansfield, and it seems to have completely escaped your logical, scientific, one-track mind, is the very fact that these people warned *you!* Whether they knew the consequences to Joel Andres or not if they also stopped the experiment, they had to warn *you* and your party! So stop your maundering on about their ethics and meddling. *I'd've* let you burn!"

Zeusman sank down into a chair, blinking at McNabb's craggy face. Then the New England senator rose, a slight smile on his lips.

"Gentlemen, we've hassled this Bill back and forth for close to two years. We've satisfied ourselves the provisions protecting the parapsychic professions, as outlined in Articles IV and V, do not threaten the safety of the citizens of this country, do not jeopardize personal liberty, et cetera and all that, and, hell, let's place it on the agenda and start protecting these poor idealistic bastards from . . . from them as don't wish to be protected."

McNabb's grin was pure malice but he didn't glance in Zeusman's direction nor was the midwesterner aware of anything but this unexpected defeat.

Op Owen reached the Center after full dark of the late spring evening. The pleasant sense of victory still enveloped him in contentment. He found himself, however, turning toward the apartments rather than his own quarters. The news that the Andres Bill had left Committee and would be presented to the Senate next session had already been relayed to the Center. He heard echoes of the celebrating which appeared to be going on all over the grounds.

A little premature, he thought to himself, for the Bill must pass Senate and Congress. There would be sharp debate but they predicted it would pass. The President was already in favor of protection for the Talented since he benefited from their guardianship.

Op Owen entered the building where the Horvaths lived. He hesitated at the elevator, then made for the steps, pleased to arrive without breathlessness at their apartment door.

He had a split second of concern that he might be interrupting the young couple but it was quickly dispelled when Lajos, still dressed, flung the door wide.

"Mr. op Owen!" The precog's face was a study in incredulous amazement. "Good evening, sir!"

"I'm sorry. Were you expecting someone?"

"No, no one. Exactly. Please, come in. It's just . . . well, everyone's been apartment hopping since the news came . . ."

"The Director is immune to jubilation?"

Lajos was spared the necessity of answering because Ruth entered from the kitchen, her face lighting up as she rushed forward to greet their guest. Op Owen was relieved at her obvious welcome: she could have developed a subconscious antipathy for him after their recent session.

"I don't think anyone expected you back tonight, sir," Lajos was saying, pressing a drink on op Owen.

"We're all so proud of you, sir," Ruth added shyly.

"I did nothing," op Owen replied. "I sat in a shielded room and listened. It was Lajos's precog . . ."

"There were three other reports, sir," Lajos said, "but is it really confirmed that Senator Andres has had a remission of that liver ailment?"

"Yes, absolutely, demonstrably true. I know we've all felt burdened with a certain . . . regret, on that aspect of the North East Incident. It is the inevitable concomitant of the precognitive gift."

"And Dr. Rizor's grant will be restored?"

Op Owen was taken by surprise. "I'm embarrassed to say I didn't think to inquire." He felt himself coloring.

"We can't think of everything, can we?" Ruth asked, her lips twitching with a mischievous smile.

Op Owen burst out laughing and, after a startled pause, Lajos joined him.

"I'll bet it will be restored," Ruth went on, "and that's no precog: just plain justice."

"How's Dorotea?" op Owen asked.

"She's asleep," and there was nothing but pride and pleasure in Ruth's face as she glanced towards the closed nursery door. "It's fascinating to *listen* to her figuring out how to get out from under the table."

Lajos echoed her pleasure. Op Owen rose, suddenly conscious of the rippling undercurrent between the two young people. His presence constituted a crowd.

"I wanted you to know about Joel Andres, Lajos."

"Thank you sir, I do appreciate it."

"It was good of you to tell us. You must be so tired," Ruth said, linking arms with her husband and standing very close to him.

"Save your maternal instincts for your children, Ruth," he said kindly and left.

Once again in the soft night air, op Owen felt extremely pleased with life. Obeying an impulse, he glanced over his shoulder and noticed that the lights in the Horvath apartment were already out. He had interrupted them after all. Sometimes, shield as he could, the stronger emotions, sex being one of them, seeped through.

He took his time walking back through the grounds, permitting himself the rare luxury of savoring the happy aura that permeated the Center. He stored up the fragrance of the joyful night, the exuberance that penetrated the dark, the hopefulness that softened the chill of the breeze, against those desperate hours that are the commoner lot of man. These times of harmony, concert, attunement came all too seldom for the Talented. They were rare, glorious, treasured.

Habit made him stop in at the huge control room. Surprise prompted him to enter—for Lester Welch, a dressing robe thrown over his nightclothes and a drink in one hand, was bending over the remote graph panels. His attitude, as well as that of the duty officer, was of intense concentration.

"Never seen anything like that before in a coital graph," Welch was muttering under his breath.

"Turned graphic voyeur, Lester?" Daffyd asked with tolerant amusement.

"Voyeur, hell. Take a look at these graphs. Ruth Horvath's doing it again. And at a time like this? Why?"

Welch was scarcely a prurient man. Stifling his own dislike of such an unwarranted invasion of privacy, op Owen glanced at the two graphs, needles reacting wildly in response to the sexual stimuli mutually enjoyed. Lajos's graph showed the normal agitated pattern: Ruth's matched his except for the frenetic action of the needle, trying valiantly to record the cerebrally excited and conflicting signals its sensitive transistors picked up. The needle gouged deep into the fragile paper, flinging its tip back and forth. Yet the pattern of deviation emerged throughout the final high—a tight, intense, obviously kinetic pattern.

Abruptly the frantic activity ceased, the lines wandered slowly back to normal-fatigue patterns.

"That was most incredible. The most prodigious performance I have ever witnessed."

Op Owen shot Welch a stern glance, only to realize that the man meant the electronic record. He was momentarily embarrassed at his own thoughts.

"What does she do?" Welch continued speaking and the technician glanced up quickly, startled and flushing. "The kinetic energy is expended for what reason? Not that she'd be able to tell us anyhow."

"For what reason?" op Owen asked quietly, answering the safest question. "For the exercise of a very womanly talent." He waited, then sighed at their obtuseness. "What is the fundamental purpose of intercourse between members of the opposite sex?"

"Huh?" It was Welch's turn to be shocked.

"The propagation of their species," op Owen answered his own inquiry.

"You mean . . . you can't mean . . ." Welch sank, stunned, into a chair as he began to comprehend.

"It hadn't occurred to me before now," op Owen went on conversationally, "that it is rather odd that a brown-eyed, black-haired father and a grey-eyed, brown-haired mother could produce a blue-eyed blonde. Not impossible. Just quite improbable. Now Lajos is precog, and we have to grant that Ruth is kinetic. So how do these genes produce a strong, strong telepath?"

"What did she do?" Welch asked softly. His eyes knew the answer but he had to hear op Owen voice it.

"She rearranged the protein components of the chromosome pairs which serve as gene locks and took the blue-eyed genes and the blonde-haired ones out of cell storage. And what ever else she wanted to create Dorotea. That would be my educated guess. Just the way she unlocked the RNA messengers for . . ." Op Owen hesitated: no, not even Lester Welch needed to know *that* bit of Ruth's tinkering—"whatever it is she has in mind for this child."

Welch had not apparently noticed his hesitation. "It'll be interesting to see the end product."

Welch was speechless and the technician pretended great industry at another panel. Op Owen smiled gently.

"This is classified, gentlemen. I'll want those records removed as soon as you can break into the drums," he told the technician, who managed to respond coherently.

"I'm glad of that," Welch said with open relief. "I'm glad that you're not blabbing all this to the world. Are you going to tell Lajos?"

"No," Daffyd replied with deliberation. "He obviously intends to cooperate. And they'll be happier parents without that knowledge."

Welch snorted, himself again.

"You sound like you're getting common sense, Dave. Thank God for that." He frowned as the drum wound the last of that Incident out of sight. "She can actually unlock the genes!" He whistled softly.

" 'One science only will one genius fit.
So vast is art, so narrow human wit!' "

"How's that again, Dave?"

"A snitch of Popery!" op Owen remarked as he left.

PART THREE

APPLE

The theft was the lead morning 'cast and ruined Daffyd op Owen's appetite. As he listened to the description of the priceless sable coat, the sapphire necklace, the couture model gown and the jewel-strap slippers, he felt as if he were congealing to his chair as his breakfast cooled and hardened on the plate. He waited, numbed, for the commentator to make the obvious conclusion: a conclusion which would destroy all that the East American Parapsychic Center had achieved so slowly, so delicately. For the only way in which such valuable items could have been removed from a store dummy in a scanned, warded, very public display window in the five-minute period between the fixed TV frames was by kinetic energy.

"The police have several leads and expect to have a solution by evening. Commissioner Frank Gillings is taking charge of the investigation.

" 'I keep my contractual obligations to the City,' Gillings is reported to have told the press early this morning as he personally supervised the examination of the display window at Coles, Michaels and Charny Department Store. 'I have reduced street and consensual crimes and contained riot activity. Jerhattan is a safe place for the law abiding. Unsafe for the lawbreakers.' "

The back-shot of Gillings's stern face was sufficient to break op Owen's stasis. He rose and strode toward the comunit just as it beeped.

"Daffyd, you heard that 'cast?" The long, unusually grim face of Lester Welch appeared on the screen. "Goddammit, they promised no premature announcement. Mediamen!" His expression boded ill for the first unwary reporter to approach him. Over Les's shoul-

der, op Owen could see the equally savage face of Charlie Moorfield, duty officer of the control room of the Center.

"How long have *you* known about the theft?" Op Owen couldn't
quite keep the reprimand from his voice. Les had a devoted habit of
trying to spare his superior, particularly these days when he knew
op Owen had been spreading himself very thin in the intensive
public educational campaign.

"Ted Lewis snuck in a cautious advice as soon as Headquarters
scanned the disappearance. He also can't 'find' a thing. And, Dave,
there wasn't a wrinkle or a peak between 7:03 and 7:08 on any
graph that shouldn't be there, with every single Talent accounted
for!"

"That's right, Boss," Charlie added. "Not a single Incident to
account for the kinetic 'lift' needed for the heist."

"Gillings is on his way here," said Les, screwing his face up with
indignation.

"Why?" Daffyd op Owen exploded. "Didn't Ted clear us?"

"Christ, yes, but Gillings has been at Cole's and his initial investigation proves conclusively to him that one of our people is a
larcenist. One of our women, to be precise, with a secret yen for
sable, silk and sapphires."

Daffyd forced himself to nullify the boiling anger he felt. He
could not afford to cloud reason with emotion. Not with so much
at stake. Not with the Bill which would provide legal protection
for Talents only two weeks away from passing.

"You'll never believe me, will you, Dave," Les said, "that the
Talented will always be suspect?"

"Gillings has never caviled at the use of Talents, Lester."

"He'd be a goddamned fool if he did." Lester's eyes sparkled
angrily. He jabbed at his chest. "*We've* kept street and consensual
crime low. Talent did his job for him. And now he's out to nail us.
With publicity like this, we'll never get that Bill through. Christ,
what luck! Two bloody weeks away from protection."

"If there's no Incident on the graphs, Les, even Gillings must
admit to our innocence."

Welch rolled his eyes heavenwards. "How can you be so naive,
Dave? No matter what our remotes prove, that heist was done by a
Talent."

"Not one of ours." Daffyd op Owen could be didactic, too.

"Great. Prove it to Gillings. He's on his way here now and he's

out to get us. We've all but ruined his spotless record of enforcement and protection. That hits his credit, monetary and personal."
Lester paused for a quick breath. "I told you that public education
program would cause more trouble than it's worth. Let me cancel
the morning 'cast."

"No." Daffyd closed his eyes wearily. He didn't need to resume
that battle with Les now. In spite of this disastrous development,
he was convinced of the necessity for the campaign. The general
public must learn that they had nothing to fear from those gifted
with a parapsychic Talent. The series of public information programs, so carefully planned, served several vital purposes: to show
how the many facets of Talent served the community's best interests; to identify those peculiar traits that indicated the possession
of a Talent; and most important, to gain public support for the Bill
in the Senate which would give Talents professional immunity in
the exercise of their various duties.

"I haven't a vestige of Talent, Dave," Les went on urgently, "but
I don't need it to guess some dissident in the common mass of have-
nots listened to every word of those 'casts and put what you should
never have aired to good use . . . for him. And don't comfort me
with how many happy clods have obediently tripped up to the
Clinic to have their minor Talents identified. One renegade apple's
all you need to sour the barrel!"

"Switch the 'cast to the standard recruiting tape. To pull the
whole series would be worse. I'm coming right over."

Daffyd op Owen looked down at the blank screen for a long
moment, gathering strength. It was no precog that this would be a
very difficult day. Strange, he mused, that no precog had foreseen
this. No. *That* very omission indicated a wild Talent, acting on the
spur of impulse. What was it Les had said? "The common mass of
have-nots?" Even with the basic dignities of food, shelter, clothing
and education guaranteed, the appetite of the have-not was contin-
ually whetted by the abundance that was not his. In this case, hers.
Daffyd op Owen groaned. If only such a Talent had been moved to
come to the Center where she could be trained and used. Where
had their so carefully worded programming slipped up? She could
have had the furs, the jewels, the dresses on overt purchase . . .
and enjoyed them openly. The Center was well enough endowed
to satisfy any material yearning of its members. Surely Gillings
would admit that.

Op Owen took a deep breath and exhaled regret and supposition. He must keep his mind clear, his sensitivities honed for any nuance that would point a direction toward success.

As he left his shielded quarters at the back of the Center's extensive grounds, he was instantly aware of tension in the atmosphere. Most Talented persons preferred to live in the Center, in the specially shielded buildings that reduced the 'noise' of constant psychic agitation. The Center preferred to have them here, as much to protect as to help their members. Talent was a double-edged sword; it could incise evil but it neatly separated its wielder from his fellow man. That was why these broadcasts were so vital. To prove to the general public that the psychically gifted were by no means supermen. Research had indicated there were more people with the ability than would admit it. There were, however, definite limitations to most Talents.

The Parapsychic had been raised, in Daffyd's lifetime, to the level of a science with the development of the Goosegg, ultra-sensitive electroencephalographs which could record, and identify the type of "Talent" by the minute electrical impulses generated in the cortex by the application of psychic powers. Daffyd op Owen sometimes thought the word "power" was the villain in perpetuating the public misconceptions. Power means "possession of control" but such synonyms as "domination," "sway," "command" leapt readily to the average mind and distorted the actual definition.

Daffyd op Owen was roused from his thoughts by the heavy beat of a copter. He turned onto the path leading directly to the main administration building and had a clear view of the Commissioner's marked copter landing on the flight roof, to the left of the control tower with its forest of antennal decorations.

Immediately he perceived a reaction of surprise, indignation and anxiety. Surely every Talent who'd heard the news on the morning 'cast and realized its significance could not be surprised by Gillings's arrival. Op Owen quickened his pace.

"Orley's loose!" The thought was as loud as a shout.

People paused, turned unerringly towards the long low building of the Clinic where applicants were tested for sensitivity and trained to understand and use what Talent they possessed: and where the Center conducted its basic research in psionics.

A tall, heavy figure flung itself from the Clinic's broad entrance, charged down the lawn, in a direct line to the tower. The man leaped the ornamental garden, plunged through the hedges, swung over the hood of a parked lawn-truck, straight-armed the overhanging branches of trees, and brushed aside several men who tried to stop him.

"Project reassurance! Project reassurance!" the bullhorn from the tower advised. "Project happiness!"

"Get those cops in my office!" Daffyd projected on his own as he began to run towards the building. He hoped that Charlie Moorfield or Lester had already done so. Orley didn't look as if anything short of a tranquilizer bullet would stop him. Who had been dim-witted enough to let the telempath out of his shielded room at a time like this? The moron was the most sensitive barometer to emotion Daffyd had ever encountered as he was physically dangerous if aroused. By the speed of that berserker-charge, he had soaked up enough fear/anxiety/anger to dismember the objects he was homing in on.

The only sounds now in the grounds were those of op Owen's shoes hitting the permaplast of the walk and the thud-thud of Orley's progress on the thick lawn. One advantage of being Talented is efficient communication and total comprehension of terse orders. But the wave of serenity/reassurance was not penetrating Orley's blind fury: the openness dissipated its effect.

Three men walked purposefully out of the administration building and down the broad apron of steps. Each carried slim-barreled hand weapons. The man on the left raised and aimed his at the audibly-panting, fast approaching moron. The shot took Orley in the right arm but did not cause him to falter. Instantly the second man aimed and fired. Orley lost stride for two paces as the shot penetrated his thigh but incredibly he recovered. The third man— op Owen recognized Charlie Moorfield—waited calmly as Orley rapidly closed the intervening distance. In a few more steps Orley would crash into him. Charlie was swinging out of the way, his gun slightly raised for a chest shot, when the moron staggered and, with a horrible groan, fell to his knees. He tried to rise, one clenched fist straining towards the building.

Instantly Charlie moved to prevent Orley from gouging his face on the coarse-textured permaplast.

"He took two double-strength doses, Dave," Moorfield exclaimed with some awe as he cradled the moron's head in his arms.

"He would. How'n'hell did he get such an exposure?"
Charlie made a grimace. "Sally was feeding him on the terrace.
She hadn't heard the news 'cast. Said she was concentrating on
keeping him clean and didn't 'read' his growing restlessness as
more than response to her until he burst wide open."

"Too much to hope that our unexpected guests didn't see this?"
Charlie gave a sour grin. "They caused it, Boss. Stood there on
the roof, giving Les a hard time, broadcasting basic hate and distrust. You should've seen the dial on the psychic atmosphere gauge.
No wonder Orley responded." Charlie's face softened as he
glanced down at the unconscious man. "Poor damned soul. Where
is that med-team? I 'called' them when he got outside."

Daffyd glanced up at the broad third floor windows that marked
his office. Six men stared back. He put an instant damper on his
thoughts and emotions, and mounted the steps.

The visitors were still at the window, watching the med-team as
they lifted the huge limp body onto the stretcher.

"Orley acts as a human barometer, gentlemen, reacting instantly
to the emotional aura around him," Les was saying in his driest,
down-east tone. To op Owen's wide-open mind, he emanated a
raging anger that almost masked the aura projected by the visitors.
"He has an intelligence factor of less than 50 on the New Scale
which makes him uneducable. He is, however, invaluable in helping identify the dominating emotion of seriously disturbed mental
and hallucinogenic patients which could overcome a rational telepath."

Police Commissioner Frank Gillings was the prime source of the
fury which had set Harold Orley off. Op Owen felt sorry for
Orley, having to bear such anger, and sorrier for himself and his
optimistic hopes. He was momentarily at a loss to explain such a
violent reaction from Gillings, even granting the validity of Lester
Welch's assumption that Gillings was losing face, financial and personal, on account of this affair.

He tried a "push" at Gillings's mind to discover the covert reasons and found the man had a tight natural shield, not uncommon
for a person in high position, privy to sensitive facts. The burly
Commissioner gave every outward appearance of being completely
at ease, as if this were no more than a routine visit, and not one

hint of his surface thoughts leaked. Deep-set eyes, barely visible under heavy brows, above fleshy cheeks in a swarthy face that missed nothing, flicked from Daffyd to Lester and back.

Op Owen nodded to Ted Lewis, the top police "finder" who had accompanied the official group. He stood a little to one side of the others. Of all the visitors, his mind was wide open. Foremost was the thought that he hoped Daffyd would read him, so that he could pass the warning that Gillings considered Orley's exhibition another indication that Talents could not control or discipline their own members.

"Good morning, Commissioner. I regret such circumstances bring you on your first visit to the Center. This morning's newscast had made us all extremely anxious to clear our profession."

Gillings's perfunctory smile did not acknowledge the tacit explanation of Orley's behavior.

"I'll come to the point, then, Owen. We have conclusively ascertained that there was no break in store security measures when the theft occurred. The 'lectric wards and spy-scanner were not tampered with nor was there any evidence of breaking or entering. There is only one method in which sable, necklace, dress and shoes could have been taken from that window in the five minutes between TV scans.

"We regret exceedingly that the evidence points to a person with psychic talents. We must insist that the larcenist be surrendered to us immediately and the merchandise returned to Mr. Grey, the representative from Cole's." He indicated the portly man in a conservative but expensive grey fitted.

Op Owen nodded and looked expectantly towards Ted Lewis.

"Lewis can't 'find' a trace anywhere so it's obvious the items are being shielded." A suggestion of impatience crept into Gillings's bass voice. "These grounds are shielded."

"The stolen goods are not here, Commissioner. If they were, they would have been found by a member the instant the broadcast was heard."

Gillings's eyes snapped and his lips thinned with obstinancy.

"I've told you I can read on these grounds, Commissioner," Ted Lewis said with understandable indignation. "The stolen . . ."

A wave of the Commissioner's hand cut off the rest of Lewis's statement. Op Owen fought anger at the insult.

"You're a damned fool, Gillings," said Welch, not bothering to control his, "if you think we'd shelter a larcenist at this time."

"Ah yes, that Bill pending Senate approval," Gillings said with an unpleasant smile.

Daffyd found it hard to nullify resentment at the smug satisfaction and new antagonism which Gillings was generating.

"Yes, that Bill, Commissioner," op Owen repeated, "which will protect any Talent *registered* with a parapsychic center." Op Owen did not miss the sparkle of Gillings's deep-set eyes at the deliberate emphasis. "If you'll step this way, gentlemen, to our remote-graph control system, I believe that we can prove, to your absolute satisfaction, that no registered Talent is responsible. You haven't been here before, Commissioner, so you are not familiar with our method of recording incidents in which psychic powers are used.

"Power, by the way, means 'possession of control', personal as well as psychic, which is what this Center teaches each and every member. Here we are. Charles Moorfield is the duty officer and was in charge at the time of the robbery. If you will observe the graphs, you'll notice that that period—between 7:03 and 7:08 was the time given by the 'cast—has not yet wound out of sight on the storage drums."

Gillings was not looking at the graphs. He was staring at Charlie.

"Next time, aim at the chest first, mister."

"Sorry I stopped him at all . . . mister," replied Charlie, with such deliberate malice that Gillings colored and stepped towards him.

Op Owen quickly intervened. "You dislike, distrust and hate us, Commissioner," he said, keeping his own voice neutral with effort. "You and your staff have prejudged us guilty, though you are at this moment surrounded by incontrovertible evidence of our collective innocence. You arrived here, emanating disruptive emotions—no, I'm *not* reading your minds, gentlemen." Daffyd had all Gillings's attention with that phrase. "That isn't necessary. You're triggering responses in the most controlled of us—not to mention that poor witless telempath we had to tranquilize. And, unless you put a lid on your unwarranted hatred and fears, I will have no compunction about pumping you all full of tranks, too!"

"That's coming on mighty strong for a man in your position,

Owen," Gillings said in a tight hard voice, his body visibly tense now.

"You're the one that's coming on strong, Gillings. Look at that dial behind you."

Gillings did not want to turn, particularly not at op Owen's command, but there is a quality of righteous anger that compels obedience.

"That registers—as Harold Orley does—the psychic intensity of the atmosphere. The mind gives off electrical impulses, Gillings, surely you have to admit that. Law enforcement agencies used that premise for lie detection. Our instrumentation makes those early registers as archaic as space ships make oxcarts. We have ultra-delicate equipment which can measure the minutest electrical impulses of varying frequencies and duration. And this PA dial registers a dangerous high right now. Surely your eyes must accept scientific evidence.

"Those rows of panels there record the psychic activity of each and every member registered with this Center. See, most of them register agitation right now. These red divisions indicate a sixty-minute time span. Each of those drums exposes the graph as of the time of that theft. Notice the difference. Not one graph shows the kinetic activity required of a 'lifter' to achieve such a theft. But every one shows a reaction to your presence.

"There is no way in which a registered Talent can avoid these graphs. Charlie, were any kinetics out of touch at the time of the theft?"

Charlie, his eyes locked on Gillings, shook his head slowly.

"There never has been so much as a civil misdemeanor by any of our people. No breach of confidence, nor integrity. No crime could be shielded from fellow Talents.

"And can you rationally believe that we would jeopardize years and years of struggle to become accepted as reliable citizens of indisputable integrity for the sake of a fur coat and a string of baubles? When there are funds available to any Talent who might want to own such fripperies?" Op Owen's scorn made the Cole man wince.

"Now get out of here, Gillings. Discipline your emotions and revise your snap conclusion. Then call through normal channels and request our cooperation. Because, believe me, we are far more determined . . . and better equipped . . . to discover the real criminal than you could ever be, no matter what *your* personal stake in assigning guilt might conceivably be."

Op Owen watched for a reaction to that remark but Gillings, his lips thin and white with anger, did not betray himself. He gestured jerkily towards the one man in police blues.

"Do not serve that warrant now, Gillings!" op Owen said in a very soft voice. He watched the frantic activity of the needle on the PA dial.

"Go. Now. Call. Because if you cannot contain your feelings, Commissioner, you had better maintain your distance."

It was then that Gillings became aware of the palpable presence of those assembled in the corridor. A wide aisle had been left free, an aisle that led only to the open elevator. No one spoke or moved or coughed. The force exerted was not audible nor physical. It was, however, undeniably unanimous. It prevailed in forty-four seconds.

"My firm will wish to know what steps are being taken," the Cole's man said in a squeaky voice as he began to walk, with erratic but ever quickening steps, towards the elevator.

Gillings's three subordinates were not so independent, but there was no doubt of their relief as Gillings turned and walked with precise, unhurried strides to the waiting car.

No one moved until the thwapping rumble of the copter was no longer audible. Then they turned for assignments from their director.

City Manager Julian Pennstrak, with a metropolis of some four million to supervise, had a habit of checking up personally on any disruption to the smooth operation of his city. He arrived as the last of the organized search parties left the Center.

"I'd give my left kidney and a million credits to have enough Talent to judge a man accurately, Dave," he said as he crossed the room. He knew better than to shake hands unless a Talented offered but it was obvious to Daffyd, who like Pennstrak, that the man wanted somehow to convey his personal distress over this incident. He stood for a moment by the chair, his handsome face without a trace of his famous genial smile. "I'd've sworn Frank Gillings was pro-Talent," he said, combing his fingers through his thick, wavy black hair, another indication of his anxiety. "He certainly has used your people to their fullest capabilities since he became LEO Commissioner."

Lester Welch snorted, looking up from the map he was annotating with search patterns. "A man'll use any tool that works . . . until it scratches him, that is."

"But you could prove that no registered Talent was responsible for that theft."

" 'A man convinced against his will, is of his own opinion still,' " Lester chanted.

"Les!" Op Owen didn't need sour cynicism from any quarter, even one dedicated to Talent. "No *registered* Talent was responsible."

Pennstrak brightened. "You did persuade Gillings that it's the work of an undiscovered Talent?"

Welch made a rude noise. "He'll be persuaded when we produce both missing person and missing merchandise. Nothing else is going to satisfy either Gillings or Cole's."

"True," Pennstrak agreed, frowning thoughtfully. "Nor the vacillating members of my own Council. Oh, I know, it's a flash reaction but the timing is so goddamned lousy, Dave. Your campaign bore down heavy on the integrity and good citizenship of the Talented."

"It's a deliberate smear job . . ." Welch began gloomily.

"I thought of that," Pennstrak interrupted him, "and had my own expert go over the scanner films. You know the high security risk set-up: rotating exposures on the stationary TV eyes. One frame the model was clothed; next, exposed in all its plastic glory. It was a 'lift' all right. No possibility of tampering with that film." Pennstrak leaned forward to Dave, though there was scarcely any need to guard his statements in this company. "Furthermore, Pat came along. She 'read' everyone at the store, and Gillings's squad. Not Gillings, though. She said he has a natural shield. The others were all clean . . . at least of conspiracy." Pennstrak's snide grin faded quickly. "I made her go rest. That's why there's no one with me."

Op Owen accepted the information quietly. He had half-hoped . . . it was an uncharacteristic speculation for him. However, it did save time and Talent to have had both store and police checked.

It had become general practice to have a strong telepathic receiver in the entourage of any prominent or controversial public figure. That Talent was rarely identified publicly. He or she usually performed some obvious service so that their constant presence was easily explicable. Pat Tawfik was overtly Pennstrak's chief speech writer.

"I have, however," Pennstrak continued, "used my official prerogative to supervise the hunt. There're enough sympathetic people on the public media channels to play down the Talent angle—at my request—but you know what this kind of adverse publicity is going to do to you, this Center and the Talented in general. One renegade can discredit a hundred honest injuns. So, what can I do to help?"

"I wish I knew. We've got every available perceptive out on the off-chance that this—ah—renegade happens to be broadcasting joy and elation over her heist."

"Her?"

"The consensus is that while a man might lift furs and jewels, possibly the dress, only a woman would take the shoes, too. Top finders are coming in from other Centers . . ."

"A 'find' is reported, Boss," said Charlie over the intercom. "Block Q."

As Pennstrak and op Owen reached the map, Welch announced with a groan. "Gawd, that's a multi-layer apartment zone."

"A have-not," added op Owen.

"Gil Gracie made the find, Boss," Charlie continued. "And the fur is not all he's found but he's got a problem."

"You just bet he has," Les said under his breath as he grimaced down at the map coordinates.

"Charlie, send every finder and perceptive to Block Q. If they can come up with a fix . . ."

"Boss, we got a fix, but there's one helluva lot of similarities."

"What's the problem?" asked Pennstrak.

"We'll simply have to take our time and eliminate, Charlie. Send anyone who can help." Then op Owen turned to Pennstrak. "In reporting a 'find,' the perceptive is aware of certain particular spatial relationships between the object sought and its immediate surroundings. It isn't as if he has seen the object as a camera sees it. For example, have you ever entered a room, turned down a street, or looked up quickly and had the feeling that you had seen just (and Daffyd made a bracket of his hands) that portion of the scene before, with exactly the same lighting, exactly the same components? But only that portion of the scene, so that the rest was an indistinguishable blur?"

Pennstrak nodded.

" 'Finding' is like that. Sometimes the Talent sees it in lucid detail, sometimes it's obscured or, as in this case, there are literally hundreds of possibilities . . . apartments with the same light exposure, same scene out the window, the same floor plan and furnishings. Quite possible in this instance since these are furnished, standard subsistence dwellings. Nothing to help us single out, say Apartment 44E, Building 18, Buhler Street."

"There happens to be a Building 18 on Buhler Street, Boss," Les Welch said slowly, "and there are 48 levels, 10 units per floor."

Pennstrak regarded op Owen with awe.

"Nonsense, this office is thoroughly shielded and I'm *not* a precog!"

"Before you guys took the guesswork out of it, there were such things as hunches," Pennstrak suggested.

For op Owen's peace of mind and Lester's pose of misogyny, it was neither Building 18 nor Buhler Street nor Apartment 44. It was Apartment 1E, deep in the center of Q Block. No one had entered nor left it—by normal means—since Gil Gracie and two other finders had made a precise fix. Gil handed op Owen the master key obtained from the dithering super.

"My Gawd," Pennstrak said in a voice muted with shocked surprise, as they swung open the door. "Like an oriental bazaar."

"Indiscriminate pilfering on a wholesale basis." Op Owen corrected him, glancing around at the rich brilliant velvet drapes framing the dingy window to the wildly clashing pillows thrown on the elegant Empire loveseat. A marble-topped table was a jumble of pretty vases, silver boxes and goblets. Priceless china held decaying remains of food. Underneath the table were jaggedly opened, empty cans bearing the label of an extremely expensive caterer. Two empty champagne bottles pointed green, blind eyes in their direction. A portable color 'caster was piled with discarded clothing; a black-lace sheer body stocking draped in an obscene posture across the inactive screen. "A magpie's nest rather," he sighed, "and I'd hazard that Maggie is very young and has been poor all her life until . . ." He met Pennstrak's sympathetic gaze. "Until our educational program gave her the hints she needed to unlock her special Talent."

"Gillings is going to have to work with you on this, Dave," Pennstrak said reluctantly as he reached for the intercom at his belt. "But first he's going to have to apologize."

Op Owen shook his head vigorously. "I want his cooperation, Julian, grudged or willing. *When* he really believes in Talent, then he will apologize voluntarily . . . and obliquely."

To op Owen's consternation, Gillings arrived noisily in the cowlike lab copter, sirens going, lights flashing.

"Don't bother now," op Owen said to Pennstrak for he could see the City Manager forming a furious reprimand. "She might have been warned by the finders' activity anyhow."

"Well, she's certainly been warned off now." Pennstrak stalked off, to confer with one of his aides just as Gillings strode into the corridor with his technicians.

According op Owen and Gracie the merest nod, Gillings began issuing crisp orders. He knew his business, op Owen thought, and he evidently trusted *these* technicians for he didn't bother to crowd into the tiny apartment to oversee them.

"As soon as your men have prints and a physical profile, Commissioner, we'd like to run the data through our computer. There's the chance that the girl did take advantage of the open Talent test the Center has been advertising."

"You mean you don't *know* who it is *yet?*"

"I could 'find' the coat only because I *knew* what it looked like," Gil Gracie said, bristling at Gillings's manner.

"Then where is it?" and Gillings gestured preemptorily to the sable-less apartment.

"These are the shoes, Commissioner," said one of his team, presenting the fragile strap and jeweled footwear, now neatly sealed in clear plastic. "Traces of dirt, dust, fleck of nail enamel and from the 'scope imprint, I'd say they were too big for her."

Gillings stared at the shoes disinterestedly. "No sign of the dress?"

"Still looking."

"Odd that you people can't locate a girl with bare feet in a sable coat and a bright blue silk gown?"

"No odder than it is for your hundreds of patrolmen throughout the city, Commissioner, to overlook a girl so bizarrely dressed," said op Owen with firm good humor. "When you 'saw' the coat, Gil, where was it?"

"Thrown across the loveseat, one arm hanging down to the floor. I distinguished the edge of the sill and the tree outside, the first folds of the curtain and the wall heating unit. I called in, you sent over enough finders so that we were able to eliminate the similarities. It took us nearly an hour . . ."

"Were you keeping an 'eye' on the coat all the time?" Gillings demanded in a voice so devoid of expression that his contempt was all the more obvious.

Gil flushed, bit his lip and only partially inhibited by op Owen's subtle warning, snapped back, "Try keeping your physical eye on an object for an hour!"

"Get some rest, Gil," op Owen said gently. He waited until the finder had turned the corner. "If you are as determined to find this criminal as you say you are, Commissioner Gillings, then do not destroy the efficiency of my staff by such gratuitous criticism. In less than four hours, on the basis of photographs of the stolen objects, we located this apartment . . ."

"But not the criminal, who is still in possession of a sable coat which you found once but have now unaccountably lost."

"That's enough, Gillings," said Pennstrak who had rejoined them. "Thanks to your arrival, the girl must know she's being sought and is shielding."

Pennstrak gestured toward the dingy windows of the flat, through which the vanes of the big copter were visible. A group of children, abandoning the known objects of the development play-yard, had gathered at a respectful, but curiosity-satisfying distance.

"Considering the variety of her accomplishments," op Owen said, not above using Pennstrak's irritation with his Commissioner to advantage, "I'm sure she knew of the search before the Commissioner's arrival, Julian. Have any of these items been reported, Commissioner?"

"That console was. Two days ago. It was on 'find,' too."

"She has been growing steadily bolder, then," op Owen went on, depressed by Gillings's attitude. And depressed that such a Talent had emerged twisted, perverted, selfish. Why? Why? "If your department ever gets the chronology of the various thefts, we'd appreciate the copy."

"Why?" Gillings turned to stare at op Owen, surprised and irritated.

"Talent takes time to develop—in ordinary persons. It does not,

like the ancient goddess Athena, spring full-grown from the forehead. This girl could not, for instance, have lifted that portable set
the first time she used her Talent. The more data we have on . . .
the lecture is ill-timed."

Gillings's unspoken "you said it" did reach op Owen whose turn
it was to stare in surprise.

"Well, your 'finders' are not novices," the Commissioner said
aloud. "If they traced the coat once, why not again?"

"Every perceptive we have is searching," op Owen said. "But, if
she was able to leave this apartment after Gil found the coat, taking it with her, because it obviously is not here, she also is capable
of shielding herself and that coat. And, until she slips that guard, I
doubt we'll find it or her."

T he report on the laboratory findings was exhaustive. There
was a full set of prints, foot and finger. None matched those on
file in the city records, or Federal or Immigration. She had not
been tested at the Center. Long coarse black hair had been found.
Analysis of skin flakes suggested an olive complexion. Thermo-
photography placed her last appearance in the room at approximately the time the four 'finders' fixed on her apartment, thus
substantiating op Owen's guess. The thermal prints also revealed
that she was of slender build, approximately 5'4", weighing 105
pounds. Stains on a paring knife proved her to possess blood type
O. No one else had occupied the apartment within the eight day
range of the thermography used.

From such records, the police extrapolator made a rough sketch
of "Maggie O" which she was called for want of a better name.
The sketch was taken around the neighborhood with no success.
People living in Block Q didn't bother people who didn't bother
them.

It was Daffyd op Owen who remembered the children crowding
the police copter. From them he elicited the information that she
was new in the building. (The records indicated that the apartment
should be vacant.) She was always singing, dancing to the wall
'caster, and changing her clothes. Occasionally she'd play with
them and bring out rich food to eat, promising they could have
such good things if they'd think hard about them. While the children talked, Daffyd "saw" Maggie's face reflected in their minds.

The police extrapolator had been far short of the reality. She was not much older than the children she had played with. She had not been pretty by ordinary standards but she had been so "different" that her image had registered sharply. The narrow face, the brilliant eyes, slightly slanted above sharp cheekbones, the thin, small mouth and the pointed chin were unusual even in an area of ethnic variety.

This likeness and a physical description were circulated quickly to be used at all exits to the city and all transportation facilities. It was likely she'd try to slip out during the day-end exodus.

The south and west airstrips had been under a perceptive surveillance since the search had been inaugurated. Now every facility was guarded.

Gil Gracie "found" the coat again.

"She must have it in a suitcase," he reported on the police-provided handunit from his position in the main railroad concourse. "It's folded and surrounded by dark. It's moving up and down. But there're so many people. So many suitcases. I'll circulate. Maybe the find'll fix itself."

Gillings gave orders to his teams on the master unit which had been set up in the Center's control room to coordinate the operations.

"You better test Gil for precog," Charlie muttered to op Owen after they'd contacted all the sensitivities. "He *asked* for the station."

"You should've told me sooner, Charlie. I'd've teamed him with a sensitive."

"Look at that," Charlie exclaimed, pointing to a wildly moving needle on one of the remotes.

Les was beside it even as the audio for the Incident went on.

"Not that track! Oh! Watch out! Baggage. On the handcart! Watch out. Move, man. Move! To the right. The right! Ahhhh." The woman's voice choked off in an agonized cry.

Daffyd pushed Charlie out of the way, to get to the speaker.

"Gil, this is op Owen. Do not pursue. Do not pursue that girl! She's aware of you. Gil, come in. Answer me, Gil. . . . Charlie, keep trying to raise him. Gillings, contact your men in the station. Make them stop Gil Gracie."

"Stop him? Why?"

"The precog. The baggage on the handcart," shouted Daffyd,

signaling frantically to Lester to explain in detail. He raced for the emergency stairs, up the two flights, and slammed out onto the roof. Gasping physically for breath, he clung to the high retaining wall and projected his mind to Gil's.

He knew the man so well, had trained Gil when an employee brought in the kid who had a knack for locating things. Op Owen could see him ducking and dodging through the trainward crowds, touching suitcases, ignoring irate or astonished carriers; every nerve, every ounce of him receptive to the "feel" of a dense, dark sable fur. And so singleminded that Daffyd could not "reach" him.

But op Owen knew the instant the loaded baggage cart swerved and crushed the blindly intent Talent against an I-beam. He bowed his head, too fully cognizant that a double tragedy had occurred. Gil was lost . . . and so now was the girl.

There was no peace from his thoughts even when he returned to the shielded control room. Lester and Charlie pretended to be very busy. Gillings was. He directed the search of the railway station, arguing with the stationmaster that the trains were to be held and that was that. The drone of his voice began to penetrate op Owen's remorse.

"All right, then, if the Talents have cleared it and there's no female of the same height and weight, release that train. Someone tried the johns, didn't they? No, Sam, you can detain anyone remotely suspicious. That girl is clever, strong, and dangerous. There's no telling what else she could do. But she damn well can't change her height, weight and blood type!"

"Daffyd. Daffyd." Lester had to touch him to get his attention. He motion op Owen towards Charlie who was holding out the handunit.

"It's Cole's, sir."

Daffyd listened to the effusively grateful store manager. He made the proper responses but it wasn't until he had relinquished the handunit to Charlie that the man's excited monologue made sense.

"The coat, the dress and the necklace have reappeared on the store dummy," op Owen said. He cleared his throat and repeated it loud enough to be heard.

"Returned?" Gillings echoed. "Just like that? Why, the little bitch! Sam, check the ladies rooms in that station. Wait, isn't there a discount dress store in that station? Have them check for missing

apparel. I want an itemized list of what's gone, and an exact duplicate from their stock shown to the sensitives. We've got her scared
and running now."

"Scared and running now." Gillings's smug assessment rang om-
inously in Daffyd's mind. He had a sudden flash. Superimposed
over a projection of Maggie's thin face was the image of the lifeless
store dummy, elegantly reclad in the purloined blue gown and
dark fur. "Here, take them back. I don't want them anymore. I
didn't mean to kill him. I didn't mean to. See, I gave back what you
wanted. Now leave me alone!"

Daffyd shook his head. Wishful thinking. Just as futile as the
girl's belated gesture of penance. Too much too soon. Too little too
late.

"We don't want her scared," he said out loud. "She was scared
when she toppled that baggage cart."

"She *killed* a man when she toppled that baggage cart, op Owen!"
Gillings was all but shouting.

"And if we're not very careful, she'll kill others."

"If you think I'm going to velvet glove a homicidal maniac . . ."

A shrill tone issuing from the remote unit forced Gillings to
answer. He was about to reprimand the caller but the message got
stunned attention.

"We can forget the paternal bit, Owen. She knocked down every
one of your people and mine at the Oriole Street entrance. Your
men are unconscious. Mine and about twenty or more innocent
commuters are afflicted with blinding headaches. Got any practical
ideas, Owen, on catching this monster you created?"

"Oriole? Was she heading east or west?" He had to stop that line
of talk.

"Does it matter?"

"If we're to catch her it does. And we must catch her. She's
operating at a psychic high. There's no telling what she's capable
of now. Such Talent has only been a theoretic possibility . . ."

Gillings lost all control of himself. The fear and hatred burst out
in such a wave that Charlie Moorfield, caught unawares, erupted
out of his chair towards Gillings in an instinctive defense reaction.

"Gillings!" "Charlie!" Les and Daffyd shouted together, each
grabbing the wild combatants. But Charlie, his face white with
shock at his own reaction, had himself in hand. Sinking weakly
back into his chair, he gasped out an apology.

"You mean, you *want* to have more monsters like her and him?" Gillings demanded. Between his voice and the violent emotions, Daffyd's head rang with pain and confusion.

"Don't be a fool," Lester said, grabbing the Commissioner by the arm. "You can't spew emotions like that around a telepath and not get a reaction. Look at Daffyd! Look at Charlie! Christ man, you're as bad as the scared, mixed-up kid . . ." and then Les dropped Gillings's arm and stared at him in amazement. "Christ, you're a telepath yourself!"

"Quiet, everybody," Daffyd said with such urgency he had their instant attention. "I've the solution. And there's no time to waste. Charlie, I want Harold Orley airbound in the Clinic's copter heading south to the Central Station in nothing flat. We'll correct course en route. Gillings, I want two of the strongest, most stable patrolmen on your roster. I want them armed with fast-acting, double-strength trank guns and airborne to rendezvous near Central Station."

"Harold?" Les echoed in blank astonishment. Then relief colored his face as he understood Daffyd's intentions. "Of course. Nothing can stop Harold. And no one can read him coming."

"Nothing. And no one," op Owen agreed, bleakly.

Gillings turned from issuing his orders to see an ambulance copter heading west across the sky.

"We're following?"

Daffyd nodded and gestured for Gillings to precede him to the roof. He didn't look back but he knew what Les and Charlie did not say.

She had been seen running east on Oriole. And she was easy to follow. She left people doubled up with nausea and crying with head pains. That is, until she crossed Boulevard.

"We'll head south, south east on an intercept," Gillings told his pilot and had him relay the correction to the ambulance. "She's heading to the sea?" he asked rhetorically as he rummaged for the correct airmap of the city. "Here. We can set down at Seaman's Park. She can't have made it that far . . . unless she can fly suddenly." Gillings looked up at op Owen.

"She probably could teleport herself," Daffyd answered, watching the Commissioner's eyes narrow in adverse reaction to the admission. "But she hasn't thought of it yet. As long as she can be kept running, too scared to think . . ." That necessity plagued

Daffyd op Owen. They were going to have to run her out of her mind.

Gillings ordered all police hovercraft to close in on the area where she was last seen, blocks of residences and small businesses of all types.

By the time the three copters had made their rendezvous at the small Park, there were no more visible signs of Maggie O's retreat.

As Gillings made to leave the copter, Daffyd op Owen stopped him.

"If you're not completely under control, Gillings, Harold will be after you."

Gillings looked at the director for a long moment, his jaw set stubbornly. Then, slowly, he settled into the seat and handed op Owen a remote comunit.

"Thanks, Gillings," he said, and left the copter. He signaled to the ambulance to release Harold Orley and then strode across the grass to the waiting officers.

The two biggest men were as burly as he could wish. Being trained law enforcers, they ought to be able to handle Orley. Op Owen "pushed" gently against their minds and was satisfied with his findings. They possessed the natural shielding of the untemperamental which made them less susceptible to emotional storms. Neither Webster nor Heis were stupid, however, and had been briefed on developments.

"Orley has no useful intelligence. He is a human barometer, measuring the intensity and type of emotions which surround him and reacting instinctively. He does not broadcast. He only receives. Therefore he cannot be harmed or identified by . . . by Maggie O. He is the only Talent she cannot 'hear' approaching."

"But, if he reaches her, he'd . . ." Webster began, measuring Harold with the discerning eye of a boxing enthusiast. Then he shrugged and turned politely to op Owen.

"You've the double strength tranks? Good. I hope you'll be able to use them in time. But it is imperative that she be apprehended before she does more harm. She has already killed one man. . . ."

"We understand, sir," Heis said when op Owen did not continue.

"If you can, shoot her. Once she stops broadcasting, he'll soon return to a manageable state." But, Daffyd amended to himself, remembering Harold sprawled on the ground in front of the build-

ing, not soon enough. "She was last seen on the east side of the
Boulevard, about eight blocks from here. She'd be tired, looking
for someplace to hide and rest. But she is also probably radiating
sufficient emotion for Harold to pick up. He'll react by heading in
a straight line for the source. Keep him from trying to plow
through solid walls. Keep your voices calm when you speak to him.
Use simple commands. I see you've got handunits. I'll be airborne;
the copter's shielded but I'll help when I can."

Flanking Harold, Webster and Heis moved west along Oriole at
a brisk, even walk: the two officers in step, Harold's head bobbing
above theirs, out of step—a cruel irony.

Daffyd op Owen turned back to the copter. He nodded to Gillings as he seated himself. He tried not to think at all.

As the copters lifted from the Park and drifted slowly west amid
other air traffic, op Owen looked sadly down at the people on the
streets. At kids playing on the sidewalks. At a flow of men and
women with briefcases or shopping bags, hurrying home. At snub-
nosed city cars and squatty trucks angling into parking slots. At
the bloated cross-city helibuses jerking and settling to disgorge
their passengers at the street islands.

"He's twitching," reported Heis in a dispassionate voice.

Daffyd flicked on the handset. "That's normal. He's beginning to
register."

"He's moving faster now. Keeps wanting to go straight through
the buildings." Reading Heis's undertone, op Owen knew that the
men hadn't believed his caution about Orley plowing through
solids. "He's letting us guide him, but he keeps pushing us to the
right. You take his other arm, Web. Yeah, that's better."

Gillings had moved to the visual equipment along one side of the
copter. He focused deftly in on the trio, magnified it and threw the
image on the pilot's screen, too. The copter adjusted direction.

"Easy, Orley. No, don't try to stop him, Web. Stop the traffic!"

Orley's line of march crossed the busier wide north-south street.
Webster ran out to control the vehicles. People turned curiously.
Stopped and stared after the trio.

"Don't," op Owen said as he saw Gillings move a hand towards
the bullhorn. "There's nothing wrong with her hearing."

Orley began to move faster now that he had reached the farther
side. He wanted to go right through intervening buildings.

"Guide him left to the sidewalk, Heis," op Owen said. "I think he's still amenable. He isn't running yet."

"He's breathing hard, Mr. Owen," Heis sounded dubious. "And his face is changing."

Op Owen nodded to himself, all too familiar with the startling phenomenon of watching the blankness of Orley's face take on the classic mask of whatever emotions he was receiving. It would be a particularly unnerving transition under these conditions.

"What does he show?"

"I'd say . . . hatred," Heis's voice dropped on the last word. Then he added in his usual tone, "He's smiling, too, and it isn't nice."

They had eased Orley to the sidewalk heading west. He kept pushing Webster to the right and his pace increased until it was close to a run. Webster and Heis began to gesture people out of their way but it would soon be obvious to the neighborhood that something was amiss. Would it be better to land more police to reassure people and keep their emanations down? Or would they broadcast too much suppressed excitement at police interference? She'd catch that. Should he warn Heis and Webster to keep their thoughts on Harold Orley? Or would that be like warning them against all thoughts of the camel's left knee?

Orley broke into a run. Webster and Heis were hard put to keep him to the sidewalk.

"What's in the next block?" op Owen asked Gillings.

The Commissioner consulted the map, holding it just above the scanner so he could keep one eye on the trio below.

"Residences and an area parking facility for interstate trucking." Gillings turned to op Owen now, his heavy eyebrows raised in question.

"No, she's still there because Orley is homing in on her projection."

"Look at his face! My God!" Heis exclaimed over the hand-unit. On the screen, his figure had stopped. He was pointing at Orley. But Webster's face was clearly visible to the surveillers and what he saw unnerved him.

Orley broke from his guides. He was running, slowly at first but gathering speed steadily, mindlessly brushing aside anything that stood in his way. Heis and Webster went after him but both men were shaking their heads as if something were bothering them.

Orley tried to plunge through a brick store wall. He bounced off it, saw the unimpeded view of his objective and charged forward. Webster had darted ahead of him, blowing his whistle to stop the oncoming traffic. Heis alternately yelled into the handunit and at startled bystanders. Now some of them were afflicted and were grabbing their heads.

"Put us on the roof," op Owen told the pilot. "Gillings, get men to cover every entrance and exit to that parking lot. Get the copters to hover by the open levels. The men'll be spared some of the lash."

It wouldn't do much good, op Owen realized, even as he felt the first shock of the girl's awareness of imminent danger.

"Close your mind," he yelled at the pilot and Gillings. "Don't think."

"My head, my head." It was Heis groaning.

"Concentrate on Orley," op Owen said, his hands going to his temples in reaction to the knotting pressure. Heis's figure on the scanner staggered after Orley who had now entered the parking facility.

Op Owen caught the mental pressure and dispersed it, projecting back reassurance/help/protection/compassion. *He* could forgive her Gil Gracie's death. So would any Talent. If she would instantly surrender, somehow the Center would protect her from the legal aspects of her act. Only surrender now.

Someone screamed. Another man echoed that piercing cry. The copter bucked and jolted them. The pilot was groaning and gasping. Gillings plunged forward, grabbing the controls.

Op Owen, fighting an incredible battle, was blind to physical realities. If he could just occupy all the attention of that overcharged mind . . . hold it long enough . . . pain/fear/black/red/moiled-orange/purples . . . breathing . . . shock. Utter disbelief/fear/loss of confidence. Frantic physical effort.

Concrete scraped op Owen's cheek. His fingers bled as he clawed at a locked steel exit door on the roof. He could not enter. *He had to reach her* FIRST!

Somehow his feet found the stairs as he propelled himself down the fire escape, deliberately numbing his mind to the intensive pounding received. A pounding that became audible.

Then he saw her, fingers clawing for leverage on the stairpost, foot poised for the step from the landing. A too-thin adolescent figure, frozen for a second with indecision and shock; strands of black hair like vicious scars across a thin face, distorted and ugly from the tremendous physical and mental efforts of the frantic will. Her huge eyes, black with insane fury and terror, bloodshot with despair and the salty sweat of her desperate striving for escape, looked into his.

She knew him for what he was; and her hatred crackled in his mind. Those words—after Gil Gracie's death—had been hers, not his distressed imagining. She had know him then as her real antagonist. Only now was *he* forced to recognize her for what she was, all she was—and regrettably, all she would not be.

He fought the inexorable decision of that split-second confrontation, wanting more than anything else in his life that it did not have to be so.

She was the wiser! She whirled!

She was suddenly beyond the heavy fire door without opening it. Harold Orley, charging up the stairs behind her, had no such Talent. He crashed with sickening force into the metal door. Daffyd had no alternative. She had teleported. He steadied the telempath, depressed the lock bar and threw the door wide.

Orley was after the slender figure fleeing across the dimly lit, low-ceiling concrete floor. She was heading towards the down ramp now.

"Stop, stop," op Owen heard his voice begging her.

Heis came staggering from the stairway.

"Shoot him. For Christ's sake, shoot Orley, Heis," op Owen yelled.

Heis couldn't seem to coordinate. Op Owen tried to push aside his fumbling hands and grab the trank gun himself. Heis's trained reflexes made him cling all the tighter to his weapon. Just then, op Owen heard the girl's despairing shriek.

Two men had appeared at the top of the ramp. They both fired, the dull reports of trank pistols accentuated by her choked gasp.

"Not her. Shoot Orley. Shoot the man," op Owen cried but it was too late.

Even as the girl crumpled to the floor, Orley grabbed her. Grabbed and tore and beat at the source of the emotions which so disturbed him. Beat and tore and stamped her physically as she had assaulted him mentally.

Orley's body jerked as tranks hit him from all sides, but it took far too long for them to override the adrenal reactions of the overcharged telempath.

There was pain and pity as well as horror in Gillings's eyes when he came running onto the level. The police stood at a distance from the blood-spattered bodies.

"Gawd, couldn't someone have stopped him from getting her?" the copter pilot murmured, turning away from the shapeless bloodied thing half-covered by Orley's unconscious body.

"The door would have stopped Orley but he," and Heis grimly pointed at op Owen, "opened it for him."

"She teleported through the door," op Owen said weakly. He had to lean against the wall. He was beginning to shudder uncontrollably from reaction. "She had to be stopped. Now. Here. Before she realized what she'd done. What she could do." His knees buckled. "She teleported through the door!"

Unexpectedly it was Gillings who came to his aid, a Gillings whose mind was no longer shielded but broadcasting compassion and awe, and understanding.

"So did you."

The phrase barely registered in op Owen's mind when he passed out.

"That's all that remains of the late Solange Boshe," Gillings said, tossing the file reel to the desk. "As much of her life as we've been able to piece together. Gypsies don't stay long anywhere."

"There're some left?" Lester Welch asked, frowning at the three-inch condensation of fifteen years of a human life.

"Oh there are, I assure you," Gillings replied, his tone souring slightly for the first time since he had entered the office. "The tape also has a lengthy interview with Bill Jones, the cousin the social worker located after Solange had recovered from the bronchial pneumonia. He had no idea," Gillings hastily assured them, "that there was any reason other than a routine check on the whereabouts of a runaway county ward. He had a hunch," and Gillings grimaced, "that the family had gone on to Toronto. They had. He also thought that they had probably given the girl up for dead when she collapsed on the street. The Toronto report substantiates that. So I don't imagine it will surprise you, op Owen, that her tribe, according to Jones, are the only ones still making a living at fortune-telling, palm-reading, tea-leaves and that bit."

"Now, just a minute, Gillings," Lester began, bristling. He subsided when he saw that his boss and the Police Commissioner were grinning at each other.

"So . . . just as you suspected, op Owen, she was a freak Talent. We know from the ward nurses that she watched your propaganda broadcasts during her hospitalization. We can assume that she was aware of the search either when Gil Gracie 'found' the coat, or when the definite fix was made. It's not hard to guess her motivation in making the heist in the first place, nor her instinctive desire to hide." Gillings gave his head an abrupt violent jerk and stood up. He started to hold out his hand, remembered and raised it in a farewell gesture. "You are continuing those broadcasts, aren't you?"

Lester Welch glared so balefully at the Commissioner that op Owen had to chuckle.

"With certain deletions, yes."

"Good. Talent must be identified and trained. Trained young and well if they are to use their Talent properly." Gillings stared op Owen in the eye. "The Boshe girl was bad, op Owen, bad clear through. Listen to what Jones said about her and you won't regret Tuesday too much. Sometimes the young are inflexible, too."

"I agree, Commissioner," Daffyd said, escorting the man to the door as calmly as if he hadn't heard what Gillings was thinking so clearly. "And we appreciate your help in the cover yarns that explained Tuesday's odd occurrences."

"A case of mutual understanding," Gillings said, his eyes glinting. "Oh, no need to see me out. *I* can open this door."

That door was no sooner firmly shut behind him than Lester Welch turned on his superior.

"And just who was scratching whose back then?" he demanded. "Don't you dare come over innocent, either, Daffyd op Owen. Two days ago that man was your enemy, bristling with enough hate and distrust to antagonize me."

"Remember what you said about Gillings Tuesday?"

"There's been an awful lot of idle comment around here lately."

"Frank Gillings *is* telepathic." Then he added as Lester was choking on the news: "And he doesn't want to be. So he's suppressed it. Naturally he'd be antagonistic."

"Hah!"

"He's not too old, but he's not flexible enough to adapt to Talent, having denied it so long."

"I'll buy that. But what was that parting shot—'I can open this door'?" Lester mimicked the Commissioner's deep voice.

"I'm too old to learn new tricks, too, Les. I teleported through the roof door of that parking facility. He saw me do it. And *she* saw the memory of it in my mind. If she'd lived, she'd've picked my mind clean. And—I didn't *want* her to die."

Op Owen turned abruptly to the window, trying to let the tranquillity of the scene restore his equilibrium. It did—until he saw Harold Orley plodding along the path with his guide. Instantly a white, wide-eyed, hair-streaked face was superimposed over the view.

The intercom beeped and he depressed the key for his sanity's sake.

"We've got a live one, Boss," and Sally Iselin's gay voice restored him. "A strong precog with kinetic possibilities. And guess what?" Sally's excitement made her voice breathless. "He said the cop on his beat told him to come in. He doesn't want any more trouble with the cops so he . . ."

"Would his name be Bill Jones?"

"However did you know?"

"And that's no precog, Sally," op Owen said with a ghost of a laugh, aware he was beginning to look forward again. "A sure thing's no precog, is it Les?"

PART FOUR

A BRIDLE
FOR
PEGASUS

Julian Pennstrak, Jerhattan City Manager, Daffyd op Owen, Director of the East American Parapsychic Center, and Frank Gillings, Commissioner of Law Enforcement and Order, had gathered in the latter's office: an appropriate setting as the four sides of the tower office were tough plexiglass so the occupants had a full panoramic view of the city they managed or foresaw and protected.

"The Maggie O affair was not without some reward," Daffyd op Owen reminded the other two. "Her . . . relation . . . in whatever degree of cousinship Bill Jones stood . . . is proving to be a sound precog."

Gillings grunted and rubbed the side of his fleshy nose, registering skepticism.

"Half a city semi-paralyzed with blinding headaches, two dead, and a lot of public lying and you say there was some reward!"

"You do tend to adopt a negative attitude, don't you, Frank?" the City Manager remarked, half amused. He was watching op Owen from the corner of his eye. He knew that the Director of the Parapsychic Center had been deeply shaken by the deaths of Gil Gracie and Solange Boshe, a.k.a. Maggie O. And the curious sparring between Gillings and op Owen dated from that incident: the one grudging admiration and the other exhibiting wistful regret. Well, Pennstrak possessed a certain empathy himself which told him not to delve too deeply into the denouement of that incident. Suffice it to say, the truth about Maggie's sudden rise and demise had been successfully obscured from public notice and, if Daffyd were satisfied that some profit existed on the black side of the ledger, the City Manager would be content. "Nonetheless," Julian Pennstrak continued, "the Professional Immunity Law is now, as of yesterday, programmed into Federal Books and State Law Machinery. What's your problem now, Frank?"

"It's this: if renegades like Solange Boshe can exist, how do we smell 'em out before they cause trouble? Now," and he held up his hand as Daffyd op Owen opened his mouth to speak, "I know you've got a subliminal TRI-D program going, Dave, but just how successful is it in routing out the odd-balls?"

Op Owen winced at Gillings's phraseology.

"Unfortunately only time will tell. We do have Bill Jones, Maggie O's cousin, and he'll be a first rate precog. Sally Iselin at the Testing Clinic has upwards of fifty applicants a day." He sighed. "Most are wishful thinkers, I'm afraid, but occasionally a live one does come in. You can't make people get Talent-tested."

"What we need," the LEO Commissioner said in a deadly voice, "is enforced testing."

"Of nine million people?" asked Pennstrak, good-humoredly aghast.

Gillings grunted. "The mavericks cost us more."

Pennstrak agreed to that.

"Better still, early testing would be a tremendous help," Daffyd op Owen said. "Our sensitives in the maternity wards do catch the occasional strong one at birth. But we lack adequate facilities and more important, the personnel. It takes a special kind of Talent, in itself, to spot embryo Talents. Sally Iselin is acutely sensitive in this area and I thank Providence for her presence in the Clinic. She's never been wrong in her assessments. But she's the only one Eastern has and she's overworked as it is." Daffyd smiled and decided against what he'd been about to confide. The dour face of Lester Welch leered at him: For Christ's sake, Dave, don't tell everybody everything you know. They don't always want to hear it. For instance, Daffyd doubted that Frank Gillings would take kindly to the notion that Sally Iselin's chief assistant at the moment was the two-year-old Dorotea Horvath, the extraordinarily Talented daughter of two of his people. Dorotea came every morning and afternoon to the Clinic, to "play" in the room full of applicants. She'd instinctively approach anyone with the least vestige of Talent so that Sally could give the deeper testing. The others could be dismissed after the routine examinations, none the wiser for the

pre-selection. Dorotea was blissfully unaware of what she could do
—she simply did it.

"Talent is sometimes latent," Daffyd told Gillings, "as it was in
Solange Boshe, springing into maturity under pressure. But different minds react to different stimuli and the powerful Talent, such
as Solange's, to another set entirely. Talent can also be consciously
or subconsciously suppressed since any Talent singles one out for
the unwelcome attentions of the less gifted. We do try to alleviate
that envy with our public information broadcasts on what Talent
does to relieve . . ."

Gillings cut him off with a brusque wave of his hand. As much,
Daffyd op Owen thought wryly, because Gillings was a latent who
had no wish to be trained or reminded of this defection.

"Sorry for the lecture," op Owen said with an apologetic grin,
"but you must realize that we are limited in what we can do even
with all the Talent at our disposal. Nor can we foresee the stray
maturing of Talent. Your LEO operatives, Frank, have all the information we've collated on how to spot the latent or unconscious
Talent. What more can we do?"

"Get your Senator friend to write a rider on that Immunity
Law," said Gillings in a growl, "that it's illegal to be Talented and
conceal it."

Daffyd returned Gillings's half guilty glare with a wide-eyed
look of surprise. Gillings's perception was not dull: he knew what
was behind op Owen's grin and he scowled fiercely at him.

"I'll suggest it to Joel Andres when next we meet," op Owen
said politely. "It's a point well taken."

"How in hell could you implement such a statute under the
conditions you've just cited, Daffyd?" demanded Pennstrak with
understandable disgust. "No facilities, not enough Talent. Besides,
latents wouldn't know and therefore wouldn't register, and a Talent who knew of his ability could claim he didn't."

"Well, it'd be a help to me," Gillings said, still in a growling
mood. Yet he glanced at op Owen with less choler. Obviously the
telepath hadn't mentioned Gillings's latent abilities to the City
Manager. The man knew when to keep his mouth shut. "I could
shut up suspects and keep them from running amok like that gypsy
girl."

Op Owen's smile faded.

"You can't suppress or contain Talent, Frank. That'd put exactly the sort of pressure on them we'd want at all costs to avoid. There's so much we don't know about the parapsychic, so much."

"Like what for instance?" asked the LEO Commissioner, steeling himself for unwelcome information.

Op Owen spread his hands wide. "I can't tell you. I'm not a precog." To which he added a devout and silent "Amen!"

Gillings unloosed another grunt. "Now, on that score, have your Talents come up with anything on this ethnic employment allocation nonsense? You guys are, I sincerely trust, pan-ethnic?"

"Demonstrably."

Gillings gave him a long look as if he suspected op Owen of facetiousness. Julian Pennstrak cleared his throat hastily.

"That's one less headache at any rate," the LEO man went on, "but your precogs haven't had any Incidents beyond this nebulous warning?" He tapped the Incident readings which had been sent to his office the previous day.

Daffyd shook his head. "The precognitive faculty is the most erratic but generally speaking, the larger the number of people involved, the greater the possibility of detailed Incidents. Or, conversely, the severer the change to a prominent person or a linked or emotional association, the more likelihood of a definitive Incident.

"The old tea-leaf and card readers attempted to tell the future, anyone's future: and while I suppose they could generalize for the average soul well enough, the best of them were only accurate when predicting the future of lives which affected a large section of general mankind. Some precogs operate only on a direct confrontation with a personality, which is why we keep key personnel folders with those sensitives. But you can't actually provoke a precog.

"In the instance of Maggie O: she was a fluke to begin with, an isolated case, unintegrated in any group or with any affiliation that would cause one of our precogs to 'read' for her. That is, until circumstances put her in a position to cross Gil Gracie's lifeline. Then we had a reading on *him*, but only because the precog was tuned to Gil.

"There are, as I keep saying ad nauseam I know, a lot of parapsychic manifestations about which we know nothing. Every time I believe I understand one combination or facet, exceptions to that comprehension appear to confound me.

"Henry Darrow said that having any Talent is like riding a winged horse, you get a magnificent view but you can't always dismount when you want to."

Gillings had waited patiently through op Owen's peroration; now he rattled the urgently tagged tapes on his desk. Pennstrak regarded the Director with new insight.

"I'd always thought that Pegasus was the symbol of poetry . . . flights of verbal fantasy. But I must say, I like your notion, Dave. A winged horse is an appropriate mount for you people. Not that I'd have the courage to hop on its back."

"If you two would deign to consider the mundane problems of the earthbound," Gillings said in an acid tone of voice, "just how in hell are we going to find jobs for all these eager mud-grubbers?"

On a morning some two months later when Daffyd op Owen reached his office, there was a message on his desk to call Sally Iselin as soon as he had a moment. To a semantically-sensitive personality, the phrasing was provocative, added to the fact that Sally Iselin was in charge of recruit-testing. Daffyd punched her call numbers as soon as he read the note, disregarding other red and white flagged tapes and messages. If only one psi-latent was uncovered in a month of public information broadcasts, the program would be worth its cost.

"Daffyd here, Sally. You rang me?"

"Oh, Daffyd!" She sounded surprised and a tinge embarrassed. "I'm not really certain if I should bother you . . ."

"My great-grandmother used to say, 'If it's doubtful, it's dirty.' "

"I'm not talking about a shirt, Daffyd," and Sally's usual levity was missing. "I'm talking about people."

"Which people?" It was like pulling screws from wood: intriguingly un-Sallyish.

"Well, Daffyd, I'd hate to prejudice you. But . . . well, would you take me out tonight? There's a place I want you to feel. I can't figure out what it is myself and I know something happened."

"Curiouser and curiouser. You've hooked me . . ."

"Oh, damn. I don't want to hook you. I've gone and done what I shouldn't ta oughta."

Daffyd laughed. "Sally, all you've done is arouse my very considerable, insatiable curiosity."

"All right, elephant's child. Pick me up at nine; you'll need the copter and *money.*" Her voice darkened with baleful implications of wild spending and debauchery, but there was a rippling undercurrent of laughter which told Daffyd that Sally was herself again. "With as many bundles as Lester will allow me. At nine!"

He depressed the comset button just as the door opened to admit Lester Welch.

"What's on Iselin's alleged mind?"

"I can't 'path over a phone," Daffyd replied, deliberately misinterpreting Lester.

The man swore and glared sourly at his boss. "All right, so you won't talk either. Maybe I've no Talent but I don't need it to know something's got Sally excited. She's so careful to sound calm."

Daffyd shrugged his shoulders and reached for the in-tapes. "Soon as I know, you will. Anything else bothering you this fine morning? And Sally says I need bundles tonight."

Lester eyed him in surprise for a moment and then snorted. He pointed to the finance-coded blue tape among the urgent flags Daffyd was fingering.

"Some local yokel from East Waterless Ford up-state wants to tax the Center's residential accommodations, same as any other apartment block. Claims the revenue on such 'high income residents' would reduce the state's deficit by 9%."

Daffyd whistled appreciatively. "He's probably right but for the fact that this is a registered restricted commune and those high-income residents turn every credit of their salaries over to the Center."

"Listen, Dave, he's building a pretty good case."

Op Owen sighed. There was always something or someone or some committee picking away at the Center, trying to disrupt, destroy or discredit it despite all the careful publicity.

"They did the same thing in New Jersey, you know, when the Princeton University Complex put up those academician villages to counteract the high price of real estate and taxes," Lester reminded him sourly.

"I'll listen, I'll listen. Now, go away, Les." Daffyd inserted Welch's tape in the console.

Lester growled something under his breath as he left. And Daffyd op Owen listened. He didn't like what he heard but the State Senator had certainly done some of his homework. Revenues from the Center's residential buildings would indeed be a tidy pile in the State's chronically anemic Treasury. Only the Center was in Jerhattan proper by a mile and a half, and therefore its revenues were the City's, if anyone's.

"Get me Julian Pennstrak, please," Daffyd asked his secretary. The City Manager might be of some assistance here. Certainly he'd be interested in what this up-state character, Aaron Greenfield (am I always to be "fielded," Daffyd wondered wryly, remembering his battle with the US Senator Mansfield Zeusman) is proposing. If Julian didn't already know. Not much slipped past Pennstrak's affable eagle-eye. Pennstrak wasn't available but his secretary tactfully put Daffyd through to Pat Tawfik, Pennstrak's speech writer who was, in actual fact, his Talent guard.

"Yes, Dave, Julian's been keeping an eye on Greenfield's proposal," Pat told him. "In fact, Julian had him in here for a long cozy chat when we first got wind of the scheme. Greenfield's like Zeusman: suspicious and scared of us supermen."

"Julian told him that the residential buildings are communal . . . ?"

"Yes and Julian showed him the figures the Center files every year, plus the auditors' reports. Cut no ice! In fact, if anything," and Pat grimaced, "it only confirmed Greenfield's notion that the Center is a rich source of additional income."

"The Center is also in Jerhattan proper."

"Julian made that point but Greenfield's one of those allocation goons: all for one and one for all . . . all monies being in one kitty —his. He's State Budget Chairman, you see."

Daffyd nodded.

"I didn't want to worry you unnecessarily, Daffyd," Pat went on apologetically.

Daffyd suppressed a tart rejoinder and sighed instead.

"Pat, it's easier to pull a weed if it's small."

"A weed? That's a good one. Greenfield's a weed all right." Pat sounded unusually acerbic. "I'll tell Julian you called and that you're worried."

"No. I'm not worried, Pat. Not yet."

"I would be if I were you," she said, all gloom.

"Is there a precog?"

"No specific ones. But frankly, Dave, I'm far more worried about the city's climate than anything old Aaron Leftfield perpetrates. And so is Julian. He's street-walking today." She gave a reassuring wave of her hand. "Oh, I sent one of the LEO sensitives with him. I can't move so fast these days." She glanced down at her gravid abdomen. "You've seen my report?"

"You sent one in?" Daffyd began riffling through the tapes.

"It should be on your desk. It'd better be on your desk."

Daffyd found the purple-backed City Admin tape and waved it at her.

"It is. Lester Welch had first crack at me."

"And he didn't mention our tape?" She made an exasperated noise. "Look, Dave, listen to it now because, believe me, it's more important than Greenfield even if Lester doesn't think so."

"Is that a precog, Pat?"

"You tell me it's my condition," she said, suddenly angry, "the way Julian does or a vitamin deficiency like my OB and I'll resign." The anger as suddenly drained from her face. "God, don't I just wish I could!"

"Pat, d'you want a few weeks relief?"

Daffyd op Owen caught the shifting emotions on her face: sullen resentment giving way to hope, instantly replaced by resignation. "Don't, Dave."

"I wouldn't and you know it. I can send out a mayday . . ."

"And overwork some other poor Talent?" Pat's chin lifted. "I'll be all right, Dave. Honest! It's just that . . . well, hell, listen to the report. And remember, it's a pan-ethnic problem this year."

"*This year?*" Another loaded phrase. Daffyd op Owen inserted the City Admin tape and his concern over the Greenfield proposal faded to insignificance as he recognized the more imminent danger of a disturbed City. He began to wonder who else had thought to save their dear Director trouble by not reporting the grim facts he now heard. Because if the Correlation Staff had slipped up on reading precogs, he'd downgrade the lot.

Brief, violent inter-ethnic quarrels over contract employment during the winter had been mediated but, within the City's ethnic sectors, the truce had been uneasy: each segment certain that another had received what plums existed. (Most of the spot employment during the winter had been make-work, paid for by funds pared from other pressing needs to give the proud their sop.) Most of the agitation could be traced to a young Pan-Slavic leader, Vsevolod Roznine. The report noted that Roznine was more feared than popular with his constituents and, although several attempts had been made to cool or placate the agitator, he had neatly avoided the traps. The report closed with the note that Roznine might have latent Talent. However, the only mental contact made had been so distasteful to the Talent that he had broken it off before he could implant any suggestion to go to the Center for testing.

"The man's public mind is a sewer," was the final comment.

Daffyd op Owen made a steeple of his fingers and, twirling his swivel chair, gazed out his window to the orderly grounds below. He felt unaccountably depressed yet he could be justifiably proud of what Talent in general and Eastern American Center in particular had been able to accomplish in the past decades. Op Owen could appreciate, and it was no precog, how much more had to be done on numerous levels: public, private, civic, clinical, military, spatial, and most important, inner. No matter what the dominant Talent, precog, telepath, teleport, kinetic, empathic, the Talented were still very human people, above and beyond their special gifts which so often complicated adjustment therapy.

They had professional immunity at long last, for all registered Talents. Another giant step forward. They had had acceptance on a commercial level for many years where Talent could steadily show profit to management. Since the first body-Talents had been able to point out assassins in crowds (even before precogs were accepted and acted on by key personnel), they'd been accepted by intelligent people. But the suspicious were the majority and they still had to be convinced that the Talented were not dangerously different.

He'd ruminated on this many times and it wasn't solving the other pressing problems before him. A city torn by the very ethnic strife that had once been hailed as a bonding compromise to the late twentieth century's lack of basic life-style values: summer was a-coming and, despite advances in weather controls, a hot dry spell which could cut the power available for city air-conditioning would only produce riot-breeding conditions.

So far, no major precogs of disasters had been recorded and for such a large unit as Jerhattan, a trouble precog was statistically more probable than one dealing with a small number of people or a single citizen. Scant reassurance, however.

And thank god, Talent was pan-ethnic, thought Daffyd. He

didn't have to worry about that ugly head rising against the Center.

He did tape an All-Talent alert on the city's climate. The great minds would now have a single thought. Perhaps they'd also have an answer.

When he picked Sally Iselin up at nine at the Clinic door, she gave him a quick appraising look. Then her anxious-puppy expression changed to a radiant smile.

"I knew it. I knew it." And she all but war-danced a circle as she inspected his costume.

"What?" he asked, turning to keep her face in view.

"You dressed just right. How'd you know? I'm sure I didn't clue you. Are you positive you're not a precog, too, Daffyd?"

"I'd rather not be."

Her vivacity faded instantly. She put a hand out, aborting the sympathetic gesture before she actually made a contact. He touched her fingers lightly in reassurance.

"Not to worry. I just had a tedious day. Felt like wearing glad threads."

Sally's eyes crinkled and her mouth tilted up as she cocked her head to one side. "You are indeed joyous," she said saucily as her glance took in his royal blue black-trimmed coverall.

"Look who's talking," and Daffyd grinned down at Sally in lime green and black swing tunic and matching high boots. Sally's puppy charm was a tonic and he wondered, as he often did in her company, why he didn't make more opportunities to enjoy it.

As he put a helping hand under her elbow to assist her up to the passenger side of the two-spot copter, she gave him a startled sideways glance. He caught the echo of mental astonishment before she started to chatter about the day's hopeful applicants.

"They come, Daffyd, swearing oaths that they'd had this or that perception. Dorotea doesn't tap a one. We go through the routine but even with maximum perceptol, they come over dead dumb and stone blind."

Sally was a compulsive talker but Daffyd became aware that her present garrulity was a shield. He wondered what Sally would need to obscure. Propriety prohibited his making a quick probe but undoubtedly there'd be clues later on. Sally was entirely too open to be devious for very long.

She directed him to Sector K, northwest of the Center, where the worn hills struggled up from old swamplands: not a salubrious area despite reclamation and renovation efforts. There were still ruins of early twentieth-century factories and it was by one such structure, a sprawling half-glass and brick affair, that Sally directed him to land.

"The place seems popular enough," Daffyd said as he had to circle several times to find a site for the copter.

Sally winced, eyeing the ranks of city-crawlers and the presence of both private and public transport copters. "Doesn't take long, does it, for the masses to latch onto a new thrill!"

"Oh? This is new?" He'd caught the worry tone of her thoughts. "Crowd bad for the project?"

"I don't know." She was more than worried. "I just don't know. It's just that . . ." She broke off, firmly pressing her lips together.

They stood in a short queue for billets, paying a credit apiece to get in.

"Milking the golden cow," Sally said with uncharacteristic bitterness as they passed the billets in at massive sliding doors which separated the outer hall from the vast factory space beyond.

"Guarding it, too," Daffyd said, noting the strong-arm types in meshed duty-alls.

"That might make more sense than you'd guess," Sally said in a very dark voice. Her mind was practically shouting "trouble."

"Will we need assistance?" he asked her, estimating how many empathic Talents might be needed to control a crowd this size.

Sally didn't answer. She was looking around the enormous open area which was filling rapidly. It didn't require Talent to appreciate the aura of excited anticipation that emanated from the audience. The hall was by no means full yet; half the tables were still empty, but most of the couches of the inner circles were occupied. Daffyd had never seen such an assortment of styles, ages and conditions of furnishings.

"They must have been scouring the Sector," Sally said. Then she indicated a table on the outer rim: a table, Daffyd noticed, which was convenient to one of the luminescent exit doors.

They were barely seated, Daffyd on Queen Anne, Sally on Swedish tubular, before a waiter inquired their pleasure.

"What's available?" Sally asked, simulating bored indifference. Daffyd was surprised that she felt the need to dissemble. "You name it," replied the concessionaire, impatient. His tables were filling up. Sally "told" Daffyd that this, too, was an innovation. "Try something simple, schatzie," Daffyd said, managing the verbal slurs of their assumed roles. "The Medboard warned you and I'm not copting you to the drain-brain again this month."

Sally affected petulance, then with dutiful resignation, asked for a mild caffeine. Daffyd, in character, asked for an esoteric blend.

"Nor am I copting you!"

"Make it two milds and bring the pot."

As the conman left, Daffyd leaned towards Sally. "Is this area disaffected?"

She wrinkled her nose. "We get a lot of hopefuls from this Sector."

Sound had come on, more frequency drone than actual note. The dim lights on the girders were beginning to fade completely, and ground spots lit up, adding their eerie moiety to the ambience. Sally looked toward the half-circle of stage which had remained semi-lit. The aura of expectation, of voracious emotional appetite increased perceptibly. Sally shivered and folded her arms across her breasts but Daffyd sensed that the created atmosphere irritated more than distressed her.

She shifted in her chair nervously when the waiter appeared with cups and the pot. He served them disdainfully—he didn't make as much commission from the milder brews—and hurried off, grimacing thanks for the carefully generous gratuity.

The auditorium was almost full now and the conversational murmur impinged on Daffyd's senses as the snarl of the unfed. Yes, the climate of the city was very uncertain indeed. He could feel the tension building rapidly now, with so many feeding it. He noticed the muscle boys spreading through the tables and couches, and he worried harder. The psychology of a crowd was theoretically understood but there was always that gap between theory and reality —that dangerous gap which could be bridged by the most insignificant event—when crowd exploded into Riot. Daffyd and Sally were far too familiar with the "tone" of Riot to be very comfortable in a pregnant situation.

In fact, Daffyd was leaning across the table to warn Sally that they might have to leave when the lighting of the stage area altered and a girl stepped into the center. She wore a white caftan-type unadorned robe and carried an old-fashioned twelve-string guitar. It had no umbilical amplifier which surprised Daffyd as much as the girl's regal poise and simple appearance.

A camouflaged hand deposited a three-legged stool and the girl took her place on it without a backward glance.

Daffyd frowned at the darkness above the stage, wondering where the sound amplification was hidden. She couldn't possibly hope to reach and hold this crowd without electronic boosting of some kind.

Then Daffyd saw the relieved and pleased smile on Sally's face.

The girl settled herself, tossed back her mane of tawny hair and, without taking any notice of the audience, began to play softly. There was no need for mechanical amplification of that delicate sound. For the first note fell into a voracious silence, the most effective conductor.

No—and Daffyd sat up straight—every nerve in his body aware of a subtle, incredible pulse that picked up the gentle melody and expanded it—telepathically!

And this, too, was what Sally had hoped he'd feel, what she'd brought him here to confirm. He saw the happy triumph in her eyes. The girl's voice, a warm lyric soprano, intensified the pulse, "sounded" off the echo as she fed the multitude with a tender ethnic admonition to love one another. And . . . everyone did.

Daffyd listened and "listened," stunned physically and emotionally by the unusual experience: unusual even for a man whose life had been dedicated to the concept of unusual mental powers. On an intellectual plane, he was incredulous. He couldn't deduce how she was effecting the total rapport, this augmented pulse. It was not mechanical, of that he was certain. Why this sensation of "echo"?

The girl would have to be a broadcasting empath: an intelligent empath, unlike poor Harold Orley who hadn't any intellect at all. This young woman was consciously choosing and directing the emotion she broadcast . . . Wait! That was it . . . she was consciously directing the emotions . . . at whom? Not the individual minds of the listeners: they were responding but they could not account for the "generation" of emotion that enveloped everyone. There had to be sensitive minds to generate emotion like that and these people were parapsychically dead. Yet she was manipulating them in some way, using some method that was non-electrical and non-sonic.

The girl continued with a more complicated tune from some early nineteenth-century religious minority which had settled in the eastern United States. And the "message" of the song was a soothing statement of acceptance. She was deliberately taking the audience out of the technocratic trap, transferring them to less complex days, lulling them into a mood of even greater receptivity. Nor was Daffyd immune to the charged atmosphere . . . except for that part of his brain which could not perceive how she was effecting this deft, mass control.

The singer finished that song and plucked the strings idly, chording into a different key. The third song, while no more intense than the first two, was a rollicking happy ballad, a spirit-lifter, a work doer.

She was preparing her audience, Daffyd realized, deftly and carefully. He began to relax, or rather, the intellect which had been alerted, responded to the beguiling charm of her performance.

Daffyd was suddenly frightened. A deep pang, covered in a flash, overladen with worry that was lyric-inspired. Only it wasn't. Sally had felt the pang, too, glancing nervously around her. The rest of the audience didn't seem to catch alarm: they were in the young singer's complete thrall, caught up in the illusion of unpressured times and ways.

The fear was the singer's and it was not part of her song, Daffyd concluded, because he could detect no other influence, no newcomer in the hall, no change of lighting or aura. Sally was concentrating on the girl, too.

Why would she be frightened? She had the audience in the palm of her hand. She could turn them in any direction she chose to: she could . . .

Her song ended and, in a fluid movement, she rose, propped her guitar against the stool and casually disappeared into the shadowy rear of the stage.

Sally turned anxious eyes to Daffyd, and they shared the same knowledge. *She's the one who's frightened. She's leaving.*

And that's the most dangerous thing she could do, Daffyd "told" Sally.

No one in the audience moved and Daffyd didn't dare. The lighting altered subtly, brighter now, and people began to shake off the deep entrancement, reaching for cigarettes or drinks, starting soft conversation.

"They don't know she's not coming back. When they do . . ."

Daffyd signalled to Sally. It was imperative they leave: they couldn't risk the psychic distortion of a riot and, once this crowd discovered that the singer wasn't returning, their contentment would turn to sour savage resentment. Caution governed Daffyd. They couldn't just leave. But they had to . . .

He reached across the table casually and deftly tipped the caffeine pot over.

"Of all the stupid jerks," Sally cried, irritably, getting to her feet and holding her flared skirt from her.

Daffyd rose, too, with many apologies. They received mildly irritated glances from nearby couples whose pleasant mood was disrupted. As Daffyd and Sally moved toward the main door, Sally kept up a running diatribe as to her escort's awkwardnesses and failings. They reached the sliding doors. The aura generated by the singer was fainter in the lobby and the close knot of men by the box office window interrupted their discussion to stare suspiciously at Daffyd and Sally.

"I can't sit around in this damp dress," Sally said in a nasal whine. "It'll stain and you know it's only this week's issue."

"Hon-love, it'll dry in a few moments. It was only . . ."

"You would be clumsy and right now . . ."

"Let's just stand outside a bit. It's warmer. You'll dry off and we won't miss any of the singing."

"If you make me miss any of Amalda's songs, I'll never, never forgive you . . ."

With such drivel they got out the main entrance. But not before Daffyd experienced a wash of such frightful lewd thoughts that he hastily closed off all awareness.

"Sally, how many minorities did you notice represented there?"

"Too many, in view of your memorandum this morning. Daffyd, I'm scared. And it's not Amalda's fear this time!"

"I'm calling Frank Gillings."

Sally pulled from him. "I'll find the girl. She's got to have protection . . ."

"Can you find her?"

"I'm not sure. But I've got to try. Once that crowd realizes she's left . . . ."

Sally turned to the right, toward the rear of the factory, slipping past the little city crawlers until she was out of Daffyd's sight. He made for his copter and opened the emergency channel to the Center.

Charlie Moorfield was on duty and he instantly patched Daffyd through to the office of Law Enforcement and Order as he was rousing the Center's riot control people. If they could get enough telepaths to the site in time, they might dampen the incipient riot before LEO needed to resort to the unpopular expedient of gas control.

"Tell Frank Gillings that Roznine is here, too," Daffyd told the officer on the line.

"Roznine? What'n hell would he be doing listening to a singer?" the man asked.

"If you'd heard the effect this singer has on people, you'd understand."

The officer swore, at a loss for other words. Daffyd wished that swearing were as therapeutic for him.

"Keep the band open, Charlie . . . ."

"Dave, you can't stay there . . . ." Charlie's voice reached Daffyd's ears even several yards from the copter. Daffyd wished he'd be quiet. He had to concentrate on "listening" for the girl. He could sense Sally's direction but he was used to Sally's mind; he could have "found" her at a far greater distance. But the singer was unknown: alarmingly unknown, Daffyd realized, because he ought to be able to "find" her. He'd been in her presence, in "touch" with her for over half an hour, long enough for him to identify most minds and contact them again within a mile radius. She couldn't have got very far away in such a short time.

The beat of heavy duty copters was audible now: coming in without lights and sirens. Daffyd looked east, willing the Center's fast transports to get here before the riot control squads. It was generally impossible to get enough telepaths during the day to quell an imminent riot unless there'd been a precog of trouble. But, of an evening, there was the entire Center's telepathic population . . . Now, if . . .

He heard the beginning of a subdued murmur from the building. The customers were getting restless. He hoped they hadn't yet realized that the singer wasn't taking a short break.

Someone opened a section of the big main doors, stood framed in the rectangle of light for a moment, peering out. Daffyd identified the stocky figure as Roznine's. Suddenly the figure of the ethnic leader froze. He stepped out, into the night, head up. The man's curses floated toward Daffyd as he slammed back into the building. Daffyd hurried in search of Sally, wondering what Roznine would do now he knew a LEO squad was on the way. Only . . . and Daffyd faltered midstride how *could* Roznine know, if he did, that the big copters were LEO. Cargo firms used the same type. Yet op Owen knew with unarguable certainty that Roznine had properly identified the aircraft.

Daffyd came round the corner of the old factory just as the personnel hatch in the huge rear door opened. He counted five of the muscle boys, each taking off in a different direction. Then a sixth man, Roznine, whose harsh urgent voice ordered them to find those effing copouts or they'd be subsistence livers for the rest of their breathing days.

"Copouts." Plural, thought Daffyd. Who beside Amalda? No time now for speculation. Daffyd sent a quick warning to Sally to leave off the search and get back to the copter. She was there when he returned, easily eluding the searching muscle men who were as noisy mentally as they were physically.

"That audience is losing patience fast," Sally said, staring at the ominous black bulk of the building. She was hugging herself against shivers of fear.

Daffyd looked eastward, saw the running lights of the slim Center transports.

"Not long now."

But too far away. Disappointment and whetted appetite rocketed to explosive heights. All along their side of the factory, exits burst open as part of the audience swarmed out, in futile search of the singer. Inside the furnishings were being thrown about and broken, people were slugging and slugged, trampled and hurt as uncertain tempers erupted.

Daffyd wasted no time. He half-threw Sally into the copter, jammed in the rocket-lift, warning Sally to hang on. The head LEO copter blared its summons before he could turn on his distinctive identity lights. As it was, he only just got out of stun range.

Once clear of the busy altitudes, Daffyd hovered, calling an "abort" to the Center transports. The situation had gone beyond their capabilities. He'd only completed one circle before he saw that the LEO copters were laying gas. It was all they could do with such a mob starting to rampage. Sally was weeping softly as he veered eastwards toward the Center.

I wasn't honestly certain, Daffyd," Sally said, curled in a small contrite ball on the suspended couch in his quarters. She kept examining her glass as if the amber liqueur were fascinating. She'd the appearance of a small girl trying to get out of a scold. Actually her public mind was wide open to Daffyd's, permitting him a review of her initial impressions of the singer. "I mean, while I couldn't think what else she might be, there was the possibility that it was all sonic amplification. You know what a skilled operator can do."

"All the more reason you should have reported it, Sally. That kind of manipulation is why mechanical amplification is strictly licensed to reputable and reliable technicians."

"And not a clue about the girl?"

"Not yet." The licensed owners of the Factory were among those drowsily helpless inside the office in the lobby of the building. They'd be questioned, of course, by Gillings's men. Perpetrators of riots could expect scant mercy from the LEO office.

"We've got to get to the girl first, Sally."

"If only I'd told you sooner . . ." Sally was floating in chagrin.

"I keep telling you, and every other member of my staff, I don't mind being bothered with so called 'trivia.' Because it isn't always as trivial as *you* might believe."

"I know. I know. I simply wasn't thinking clearly." That was what she said, but what Sally was thinking, also for him to see, was that she hadn't wanted to disappoint him, or herself, in case her initial impression about the singer had been wrong. The girl had been almost too good to be true.

"Was she afraid of that crowd, Daffyd? It was three times the size of the one the other night. In fact, the size alone put me off."

"You first heard her . . ."

"Just two days ago. I tried to get backstage to see her . . ." Sally shrugged her failure.

"Muscle boys?"

"No." Sally was astonished. "Everyone else wanted to get next to her. I'd never have had a chance to find out for sure with so much interference, much less suggest she come to the Center."

Daffyd began to stroll about, his arms crossed over his chest, his head down.

"We both sensed her fright?"

Sally nodded.

"We are both agreed that she is a broadcasting empath?"

Sally nodded again, more emphatically. "Could she also receive? I mean, that would account for that 'echo' phenomenon, wouldn't it? She throws the emotions out and then magnifies them on retrieval"

"That's one explanation."

"Hmm, but you don't subscribe to it with any enthusiasm."

Daffyd grinned at Sally. "It doesn't fit all the circumstances. Besides, Roznine used a plural . . . 'those effing copouts.' "

Sally's eyes rounded with surprise. "She links. That would account for the amplification and the echo." Daffyd nodded. "Then who's the other empath, or empaths?" Daffyd shrugged. "Doesn't she realize what she is?"

"Probably not. We shall have to inform her."

"And how do you plan to do that?"

"I think we ask for Frank Gillings's help . . ."

"But . . . but . . . she started the riot. You know what happens to riot provokers."

"Yes, but I also know that Frank wants all Talented people registered, trained and controllable. So when he's had a chance to question the sleeping beauties . . ."

"We can trace Cinderella and fit her out with glass slippers . . ." Sally grinned saucily as she picked up the analogy.

"Before Pegasus flies away with her."

"Pegasus? He's a myth, not a fairy tale. That's not fair, Daffyd!"

"But the analogy is most apt," and op Owen was grimly serious. "And we've got to put a bridle on her Pegasus or she'll end up with singed wings."

Although the LEO Commissioner and the Director of the Eastern American Parapsychic Center were on good working terms, the Commissioner avoided coming to the Center. Respecting this whimsy, Daffyd called through to Gillings's office the next morning, asking for an appointment and specifying his business as the Fact riot.

"How did you happen to be there, Dave?" Gillings greeted him, rising from his chair as op Owen was ushered into his tower office.

Daffyd spent a moment admiring the 360° view of the sprawling hazed metropolis.

"Tracking a rather unique Talent."

"That singer?" And Gillings swore when Daffyd nodded. "Do you know the toll on that caper?"

"No, but it's one helluva lot cheaper than it would have been if we hadn't alerted riot control."

Gillings frowned. "She shouldn't be allowed a public performer's license."

"I wanted to find out if she had one."

Glaring, Gillings icily banged at his desk comset and demanded to be put through to ID. No license had been issued to anyone answering the description of the singer, Amalda: nor had there been a license issued to the Fact for solo entertaining. There were, however, specifications on record as to what mechanical amplification was permitted the management of the Fact, the frequency of the programming and the nights on which public gatherings could be held and the maximum number of people permitted to gather. Last night's performance, it transpired, was completely illegal. Gillings issued a summons for the owners, brothers named Dick and Harry Ditts, who had told an entirely different tale the previous evening when they had recovered from sleepy gas. Five minutes later, Gillings was informed that neither Dick nor Harry Ditts could be located at their residences on record.

"Have they any known connection with Roznine?"

"Roznine?" Gillings regarded Daffyd with a combination of disgusted annoyance and startled concern which faded into deep reflection. "You saw him there?"

"Yes, he was at the Fact. When we were withdrawing from the scene of the imminent riot, he was deep in conversation with several types in the lobby. Later he spotted the LEO copters on their way in and made his way out. Funny he didn't suggest to the Ditts brothers that they leave with him."

"Don't be naive. Roznine looks after Roznine, first, last and al-

ways or I'd've had him cooled long ago. But Sector K is far from
his bailiwick . . ." Gillings stared out across the city with narrowed eyes. "He's been getting too damned powerful in the City
and not just with the Slavs. A megalomaniac is what he is and they
operate with a curious ability to avoid minor disasters . . . until
they get overconfident. Roznine hasn't made that mistake . . .
yet . . ."

"I shouldn't wonder that there's some Talent in a megalomaniac,
apart from his madness."

"Talent?" Gillings erupted as Daffyd had known he would.
"Christ, that's all I need is a Talented pan-ethnic leader. Goddammit, why don't you people get on the ball and round up all these
goddamn freaking Talents before they go haywire. We've got
enough problems keeping that . . ." and his blunt-fingered hand
described a circle at the panoramic metropolis outside the plexiglass, ". . . from exploding as it is without unnatural hazards like
latent Talents . . ."

". . . Then help us find Amalda. She can be immensely useful . . ."

"She's a riot provoker . . ." Gillings's eyes narrowed with a
flash of vindictiveness.

"Are you going to help me, or hinder me, Frank? The girl is
valuable to both of us but not in your cooler as an RP. She's an
intelligent broadcasting empath of tremendous range and power. I
don't think she realizes what she is . . . or didn't until possibly
last night. Something frightened her out of her wits halfway
through her third song. She ran! I don't know what it was nor do I
know exactly how she can broadcast the way she does, but it's
imperative that the Center find and protect her."

Gillings's eyebrows rose in ironic surprise. "You and Iselin were
there. Why didn't you get her then? What happened?"

"Among other things, a riot. Some people shield automatically,
Frank, and if you can't trace the mind, you can't catch the body."

"All right, all right," Gillings said, irritably waving aside Daffyd's mild reproval. "But how come she doesn't know what she is?
All right, all right. I know the answer to that, too. All right, what
do I do?"

"I want a tracer on any young singer of her description applying
for a performer's license anywhere in the country. And I want to
know where she has sung, where she trained, where she came

from. She's gone to cover and she won't find easy. In the first place, she's terrified of whatever hit her last night. And secondly, she'll have a good idea what happened when the audience found out she wasn't going to sing again. She has two very good reasons for being scarce. I also don't want her frightened out of her wits so let me handle the actual search with my people. I'll get my propaganda team to alter some of the public info broadcasts subliminally. We might get her to seek us out spontaneously which would be preferable," Daffyd added, rising.

"Okay, you handle it, but I want that girl found and trained or whatever it is you do with them. And quick. I'll shunt the report on her to your computer. Shouldn't take long to trace her."

It took two days to trace the girl known as Amalda. And the print-out had many gaps.

She'd been born and reared in a small Appalachian commune: educated to her sixteenth year in the County School system which she quit to "travel" . . . a not uncommon pattern for an undirected or unmotivated youngster. There was no record of formal music instruction but music was a feature in her environment: no official record of her for several years until she took work in a Florida food control complex. Two applications for performer's license in Florida were denied by the Audition Board there. The third application was provisionally granted and lapsed without formal request for an extension, but several short term engagements were on record for her as an unamplified, string-instrumented folk singer. A new application as apprentice, non-singer, had been filed in Washington, D. C. four months before: one engagement was listed without a termination date. Then Daffyd had a check made on the play in which she had appeared. Amalda, who had started as a walk-on, had been abruptly promoted to an important supporting role. The play was scheduled for a metropolitan opening in three weeks.

Although Daffyd had only a superficial acquaintance with the mechanics of the Performing Arts, there were several glaring contradictions in this report. And no explanation for Amalda's sudden appearance as a self-accompanied soloist in a minority entertainment hall of dubious reputation.

In the meantime, he and Sally worked with the propaganda de-

partment to include in the public information broadcasts a subliminal appeal for someone in Amalda's situation. Daffyd also got in
touch with the play's producer.

"I've had enough trouble with that flitting bird," Norman
Kabilov told op Owen. "If she does show up, I'll tell her straight:
she gets no more contracts and she shouldn't ever hope to get a PP
license approved. Not if I have any connection with the PA."

"What kind of trouble did you have with Amalda?" Daffyd
asked, injecting placatory thoughts at the irritated little man.

"Troubles, plural, not trouble singular," and Norman Kabilov
glowered at op Owen.

Daffyd knew the man was considerably perplexed by the Center's interest in his ex-actress.

"First, she latches on to my stage manager, Red Vaden . . .
good man, Vaden. Solid. Dependable. Only this little twit has him
hopping to her tune like he'd never tried to brush off a stage-struck
tail before. Red doesn't ask many favors so when he wants this bird
in the cast . . . so when the show travels, he's not lacking what
he's been having regular . . . I say, yes. What harm? Suddenly I
got Red begging me to give her an audition for one of the secondary leads. I already got a good PA picked out for the part . . ."
Kabilov's expression told Daffyd that his choice had been personal
rather than professional. ". . . but I gotta keep 'em happy so I
audition the girl." The little producer frowned now, his thoughts
vivid to Daffyd. The man had been surprised out of boredom at the
quality of the audition and immediately signed Amalda for the
role, despite the fact that he'd known he'd be in for a heavy time
with the disappointed candidate. "Mind you, it wasn't that great a
part until that kid reads it." Another headshake of perplexity. "I
dunno how she did it because she sure had no theatre arts credits
but I couldn't *not* give her the part. And then the author comes to
rehearsal and hell, he's rewriting the part to give her more. I damn
near have a jeopardy action from Carla Jacobs who's the name in
the play. Only Red goes to work on *her* and she quiets down like a
lily. And you gotta believe that Jacobs don't handle that easy. She's
pushing fifty, y'see, and any new bird is a threat. Funny thing,"
and Kabilov stared off above Daffyd's head, his mind taking up and
discarding a hundred different glimpses of Carla Jacobs in high
tantrum, Carla Jacobs soothed and very few snatches of Amalda.
The man was unconsciously censoring those recollections. "Once

La Jacobs got to working with the kid, things were okay. Wanta see the reviews we got?"

Daffyd hastily assented but he was given no chance to do more than glance at the commendatory headlines in the fasc sheets.

"As long as we were in Washington, it was okay. But the minute we got to Jerhattan, troubles! La Jacobs storms in here with her lawyers and her current man and she won't play with that creature anymore. In fact, she gets so absolutely violent we gotta trank her. Now I can't lose La Jacobs or I lose the theatre *and* the play since that's the contract. So I tell Red to find his bird another nest. I can't afford trouble. And they both walk!" He was indignant. "Just like that. He walks. A guy I'd sworn was 100% dependable walks out of the show two weeks before opening. On a account of a scrawny bird!"

If Norman Kabilov looked the picture of outraged innocence, he "sounded" like a man reprieved from an unknown ordeal. However, he did have publicity shots of Amalda and Red Vaden, which he appeared relieved to give Daffyd: as if by getting rid of everything reminding him of this unsettling episode he could erase it from his memory.

Daffyd op Owen had his best finders scan the pictures, he sent copies to the LEO office and, on an off-chance, gave a final print to his best precog.

"You better find that girl," Gillings told op Owen, "or I'll find her and make her answer—officially—for that riot."

"Frank, don't provoke another Maggie O."

Though the comset was not color, Daffyd was certain that Gillings's face changed shade.

"We're doing all we can," he went on soothingly, "to find her but there's no way of forcing her to come to us."

Gillings growled something dire as he broke the connection.

There were days when Gillings was not Daffyd's only cross. He and Sally had spent most of the morning trying to figure out a way to attract Amalda to them. Lester Welch walked in, listened a few minutes and then snorted in disgust.

"Why don't you just find out where this Red Vaden lives? If he was so gone on the girl he'd leave a successful show, he's probably tied up tight with her. And if he's at leisure," and Lester grinned

intense love-hate auras swirling in the room and among them the
sure knowledge that the chestnut-haired girl seated facing the door
was a powerful and violently agitated empath; that the red-bearded
man standing by the window was linked to her in a desperate,
despairing bond.

"I'm Daffyd op Owen," he said, "and this is Sally Iselin, head of
our Clinic Recruiting Team. We've been looking for you." Daffyd
poured out waves of sympathy/reassurance/overt love and respect.

"*We* found you," replied the man. "I'm Bruce Vaden."

"We tried to locate you at the Fact last night," Daffyd said, turning to Amalda. His second impression was that the girl was about
to implode.

At that point, Sally gasped and made a movement towards
Amalda as the impact of fear/confusion/hatred/love/horror/re-
vulsion/affection lapped over the two Talents.

"That's just a sample of what I can do." Despite a southern
softness, the girl's voice grated in their ears and was echoed by an
intense mental shout that caused both Daffyd and Sally to shake
their heads. "I don't want this. It doesn't matter any more if Red is
in or out of the room. It works anywhere now." She was drenched
in bitterness, but there was pity as well as satisfaction to be read
from her glance as she watched Sally beginning to shake with reaction.

Daffyd curtly gestured Sally from the room. She resisted until he
reinforced the order mentally, telling her to get Jerry Frames over
here on the double. He duly noted that she was rebellious and not
bothering to hide the fact in her public mind or her expression.
Daffyd winced slightly as Sally slammed the door behind her.

"You're an empath," Daffyd told Amalda, trying to reach
through her broadcast to soothe her stampeding emotions.

"I don't care what I am. I want you to stop it. Now!"

"I can't stop it, my dear," he said in his kindest voice, but he had
a vision of a bridleless winged horse bolting across the heavens.

Amalda rose, in a single fluid movement, her eyes blazing.
"Then I will!" Her words rose to the edge of a scream as she
launched herself at the window. Daffyd moved to intercept her,
physically and mentally, but not as swiftly as Red Vaden. Not that
she could have achieved her end, since the window was unbreak-
able. So she hit the plastic hard and crumpled into the arms of the
redhead, sobbing hysterically and broadcasting such conflicting

as he used the performing arts' euphemism, "he's surely checke
into the PA Casting Agency."

Op Owen closed his eyes briefly before he thanked Lester with a
good grace.

"I'm not sure what we'd ever do without your common sense,
Les."

"Oh, someone else'd tell you your nose is on your face." And Les
left.

"This is one time I wish I were a kinetic," Daffyd said with a
wistful sigh, thinking all kinds of disasters, of a minor sort, to
befall the dour New Englander on his way down the aisle to his
own office. Then he caught Sally grinning at him, her eyes sparkling. "And if you repeat any of what I was thinking . . . ."

She composed her face into solemnity, raising one hand. "Dai,
you know I can't 'path that accurately." But in her mind was a
vivid picture of Lester stuffed into one of his wastepaper baskets.

Daffyd placed a call to the Casting Agency. Bruce Vaden had
reported his availability and a new address. However, the Agency
informed him, the address was naturally restricted. Daffyd explained who he was and that he urgently needed to get in touch
with Vaden and was informed that Performing Artist Vaden
would be contacted and would return his call if he were interested.

" 'If he were interested' indeed," Daffyd repeated, breaking the
connection with uncharacteristic irritability.

"Shall we think Lesterish, and perhaps drop a word in the omnipotent ear of our local lion?" asked Sally.

Her suggestion elicited the needed address in five minutes and in
less than half an hour, they were on their way by copter to an
isolated area of the Coast. The small sea-silvered cottage was
tightly locked and obviously untenanted. Rather depressed, Sally
and Daffyd returned to the Center. Lester met them at the roof
stairs.

"You're covered with canary feathers," said Sally.

"I thought you couldn't read my mind," Lester replied, startled.

"With your expression I don't need to."

But Sally hesitated at the door of Daffyd's office. Rather more
aggravated with circumstance than Sally, Daffyd took her firmly
by the arm and pushed her into the room. He was instantly overwhelmed by several devastating impressions: contact with Sally
informing him that her emotions were highly unstable; there were

and powerful emotions that, out of pity, Daffyd reached for the trank gun in his desk and shot her.

There was absolute silence on every level in the room as the two men stared down at the limp figure in Vaden's arms.

"I suppose that was necessary," the man said in a bleak voice as he swung her up in his arms.

Daffyd could read the relief in the man's mind which had been bruised by confusion, fear and an unquestioning devotion to the girl. Op Owen gestured towards the couch.

"All right, op Owen, what now?" Vaden asked after he had arranged Amalda gently in a comfortable position. The man's eyes were a cold, troubled blue.

Daffyd returned the gaze, probing deftly and finding in Vaden's outer thoughts that their visit here had been his suggestion, a last possibility of assistance, since Amalda had been determined to end her Talent even if it meant taking her life.

"First we have the Center's doctor prescribe sedation," and Daffyd nodded towards the painfully thin arm of the unconscious girl, "and a decent diet."

Vaden snorted as if practical advice was the last thing he'd expected from op Owen but he took the chair Daffyd indicated to him.

"Then the Center teaches her to control this Talent."

"Talent?" Vaden exploded. "Talent? It's an effing curse! After the other night, she's scared to go out of the house. She'll never perform again . . . She won't even . . ." and he clenched his teeth over what he'd been about to add but not before the thought, "audible" to Daffyd, made him pity the two more.

"Any Talent is a two-edged sword, Vaden," op Owen said, swinging his chair a little, a soothing motion.

"What kind of a freak is she?"

"She's by no means a freak," Daffyd answered in rather severe tones. "She's a broadcasting telempath . . ."

"And I'm the booster station?"

"I think that would be a good analogy."

"Look, op Owen, I've read a good bit about you Talents and nothing was said about what Amalda does . . ."

"Quite likely. We're just beginning to appreciate the mutations possible in the parapsychic. We have only one true telempath here. He unfortunately has no more mind than a rabbit and he only

receives. Amalda can apparently transmit exactly what she
chooses. I gather the phenomenon only began when she met you?"

On the top of Vaden's mind was the actual first meeting: a sort of
dazed comprehension that they were "meant for each other."
Their first love-making had been a revelation to the blasé, sex-
wearied Vaden and each succeeding day had strengthened their
interdependence.

"She was down and out," Vaden said aloud in an expressionless
voice. What he wasn't saying was vividly and pictorially flashing
across his mind, elaborating with every shade of the emotional
spectrum a dry recital of fact. "Thank God it was me she approached . . ." and beyond the flashes of memories, Daffyd saw
that Vaden had never allowed himself the luxury of loving or caring for anyone for fear of being hurt and used. In a transient profession, constantly besieged by stage-struck youngsters who
thought a PA license was "all" they needed to achieve fame, he had
been invulnerable to physical charms and ordinary ploys. But he
had absolutely no defense against the impact of Amalda's mind in
his. Now he ran nervous fingers through his crisp red hair. "We
went everywhere." He'd been haunted with the fear that she'd
leave him or be taken from him. "Even to rehearsal. Then the girl
who was to play Charmian was late so I asked Amalda to fill in and
read it 'til she came. I've never heard a better first reading. She
even lost every trace of her regional accent and became the hard-
voiced trollop. We all loathed her. It was such a total characteriza-
tion! I've never seen such a thing in all the years I've been a PA. I'd
expect such expertise from someone like Mathes or Crusada, but a
novice? An ex-canary?" Vaden looked toward the unconscious girl
and gave a sort of incredulous shrug. "She was so pleased to think
she did have ability. She'd tried often enough to qualify as a vocal-
ist." Vaden made an exasperated noise in his throat. "The first time
she sang for me I couldn't credit that she'd been refused a license."
He turned back to Daffyd. "It just didn't make sense."

"I'd hazard that you were the missing factor."

"A modern Svengali?" Vaden was bitter.

"Not exactly. But the brain generates electrical currents. And in
the same way that a receiver must be tuned to a certain wave-
length to get a message broadcast on that same wave-length, minds
must be broadcasting on the same frequency. Yours and Amalda's
are. Were either of your ever parapsychically tested?"

"Not that I know of."

"Well, we can sort out the pure mechanics later during testing but there is one other pressing question I must ask."

Vaden did have Talent, whether it had blossomed through contact with Amalda or not was immaterial, for he instantly perceived what was on Daffyd's mind and stiffened. Daffyd continued, feeling it wiser not to let Vaden realize that he was in the presence of a strong telepath . . . at least not yet.

"Granted you serve in the capacity of an amplifier for whatever mood Amalda creates, what happened the other night at the Fact? What terrified her so that she fled from what obviously was a smash-success? She had that audience in the palm of her hand."

An expression akin to terror crossed Vaden's face, ruthlessly suppressed in a second.

"You were in the audience?" Vaden asked, temporizing.

"Yes, Sally Iselin had heard Amalda two nights before and wanted me to confirm her suspicion that Amalda was a high-gain empathist. What scared Amalda off that stage? And sent both of you into hiding?"

There was nothing helpful in Vaden's mind except a repetition of what Daffyd and Sally had felt in Amalda's projection. Instead, Vaden's thoughts became despairing.

"That's why you've got to help us, op Owen. Turn Amalda off!"

Vaden didn't attempt to disguise his fear now. And he didn't strike op Owen as easily frightened. He was tough, able to take care of himself from the look of his bearlike build. And had taken care of himself, to judge by the scars on his knuckles and face.

"Fortunately, no one can turn Amalda off. Nor do I yet see the necessity." Only a nebulous but overwhelming fear in both Vaden and Amalda.

"You'd better see," Vaden cried, leaning urgently toward op Owen. His eyes were blazing with anger, fear and a sense of impotence which would be more frightening and humiliating to a man of Vaden's temperament. "You'd better see that it's crushing Amalda to the point where she was willing to commit suicide rather than live with what she's become!"

"You haven't told me *what* frightened her and what, if I may speak candidly, is bothering you as well."

Vaden got a grip on his fear and anger. "There was someone else in that audience," he said in a harsh controlled voice, "who suddenly linked up with us. Someone who was trying to dominate. Who was determined to control what Amalda can do. She got the brunt of it, of course, then I caught it."

Op Owen was certain then, with an awful instinct, that Roznine was the third person. And the ramifications of that premise were decidedly unsettling. He managed to smile reassuringly at Bruce Vaden. He swung his chair idly from side to side with counterfeit unconcern. He had lost Solange Boshe but he wouldn't lose Amalda . . . and Vaden . . . *and* Roznine.

"That's very interesting," he told Vaden. "Does Amalda have any idea of the man's identity?"

"How could she?" Red Vaden asked scornfully. He was making a notable effort to cover his inner perturbations. He couldn't bear even the notion of sharing Amalda with anyone. "The minute she realized what was happening, how strong the guy was, and what he wanted her to do, she made as if she was taking a short break. And told me to follow. But she won't ever sing again. You don't know what it does to you . . ."

"I probably more than any man," Daffyd said with a slight smile.

Vaden discredited the statement with a cutting sweep of his hand.

"You've got to understand that Amalda must be turned off."

There was an edge in his voice now: he was hitting an emotional high, too. Daffyd reached surreptitiously for the trank gun.

"Don't you dare!" Vaden moved with surprising speed and grabbed op Owen's hand.

"I thought you'd understand, op Owen. Whoever that guy is is double dangerous!"

"You'll have every bit of protection the Center and every other Center in the world can offer you, Vaden," Daffyd replied, allowing his voice to take on strength without volume. "Which is not inconsiderable, I assure you. What *you* don't understand, Vaden, is that Amalda's main problem is simply lack of control of her rather breath-taking ability."

"*You* don't understand." Vaden was desperate. "She can control masses of people. Those subbies in the Fact . . . she could have made them do anything. That's what's terrifying her. And me. And that other freaked-out mind . . . *he* wanted to *use* her to control that kind of a dangerous mob. God, man, I know what riot is. I've seen them. I've been caught in them. I know what happens.

She could *cause* one. She even started one by not being there. She could incite the entire goddamned Jerhattan complex . . ."

"How?" asked Daffyd blandly.

"By . . . by . . . doing what that mind wanted her to do the other night."

"But," and Daffyd matched Red Vaden's urgency with his own, "she didn't! And she couldn't! And nothing on this world, not even some freaked-out mind with a megalomaniacal bent could make her. And once she's learned to control this . . . winged horse of hers, I think you'll all find this not so cursed a Talent."

"I don't believe you."

"How old is Amalda?"

"What? What has that got to do?"

"How old?"

"She's twenty-two. . . ."

"Twenty-two. And rather young for twenty-two, I should imagine. That's still a tender age." Daffyd could've wished for some of Amalda's empathic strength but he was getting through to Vaden's basic reasonableness. "And she has become emotionally involved with you . . . No offense, please, Mr. Vaden. From a rather humdrum frustrating existence, she has erupted onto the stage, into prominence . . . Even a mature personality could be dazzled. Then she is thrown into a highly charged situation—the concert at the Fact—it was unnerving for me as an observer, and I'm well in command of my emotional responses. She is frightened and runs! For which I don't blame her at all. In short, Amalda has been operating on high for some time. We are still frail masters of our powers, Mr. Vaden. And that receiver/broadcaster unit which is Amalda is overcharged.

"No, Mr. Vaden, we can't turn her off. We don't want to. But we can teach her how to channel her Talent, how to discipline it so it won't run away with her as it has just done. We can also show you how to help her put on the brakes. On, yes, you can apply what, to all intents and purposes, are circuit breakers. She will need your strength and aggression, Mr. Vaden. In fact, and this is between us, Amalda is not as important as both of you. So I will consider you a team, because that's what you are."

"Then you can help?" asked Vaden. He didn't quite believe op Owen but the aura of belligerent desperation was fading.

"I just said so."

"No," and Vaden shook his head angrily as if he'd thought Daf-fyd would "know" his exact referents.

"Emotion is as much a tool as a pen or a pneumatic drill . . ."

Vaden stared at him, and then unexpectedly chuckled. "And Amalda's been swinging the drill?"

Inwardly op Owen cheered. Thank God the man had a sense of humor.

"Exactly. Amalda has all the finesse of a tyro. If you had been the focus instead of this rather impressionable and previously frus-trated young woman, I think matters might have progressed more circumspectly. As it was . . ."

"I don't think Amalda's going to believe you, op Owen," Vaden said, looking sadly down at the unconscious girl.

"I don't think she'll have any alternative," Daffyd replied se-verely. Vaden frowned, his eyes narrowing, but op Owen returned the look, adding a mental reinforcement. "She is exhausted from the look of her, which is what happens when you run an engine on full power for any length of time. We'll sedate her sufficiently to let her body and mind rest. And we'll keep her sedated until she be-gins to realize that she cannot control everything around her with the grip of a tyrant . . . for that seems to be her main fear. Rather commendable, actually."

"And?" Vaden said in a flat, no-argument voice.

"And, in the meantime, you will have to learn how to aid her. You've been more or less passive. Shall we say," and Daffyd smiled slightly as he bowed to Vaden, "you are both engaged for a long-term contract with no options."

The door burst open to admit Jerry Frames, the Center's physi-cian and Sally Iselin, who glared her way back into the office. Daffyd smiled as he stepped aside to let them through to Amalda.

"What took you so long?" he asked Sally.

"What d'you think I am? A lousy pop Talent?"

She's able to cover completely now, Daffyd," Sally said with understandable pride.

They were watching through the one-way mirror as Amalda fed Harold Orley. The witless empath was neatly eating, with appe-tite, and often a small smile of pleasure on his child-like features.

"Never thought we'd use Harold as an instructor," said op

Owen. Sally grinned at him, her eyes sparkling. "Harold's a useful old tool."

Daffyd thought fleetingly of Solange Boshe.

"Don't, Dai!" Sally's one word was reinforced by her mental command behind which Daffyd sensed sympathy, pity and, oddly enough, annoyance.

"She's off all tranks now?" he asked, grateful to her.

"Heavens yes. She's got to concentrate on Harold, you know."

"Then let's start them moving about outside."

"I would if I were you. The Red Bear's about to go stir crazy."

"Red Bear?"

Sally wrinkled her nose. "That's what I call Vaden."

"Then Amalda's Goldilocks?"

"Good heavens, no. She's Cinderella, remember?"

"Cinderella and the One Bear?"

"Cinderella, the One Bear and . . . the Wolf!"

Daffyd frowned. "I thought I was a better therapist than that."

"Oh, it's just a back-of-the-mind worry. She's not going to trust herself until she does meet and vanquish the Wolf. And then we can all live happily ever after."

There was a tinge of bitterness in Sally's bright voice that made Daffyd look at her closely. He was tempted to probe but that wasn't ethical, particularly since Sally would be instantly aware of the intrusion. So he observed Amalda for a few more moments before leaving the Clinic.

In the month Amalda had been at the Center, the over-thin, intense girl-child had been replaced by a still slender but composed young woman. Her fears had slowly been eased by Daffyd's adroit therapy and by her own ability to discipline her emotions, to channel the vital energies deftly.

The first sessions with Harold Orley had been conducted with Amalda fairly well sedated. The girl had been revolted by Harold's witlessness. There could have been no clearer mirror for her reaction. Pity for the moronic empath had been quickly suppressed because Harold would disconcertingly burst into tears. At first Amalda had rebelled at being forced to work with Harold but she could not refute the fact that he would react instantly to her emotions and until she could control them in his presence, she couldn't expect to be able to control them sufficiently in public.

In the first days at the Center, she had also demanded, even

under heavy sedation, to be lobotomized: an operation which
Amalda erroneously supposed would suppress her gratuitous Talent. Then she met Harold and realized that the psionic portion of
her brain would not be excised by such an operation. Step Two in
Amalda's rehabilitation was her introduction to the Center's star
young Talent, two-year old Dorotea Horvath. It didn't take
Amalda long to recognize the lesson which was thus demonstrated
to her.

Small Dorotea was playing contentedly with six-sided blocks.
When they tumbled, her fury exploded . . . to be checked, unconsciously but firmly, by her mother. The young telepath's thoughts
were so loud and clear that Amalda couldn't fail to recognize the
analogy.

"So I discovered a bright new toy in my mind and it won't play
with me, is that it?"

"You have to learn to balance the toy just as Dorotea does . . ."
Daffyd said gently.

"So they won't all fall down and go boom?"

"With you underneath," added Sally. "Like the night at the
Fact."

Despite sedation, Amalda paled and shuddered.

"He can't find me, can he?"

"Not here, behind shielded walls, my dear," Daffyd reassured
her.

Once Amalda could control her emotions, Vaden began to take
part in the exercises. It was during these sessions that the phenomenon of the second Fact concert was harnessed. Amalda, with Red,
could dominate the emotional atmosphere of any large room, could
project, even to the minds of sensitives, any emotion she chose. But
the force that Daffyd and Sally had felt at the Fact was absent.

"The team right now is limited," Daffyd said to Sally, somewhat
ruefully.

"Limited?" Sally was surprised.

"Yes. As long as there are no dark emotions being counter-broad-
cast, she can project what she wants of the lighter ones. But I was
rather hoping that she and Vaden would be strong enough together
to counteract . . ."

"An incipient riot?"

"Yes," and Daffyd leaned forward eagerly. "That would placate
Frank Gillings and wipe out that RP he's still got against her. And

think what it would mean in riot control techniques: two people instead of twenty sensitives, if we have 'em available when we need 'em, or instead of the gas."

"Well, so that's what you've had in mind."

"As it is, I think we'll let them operate as a team in those gatherings that tend to develop brawls: conventions, fairs, industrial shows."

"And what about the Wolf?"

"Ah, yes, but you see, I want him to come out of the woods."

"And Amalda?" Sally "sounded" furious with him.

"Which would you wager on? A Wolf or a Bear?"

D affyd op Owen was by no means as callous of Amalda's safety as Sally might think, for he'd circulated a warning to all sensitives for any inquiry about Amalda or Bruce Vaden and any unusual activity on Roznine's part. Ted Lewis, the chief police Talent, gave them their first hint of interest. A well-known and respected Performer's Agent who just happened to be Polish, asked for assistance from Central Casting to find a missing PA, Bruce "Red" Vaden who was reportedly employed but who had obviously not appeared with any working company.

"Now that could be legit," Ted Lewis told Daffyd. "The guy really is forming up a variety show for the Borscht circuit but for that he doesn't need a stage director with Vaden's rating."

"What about an unamplified folk singer?"

Ted Lewis shook his head. "Now Roznine may have found out that Amalda is Vaden's bird but it's also fairly common knowledge that Gillings is still after the folk-singer who started the riot at the Fact. Stupid Roznine isn't. Devious, yes."

It suited Daffyd that Gillings had not yet dropped that charge, for while Amalda was recovering herself and learning to control her abilities, the charge would provide her with a certain protection.

What did puzzle Daffyd was what Roznine intended doing with Amalda if, as, and when, he got possession of her. To be sure, the public was informed, in broad terms, about the capabilities of the Talented but nothing had ever been released about the more bizarre possibilities of psionic powers. Certainly nothing related to Amalda's ability for the very good reason that until Amalda had met Bruce Vaden, such a Talent couldn't even have been conjectured as possible. Therefore, what could Roznine's active imagination have suggested to him? Did he realize that he, Roznine, was Talented? Since he had domination over his ethnic group, did he plan to dominate the entire City through Amalda?

"Vsevolod Roznine is no man's fool, boss," Ted Lewis was saying to Daffyd's further agitation. "He's got every single employment and patronage plum available for his Slavs. Oh, all very legal; a bit dicey if you're looking at it from some other ethnic corner, but legal. And he's fast moving out of his own bailiwick. He's been getting cooperation where no Pan-Slav has ever got it before. How, why, what he does, we don't know. He may use a common garden variety of blackmail or he may even have a genuine Talent. Though Gillings'll flip if he's got to deal with a Talented ethnic leader!"

"There could be worse things," Daffyd said, though obviously Ted Lewis wouldn't agree. "Have you got the LEO precogs sensitive to both Roznine and Amalda?"

Ted Lewis shot his superior a disgusted look. "They're all sleeping on papered pillows."

"And?"

"Boss, you know you can't force a valid precog."

"No Incidents at all?"

"Nary a one. Only vague feelings of uneasiness." He was evidently repeating a frequently reply, which satisfied him no more than it did Daffyd.

"Keep an open mind on Roznine. And don't let Gillings know we suspect Roznine is Talented. I'm going to start using Amalda and Vaden as a team. Sooner or later Roznine will discover her again."

"You want that?"

"Very much." And in Daffyd's mind, as he left Ted Lewis, was the memory of Solange Boshe's wild demented face before she teleported through a steel door in the parking building.

Gillings was delighted to use Amalda and Bruce Vaden as riot prevention. He even offered to take the charge off the books but Daffyd suggested that it remain a while longer. The team was instantly assigned to a round of rallies, meetings, conferences, and conventions. Such gatherings were encouraged to divert a population with too much unoccupied time but any one of them might explode into a riot, given the proper stimuli. Decibel alarms were legally required in every meeting hall, including churches, but clever agitators could and had sabotaged them so that the suppressant gases were not released when the "noise" level reached the sharp pitch of incipient riot. The professional agitators had also learned how to modulate their voices below the danger level, carefully goading their victims into the spontaneous combustion which neither gas nor water jets could control. And which no precog could be expected to accurately predict until too late for effective action.

Fortuitously, as Amalda learned to control herself, she learned to read Harold with an accuracy and perception that surpassed Sally's. Harold could serve with the team, Daffyd decided, as a gauge for the general atmosphere of a group and as, in an emergency, a body guard for Amalda. (You learned things, even from disasters, Daffyd told himself positively.) Partnered with the empath, Amalda would sit in the center of an audience or circulate through a crowd. Vaden would be on the periphery, ready to "broadcast" if it became necessary. They could also be expected to keep up a running projection of whatever aura the LEO authorities or the sponsors of the occasion requested, if this were not a commercial affair. Subliminal pressures for mercantile purposes were, of course, an illegal and unethical use of Talent.

The team was extraordinarily successful in unexpected ways. The Motorboat show had the lowest incidence of petty pilfering in its history: the Home Show reported no lost children and a remarkably quiet, well-behaved quota of siblings following their parents through the exhibits. Two conventions, noted for the inebriation of their members, had their damage deposits reduced as a result of genial but undestructive behavior.

And Amalda began to gain confidence to the point where Sally remarked that even Bruce Vaden had been seen to smile occasionally.

I was surely right about the menu today, Amalda thought as the waiter plunked down the mock chicken, lumpy reconstituted potatoes and shrivelled snap beans. *Oh, well, all part of Life's Rich Pageant,* she added and started broadcasting recklessly intense delicious taste feelings. Harold began to beam beside her, attacking his food with relish.

She glanced casually around at her table mates, as pompous a crew of convention goers as she'd ever seen and she was now an authority. (Did they always use the same "masks" at conventions? Or could it be the same group of people as the Plastic Container Manufacturers last week, and the Fabric Finishers Association on Tuesday-week?) They responded to her prompting as rapidly as Harold, all grunting with pleasure as they ate their cardboard food. Amalda sighed. Too bad she and Bruce couldn't get a kick-back from the catering staff for "improving" their food beyond the call of duty.

Now there I go again, she thought, *but it does seem that the Talented were letting an awful good thing go the way of Duty and Honor.*

She was rather pleased with her broadcasting today. She had begun to bother with such fine points in their assignments, more to amuse herself at first—like stopping all those kids from whining at the Boat Fair. But it had sounded like home, all her brothers and sisters whining at once, before they'd tied Ma off. If she never heard another child whine it would be soon enough. And making food at least "seem" tasty was in defense of her poor abused digestion. According to specifications, all the nutrients and vitamins were in the food and would be absorbed by her system. But she'd come to prefer "tasting" things. It made these convention luncheons bearable. What a way to earn a living!

And yet, Amalda reluctantly admitted, she didn't dislike it. If only . . . She wouldn't think about that. It'd ruin her appetite. After all, now she'd got the hang of this trick mind of hers, she could make whole bunches of people feel what she wanted them to. When the time came, she could control *him*, too. Bruce was never far from her. She smiled, the warmth of his infinite love a presence to counteract any nibble of fear. Sometimes when Bruce made love to her, she wanted to embrace the whole world with its beauty, but that sort of broadcasting wasn't even moral: that was private between her and Bruce and . . . *He'd* thought things at her that night . . . Things she didn't even dare to think about . . .

Harold was getting restless. She curbed her reminiscences.

And then, the jab. So sharp she gasped, so hard it was physical yet the prod was in her mind . . . and all too familiar. *He* was here.

Harold whimpered, empathizing with her. She hastily damped down her shock of fearful surprise. *He* was as abruptly gone from her mind. She shivered, unable to suppress the lingering sense of revulsion that that recognition touch evoked in her. She overcame the feeling, smiling inanely around at her table mates. She patted Harold soothingly on the arm. He grinned, restored to equilibrium. Good, she must keep this to herself.

But she couldn't keep from glancing around for Bruce: he was at table 4, near the dignitaries. He glanced up, nodded at her, and was then required to make some answer to his partner, a female who simpered up at him.

Sometimes, Amalda thought, *Red has the harder role to play.*

Part of her mind wanted to search for *him,* but her strongest desire was never to be touched by *him* again, ever. She scanned the room now, certain she'd be able to locate his evil self. She'd certainly studied his IDs long enough to spot him physically anywhere. Waiters were coming and going from the kitchens. He wasn't one of them. He wouldn't be one of the conventioneers. She'd've identified him long before now. She opened her mind, making it, as Dave had suggested, like the lens of a camera, slowly widening. She didn't really want to: too much of an appalling and revolting nature seeped in. She wondered how Dave, who was a full telepath and "heard" actual thoughts, not just emotions as she did, could bear it. She wondered how much he had "conditioned" her mind to accept her Talent. She knew he had: he'd told her so. She didn't mind . . . probably Dave had done that, too. But he was so kind. Now if only he'd . . .

No, she told herself sternly, *these thoughts you may not have. Sally loves Daffyd op Owen.* She grimaced. *For a perceptive Talent, Dave could be awfully dense. For the Lord's sake, you didn't even have to be a telepath to see Sally Iselin was madly in love with him. Or maybe Dave knew and couldn't do anything about it? Couldn't someone condition Dave? Hmmm. Maybe I'll get to work on it. No,* and Amalda gave her head a little regretful shake, *that would be tampering and that's not ethical.*

She sighed. Being a Talent imposed certain rules and regulations which absolutely couldn't be broken. In the first place, you got found out too fast. Not much of a bridle on that winged horse Dave's always talking about but it kept you from falling off . . . morally . . .

The waiter was bending over her. Amalda leaned toward Harold to permit the waiter to remove her plate. Instead he mumbled something.

"I'm sorry. I didn't hear you," she said, smiling up at him.

He gave her a stare and said something in the same unintelligible mumble. She could, however, sense his urgency. He had something she must do?

"I'm really very sorry, but would you repeat your question?" She gestured at the chattering diners by way of explanation.

The little man looked angry. In a clear voice, he asked the waiter at the next table to join him.

"I ask her a simple question and she gives me this so-sorry routine," he said. But he was incensed about something. And his urgency intensified.

"Really, there's so much noise," Amalda said.

The second waiter, a burly man, gave her a fierce scowl.

"What's your problem, miss? You got delusions? Ain't you conventioneers satisfied with nothing? Do like he says and there'll be no trouble."

"I certainly don't want to cause trouble." And Amalda began to broadcast soothing thoughts.

Suddenly a third man was pulling her chair from under her and the first two had her by the arms.

"You just come with us, miss. You just come with us."

They were scared: they were prompted by an urgency which was unnatural and artificially induced. *He* had instigated their actions.

She got Harold to his feet. The poor witless fool was momentarily as confused as she was. She felt Bruce reacting. But she was being physically manhandled away from the table by the two waiters. If they did get her out of the hall—it wasn't that far to the kitchen entrance—Amalda tried to keep from panicking. The next thing she knew Harold reached out and grabbed the waiters by the shoulders, had torn their hands from her arms, and banged their heads together.

Then Bruce and two officials closed in on the knot of people and somehow the unconscious waiters were being whisked from the banquet hall.

"Calm 'em, Mally," Bruce hissed at her and she began to pour out such sweetness and light that everyone at her table stopped eating to beam at each other. She modified the broadcast, got Harold and herself reseated. She even managed to keep her trembling reaction inward so that none of it boiled over to erase the idiotic smile from Harold Orley's face.

By the time the luncheon ended, however, the effort began to tell on her and was reflected in Harold's nervousness. She felt physically drained. What if *he* had been able to get her away before Harold could react? Before Bruce, on the other side of the hall, had been able to get to her? Supposing *he* had . . .

Bruce was at her side, his face set and determined. She knew that look. But now she was afraid of leaving the semi-protection of so many people. If he had actually tried to kidnap her in the middle of a convention . . .

A plainclothes LEO man was bearing down on them. She rose, smiling brightly. Harold twitched his hulk to his feet, but his brow was clouding with childlike anxiety.

Disgust at her spinelessness buoyed Amalda's weakening knees. The instant Red put his arm around her protectively, she almost crawled into him.

"Let's get her out of here," Red said and gestured the LEO man to lead Harold.

"Come this way," the LEO man said, gesturing to the draperies at the side of the huge banquet hall. A door in the paneling gave onto a small anteroom. "The Waiters Union is screaming over those busted skulls. We got to get you out of here quietly. What'n'hell did happen, Amalda?"

"I don't quite know," she murmured, aware that exhaustion was overcoming mental resolve. "Is it all right to leave?" She looked back over her shoulder at the diners dispersing slowly.

"The hell with them," Bruce said in a savage voice.

"I'm so sorry. So sorry." Amalda had a sense of failure. The first time she came up against *him* she had fallen apart. She wanted to cry. She was a failure. After all Daffyd and the others had done to help her . . . to swoon like any vapid female . . .

"I'll get you. I'll get you the next time." The voice was as loud in her ears as Bruce's exclamation.

"Bruce . . ."

Charlie Moorfield came through Daffyd's door without bothering to knock.

"They did it," he cried, halting his forward momentum just short of gouging his thighs on the desk edge.

Daffyd picked up the images so vivid in Charlie's mind, and despite the fact that he could also perceive that the emergency was over, he sprang to his feet.

"Who did what?" demanded Sally, excitedly. She wasn't accurate enough to 'path the sequence.

"They tried to snatch Amalda at the Morcam Convention luncheon," Daffyd told her.

"Only she got Harold to bash their skulls in."

Sally gasped.

"Gillings said the attempt and the arrest were handled so quickly that no one at the table with Amalda and Harold knew what happened," Charlie went on. "Waiters Union is screaming over the quote unwarranted unquote arrest of three members. There's hell to pay."

"Not necessarily," said Lester but he was glowering as he walked into the room and carefully closed the door behind him. "This is a clear case of professional immunity."

"How do you construe that?" Daffyd asked.

Lester sighed as he regarded his boss with a tolerant expression.

"Amalda is a registered Talent, right? She was present at the Luncheon in a professional capacity. Therefore no one, not anybody, has the right to interfere. The waiters did, by trying to remove her from the hall. They broke the law. Amalda hasn't. Neither has Harold. Even if he was a little overzealous, he is now protected from the consequences of his Talent."

"Wait a minute, Lester," Charlie said, "that Immunity Law only means that you can't get sued when . . ."

"It also means," and Lester waggled a bony finger at Charlie and Daffyd in turn, "according to the way Senator Joel Andres and our legal eagles interpreted it to *me*, that any citizen attempting to interfere with a registered Talent's performance of his duty is violating that law."

"This would be the first time we've had to invoke the law," Daffyd said.

Lester raised his eyebrows in surprised alarm. "So what's wrong with that? Or did you break your . . ." he glanced abruptly at

Sally who stifled her laugh . . . "your bones arranging protection *not* to use it?"

Op Owen made a cut-off gesture with one hand. Lester Welch muttered in disgust.

"I thought by this time you'd've learned the cost of idealism, Dave. We sweated out that Bill: it damned near cost us Joel Andres's life; we have a clear case of an infraction and by God's little chickens, you're going to invoke it. If Gillings hasn't already."

The comset on Daffyd's desk lit up, flashing red. He pushed the toggle down.

"Commissioner Gillings, sir, urgently."

Daffyd nodded acceptance.

"Op Owen, we're getting a lot of static from the Waiters Union, about Amalda, false arrest and all that crap," Gillings stated with no preamble. "So far I've played it that their member was pushing a lust act and got told to bug off: that the lady-in-question is sufficiently upset to invoke female citizen's rights. Then we got the honest-employees, good union men with clean sex records and she's a pervert-after-the-damages claim." Gillings sighed with heavy disgust. "You know, the usual convention static. Now, we can clear all this up by invoking the Professional Immunity Act but . . ." and Gillings waggled a thick finger at Daffyd. "I'm not all that eager to break the team's cover. Bruce Vaden told my men that something had scared Amalda and the only thing I know she's scared about is what happened at the Fact. Was there a repeat at the Morcam?"

"I haven't talked to Amalda yet, Frank," Daffyd said. "I assume she's on her way back here with Vaden?" Gillings nodded. "Give me a little time."

"Don't take too much. That Waiters Union packs quite a wallop."

As soon as the Commissioner's face had faded from the screen, Daffyd asked for Ted Lewis in the LEO Block.

"Ted, you heard about the snatch attempt on Amalda?"

"It's all over the place. Say, why don't you just invoke the Immunity Act . . . No?" Ted was as perplexed as Lester.

"Is Roznine involved in any way in the Waiters Union?"

"Hell yes. There isn't one Union he isn't involved with right now."

"Any chance of finding out if he was at the Morcam Convention Hotel this afternoon?"

Ted Lewis held up a hand, flicked on another switch, his words and the reply indistinct, being off the receiver limit of the comscreen. He looked more confused.

"We've had Croner sort of keeping him under the eye/ear. Croner says he's at a TRI-D on Market and Hall. Huh, how's that, Croner? Hey, boss, Roznine has been watching a lot of TRI-D lately."

"Then he suspects he's been under surveillance and is ducking out the other exit of the TRI-D. Fine." This was an unsettling development because it could mean that Roznine was developing as a Talent. If he got pushed too hard. . . . op Owen shuddered. "Let's go see Amalda."

It was *him*," Amalda told Daffyd. She looked white, shaken and small as she huddled against Red Vaden on the couch in the living room of their suite.

"How close to you?"

She shook her head. "He wasn't in the room. I'd've seen him. But he was near enough to recognize me. My mind, I mean." She gave a delicate shudder. Had he recognized her because she'd been thinking those thoughts about him? She wanted to ask Daffyd but she didn't dare. She'd let him down enough already.

"Were you aware of anything, Red?" Daffyd asked.

"Not at first. Then only Amalda's surprise. I looked up and saw the waiters grabbing her. But before I could get across the room, Harold had acted." There was admiration on Vaden's face for the maneuver. "I should apologize to the guy. I think we got things quieted down before any of the convention crowd got wise."

"After the attempt, were you aware of Roznine's mind, Amalda?"

"Not until we were leaving the hall." She closed her eyes. "He said 'I'll get you. The next time I'll get you.' "

Daffyd looked questioningly at Red who shook his head.

Had you ever received words before, Amalda? Daffyd asked.

Amalda looked at him startled and then shook her head, smiling shyly. "Only from you. Before now." She was aware of his concern. "That's bad, ain't it?" she asked, her soft southern inflection intensifying her regret.

"Not necessarily. We have a problem," he began, choosing his words carefully. "We know that Roznine would like to . . . get you, Amalda, to accomplish his own ends which, knowing your capability, must be illegal control of men's emotions. We have to assume he's been trying to locate you. We must also assume that he may not realize that Bruce is part of your ability. And that's a link that can and will protect you, Amalda." Daffyd reinforced that notion with a stern telepathic voice. "Roznine couldn't succeed in kidnapping you today, could he? Well, he damned well won't be able to anywhere else either."

"You can't be sure of that, Daffyd," she said in a very small scared voice.

"I don't intend to put it to the test, Amalda," Daffyd continued smoothly, smiling at the apprehensive girl, "but kindly remember that you have successfully eluded him twice now. Once by running away and hiding—successfully. And today by direct action against his agents."

Amalda slowly nodded her head in agreement.

"Now, while Roznine is keen to get his hands on you, we . . . and I include the Commissioner . . . are very anxious to get Roznine."

It was Bruce Vaden who stiffened and looked with an intensity close to hatred at Daffyd op Owen. The telepath returned that look calmly, knowing in that exchange that Vaden understood the implication even if Amalda didn't.

"Roznine is obviously a latent Talent. We know he fits minds with Amalda. We don't know what else he can do, and he is in a peculiarly sensitive position in the ethnic situation of this city: in a position to do a lot of damage or a lot of good. We can't push him too far and we can't let him go. We do want him, preferably on his own initiative as you did, to come to the Center. You know what it's like to have an unmanageable Talent . . ."

Daffyd was speaking more to Bruce Vaden than Amalda but it was the girl who answered.

"It's awful . . . awful lonely, awful wonderful." She gave Daffyd a smile, tremulous, and though she held her chin up in an attitude of confidence, he could see the indecision and fear of her mind.

"Now," he went on briskly, "in using the Waiters Union to snag you, Roznine has put us in a difficult position: we can easily use the Professional Immunity Act to protect you but that would necessitate your appearance in court. And believe me, everyone interested in our cover agents would be there to identify you. Your team usefulness would decrease . . ."

"Does *Amalda* have to appear in court?" asked Red suddenly.

"Well, yes. Oh, I see what you mean," and Daffyd started to grin. He managed to keep his smile normal despite what he had read in Bruce Vaden's mind under the cover of the constructive suggestion. "Very good point. Two ways. Yes, I suppose we could make Amalda up to look different . . . or we could have a stand-in for her. In that case, Amalda would have to be physically present because Roznine would be there and he'd know if she weren't present, which could score against us if an EEG reading is requested by the prosecution. Hmmm. Good notion."

"What can Roznine hope to achieve by forcing us into court?" asked Red. He was trying to cover his earlier thoughts before they came apparent to Daffyd. Present now was a thread of hopelessness, a presentiment that the intense happiness and rapport that Bruce Vaden had enjoyed with Amalda was to be sundered: too good to last. Daffyd could only answer the spoken question.

"Now that has me stumped," he said, and meant it on several levels.

Stand-in?" Gillings appeared to reject the stratagem instantly and just as abruptly, he frowned thoughtfully. "Why? You don't think anyone would be crazy enough to try and snatch Amalda in court, do you? Although . . ." he glanced over at the windows, "the atmosphere is damned unstable . . ."

"I know," Daffyd agreed. Even during the short copter flight to the LEO Block, he'd been aware of the pervasive "darkness" of the city's emotional aura. The weather had been miserable, which didn't help; general employment was down; there'd been the usual complaints about the subsistence-level foods; gripes about the TRI-D programming; nothing out of the ordinary . . . yet. There might indeed be the makings of a major blow-up.

It would take two weeks for an improvement in the food to have a perceptible effect: TRI-D programming was undoubtedly being altered but even the most perceptive Talents could be fooled over what the public really wanted on the boob tubes. The variety of "circuses" available was almost as infinite as food-tastes and yet one never knew precisely what would satiate the public appetite. Op Owen made a mental note to check all precog rumblings. Strange there hadn't been any definite Incident by anyone when such a large population unit was involved.

"Look, op Owen," Gillings was saying, "I've got to have the team available for riot spotting. Particularly right now. And I can't have them identifiable."

"Then we send Amalda to the hearing made-up."

Gillings muttered under his breath about fancy dress and sow's ears and then suddenly swung round to fix op Owen with a startled glare. Daffyd hadn't expected to keep Gillings in the dark long.

"Okay, op Owen, what's behind all this pussy-footing? Who was trying to snatch Amalda at the Morcam Luncheon? Was it the same guy who was at the Fact? Because if it was, let's get him and cool him. I need that team operating. And there's that open charge of riot provocation . . ."

Op Owen took a deep breath. "I don't think it would be advisible to cool Roznine."

"*Roznine?*" Gillings exploded from his chair with all the frustrated astonished exasperated impotence of the strong man suddenly discovering himself in an untenable position. "Roznine! Christ, op Owen, do you know what would happen to this city, in the present mood, if I arrested the Pan-Slavic leader?" He fumed on, in much the same vein, for moments more until either Daffyd's placatory thoughts or his own lack of breath brought a stop to the flow of recriminations.

"I haven't suggested you arrest Roznine. In fact, that would not only be impolitic but dangerous."

Gillings glared at him, snapping out one short explosive word. "How?"

"Because Roznine is a latent Talent. That's what scared Amalda."

Gillings erupted again, thoroughly enraged. This time the shield of his public mind slipped sufficiently for Daffyd to see past the anger to the panic his confession evoked.

"*No!*" Daffyd's negative, forcible mental as well as audible, carried weight on every level and blocked those avenues of action which he could perceive Gillings already plotting. "Roznine is contained . . . at the moment. But—this time we don't force a latent into a position where he can become dangerous to an entire city. I want to avoid another Maggie O far, far more than you do!"

Gillings had no escape from Daffyd's mind, so op Owen did not relent in the pressure until he was certain of Gillings's uneasy and resentful cooperation.

"Roznine is no threat to us . . . yet. But he does threaten Amalda," Daffyd went on. "That threat is real. It would be stupid," and he paused to let that word be absorbed, for Gillings was not a stupid man, "to get Roznine so frustrated that additional facets of his Talent—whatever it is—are stimulated."

Gillings's face was a study of frustration. He gave vent to a stream of profanity which so delighted and enlightened op Owen that he could ignore the fact that he was the victim of the spiel. But, with the avalanche, Gillings recovered his mental equilibrium.

"I told you a couple of months ago that what you guys really need is a law that makes it illegal to conceal Talent."

Daffyd laughed wryly. "Roznine may be unaware that what he uses is Talent!"

"Unaware? My effing foot. With all the publicity you guys have been larding the TRI-Ds with, he's got to know what he is—especially if he's been playing mental patty-cakes with that Amalda. Op Owen, I don't need a Roznine in this city! You Talents put him where he belongs and bridle him or lobotomize him or something. Or I'll invoke whatever law on the books suits me and cool him permanently. I can't have this city turned into a battlefield. Or have you forgotten Belfast?"

His buzzer winked the urgent red. Gillings raised one fist as if to squash the unit and then, swearing viciously, slapped the toggle open.

"Well?"

There was a moment's hesitation. Daffyd could almost see the caller swallowing hastily, probably wishing he didn't have to continue.

"Commissioner, the lawyers for the WU are here with bail for their members. Do we release them?"

"I want to scan them," Daffyd said in a swift undertone.

"Delay 'em. Someone's on the way down from this office. Then permit bail."

Gillings tossed an oddly designed coat button to op Owen. "This'll get you anywhere in the building. And keep it."

Daffyd thanked the Commissioner, and left. Prowling the LEO offices would not be a frequent pastime: the "neural" noise level was more than a telepath of Daffyd's sensitivity could bear.

The Waiters Union had sent a battery of lawyers to procure the release of their incarcerated members. They had been shown into a waiting room, just off the main admissions hall of the retention section of the LEO Complex.

Daffyd sauntered by, scanning each man's mind quickly. What he "heard" he didn't like, but it confirmed the fact that Roznine was organizing the proceedings. None of these men knew more than his own assignment. But each was moved by an intense desire to complete it expeditiously and successfully or . . . The "or else" held dark, dire and fearful consequences.

Daffyd returned as quickly as possible to the shielded calm of Gillings's private eyrie. The Commissioner was absent. Daffyd used the few moments' respite for some solid thinking.

There were times, he finally concluded, when a man had to operate on the "feel" of things alone. He was not, God forfend, a precog, but there were also times when a man simply had to dispense with rational thought and its consequences. Particularly when faced by a free agent like Roznine who could not be expected to have predictable responses to stimuli and pressures.

The similarities between Roznine and Maggie O were inescapable, but this time Daffyd had a tool and a resolve.

"We've been fighting fire with old-fashioned water, Frank," he said to the Commissioner when the man stalked back into his office. "From now on we use modern methods, foam and tranquilizers."

"What are you jibbering about?"

"I can't explain, but will you trust me?"

Gillings glared back at him, but his tight natural shield leaked conflicting emotions of desire-to-believe, distrust, and irritable frustration.

"I goddamn well have to, don't I? But, goddamn it, Dave, if you Talents don't contain Roznine . . ."

"*We* can," and Daffyd op Owen began to grin with utter malice for the underhanded, immoral, unethical use of Talent he was about to invoke. Lester wouldn't approve either, but then, he didn't plan to tell Lester Welch.

The stratagem did require the invocation of the Immunity Act. What Daffyd didn't count on was the hue and cry when the news of the hearing was announced on the media. Suddenly Aaron Greenfield vociferously supported the Waiters' Union in their outraged cry against Talent abusing unTalented people and hiding behind the law. The Morcam Convention Committee tried to evade any responsibility by claiming that they had not hired a Talent team for their Luncheon . . . their defense being that *their* convention members were law-abiding peaceful people with no record of violence, so a LEO team was unnecessary and an insult to their good name, etc. Greenfield made political hay of this as well. He'd never been in support of the Immunity Law because "obviously it was a screen for illegal, immoral, unethical invasion of privacy: one more instance of establishmentarianism and totally unwarranted minority privilege." "Repeal the Immunity Act; no extraordinary privilege for minorities!" "Make them Pay Their Own Way! Taxation for all on an equal basis."

Precogs began to have troubled Incidents. To alter circumstances, the team began wearing disguises, with Amalda and Bruce Vaden both paired to combat-trained LEO men. They were also on twenty-four-hour call, hopping from one gathering to another, trying to forestall explosions—usually at rallies designed to bring their own downfall. Twice Amalda felt Roznine's mind searching for hers. She'd break off all broadcasting and the team would leave that area instantly.

The weather remained unseasonably hot and humid. There were unprecedented foul-ups in the food supply and a heavy drain on the power sources necessitated cuts of the entertainment circuits. More trouble.

Roznine's stratagem also suffered from his zealousness. On the day of the hearing, there were so many people wanting to attend this test of the Immunity Act that he couldn't possibly have attempted a kidnapping. The press of hopeful attendees provided the LEO officials with an excuse to be selective and, naturally, the audience was conveniently packed with out-of-town Talents whom Daffyd had invited. Sensitives at the Court Block entrance tipped the LEO men off whom to exclude and the Pan-Slavic contingent was decimated. In the wake of the prosecuting force, Roznine was admitted in his capacity as Pan-Slavic leader since one of the waiters was his ethnic. It was the first opportunity Daffyd op Owen had had to get a good look at the man and he was somewhat surprised by Roznine's physical appearance. Daffyd would have liked to "scan" him but the emotional aura of the courtroom made that mentally and physically impossible. The telepath pondered on the subconscious impressions he'd been receiving from Gillings and Amalda, for Roznine was a perfectly presentable, personable looking chap, quietly dressed in a moderately expensive tunic, his heavy head of black hair cut to his shoulders and his thick black moustache trimmed to join the sideburns, leaving the rest of the strong face bare. Roznine took a seat by the wall and turned for a careful survey of those already seated.

Op Owen sincerely regretted the impossibility of probing the man's mind. He must have planned something. He had a "waiting" about him, calmly composed in the midst of a hectic scene.

But there had been no precogs on the situation. There'd been incidental auguries but of too varied a nature to be useful or indicative of the trend of the day's events. Daffyd could only conclude, as the Correlation Staff had, that it didn't matter how the hearing went today. That in itself was unsettling. However, plans had been made for such contingencies as common sense indicated. Daffyd had warned Vaden, among other things, and then "conditioned" Amalda with strong confidences. There were Talents unknown to the girl in the audience and they had their instructions.

Bruce Vaden entered, slipping into an aisle seat at the rear. He, too, glanced around, his eyes sliding past Daffyd's. He's looking for Roznine, Daffyd thought, as Vaden's eyes lingered once on some bull-chested man but not on Roznine's mustachioed face. Roznine's attention was held by a wiry little man in sloppy tweeds of ancient manufacture who pranced conspicuously down the aisle to a seat reserved for him by the prosecution's table.

So, thought Daffyd, Aaron Greenfield had a small man's push! Greenfield leaned over, tapping one of the prosecuting attorneys on the shoulder and engaged him in a guarded conversation, all the time glancing around the audience, pointing at last to the very empty seats on the defendant's side.

The hearing lights went on and the "judge" sounded his electronic gavel for the court to come to order. One of the prosecution team rose to protest the absence of the defendant and counsel but that was Amalda's cue and she, and her escort, made their entrance.

There was, of course, the anticipated cry of protest from the prosecuting attorneys. The defendant arrived garbed in voluminous robes, bewigged and made up *à la japonaise*, escorted by two women exactly the same to the last hair and measurement. Even as the prosecution leapt to its collective feet, the three figures shifted in a complicated pattern, making it impossible for any unTalented person to know which one was which.

However, as this was a preliminary hearing, necessarily conducted in front of the legal computer, the "hearing judge" had no directives about the dress or escort of the defendants and/or attorneys so long as they appeared clad and reasonably clean. Prosecution replied that the defendant was deliberately obstructing justice by appearing with look-alike escorts. One of the Amaldas rose, presented two sets of credentials as legal counselors for the defendant and asked the "hearing judge" if it was programmed to refuse defendant's counsel on the basis of similarity in shape and appearance to defendant. The objection was overruled.

Prosecution instantly demanded EEG readings to prove that the women so attired were in fact the aforesaid attorneys and the defendant.

Defense had no objection and EEG readings were promptly taken, establishing beyond controversy who were the attorneys and who the defendant. At which point, the three women repeated their rapid "shell-act." Daffyd op Owen watched furious anger suffuse the faces at the prosecution table, evidence that the ruse was successful. The audience murmured, half in amusement, the other half totally confused by the antics.

The hearing proceeded with the charge being made of illegal arrest and restraint, countered by the defense invoking the Professional Immunity Act, requiring that the complaint against Amalda, Registered Talent, be dropped.

Rather smug, Daffyd missed the first twinge of Amalda's alarm.

"Daffyd," she said, her mind tone anxious, *"he's after me."*

"Make everyone laugh," Daffyd said and so quickly did she react, with such forcefulness, that Daffyd didn't need to call in the reserve empaths to help.

For a moment Daffyd wondered if fear prompted her outrageous strength, for everyone in the audience, himself and the planted Talents, were struck by an epidemic of giggles. It would appear that the audience was attempting to laugh the complaint out of court.

Daffyd suppressed Amalda's projection sufficiently so that he wasn't doubled with uncontrollable mirth. Roznine had a rictus-like grin across his face: he'd leaned back against the wall in an effort to control his body and he was forcing his head to move so he could scan the audience. Daffyd bent over slightly, counterfeiting excessive mirth, and noticed that Red Vaden and the other Talents were doing the same thing.

Grand! Let Roznine think only Amalda was responsible! But could Amalda—even with Red helping—broadcast so strongly? Could she actually use Roznine without his consent? If so . . .

The "hearing judge" mechanically sounded the gavel and called for order, its voice getting louder and louder as the giggles continued. It ordered the courtroom cleared of "obstructionists." The paroxysms which had afflicted everyone abruptly ceased and people weakly wiped their eyes and ordered their clothing. Aaron Greenfield looked anxiously around, his face flushed with anger. The man was no fool, Daffyd realized. He'd know that Talent had been responsible and, with his prickly dignity offended, he'd redouble his efforts to get the Talented taxed. Oh, well, you couldn't make an omelette without breaking eggs, thought Daffyd philosophically. He nodded approvingly at Amalda who, with her twins, had sneaked a glance at him.

Prosecution then announced possession of a sworn statement from the Morcam Convention Committee that it had requested no LEO surveillance. Defense replied that all convention situations fell under the Riot-Prevention Act and the LEO Commission was quite within its jurisdiction to use such riot prevention techniques as seemed advisable. The uncertain climate of the city was cited to be in the "unsettled" percentile which permitted the LEO Commission to take such precautions as it deemed necessary to ensure law enforcement and order. The defense counsel reminded the "judge" that any gathering of 200 or more persons (and the Morcam Luncheon had had 525 paid and consumed covers) was liable to auxiliary surveillance whether requested or not when the climate of the city registered in the "uneasy" percentiles. Prosecution demanded to know exactly what riot prevention technique was employed by Amalda. Defense responded that she was a registered empath of a + 15 sensitivity and a perceptive rating of + 12, and offered to produce positive testimonials from organizations which had employed Amalda in her capacity as a Talent for riot prevention. Prosecution repeated its demand for an explicit description of her crowd control technique and defense invoked the provisions of the Law Enforcement and Order Commission.

Daffyd wasn't certain whether the prosecution wanted to separate Amalda from her look-alikes or discover the exact procedure she used.

Defense again requested that the charge be dropped: she didn't wish to waste the Court's time and public money when the evidence clearly pointed to a *nolle prosequi* situation.

Prosecution insisted vehemently that this was a clear case of personal infringement and misuse of privilege just as the time-limit light came on. There was the rumble as the "hearing judge" searched its programming for precedents. That didn't take long. Moments later the date for a trial appeared on the screen: a date seven weeks hence.

Not bad, thought Daffyd, although he'd half wished that the computer would throw the case out. With no precedents, there'd been slim chance of that.

Amalda's fear was like a knife in his own guts. He tried to get through to Roznine, to fathom what the man was doing. Bruce Vaden jumped to his feet, started down the aisle, his progress blocked by others who were beginning to leave the courtroom.

Daffyd had the sense that every Talent in the audience stiffened suddenly and then Roznine, half rising from his seat, stunned amazement on his face, began to topple slowly over onto the people in the row in front of him.

"Hey, this guy's passed out," someone cried. "Is there a medic around?"

Bruce Vaden kept trying to reach Roznine. Daffyd signalled to two other Talents to assist. If they could bring Roznine to the Center this way . . .

"I'm a physician," a woman said in a firm loud voice, three rows away, holding up her emergency pouch. There was a slight scuffle as Bruce tried to intercept her, but suddenly the Pan-Slavs moved, jumping over seats, knocking people aside in an effort to protect their fallen leader.

Daffyd caught Vaden back, called off the others.

The bailiff scurried from the court, yelling for an ambicopter, as the woman medic and three Slavs lifted the stricken man and carried him to the prosecution's table. The "hearing judge" began to call for order, for the next case, for the obstructionists to be removed from the courtroom. Its voice got louder and louder until it finally called a recess until the court could be humanly cleared.

All right, all right, we've got him under heavy sedation in the Court Block infirmary," Frank Gillings told Daffyd, "but that took doing. The place is crawling with Pan-Slavs. We can't arrest a man for collapsing in court . . . and how did you do it?"

"One of the teleports gave him a 'punch,' " Daffyd said with a rueful grimace.

Gillings stared at him with awe and respect.

"One has to be very careful," Daffyd explained almost apologetically, "pressing against the carotid. But he was pressuring Amalda."

"You expected that! But I expected you guys to grab him there. And that goddamned hearing is affecting the entire city. Now don't tell me you expected that!"

Daffyd looked at Gillings and, for a micro-second, hesitated.

"No, not exactly, but we're doing our very best."

"What? What in hell do you mean by that?"

"I mean, we've set the trap and baited it and we simply have to have patience."

"Patience? With this city about to erupt?"

"Curiously enough, Gillings, I don't think the city is going to erupt. Oh, we've recorded some Incidents, minor ones, involving Talents . . ." and Daffyd frowned because the Incidents were distressing and so vague that only a general all-Talent warning could be issued.

Gillings gave one of his disgusted growls. "You guys make me sick. You can't even protect yourselves."

"We'll do what we can," and Daffyd's voice turned steely enough to reprimand Gillings. "What concerns you, Commissioner, is the fact that our precogs have predicted no major Incidents. Your city is going to be safe!"

"Prove it!" demanded Gillings but Daffyd op Owen made no reply as he left the Commissioner's office.

It took the telepath the entire trip back to the Center to get control of his inner perturbation. Of course, Gillings had to be ruthless and consider only the larger aspect, the safety of the City, but it galled Daffyd to think that Gillings could so off-handedly dismiss the personal trials of the Talented. It grieved Daffyd that there would be more precedents on the newly-programmed Immunity Law after the next few days. The fact that Talents would now have redress for the precogged personal assaults on them was no satisfaction. He'd really have preferred never to have had to invoke that Law.

It would serve Gillings proper notice if Roznine did burst out of bounds . . . And how in hell were they to promulgate a law that made it illegal to conceal Talent? Latent Talents were always cropping up when the right connections were made . . .

And not a single Incident connected with Amalda or Red or Vsevolod Roznine. And he'd had every precog in the Center sensitized to that unholy trio. How could that possibly be?

Daffyd's state of mind was grim as he landed the copter on the roof of the main administration building of the Center. He tried to drain the poisons of bitterness and anger from his mind as he descended the stairs. He paused at his office door but swung away. He had to calm himself. This excessive reaction was self-defeating. Gillings might be a latent Talent himself but he remained obdurately impervious to the problems of the Talented, especially when they interfered with the law enforcement and order of his precious city.

While Roznine was unconscious in the Court Block infirmary, Daffyd had managed to implant a suggestion that Roznine seek Amalda out at the Center. It was the only feasible practicable method . . . make the mountain come to Mahomet. And the mountain must apparently come of its own volition. Now, if he could just get Mahomet to do a Lorelei . . . it would speed matters up, and maybe so many Talents wouldn't get hurt.

That brought Daffyd back to the point of anger he'd reached in Gillings's office and the whole thought sequence started again.

His path led him past the play-yard where he could hear the children yelling and screaming, arguing over some violently important triviality. Triviality? To him, perhaps, yet they were as devoted to their separate sides of the argument as he was to . . .

"Well?" Sally Iselin stood in his way, her fists planted on her hips, a mock-ferocious expression on her pert pretty face. "Aren't you pleased with the outcome of the hearing?" She frowned, sensing his uncertainty. "But you were able to plant a suggestion in Roznine's mind? Oh, that Gillings. What is it about a cop that sours the man?"

It was Daffyd's turn to be surprised. "That's pretty good reading, Sally."

As suddenly he felt her mind tighten and the contact that had begun to lift his depression was taken away.

"What does Gillings expect of us anyway?" she asked.

"A happy ending!"

Sally eyed him speculatively and then fell in step with him, grinning.

"There has to be a happy ending to every fairy tale, after all. Though I shouldn't have expected it of Gillings, fer gawd's sake."

Her switch of mood, while it obscured her thoughts from him, lifted his spirits. Nonetheless, he said rather gloomily that there hadn't been a precog of any happy ending for Cinderella.

"Oh, you . . . honestly!" Sally sounded peeved and her eyes flashed at him irritably. "Your trouble, Daffyd op Owen, is that you don't really believe in Talent."

"I beg your pardon?" Daffyd stopped and stared down at her.

"Just because no one has precogged a disaster of some monumental proportion resulting from this fairy tale affair, you're down in the doldrums. Does everything Talented *have* to end in disaster? Are you going to be committed to grief for the rest of your born days? Or are you willing to admit that there hasn't been a disaster precog because there isn't going to be a disaster? That things will work out right? All the sensitives are edgy, but *not* miserably so. Good God, do we have to wallow in sorrow all the time? Do we have to run around wondering if we have a right to be happy?"

Daffyd thought he knew Sally Iselin fairly well but this—from a girl characteristically full of puppyish good-nature and exuberance?

She turned on him, her brown eyes flashing with anger as she

stamped her foot. "And I am not a good-natured puppy! I can be
just as much of a bitch as any other woman!"

In that outraged mood, she forgot to shield her inner thoughts. It
was all there, what propriety had kept Daffyd from "perceiving"
and her sense of honor had prevented her from showing him more
openly.

Abruptly Daffyd reached out and drew her into his arms, savoring the miraculous disclosure. Unaccountably Sally struggled, and
courtesy disregarded, Daffyd probed deeply into her mind, past the
barriers she had carefully erected, past the pert verbosity with
which she masked those inner feelings. With a strangled sob, she
relaxed against him and let him perceive the whole of her conflict.
The older man/much younger woman, her yearning to be tall/
elegant, an appropriate spouse for a man of his status/abilities, the
puppy image of herself from his mind, her feeling of inadequacy
because she couldn't locate more and more Talents to relieve the
burdens on him . . . all the small sins and great vanities that in-
habit the soul of any human being. And what he saw in that instant of perception only endeared her to him more.

With one hand he tilted her head back, forcing her to meet his
eyes, amused that a telepath required a look. Her mouth lifted
slightly in a smile as she shared his thought. He felt a pressing
need to articulate the thoughts he was transferring to her mind but
all he could say was her name before he kissed her. No more was
needed.

The next morning the nebulous anxieties of the sensitives were
translated into attacks on the Talented. One of the finders attached to the LEO Block was beaten up on his way to the Center.
A Talent mechanic at the big Mid-Town Parking Complex was
seriously mauled and shoved into the boot of the car he'd been
servicing. Two healers in the General Hospital were raped and
shorn of their hair but their assailants were caught because the
girls had the ability to "call" for help.

In the clear light of that morning, Daffyd bitterly wondered if
indeed he had a right to any personal happiness.

"And if that isn't a piece of outright antediluvian puritanical
nonsense, I don't know what is," Sally said, popping out of the

bathroom with all the savagery of a miniature . . . ". . . I am not a miniature anything, Dai op Owen."

But she was comical enough in her undressed state, mentally bristling at his thoughts and aggravated by his pessimistic rumination to put the morning's disasters in their proper perspective.

"I'm not sure what good it'll do to have Roznine marching in here now," she went on, pouring out coffee.

"I'd hoped he'd come as soon as he regained consciousness."

Sally's eyebrows flicked up. "You've never failed of your mark before. Unless . . ." She pursed her lips, frowning.

"Amalda's inhibiting him?" Daffyd caught the half-suppressed notion.

"You know she's scared of him. I mean, scared as a woman is of a very domineering man . . . sexually, I mean. Oh, you *know* what I mean and then there's Bruce Vaden and all that."

"Amalda had proof positive yesterday that Roznine couldn't dominate her."

"Perhaps . . . I mean, intellectually, Talent-wise, yes. But it's Bruce that's holding her back. He's already at the top of the Glass mountain and Amalda doesn't dare roll the other apple."

Daffyd caught the unarticulated ramifications of Sally's thinking. Part of Amalda's reluctance to admit Roznine's attractiveness to her stemmed from a fear of losing Bruce Vaden, to whom she was equally attracted but for different reasons.

"She's not one to drop the bone she's got in her mouth for the one she sees in the water," Sally said.

"Now it's fables?"

"Why not? You added myths to my fairy tales so it's my shot."

"That only leaves me proverbs."

"So?"

"So! That leaves us with Amalda inhibiting Roznine?"

"He should've been here otherwise."

Daffyd was turning over this interesting possibility in his mind when the comset beeped.

"Boss, we got pickets out in front," said Lester in a thoroughly disgusted tone of voice. "Pay your fair share. Everyone else is taxed. Why not you? No Minority priviliges."

Daffyd sighed long and deeply.

"Pete's on reception and he says they've got legal political platforms, their IDs are upstate and they're registered party members.

Legally, under the Political Platform Act, they can picket the grounds because there *is* legislation concerning our tax status before the State Senate right now."

"Did you inform Gillings?"

"Hah! They informed us about the time the first picketers foregathered on our gatestep. What'n'hell happened to your Machiavellian nonsense of yesterday?"

" 'There's many a slip twixt cup and lip!' " Daffyd replied. Sally gasped and signaled surrender.

"Huh?" Lester wanted an explanation.

"I must ask Gillings if Roznine's had a visit from Aaron Greenfield since the hearing yesterday," was Daffyd's reply.

"Did you goof, boss? Now what do we do?"

"Keep tabs that the on-lookers remain quiescent, and alert riot control."

"Amalda and Red?"

"No, plunk Harold in the gatelodge with Pete. Ask Gillings . . ."

"Ask him yourself: Charlie says he's just called through."

Before Daffyd could request a deferment of that call, Charlie had patched it through and Daffyd hoped his flinching wasn't apparent to the LEO Commissioner.

"You got troubles?" Gillings's face was impassive.

"Nothing we can't handle . . ."

"Oh, the trap's sprung?" Gillings looked almost pleased.

"Hmmmm . . . but I'd like a few of your riotmobiles around." Gillings's expression changed rapidly to sour discontent.

"Like that, huh? I thought Roznine was supposed to come like a lamb?"

Daffyd shot a glance at Sally who was muttering something about metaphors being illegal. Her levity was not appropriate to the gravity of the present situation and yet . . . it helped.

"Roznine's a strong personality . . ."

"I'm going after him . . ." Gillings now looked like a trap sprung.

"Gillings," and Daffyd's tone of voice was far sterner than people were apt to use in addressing the LEO Commissioner, "don't go after Roznine. We've exerted all the pressure possible under the circumstances. He'll come . . ."

The Commissioner regarded the Director for a long moment.

"You better know what the hell you're doing, op Owen."

"I do."

"Well, you sound as if you do," Sally said when the call was disconnected.

"I really think I do, Sally." Daffyd looked out of his window toward the building which housed Amalda and Red. "Two birds in one bush, two baskets with the same eggs, two minds with the same great thought . . ."

"Spare me! Uncle! I yield!"

"Good, then let's figure out how to unwind Amalda. I did not suggest to Roznine that he bring Great Birnam Wood to Dunsinane."

"I should have guessed that Shakespeare would be next."

"Considering my propensity for quoting Alexander Pope, I wonder you dared."

He's coming for me," said Amalda when she and Red noticed the circling picketers and the gathering of curious by-standers.

Bruce Vaden threw back his head and roared. He wasn't counterfeiting the amusement though it had a bitter note. But her woebegone expression was ludicrous and his laughter was not the sympathy she'd expected.

"My dear child, if Roznine has to salve his Slavic ego by resorting to that kind of subterfuge . . ."

"What on earth do you mean?"

"I mean that Roznine simply can't walk in here, no matter what suggestion op Owen planted in his mind when he was unconscious."

Her irritation was replaced by a shudder. Vaden could feel the repugnance she experienced when touching Roznine's mind. But her impression no longer dominated his reaction to Roznine. Not after seeing the man in Court yesterday.

"Did you really look at Vsevolod Roznine yesterday?"

Amalda gave him that wide-eyed innocent stare and he felt her going "dead" on him. At first Bruce thought it was because she was afraid of Roznine and censored any references to him. Now he knew differently.

"Mally hon," and he took her by the shoulders, forcing her to

look him in the eye. "I looked *at* Roznine. I looked him over good
and strangely enough, I liked what I saw." That got her where she
lived, and Red took a deep breath, opening his own inner mind so
she couldn't fail to see the sincerity of his words. "He's the kind of
guy I'd trust and respect even if I could probably take him apart in
a fair fight. Oh, I know. I've heard all this static about his sewer-
sink mind and his power in the city and I don't know as my public
mind would be all that clean and pure. I've learned to do my improper thinking carefully but no one's warned Roznine that
there're guys around reading him now and again."

Amalda was staring up at him. Her eyes had gone all big and her
lips were parted. He wanted to kiss her, to love and reassure her,
but not just then.

"Mind you, I don't think Roznine's a crusading saint but feck-
itall, Mally, he's up against City Hall and when you're fighting
City Hall you use every advantage you can beg, borrow or," he
clipped her lightly on the jaw, "kidnap. Not that I blame him for
flipping his nut over you." He couldn't keep his voice steady and
he knew he was playing-back their initial meeting. "If you affect
Roznine the way you do me, I'm damned sorry for the poor guy. It
must be hell for him to want you and not get you."

Amalda discarded all restraint and now remorse/love/apprecia-
tion/agreement/understanding/pride/loyalty washed over him.

"Don't do that, Mally. I've got to think."

She bit her lip apologetically and "buttoned" her emotions up.

"Thanks. Now, where was I? Yeah. As of yesterday, I don't think
Roznine could use you. Not now. Or only if you let him. And you
won't. If that's what's bugging you, forget it. Or don't you remember how easily you knocked him out? You gotta take it easy on the
guy, hon. He loves you even if he doesn't know it."

"It's you I'm worried about, Bruce," she said in a very low voice,
her eyes wide and full of tears.

So he embraced her, pressing her slender body against him, so
she'd "feel" all he couldn't express. His knowledge that you aren't
selfish with Talent, whatever kind you possessed: that they had a
relationship too strong to be broken or diminished by the acceptance of a third party: that Talent had obligations beyond the personal and this was one of them, for both Amalda and Bruce.

She reached up tenderly to stroke his face, her fingers enjoying
the tactile contact with the silky hair of his beard, letting her fin-

gers express what she didn't articulate. As she had learned to accept Bruce's right to decide for them both, she accepted his decision now.

"The stage is set, honey," he said finally. "Extras all milling about, waiting for the director. Are you going to let him come?"

She gave an impatient little shrug, then squared her shoulders and smiled at him, ready to move mountains, from the look of her. He liked that about Amalda, among a thousand other things. He conveyed that approval with a gentle, mind-blown hug. Talent has advantages, too.

R oznine rubbed at his temples, wondering what kind of fake powder the medic had sold him as a headache remedy.

They had done something to him when he was unconscious. Just as he, Vsevolod Roznine, knew that *they* had caused him to black out at the hearing. No, not "they"! *Her!*

The conviction that he had to get to her, be with her, returned with renewed and irresistible force. And Roznine fought it again, fought it as his head throbbed, and his hands clenched into fists of effort to withstand the compulsion.

He flung himself from the table, catching the leg with his foot and upsetting the untouched meal, half-stumbling against the door and striking his temple on the frame. He hit his head a second, a third time. And clutching the molding, threw back his head in bitter laughter.

"Roznine has to beat his own head, because it feels so good when he stops!"

His fingers dug into the frame until his nails bent against the durable plastic. His head turned slowly, as if he could see straight through concrete and plastic, across the miles to the Center in which direction he unerringly turned.

"*NO!*" This time his fists thudded into plastic. "Roznine does not come at a woman's call. She comes to him!"

How had they done this to him? How could she call him? Once he'd known her name and that she was at the Center, he'd had his people find out all they could. She was registered as a telempath. Roznine had looked that up and the answer had only confirmed what he'd guessed himself: she could transmit emotions and probably receive them.

Roznine pounded the wall viciously, transmitting such hatred and discontent as boiled up in him from the frustration of not having her and the humiliation of being knocked unconscious . . . in full view of his constituents . . . by a slip of a girl he could break in two pieces with one hand.

And who was the redbearded man who worked with her? How close did he work with her?

Jealousy was added to the seething emotions of Vsevolod Roznine. And the skin of his skull pulsed with a surfeit of his angry blood.

The intensity of his desire to see Amalda reached another peak. He fought it. He would not go to her. She must come to him! He could not go to her. She had to come to him. She, who could read his thoughts, let her read that one. Let her read his feelings . . .

"No!"

Roznine stopped. Everything about him stopped, his heart, his lungs, the oxygen molecules in his blood. Then he took a deep breath and exhaled, his wide mouth forming an odd smile in a suddenly calm face.

No wonder she had not come to him, the little one. She *could* read his thoughts. She would be terrified of him, Roznine: terrified of the anger he had felt toward his little bird. He had felt her fear before, felt her spirit fluttering away from him. That was why she had run from the Fact. But she shouldn't fear him, Vsevolod Roznine. Every man, boy and adult she should fear but not Vsevolod Roznine. He would go to her. He would explain.

Chort vozmi! Would his head never stop aching?

His comset buzzed. The noise stabbed piercingly through his skull. He grabbed frantically for the set to stop the noise, answering in a savage tone.

"Everyone's in position, Gospodeen."

"Position?" Roznine shook his battered head, unable to recollect which position and where.

"The picketers have been checked by the Center's guards, who are two old men: nothing to worry about."

Picketers? Pickets? At the Center? Oh, yes. He'd discussed that with the little man from upstate. How could he have forgotten?

"And the riot squad?"

"Parked at or working conveniently nearby. The disposal men . . ."

"Good enough!" His head pounded like a drill press but he remembered. How could he have forgotten? So she was a riot control team, was she? Well, let her control this riot! Men would pour in to the Center's so private, so secluded, so sacrosanct grounds from all over the city: men from many ethnic groups so it couldn't be blamed on his section. It had meant cancelling half the favors he was owed but, just let him get his hands on that little riot controller and . . .

He threw open the illegally unsealed window and slid down the airshaft on the escape line. He opened the window in the rear flat, which conveniently belonged to a relative who was blind anyhow, and exited through the back door. Found the iron pry-bar and flipped up the sewer lid, snagging it deftly back over the manhole when he was within. He walked briskly over the thin stream which trickled down the pipes at this time of day. Two rights and a left brought him to a wider section conduit with a catwalk on one side. Two more rights and two lefts and he climbed a ladder. The manhole had been shielded and a Disposal truck was just drawing up. Swiftly he was within the truck and issuing orders to the driver.

The sensitive signalled LEO headquarters that Roznine had left his quarters. Immediately Gillings warned the Center and circulated the alert to all stations.

Charlie Moorfield ran through to Daffyd's quarters.

"Ring Amalda and tell her I'm on my way over."

Sally was struggling into her coverall, excitement making her fingers fumble so that Daffyd held the collar until she could find the armholes.

"He is coming. You were too much for him."

"Possibly."

Daffyd could also see another interpretation of Roznine's secret exit, particularly with the picketers outside and the observers forming a larger and larger ragged semi-circle beyond the gates to the Center.

"Yes, I see what you mean, Dai."

"Let's reinforce Amalda."

The buzzer sounded again. "Boss, I get no answer from Amalda."

"Tell Gillings to get all riot units here on the double. Alert ours."

Daffyd op Owen swore as he grabbed Sally's hand and pulled her out the door. Short of teleporting, he'd never been down the stairs so fast. Afterwards Sally told him her feet had touched the steps only three times.

Amalda and Bruce Vaden had exited through one of the side-gates in the grounds. They'd come up on the picketline from one side, mingling with the onlookers until they were directly opposite the main gates. The picketers were dutifully chanting the slogans they carried, the four LEO men routinely assigned a picket, were almost as bored with the proceedings. A passenger conveyance settled to the public landing some hundred yards from the gates and the occupants, carrying collapsed signs, descended in an orderly fashion.

"Those are bully boys, not bona fide picketers," Bruce told Amalda in a quiet voice.

She nodded for she'd unerringly sighted the one man who was important. "*He's* with them."

"Well, this is the last place he'd be looking for us. Are you shielding tightly?"

Amalda nodded again but she didn't take her eyes from Roznine.

He really was attractive, she thought. There was something proud and fierce in his manner. Bruce was right: she hadn't really seen him before. She's been just so scared of his mind . . .

She stopped thinking because Roznine was suddenly glancing over his shoulder, at the crowd, frowning slightly. He stood near the copter, to one side of the new shift of pickets. They were milling about . . .

"Warn Dave, Amalda, and get set. See how they're maneuvering?" Even as he spoke, Bruce glided to a more advantageous position for teamwork.

The new arrivals, for all their aimless movement, could now be seen aiming for LEO men and the Center's two guards, mild-appearing gentlemen who were in fact top kineticists and could hold a grown man immobile on the ground without lifting a physical finger.

The old shift broke from their circuit, grounding and collapsing their signs, preparatory to leaving. Some elements of the crowd which had watched pacifically from the footpath began to move toward the grounds.

Amalda began to broadcast, gently at first, the feeling of immense fatigue, utter boredom and a dislike of this activity.

Bruce moved further across the street, picking up and increasing the intensity of her broadcast. But he watched Roznine, saw the man stiffen, his head turn slowly, unerringly towards Amalda. The group in which she had been standing shifted and she was by herself.

The setting of the confrontation was superb, Bruce Vaden told himself with a curious objectivity. As if by magic or common consent, everyone melted from the two principals, leaving a clear path between them.

"Don't get scared, honey baby," Bruce told her under his breath, fighting in his mind to hold the broadcast and disguise the inner reluctance of sharing Amalda with anyone at all.

Suddenly he felt buoyed up, felt the indescribable mental support and touch of Daffyd op Owen, speaking through him to Amalda. And it wasn't just Dave, but something . . . . no, *someone* else.

The area was blanketed with silence by Amalda's projection which began to waver slightly. Bruce intensified it, imagining as he'd been taught, that the emotion was something visible which he was manipulating tangibly, as visible and tangible as water falling over a specific area, drenching everything with its cascade.

Everything went at half speed. Roznine pulled first one heavy leg forward, then the other, like a man treading through molasses, sticky, cloying. The man's face was contorted with effort and concentration.

Amalda just stood, her chin slightly raised, looking as regal and poised as she had on the Fact stage, so sure of herself that she almost fooled Vaden.

The action was all slow motion: the picketers, real and bogus, discarding their all too heavy signs, inexorably sinking to the ground, sprawling in poses of utter exhaustion. It affected the LEO men though they tried hard to resist the pressure, falling to their knees and hands, faces down on the ground.

Then only she, Bruce and Roznine were standing. She took a deep breath and looked straight at Roznine's eyes: the first time she had done so.

And Bruce was right that Vascha (she found his nickname easily: though he thought of himself, self-importantly, only as Vsevolod Roznine, the Vascha personality was there, too) was nice looking, with a strong body and sensitive hands. She liked long, well-shaped fingers on a man—she liked to have such hands on her body.

"All right, here I am," she said out loud and dared him in her mind to overpower her.

His eyes seemed to eat her flesh hungrily, as if starved for the essence beneath the covering tissue.

"You're mine. I, Vsevolod Roznine, say you are mine." That was his thought, beating away at her. She wanted to laugh, to sing out because his thought couldn't go any further than her mind. It couldn't reach Bruce, standing not more than five feet away. Not unless she wanted it to go further!

"Well, what are you waiting for?" she asked gently because the knowledge of such total power over another human being humbled her.

Some of his bully boys were getting to their feet for she'd turned off some of her blanketing projection to deal with Vascha. Through Vsevolod Roznine she sent a fleeting thought of nausea that instantly reduced them to retching bodies on the grass. And as abruptly, she deflected the actual illness. Then she turned off the empathetical broadcast completely, knowing its cessation would leave the victims disoriented enough to cause no further trouble.

"I think you'd better come with us, Vsevolod," she said to Roznine and took his hand, turning and leading him toward the Center as if he had no other choice. He didn't because Bruce fell in on the other side, their strides matching.

Roznine was dazed, his lips compressed into a thin line. He glared down at Amalda as she led him, at arm's length, like a mother dragging an errant child home.

The gateman nodded to the trio as they passed into the Center's Grounds.

What'n'hell has happened to your common sense, op Owen?" Frank Gillings demanded. "Letting not only Amalda and Vaden but Roznine into the City Council? For Chrissake that's what he wanted Amalda for . . ."

"Easy, Frank. The team's on assignment, completely legitimate."

"Council isn't a riot situation . . ."

Daffyd raised his eyebrows in polite surprise. "No? According to Roznine, the tempers get so hot no constructive work is ever done. Each ethnic group insists that its members are being discriminated against with accusations and counter-accusations until the mediator adjourns the hearing with nothing accomplished except exhibitions of parliamentary bad manners. Sorry. The team is going to cool things long enough for common sense to prevail. Roznine's reason for wanting Amalda's Talent in City Hall was valid." Daffyd also neglected to add that that was the bargain he'd struck with Roznine to join the Center. All the man wanted was to be certain the employment allotments were impartially assigned. Well, not all, Daffyd amended to himself, but Roznine had gone about it the wrong way.

Daffyd grinned reassuringly at Gillings's image in the comset. "He's part of the team now and *she* follows orders."

"But does Roznine?" asked Gillings sarcastically.

"As I've explained to you, Frank, Roznine is paraphysically dead to anyone else. Oh, Bruce Vaden empathizes with him to some extent now they've both had training, but Roznine's is a one-way Talent, right to Amalda. She's the focus of the gestalt. You might say, he's been check-reined."

Frank Gillings grunted, somewhat mollified. Then, jutting out his chin, he glared at the Director. "You going to start lobbying for a rider on that Talent Immunity Law?"

"Immediately. In fact," and Daffyd's smile broadened with sheer malice, "Senator Greenfield is helping us get an interim rider through the State Senate on a Bill he has coming up on the Agenda next session."

"Greenfield?"

"Yes. Roznine invited him here at the Center for a chat. The Senator was most amenable to the suggestion."

The LEO Commissioner's frown was partially perplexity. "What'd you guys do to Greenfield? Blanket him with loving kindness?"

"Good heavens, no. It was merely pointed out to him that the Center is not a minority, but a collection of minorities since all ethnic groups are represented. He took a tour of the grounds and instantly perceived that the housing was by no means as luxurious as he'd been previously led to believe, with swimming pools or wasted space that might house additional families. In fact, he complimented us on our planning and thrifty use of facilities."

Frank Gillings was by no means taken in by Daffyd op Owen's bland manner. He growled something under his breath.

"What did Roznine have on him, Dave?"

"I don't know what you mean, Frank."

The LEO man made a gesture of disgust.

"Dave, don't give me any more problems for a while, will you?"

"Nothing's coming up in the foreseeable future."

The screen went blank on Gillings's incredulous expression.

"Daffyd, that was highly immoral, unethical and downright dirty," said Sally, half scolding as she rose from the couch where she'd been sitting out of line-of-vision of the comset. She walked in under his arm, linking him around the waist. He nuzzled her curls and kissed her forehead.

"Probably. Les is always reminding me that it's bad policy to tell all."

"It's a shame about Vascha though." Sally sighed.

"Why?"

"Oh, it's rather sad, his being a psychic mule, her Pegasus."

"Thank God he is," Daffyd said so fervently she looked up, startled. "With the ambition and drive that young man has, he'd rule the world in half a year if Amalda and Bruce weren't there to stop him."

PEGASUS
IN FLIGHT

This Book is respectfully
and gratefully dedicated to
Diana Tyler
and
Diane Pearson.

PROLOGUE

During the late twentieth century's exploration of space, a major breakthrough occurred in the validation and recording of extrasensory perceptions, the so-called paranormal, psionic abilities long held to be spurious. An alternate application of the Goosegg, an extremely sensitive encephalograph developed to scan brain patterns of the astronauts who suffered from sporadic "bright spots," temporarily diagnosed as cerebral or retinal malfunction, was inadvertently discovered when the device was used to monitor a head injury in an intensive-care unit of Jerhattan. The patient, Henry Darrow, was a self-styled clairvoyant with an astonishing percentage of accurate "guesses." In his case, as the device monitored his brain patterns, it also registered the discharge of unusual electrical energy as he experienced a clairvoyant episode. For the first time there was scientific proof of extrasensory perception.

Henry Darrow recovered from his concussion to found the first Center for Parapsychics in Jerhattan and to formulate the ethical and moral premises that would grant those with valid, and demonstrable, psionic talents certain privileges and responsibilities in a society basically skeptical, hostile, or overtly paranoid about such abilities.

Extrasensory perception—or Talent, as it came to be called—came in varying strengths and forms. Simple, short-range telepathy was fairly common, once inhibitions were discarded. But there were also one-way telepaths, people who could send their thoughts but not receive those of others, and people who could receive thoughts but not send. Others were empaths, able to adjust immediately to the moods of those around them, sometimes quite unconsciously. Telempaths could sense and react to extreme or more distant emotions; some of these were able to redirect emotion, by broadcasting other emotions or by neutralizing the negative—such Talents proved to be invaluable in crowd control, for they could keep a throng from turning into a senseless mob. But the most valuable of the telepaths were those who could both receive and broadcast thought, speaking to other minds anywhere in the world.

Telekinetics—Talents who could move physical objects by sheer mental power—were also invaluable, their abilities ranging from lifting heavy machinery to manipulating on micro levels.

Clairvoyants or precogs could see future events, either close at hand, or at some remove from their present. Very often their visions allowed the future to be altered and disasters to he averted. Some clairvoyants had special affinities: some sensed events revolving around fire, water, or wind; others were more apt to perceive children, or violence, or criminal intentions.

Finders also had affinities—some could locate people or animals, while others were able to sense inanimate objects—and their abilities could vary greatly in range.

Talent came in many forms and guises, and not all of the viable types had, as yet, been recognized. The various centers, worldwide, constantly searched for the less dramatic gifts because the need had now far outstripped the supply. For those potential few, the training was arduous, and the rewards did not always compensate for the unswerving dedication required by their taxing positions.

And yet to be found Talented became the aspiration of many, and the triumph of few.

They have been at a great feast of languages,
and stolen the scraps.

—William Shakespeare.

CHAPTER 1

Tirla took a quick look from the alley into the Main Concourse of Residential Linear G, then pulled back instantly, flattening her thin twelve-year-old body against the plasslab wall. Public Health officials were swarming all over, rounding up the early-morning crowd of able-bodied workers who had been scanning the employment board for a day's work, the mothers with their handicapped kids making their way to the Rehab centers, and the legal children on their way to the Linear's physical-training facility.

Cautiously she took another look, to see what the PHOs were setting up on their tables: vials and the big compressed-air bottles that operated the hyposprays. She withdrew, having seen enough to recognize another wholesale vaccination effort. Strange, she hadn't heard of any new 'mune plagues. To give them their due, PHO was swifter than rumor to avert disaster.

Rapidly Tirla ran through her head her current list of those mothers of illegal children whom she should inform: first, because they would pay her for warning them to hide the kids; second, because those who could afford to would pay her for stealing whatever vaccine was being administered. She counted on her fingers: Elpidia, certainly; the old bouzma, Pilau; Bilala, and Zaveta, Arisan, and Cyoto—and she had better ask Mama Bobchik if there were newborns, for they would need the Five-shotter. She would want one for herself, as well, and could possibly finagle a box, depending on how the current stuff was packaged. It all depended. Mirda Khan, yes—she had best tell that old wagon right after she warned Mama.

She would have to change into clean clothing issue—she had washed, but this week's issue was five days old and looked eight. Public Health were quick to notice details like that. Mama Bobchik was always good for fresh wear, especially if Tirla went to her first with her news. This could be a very good day, Tirla thought with a rise of spirits as she slipped back down the alley for the center-shaft emergency stairs on her way down to Mama Bobchik's pad.

Most of Tirla's twelve years had been spent in scrounging a totally unofficial living in the multi-ethnic thirty-storied community of the Linears. She could not afford to miss a single trick, like today's unexpected Public Health roundup, to escape the stringent controls, clever obstacles, and little traps ingeniously set up by the Jerhattan Complex Administration Council and the Law Enforcement and Order Organization to identify and control each member of the restless population.

Officially there had never been a record of Tirla's birth. She was, however, the fifth child born to Dikka—only the first, Tirla's brother, Kail, was legal. The government tied a woman off when she gave birth to a second child. Consequently Firza, Lenny, Ahmed, and Tirla had all been born in Dikka's single-parent squat with the aid of Mama Bobchik, who had had an illegal child every year until her womb had dried up. Kail had been official until Dikka had sold him at ten. Firza had had the use of Kail's wrist ID for two years until she was profitably disposed of. In the next year, Dikka, Lenny, and Ahmed died of one of the immune plagues that sporadically flared up to decimate the Linears. In the haste and confusion of body disposal, Dikka's death had not been officially noted. So Tirla had been left with two ID bracelets—a fine legacy. Self-sufficient and resourceful, she had managed to retain the squat, drawing two subsistence rations, until Dikka's ID was canceled after her failure to appear for a routine medical examination.

Wise in the ways of her society, Tirla had not been caught short by the lockout. She knew Tenancy Articles, Paragraphs, and Subsections by heart, so figuring out the cancellation date had been no problem. Two days prior to the eviction, she moved her few possessions—hotter unit, the best of the sleep sacks, the 'corder, and the pretties Dikka's men had given her from time to time—into new quarters five levels below the Main Concourse, in the maintenance segment of Linear G, right beside the charged security grille that protected the engineering section from unauthorized entry.

Only a slight and agile person like Tirla could reach the eyrie, where massive ducts formed a broad platform before bending up the inner wall. She patched her hotter and 'corder wires into the overhead cables, certain that her small use of electricity was unlikely to be discovered, and settled in. She did miss the all-night informational programs on the squat's tri-d. The big public tri-ds on the Concourse stopped 'casting at the midnight curfew. Tirla, with her clever, shrewd, and organized mind, was thirsty for knowledge. She even used Kail's ID to log into school. One of Dikka's men had said that one had to know the rules before one could break them. Tirla had never forgotten.

For another two years, Kail's bracelet supplied his small sister with daily subsistence, weekly clothing issue, and other amenities until "Kail" failed to appear at Evaluation Center within three weeks of his sixteenth birthday. The cancellation caused Tirla no problem, for by then she was well-established, almost indispensable to most of the Residential clients and gang bosses in the neighborhood industrial complexes. Her ability to translate any of the nearly ninety dialects and languages used in the subsistence-level Residential Linears saved clients hours at official transspeech centers, or worse, misunderstanding. She knew when to be ingratiating or stand firm. She knew what courtesies were due whom and never failed in performing them. Everyone who knew her knew very well that she was illegal. Because she was so useful to the residents of Linear G, as she would be today with her warning about the Public Healthers, and because officially she did not exist anyway, there was no profit—yet—in reporting her illicit existence.

The various errands she did—and she was scrupulously silent about them—often brought in "floating" credit chips. Floaters were legal tender—*Pay to Bearer*, untraceable chips that changed hands frequently. Jerhattan Treasury and all the merchant and banking houses wisely ignored the circulation of minor amounts of floaters, just as they ignored the petty small traders as long as they made no trouble and their merchandise was harmless. Tirla, and others like her, relied on floaters to support their illegal existences in the Linears.

Linear G thrust thirty massive levels above the squat, featureless F and H commercial blocks where residents of Linears E, G, and I worked. Once, on a Free Day, while Tirla still had her brother's

ID, she had gone with Mama Bobchik to the Great Palisades Prom-
enade, where thousands upon thousands of people had swarmed to
enjoy a brilliant spring day, to overlook the exclusive hives, platforms, and great cone complexes of Manhattan Island, and to ooh
and aah at the monorail cars, large and small, that zipped along the
tracks which garlanded the buildings like colored tinsel strands.
That was the first time Tirla had seen ships floating on water or
the great pleasure skycars. There had even been a special issue of
holiday food, yards above the standard fare, at dispensing banks.
Buril, Mama's son, had a tripper key that he used on the dispers, so
they had managed to stuff themselves before the mechanism's malfunction alarm was triggered. It had been a super day for Tirla.
She had never dreamed that the world was that big.

That was the same day that Buril explained to her all about the
space platform that was being built, which needed so many workers. When it was completed, he said, all the people living on Manhattan who had enough credit and were the "right kind" would be
able to go off into space and find other worlds to live on. Then all
those beautiful buildings would be empty and there would be
enough space for everyone crammed into Linear squats to live in
proper big apartments with a bedroom for each family member
and no more Public Health or LEO men and women tying men
and women off, shaming a virile man.

This morning, as Tirla scratched on Mama Bobchik's door to tell
her of the PH presence in the Linear, she heard the old woman
gasping and groaning as she struggled off the bedshelf.

"*Kto stuchitsya? Perestan'te udaryat'sya. Okh, kak bolit golova!*"

Tirla grinned. So Mama had a big head this morning, caused by
the vodka she had made from the potatoes Tirla had nicked for her.
In that state, she would be easy to wheedle out of a credit.

"It's Tirla, and the Public Health are already on the Concourse."

"*Boje moi! Eto tak?* Have I not enough pain in my life?" But the
door was pushed open wide enough for Tirla to slip inside. "What
have you said? The Public Health again? So soon? Why?"

"Another vaccination by the looks of it. They're grabbing everyone, able-bodies, students, handies and their mothers."

"Ah, we must hurry. Elpidia, Zaveta . . ." Mama Bobchik began reciting the names of her usual maternity patients.

Tirla tugged her arm.

"Nu, what do you want from me?"

"I cannot help unless I have clean issue," Tirla said, managing to look piteous and sound efficient at the same time.

Buril had fixed the clothing-issue slot in his mother's squat so that it could be coaxed to extrude more than it ought. His taking ways had been very useful until Yassim—Tirla made the warding sign at just the thought of *that* man—had paid Mama a huge sum for him. Buril's unusual talent for "fixing" official equipment made him quite valuable—he had not gone the usual route of Yassim's purchases, and Mama had been paid enough floaters to keep her comfortable in her old age.

Mama Bobchik blinked her reddened and bleary eyes and looked at the tiny girl. "*Da,* that is so!" She patted Tirla's head before she went to the clothing slot and did something that her heavy frame obscured from the girl's sight. When she turned back, she had a packet in her hand.

"I washed this morning," Tirla said, immediately unfastening and stepping out of the old suit. She had to roll up the sleeves and legs of the fresh issue, but when she had neatly folded each roll over wrist and ankle and pressed the edges to seal them, sleeve and leg bloused out nicely to give her apparel more style. She retied the pretty braided rope belt that she had inherited from her mother and tucked the excess material neatly back. "Now, I'll tell Mirda Khan, do this level, and then up and down. That'll be all I think I have time for. What'll I do for an ID? They'll grab me if my wrist's bare."

What Tirla wanted most in her life was a genuine, valid ID bracelet that would allow her a squat right, the use of a tri-d, three meals a day, and a fresh weekly issue of clothing. An ID that was all her own and had never been anyone else's! One that would allow her into the school programs that so few of the kids she knew seemed to care about at all.

Now she cocked her head at Mama Bobchik, knowing perfectly well that an ID was essential when the PHOs were swarming the Linear. Mama Bobchik pretended to consider, giving Tirla just a few moments of anxiety.

"*Eto tak!* For PHOs, we use one." With a flounce of her skirts, for Mama would not wear the single-piece coverall without proper skirts to conceal her limbs, she turned her back on Tirla again. No matter how hard Tirla listened, she could not tell where Mama secreted those precious counterfeit IDs that Buril had also contrived. They were good for one day's use only—one day, because while the band would be accepted by a portable reader such as the PHO would have to record vaccinations, it would show up as a fraud later, when the day's entries were checked.

Mama Bobchik turned around, dangling the precious ID band. "You split the take for the warning with me. As usual."

Tirla nodded solemn agreement to the terms, her eyes watching the swing of the band.

"And if you can steal enough vaccine, I will give you thirty percent of that take," Mama added.

Tirla gave an incredulous snort. "Sixty. I could get caught stealing."

"Forty, then. No one has caught you yet. After all, I gave you the ID at no cost to you and have the expense of the spray gun."

"Forty-five!"

The two hagglers eyed each other, and then Mama's broad face beamed down at Tirla's unyielding expression. She spit in her palm and engulfed Tirla's delicate hand in her own to seal the arrangement.

"You are a clever one. You must hurry now."

The girl was already slipping through the half-opened door and down the hall to spread the warning.

Despite her speed, Tirla barely finished her route before the PH officers began to penetrate the levels, checking the IDs of each squat's occupants and herding them out and down to line up for their hypospray. She soon learned that the health threat was not a 'mune plague but a virulent intestinal disease that had started in Linear B with devastating results. All Linears were being vaccinated in an attempt to stem the spread of the ailment. The PH public-address system droned on constantly giving a short explanation in all the languages registered in Linear G; Tirla did some rapid translations of her own when requested by nervous mothers.

"It's only another food contamination," she assured the skeptical. "They've isolated the source, who have been heavily fined and lost their license."

"Huh!" Mirda Khan said, her dark eyes glistening with skepticism. "That will be gone as long as it takes to send in enough credit to reissue it. How long will the protection last us?"

"Oh, this one'll do us for a year!"

"A year? They are improving."

Trudging forward step by step in the long line, Tirla and Mama Bobchik finally reached the PH, dropped their wrists across the reader, and received their shots. Immediately Mama pretended to become faint and staggered against the table. While the PH woman was coping with that, Tirla swept an entire tray of the vaccine ampoules into the shopping sack Mirda Khan had ready as she, too, came to Mama's assistance.

"*Okh, kak bolit golova!*" Mama said in an appropriately wispy tone, the back of her fat hand against her head. The pain in her voice was not entirely faked, considering the hangover headache.

"What's she saying?" the PH officer asked, hovering between concern and annoyance.

"Her head hurts," Tirla replied.

"Not from this injection," was the callous response of the PHer. "Now move along!"

Solicitously Mirda Khan and Tirla propped up Mama Bobchik as she made her way slowly toward the nearest side aisle. Once safely out of sight, Mama immediately reached for Mirda's sack and peered inside it.

"One whole tray? Miraculous, Tirla, truly miraculous. There are more than enough. Run ahead and tell them to come in small groups. The PHOs have already checked our three levels. It will be safe."

In the course of her errands, Tirla tried her ID bracelet on as many public dispensers as she passed, no matter what commodity emerged from the slot. She tucked each purloined item into the extra material at the back of her coverall, or into a sleeve or a trouser leg. It became harder to move quickly, but she managed. By evening, she had enough small floaters and illegally acquired items to keep her well fed and content for the next month. If she stretched a bit, it might even be six weeks before she need bother about working again.

CHAPTER 2

There was no aura of menace or threat," Rhyssa Owen told Sascha Roznine as he stood glaring down at her. To reduce his threatening glower to a more productive, thoughtful mood, she touched his arm, reinforcing her statement with a mental *See? Curiosity. An impingement, not a threat.*

Sascha subsided, but he continued to glare at the graph recording of Rhyssa's early-morning sleep pattern, where the wide black mark of the spoke showed that she had been roused from an REM dream sequence to full alertness by a mental intruder.

As the director of the Center for Parapsychic Talents on the North American East Coast, Rhyssa Owen lived on what had been the Henner estate, a reserve of trees, lawn, and mature gardens above the Hudson River on the Palisades. This archaic remainder of the twentieth-century residential suburbs interrupted the flow of Linear structures that housed the millions who lived and worked in the massive Jerhattan complex. Rhyssa's quarters were undistinguished from any of the other three-story apartment blocks set among the gardens and trees. As with all dwellings for the Talented, these were secured and shielded from unannounced entry. In fact, even those who tenanted the Linear constructions running on the long sides of the Center's extensive grounds did not know of its existence, so artful were its screens. No one should have been able to intrude on Rhyssa, much less in her sleep.

"Awkward, rousing you so thoroughly. You need all the rest you can get." Sascha projected a vision of himself and Rhyssa curled together in her bed, the double-thick duvet tucked around their spooned bodies.

Yes, yes, Rhyssa replied. She responded with a vision of a firm foot pushing the Sascha body out of the bed. *But even if you had been there physically, you couldn't've helped, Sascha-bear. It was all in my mind, in my dreams. And that's your duvet, not mine. I never use plaids.*

Rhyssa smiled up at him, fluttering her eyelashes to mock his projection. He raised his brows in resignation. They both enjoyed this game. They had been playing it for years.

Picky, picky. Don't avoid the issue, Sascha said. "Who, I'd like to know, could knock in on your mind? And why?"

"Indeed!" Rhyssa crossed her arms and stared off into a view of the lowering clouds and dismal rain that obscured a usually breathtaking view of Jerhattan. *That's what perplexes me.*

Don't range, Streaky. Sending your mind out searching for him takes too much out of you. You're going to need all your energy to deal with the Zealots. He projected the vision of three persons with limbs so entangled they resembled an Oriental fetish, each caricatured face wearing an expression of mixed intransigence and skepticism.

Oh, don't! She laughed as her return image untangled arms and legs and set each person upright, a whiskbroom smoothing tunic and trousers while emblems of rank were straightened. *I can't remember that when I have to deal soberly with their urgent requests for Talents I don't have. They're laughable enough as it is.*

"Good. That's all they deserve. Shall I have Sirikit check back and see when this phenomenon first registered?" *Sheer impudence!* Sascha snorted his annoyance.

"That's an idea." Rhyssa smiled ruefully as she pulled clothes from drawer and closet. She continued to talk as she dressed in the bathroom. "I only thought of checking my graph this morning. I really do need my sleep."

"Probably some emergent Talent who doesn't understand protocol. I do wish they didn't always feel required to overreact to their newfound mind-powers."

"Damned strong one!" Maliciously, Rhyssa projected an image of a very young Madlyn Luvaro, mouth wide open, and the circle of people cringing away from the waves of sound emanating from her.

Sascha grimaced. Madlyn Luvaro had a mental shout that could penetrate to the space station and any of its peripheral dockyards. It had been Sascha's task, as he was nominally in charge of Training and Development, to teach her how to focus and moderate her mental voice. Madlyn adored him passionately and was embarrassingly possessive of him, an adulation he was finding increasingly difficult to discount—it was the reason that he assiduously cultivated the notion that he and Rhyssa were on the brink of a total partnership. Kindly, Rhyssa did not disclaim the rumor.

"I'll have Sirikit run a check on possible emergents," he told her, then sent the request to Sirikit in the Control Room, also asking her to check Rhyssa's encephalograph charts for the previous months.

Emerging washed and dressed, Rhyssa beckoned Sascha to follow her through to her office, which adjoined her living suite. She yawned as she sat down at her desk, kinetically pulling some pencil files into her reach, fanning them out, and turning each until the index-code side was visible. She selected the one she wanted and neatly piled the others in front of her, code side outward, as her first selection inserted itself in the reply slot. Simultaneously the reader net came off its hook and settled lightly on her head. With one finger, she poked the left contact pad against her temple in a final adjustment.

"We won't find him there," she said, and was as startled as Sascha was that she used a gender. "Well, I know a trifle more than I thought I did from that fleeting nudge."

"A secret lover?"

"Could be," Rhyssa murmured, projecting an image of a sly grin and a come-hither expression directed at an amorphous shadow. Although her tone was light, Sascha perceived that her surprise at making any kind of an identification went deep.

"I'll follow through," Sascha said, and left her office. As he took the antigrav shaft down from her tower to the vast basement complex where most of the Center's training and research was conducted, he carried with him a vivid mental picture of Rhyssa Owen at her desk, the reader net covering her black hair, a spiderwebbing across the wide silver lock that she had had since her early teens. That streak grew broader every year, and by her late thirties her hair would be all Celtic silver.

Rhyssa would always have a young face, Sascha thought, as both her father and her illustrious grandfather, Daffyd op Owen, had had: young, vibrant, with dark blue eyes that sparkled and gleamed with intelligence, humor, and unassailable energy. Rhyssa was nearly as tall as the males in her family and a shade too thin; she clothed her long bones in elegant, if often bizarre styles: generally long flowing garments that set her off in a society which had stripped apparel to the minimum.

She was not pretty—her features, though small, were too uneven and mismatched, her right eye socket canted above the cheekbone, giving her a gamine expression that no one who knew her would misjudge. Her nose had a slight bump, making her profile look haughty, and her mouth was too generous above a strong jawline. Still, one forgot such details within moments of meeting her. She had inherited the full measure of charismatic personality, as well as the strong psionic talents, of her parents—and of the grandfather who had battled to secure the position of Talents in the present socioeconomic-political atmosphere.

Sascha Roznine, himself a third-generation Talent and younger than Rhyssa by three months, preferred his current role as chief trainer and recruiter in the Center. Not for him the petty power ploys that Rhyssa coped with admirably, for he had struggled all his life to manage a quixotic temper. The nerve-racking sessions with Jerhattan's managers and all the picayune details she had to deal with would have set him raging in five minutes. Sascha, on the other hand, had immense patience with emergent Talents, coaxing, cosseting, and curbing, gently allaying their doubts and building their confidence. When Rhyssa had once pointed out that, in their own way, emergent Talents were as obnoxious as managers, Sascha had replied that at least Talents learned from their mistakes.

There were so many strengths and varieties of Talent. Of the precogs, there were those who could foresee events, generally those which would have a major effect on a large number of other people; those whose prescience was limited to people they knew or were assigned to watch; and those whose precognitions had affinities with fire, water, males or females, children—there was as wide an assortment of focus points as there were strengths of perception.

Telepathy was the most common Talent, though some people could only receive thought, and others only send it. Telepaths felt emotions and responded to the pervading ones. A trained telempath could either dampen negative auras or reinforce positive ones, a Talent useful for altering the tension in a crowd, preventing rampaging emotions from turning groups of people into disorderly mobs.

Finders were those Talents who could locate things, using only a facsimile of the desired item, or, in the case of a missing human or animal, a garment or some other personal object.

Telekinetics could work on the largest objects, or the most minute particles that could not be seen with the naked eye or even a microscope, though there had only been one known genetic manipulator, Ruth Horvath. Telekinetics were invaluable in so many walks of life that those with this Talent were encouraged to have as many children as possible.

The rarest of the Talents were the pure and double telepaths—like Rhyssa, who could send and receive communications across the world as long as she had met the person she wished to contact. She could penetrate any mind not shielded by the thin metal caps the nervous wore or by the natural mental shield that some normal people were born with.

Sascha, also a strong double telepath, lacked the phenomenal range that Rhyssa possessed, but he never resented her for it. Once her strength had been established by her grandfather, Rhyssa had been committed to a Center directorship and all its responsibilities —responsibilities that Sascha would never want to take on. As far as he was concerned, Rhyssa was welcome to her Talent.

He heard Madlyn Luvaro before he landed on the shaft cushion at the basement level. She was trying to be quiet, but she was as successful as if she had been tap-dancing across a sound-resonant surface.

Until you learn to damp down your aura, it won't work, Madlyn, he told her. *Improper flow! Low positive energy is what you need to be "silent."*

Dammit, I thought that's what I had! Her mental response was contritely discouraged.

Sascha pushed out of the shaft and there she was, flattened against the wall.

"I did 'hear' you coming," she said aloud.

Sasha: Giant step forward! Madlyn was a powerful sender, but generally she could "hear" only those in her immediate vicinity.

He tugged a strand of her tangled mane of black hair as he passed, and she fell into step behind him, her large and expressive eyes rueful. Madlyn was a voluptuous eighteen-year-old with a sensual nature to match her appearance. She, and her Talent, had matured at fourteen, and since then Sascha had been struggling to teach her the necessary discipline that any Talent had to master, and that she would certainly require before her penetrating mental shout could be utilized.

Sirikit's already checking Rhyssa's Goosegg readings. Sascha had not tried to dampen his immediate concern. With so many telepaths aware of the alarm, keeping the investigation under wraps had been impossible.

Someone actually intruded on Rhyssa? Madlyn projected an image of herself throttling a large, amorphous intruder and squashing it into a little ball which she then flushed down the toilet.

Sascha snorted. Madlyn was quite capable of attacking anything that threatened Rhyssa. Who in the Center wasn't?

They found Sirikit already scanning Rhyssa's Goosegg encephalographs for the previous month. Several were paused at the spoking that indicated intrusive wakenings. The Goosegg, initially developed to monitor the odd light flashes experienced by astronauts, was especially sensitive in registering delta brain waves, which had been discovered to be the seat of paranormal or extrasensory perceptions. A Talent, trained to recognize his or her own slight mental alteration prior to paranormal activity, slipped on a net that could read brain activity. Many Talents, particularly the precognitives and clairvoyants, wore them night and day. They were lightweight, of a strong fine mesh matching the wearer's hair color. The net transmitted to the Center's main banks, so that Incidents of paranormal activity could be officially recorded, studied, and consulted. It was proof positive to any skeptics that the extrasensory perceptions did occur.

"Look at Rhyssa's recordings, Sascha. There's no question that the Incidents have been increasing," Sirikit said as Sascha strode to the bank of horizontal spindles used in such comparisons. "First one three weeks ago, second four days later, then three, and this past week once a night—about four-ish."

Sasha: *Odd time for a voyeur!*

Sirikit: *With three-quarters of the population asleep in bed.*

Madlyn: *Insomniac?*

Sascha smiled, for not only was her mental tone appropriately soft but she had caught the quick exchanges.

Sasha: *An adolescent generally has to be pried from his sleep. Rhyssa thinks it's an emergent Talent.*

Madlyn: *You keep telling me that emergent Talents follow no rule.*

"Any statistics on insomniacs?" Sirikit asked.

"I'll program it," Madlyn said, flipping her hair back as she seated herself at a monitor, keying in directories that could access any computer bank in the world under the special concessions granted the Centers. She was cleared for normal use, although passwords were needed for any sensitive files. Madlyn might have been blatant in her sexuality, but her mind, open to inspection at all times, was as transparently guileless as a child's. "Well, this won't be productive. Anyone can have insomniac phases. Anxiety is the biggest cause. There are some people, the elderly in particular, who can get along on only four hours of sleep a night!" Her mental picture was of a horrified grimace superimposed on a tossing body in a rumpled bed. "I'm wrecked without eight hours!"

Sirikit leaned back from the spools, which had all paused to display the telltale spoke of intrusion.

Sirikit: *Three-thirty to four, predawn, too early for most shift workers, even air and road haulers.*

Sascha bent over her shoulder, studying the reels as if he could glower the riddle into the open.

Sascha: *Rig her net.*

Madlyn gasped and stared at him. Sirikit blinked, sighed, and then, rising from her stool, went to the main board to enable the necessary program.

"Some early-morning joy seeker *has* to be overflying the Center. Set an alarm through her net, and we can catch the bugger in the act." Sascha's voice was vindictive.

Madlyn shot him a worried glance. She could feel the wave of high negative energy he exuded.

CHAPTER 3

Barchenka, Duoml, and His Highness Manager Prince Phanibal Shimaz arrived promptly for their meeting with Parapsychic Center Director Rhyssa Owen at the Jerhattan City Manager's Tower, a massive structure in the center of Central Park, the last vestige of nineteenth- and twentieth-century Manhattan. The tower, rising above the tallest of the mercantile buildings, was crowned by ziggurats of communication dishes, giving it an appearance from any distance of a grotesque bunch of stiff daisies rammed into an immense glass brick. Skycars of varying sizes at the landing level stuck out like a fringe of angular, multicolored leaves.

Space Station Construction Manager Ludmilla Barchenka entered first, her odd bouncing gait indicating that she was wearing her antigrav boots. Her infrequent visits back to surface gravity were difficult for her—but they tended to be worse for those she confronted. The woman's appearance did nothing to mitigate her abrasive personality: she was stocky, big-boned though not fleshy, with a flat, broad face and unexceptional features. Pale blue eyes and short-cropped hair only added to the image of a tough persona —cold, inflexible tenacity. To top that off, Ludmilla invariably wore a thin metal skullcap, a shielding device that was almost an insult to Rhyssa in her capacity as director of the Eastern Center. Rhyssa was not sure if Barchenka used the shield merely out of concern for security or because she was pathologically wary of the Talents whose services she desperately needed even as she deplored their abilities. Sascha was convinced that Barchenka had some sort of Talent, even if it could not be scanned, and that she refused to acknowledge the possibility.

Despite her total lack of social graces, the Exalted Engineer's dedication could not be faulted. Padrugoi Station was due to be completed, and on budget, at the end of the current year.

With interstellar voyages now possible and habitable planets located in two near systems, the pressure to implement the colonization program was incredible. But first the Padrugoi Station, the essential springboard to the stars, had to be completed. The project had worldwide priority and the enthusiastic support of every political and economic faction on Earth.

Considering that the first laboratory station had gone over budget by trillions and had been five years late in completion, Barchenka's achievements so far were considerable. But Rhyssa knew the truth: that the Exalted Engineer was beginning to fall behind schedule despite all her efforts. It was rumored that the woman slept no more than four hours a night and daily accomplished a prodigious amount of work—but that she expected the same dedication from everyone on the project. Unfortunately she did not have the charisma or leadership ability to generate either loyalty to herself or to the project. Initially many Talents had volunteered to assist, but one after another they declined to renew their contracts. The many enticements to return with their unique capabilities to work on Padrugoi Station had met with failure.

Personnel Manager Per Duoml, coming in behind Ludmilla, moved with the heaviness of someone accustomed to lighter gravity, but he managed without the antigrav assists. A Finn, as capable and dedicated as Barchenka, he was slightly easier to deal with. And though he, too, tended to wear a metal shield, the Talents had liked working with Duoml: he was fair, competent, and had succeeded in persuading a few Talents to return for special, short-term assignments. But still most had declined to extend their employment, and they could not be conscripted. And though Rhyssa had dutifully asked the directors of every Center in the world, she had no takers to offer Duoml.

Program Manager Prince Phanibal Shimaz pounced in behind Per Duoml, and his presence was neither essential nor welcome to Rhyssa. Peculiarly arrogant and impervious to her continued, and lately overt, distaste for his company, he used any excuse available to press his suit on her. Rhyssa often wondered why he had bothered to develop an impenetrable mind shield when his face revealed all that most men would have had the courtesy to hide. The prince was a computer genius—some said he had thought in binary codes in his creche and teethed on chips—and when he was barely out of his teens, he had mastered the use of the Josephson junctions in what he termed an "idiot proof" application to regulate with complete safety the vast flow of skycars and drones in and out of major Linear depots and over densely populated areas. He was currently applying his efforts to create a similar basic and safe flow of spatial traffic.

Rhyssa composed her face and her mind, smiling with a warmth she did not feel as the three settled themselves.

"I do *not,*" Ludmilla began with no preamble, her deep voice guttural with only a slight trace of her native language, "have the required personnel." Her pale eyes accused Rhyssa.

"As I have told you repeatedly, Manager, I cannot and will not order the Talented into space."

Ludmilla brought her fist down with a wince that revealed that, in her frustration, she had forgotten the gravitational differences. She brought the bruised hand up in a gesture that in the space station would have been flamboyant but was less graceful on Earth.

"You *must* insist—"

"I can insist, but they can resist," Rhyssa replied equably.

"How can I maintain schedules without the personnel to perform the necessary tasks? Day by day we fall minutes behind: minutes which your diffident workers could make up in seconds. I will not fall behind the schedule. We will make our completion deadline. We must have the suitable personnel. You told me that you have them, and I have here the proof." Triumphantly Ludmilla extracted a pencil disk from her tunic and brandished it at Rhyssa.

"In that reply I said that I would certainly approach all Centers with your specific requirements. I most certainly did not promise to fill the vacancies."

Barchenka narrowed her pale eyes into a basilisk stare. "You recruit constantly. It is public knowledge that you find new Talents—"

"It does not follow," Rhyssa inserted smoothly, "that those we recruit are the kinetics that you specifically request. Certainly I could not ask untrained Talents to go into the hazards of space."

"Why not?" Ludmilla dismissed that consideration with a broad wave of her hand, inserting the pencil file back into its pocket at the end of the gesture. "We will train them on the job—to be useful, to be careful, to be specialists. They will love space. They will make many credits and be wealthy."

"The Talented do not accumulate wealth, Manager," Per Duoml stated in his flat, nearly toneless voice, his patient eyes never moving from Rhyssa's face.

"Nonsense! Everyone acquires wealth." Ludmilla had more than the usual contempt for altruists. "In the beginning we had many Talents working for us."

"We wished to assist the world project," Rhyssa said. "But you would not accept their stipulations when their contracts came up for renewal."

"Stupid clauses, untenable for us. Shifts of no more than six hours when we work twenty-four on the platform. Special shielding for noise. There is *no* noise in space." Her scornful gaze rested hotly on Rhyssa.

"No noise which is audible to you, Madame Engineer, but which is extremely unpleasant to sensitives."

"Bah! Sensitive!" Once again Barchenka summarily dismissed that consideration. "Spoiled, pampered, catered to."

"No, Madame Barchenka, not pampered or spoiled, but yes, catered to," Rhyssa flashed back. "The Talented are skilled personnel and require some minor considerations to enable them to perform at their best in the hostile environment of space."

Barchenka plowed on as if she had not heard. "It is incredible that such a minority can exert so much influence on the economic life of our world. In the airport, in the spaceport, in industry where, while I order matériel, I see the very Talents I must have to complete the most important project of the world, a project which has universal approval, which means mankind may reach beyond the limits of this solar system and explore the very stars themselves. Yet you and the other Center managers do not permit me to hire the specialists I need."

"It is not the permission of the Center directors that is required, but the consent of the employed," Rhyssa reminded the engineer. "Center directors negotiate the individual contracts with the necessary safeguards."

"I can buy the contracts." Barchenka's challenge was also a threat.

"Such contracts cannot be sold, Engineer Barchenka, and if you

would accept the necessary safeguards, you might be more successful in attracting Talent!" Rhyssa replied sternly, beginning to lose
patience with the woman's dogmatic pursuit. She could ignore Per
Duoml's mournful expression and even keep her gaze averted from
Prince Phanibal's hot eyes, slightly wet lips, and nostrils that flared
slightly from his rapid breathing; but all three glaring at her were
an unnerving combination. She kept a smile on her lips, deliberately increasing the flow of her limbic system.

"You can insist," Ludmilla repeated. "It is in all your contracts
that 'it can be voided at the discretion of the Center in emergencies.' "

Rhyssa suppressed a rush of anger that Barchenka had been
given access to a Parapsychic Contract and had to remind herself
that such contracts were public knowledge. "My fellow directors
do not consider that you have a true emergency, Engineer
Barchenka."

For the first time Barchenka flared angrily. "I say this is an emergency! I say I must have a larger work force to complete this world
priority project."

"You have unlimited access to the conscriptable pool of workers."

"Bah! They are useless—sterile, uneducated, untrainable grunts!
I cannot build a space platform only with grunts. I will have the
kinetics I need. I promise that, Director!" With that she wheeled
and, in a dangerous imbalance, made a lurching exit, Prince
Phanibal following her.

Per Duoml took one step forward, bowing slightly at the waist.
"Even half a dozen kinetics would improve the situation tremendously."

"As I have explained repeatedly, Per Duoml, insure the Talents
shielded quarters and a six-hour maximum shift and they will be
amenable. Surely if there's credit enough in your budget to support the number of trips back to Earth that have been made for the
purpose of recruiting Talents, the funds can be found to supply
their basic needs on Padrugoi!"

"Engineer Barchenka must adhere to the budget. No alterations
can be made to existing staff accommodations."

"Then Engineer Barchenka is stuck with the result." Rhyssa
fervently wished that Per Duoml would relax his mental shield
long enough for her to place directly in his mind the information

her words patently did not convey. "You require kinetics to shift objects of mass proportions in the assembly of Padrugoi. You also need kinetics who can assemble chips of the most complex delicacy in the total vacuum of space. The kinetic energy required by both tasks is the same and exhausting. They need quiet to restore their strength—they are sensitive to the metallic vibrations of Padrugoi itself, the inhumanly close quartering, the lack of privacy, and the appallingly bad rations which are insufficient to replenish their bodies and minds."

Per Duoml nodded impassively and then shrugged, unwilling to comment before he, too, turned to leave.

His departure left Rhyssa with an uneasy sense of foreboding. She directed a query to Sirikit on duty in the Control Room of the Center. *Any precogs in just now?*

Sirikit: *None. You're expecting one?"*

Rhyssa projected an image of Ludmilla Barchenka's grim visage: *Possibly!*

CHAPTER 4

The boy blinked three times, and the channel on the ceiling screen changed again. He sighed. Yet another oldie he had already seen often enough to have memorized the good parts. He blinked the switch signal again, and realized that he had been through enough of the channels to be sure that there was nothing on to catch his attention—not even an educational program unfamiliar to him. The first few weeks he had been in the ward it had been lots of fun, watching the tri-ds all through the long nights. Kept his mind off—things—after his headaches had eased. Sometimes he almost missed those headaches, because at least then he had been feeling something in his body.

He sighed. He could do that, too, he reminded himself, thinking positively as Sue, the therapist, said he must. He didn't understand a lot of what she told him, like imagining himself walking and running, thinking hard of how he used to do it—before he had run alongside the ruins and that brick wall had collapsed on him.

Why? The agonizing question made him gasp. He had thought he had stopped thinking about that. Asking "why" was definitely negative and always depressed him terribly. Why had that wall come down just as he, Peter Reidinger, had been running past it? Had he kicked a stone that had been enough to trigger the collapse? Had one of the boys chasing him lobbed a stone at the wall? Why, since it had been standing for fifty or a hundred years all by itself, why had it picked that moment to come down? Three seconds later, he would have been safe—safe from both the wall and the boys chasing him. Why had he turned into the forbidden area, anyhow? He'd had a choice at the end of the alley: over the wall, only it seemed very high to him and he had nothing to give him a leg up; to the right, only that took him back into the Alley Cats' territory and possible ambush; or to the left, *weaving his way through the ruins, making it more difficult for them to know which way he would go.* Why?

Negative! Negative! Peter screwed up all his face muscles and then made them relax, group by group. Then he smiled, slowly and consciously spreading his lips and bringing the corners of his mouth up, stretching them until his cheeks lifted, his chin dropped, and his lips parted over his teeth; willing the nerve impulses in his face to change the limbic system. As Sue had taught him, he pulled his most happy moment out of his mind: his eleventh birthday, when his father had come home on leave from the space station in time for the party.

Planting that memory firmly in front of "why," Peter rehearsed the details of that happy experience until he could relive the entire scene from the moment the door chime had announced that his father had made it home until Dad had tucked him into his bunk. He had gotten so he could even feel the touch of his father's hand on his forehead.

Good thing Dad had touched him there—one of the only places he still had feeling. Peter sighed again and refelt the touch. Then he closed his eyes and "heard" his father leave the room, "heard" the muffled sounds of his parents talking and laughing. He expelled another deep sigh.

He was lucky. He could breathe on his own now. Sue had been so proud of him when that autonomic reflex had returned. He filled his lungs, knowing that his chest was rising, his diaphragm tightening. He could feel the air in his windpipe. He held his breath until spots came in front of his eyes; then he expelled it.

Immediately he heard the steps of the duty nurse. Miz Allen did not like to be disturbed, especially when he knew that they had a critical case on Pie 12. He counted ten steps and then she was peering down at him, making eye contact. She then peered at the wall panel that displayed the readings from his monitors.

"Why was there a respiratory fluctuation, Peter?"

"Aw, I was just doing my breathing exercises."

"You were not." Miz Allen glared at him a moment, and then her long thin face relaxed. She laid a light hand on his forehead and then drew one finger down his cheek to press it against his lips. "You were fooling. Don't fool with your breathing, Peter. Your brain needs oxygen. And it needs sleep, too. It's quarter of four. You should sleep. You know how to achieve relaxation, Peter. Do your progressives, there's a good boy."

They both heard the sudden whimpering of the burn girl on the other side of the circular ward.

Miz Allen, reproving smile and all, disappeared, and Peter counted her steps, twenty-one, to get to the critical case. Then he counted to thirty, and the whimpering ceased. He knew burns hurt. He wished he felt something, *even burns!*

He immediately put his mind to the few progressives available to him: the relaxation of every muscle in his face, head, and neck. He could not move his head, but he had sensation in his neck. He reached total slack and thought carefully of his *place, feeling the spring of grass under his feet, hearing the shimmer of leaves as a wind soughed through them, smelling the fragrances of the garden, gazing up at the sky above, the sun warm on his back. He began to float again. He had the sensation of drifting up, out of the supine body resting on its cushion of air, amazed and annoyed at the various tubings and wires shunted into him that he never felt.*

The garden of his dreams was miles away from Jerhattan. It had been part of the vacation farm to which his parents had taken him when he was eight. For someone raised in Linear Jerhattan, surrounded constantly by the noise and smell of people and maintenance machineries, he had been totally entranced by the farm. Peter knew that there were small green belts throughout the Jerhattan complex; he had even been to several, trying to relive that vacation, but none had evoked the same response in him, being too small and cramped to close out the eternal noise of the city.

He had found a place, though, where he could float when he got to the proper state of relaxation. It had grass and trees, barely visible in the eerie predawn light. And he was strangely attracted by other inexplicable strands, comforting wisps of thought, enticing him to linger. One in particular intrigued him, and he hovered as close to it as he could, tantalized by a sense of tranquil familiarity.

All of a sudden he was nearly blinded by powerful lights that flooded the scene. He felt a moment of terror. He could not suppress his scream, steadying only when he heard Miz Allen's steps. He did not open his eyes until he felt her hand on his forehead and knew *he was safe back in Bed 7 of Pie Ward 12.*

"What's the matter, Peter?" Miz Allen always knew if a patient was shamming and she did not tolerate false alarms. Her eyes flicked to the wall panel. "Bad dream?"

"Yes, bad dream." Despite himself, his voice quavered, and her expression softened.

"Yes, your endorphin level shot up. I think you'll have to have some sleep."

Peter nodded, relieved at her decision. "I've got VMR tomorrow . . ." He began, but then darkness overwhelmed him.

You scared him off! Rhyssa accused Ragnar, fuming that someone had triggered her net to alert the Center's security forces if her pattern spiked during the night. The field lights had blazed up. Moments later she had heard the thrumble of the skycars, shooting off in all directions. *Sascha!* she roared. He was the only one empowered to set surveillance on her!

Sascha: *We'll catch the bugger!*

Not that way! Rhyssa forced controls on herself to disperse the white-hot fury. Sascha had exceeded his authority—even the boundaries of friendship.

Sascha: *I have not!*

She inhaled deeply, aware that she was still trembling with anger. She expelled the breath right down to her toes, continuing to press downward until her belly muscles were taut. *There was* NO *threat!*

There was *intrusion!* His mental pattern broke briefly as he responded to some exterior stimulus. *That's bloody strange,* he said a moment later. *There was no intrusion. Not a physical one. Not a blip on any screen that can't be accounted for. And nothing—read that—nothing in our airspace.*

An emergent! Rhyssa colored the thought with satisfaction. *That is, if you haven't scared him out of his Talent!* She sent an image of herself turning back onto her stomach, hauling the duvet in its pastel print tightly around herself, and dragging a matching pillow firmly over her head—which was what she did.

An emergent from where?" was the question that circulated the Control Room.

"Who's awake at four o'clock in the morning?" Sascha asked.

"I can do a probability curve," Madlyn suggested, "eliminating all the obvious shift workers."

"Why eliminate them?" Budworth asked.

"If they're working, they're not doing o.o.b.," she replied.

"And who says this is an out-of-body job?" Sascha asked, turning on Madlyn with surprise.

"What else could it be?"

Sascha grinned. "You may very well be right, Madlyn, and it's so obvious I wonder none of us thought of it before. Okay, who would go o.o.b.?" It was a leading question to which he already had an answer.

"Someone who doesn't like the bod they're stuck with," she replied.

"But o.o.b.'ing *is* Talent," Budworth said, "and all of 'em are registered, so they have better things to do than o.o.b."

"*If* they're registered," Sascha pointed out.

"I see, so we run a check on new ones."

"That's right. With the hospitals."

Madlyn groaned. "D'you know how many hospitals there are in Jerhattan?"

"Not intimately," Sascha said with a grin, and pointed an index finger at her. "Think of it as a survey question in your training. Ask for paralytic cases, teen, preteen, insomniacs . . ."

"Why blame the teens?" Madlyn asked, bridling.

"They won't have been scanned for Talent yet. Okay," Sascha added graciously, "try anyone faced with a sudden lack of mobility. I'll add the prison systems, too." He grinned at Madlyn's groan. "One of the most famous was a guy escaping a sadistic jailor."

Madlyn's eyes widened. "Can the Center get prisoners released?"

Budworth chortled. "Don't you remember your Center history? This place was started by rejects from prisons and mental institutions—" He shot a sly look at Sascha. "—and all kinds of otherwise asocial and/or eccentric personalities."

"If my brother were here . . ." Sascha waggled an admonitory finger at Budworth.

"Huh!" Budworth snorted. "I'm not afraid of your brother even if he is the high-and-mighty Law Enforcement and Order commissioner."

"I would be," Sascha replied. "Which reminds me, I'm late for that appointment. Get the program started on checking hospitals and prisons. And buddy boy, you can do the mental institutions. I appreciate the reminder."

"Ha!" Madlyn said to Budworth as Sascha left the Control Room.

How can there be that many illegal children in the Residentials?" Jerhattan City Manager Teresa Aiello demanded of Medical Chief Harv Dunster. "Your people are supposed to tie off after a second pregnancy."

Harv's angular face was grim. "Only if we get to deliver 'em. You know that some ethnic groups still refuse to practice contraception. Until we have the right to use infertility drugs in subsistence-level food, there'll be unreported births—and continued traffic in preadolescents for sexual perversions, or cheap labor in illegal factories. And the ones with the right blood factors and healthy organs will still be stashed away by the very rich for transplants as needed." He gestured at the fax sheets on Teresa Aiello's desk.

"And ruthless people will still dispose of the used ones," added Boris Roznine, commissioner of Law Enforcement and Order. "Even illegal kids have rights." He glanced obliquely at the faxes scattered on the worktop.

Teresa inadvertently glanced down. She was a tough-minded woman, but she had a ten-year-old daughter, and the fax of the bloated bodies discovered as flotsam off the North Shore of Long Island spared no one's sensibilities. She averted her eyes. The coroner reported that the oldest had been twelve, the youngest five.

Boris Roznine had contacted her the moment the appalling discovery had been made. The temper of Jerhattan was always uncertain when faced with such news, and Teresa had called an emergency meeting of her commissioners to prepare for a possible eruption if the news was leaked to the media. Boris's twin brother, Sascha, was due to arrive with the Parapsychic Center's suggestions. To insure the tight security around the tragedy, the four were meeting in the shielded privacy of the city manager's tower office.

"Ah," Boris interrupted what Teresa had been about to say, his right hand lightly touching his temple in indication that he was receiving a telepathic message. "Positive ID of one, the Waddell girl who was kidnapped six weeks ago . . ."

Teresa winced and let out a groan. The Waddells were acquaintances of hers, high-tech executives; the child, bright and extremely pretty, had been a school friend of her daughter. Teresa had put a top priority on the abduction, and had officially requested that Rhyssa Owen assign her best finder to the case.

"Two others are listed as runaways, reported missing two months ago. Of the others . . ." Roznine shrugged, glancing at the medical officer. "The best the lab can do is genotypes, and it's all-sorts."

Every citizen of the United World was permitted—provided they did not carry the proscribed genetic recessives—to produce a replacement. One parent, one child. Two parents, two children. ZPG was stringently enforced until the pressure of Earth's population could be released on the new habitable worlds, identified but not yet attainable. The Propagation Laws were easier to enforce in rural communities than in the huge residential warrens of cities like Jerhattan, with its population of over thirty million.

Teresa turned to the LEO commissioner. "You haven't stopped the spot checks, have you, Boris?"

"Hell, no, but we're still not locating the early pregnancies no matter how we try. If I had the personnel to mount simultaneous level searches, we'd catch more." Boris brought his clasped hands together as if closing a net. He gave a ghost of a grin. "We did pretty well at the Residentials, six weeks after the last big power outage, but that was a once-off." Then he spread his hands wide, matching Dunster's resignation. "You know our situation. We manage to keep a lid on most of the trouble—if we're all sitting down as hard as we can. It isn't as if we need more bodies."

"The ones that ignore the legal control," Harv said dejectedly, "are exactly the ones educational and hygiene programs don't reach—in any language."

Teresa grimaced. "So there's no indication where the rest of those poor kids were snatched?"

Roznine shook his head. "Could have come from any subsistence level."

"In the last gruesome chucking, three months back or so, only four were recognizable ethnic types," Harv Dunster said grimly. "Near Easterners—Lebanese and Arabic. Two were Tay-Sachs, ten were dark-skinned, and one was an HIV carrier—which may well be why they were all . . . disposed of." The medic sighed heavily. "I suspect Lab may also find anti-body positives among this latest—"

"Spare me, Harv," Teresa said firmly, and called up the main Jerhattan map on her screen. "We've just had a go-round of the Residentials with Public Health. We haven't got the funds available for another. Exactly where were the bodies found, Boris?" Her fingers hovered over the terminal as she waited for an answer.

"Washed up out by Glen Cove, not far from some of the more exclusive residential hives bordering the Sound."

"Great!" Teresa's frustration came out as sarcasm. "No Incident logged?" she asked Boris, though that would have been included in the initial report.

"The storm, yes. The flotsam, no."

"Shouldn't your brother be here by now?" Teresa frowned, glancing at the clock ticking off the seconds in the corner of the main screen. "We need all the help we can get on this."

The focus of Boris Roznine's blue eyes locked briefly as he linked minds with his younger brother. "Traffic snarl's breaking up. But he says"—his voice suddenly deepened as the Talent peculiar to the twin brothers allowed one to speak through the other— "Look, I want to save time—yours and mine. These murders go deeper than the loss of thirty juveniles. Forget the HIV factor—it's irrelevant here. They were disposed of because we'd got too close to them, but not close enough, soon enough. Teresa, Carmen's been on search-and-find duty ever since you handed us the Waddell kidnap file. She got a whiff or two of terror, but never enough light to pinpoint. Except that she got a hint of water." Boris's wide mouth quirked briefly, reflecting his brother's chagrin. "Most of those children had to be illegals. We all know that that group of pederasts is active—and supplied—despite international efforts to eradicate that sort of traffic. We know that kids are bought as cheap labor and shipped who knows where. And that some are also secreted as possible transplant donors.

"We haven't been idle," Sascha's voice continued. "This could, in fact, be the break we've been waiting for. We got too close. It'd be nice to know—" and at that word the door to Teresa Aiello's office swung open and Sascha Roznine strode in, smiling at everyone. As he gave his brother's shoulder a grateful squeeze, he continued, "where exactly we got so close. We're working on it, and with your assistance, Harv and Teresa, I think we have a line to throw out to those sharks." His smile took in each of his listeners, but he cocked his head at his brother and winked.

Slowly a smile began to lighten Boris's face as he read the detailed thoughts in Sascha's mind. "Tag kids with strands through the school system? That might just work! We might even catch the bastard child-stealers this time." Boris leaned forward across the table. "You are all familiar with the restraint filaments that were recently developed? Sometimes those we tangle with the strands escape before they can be secured. A second application has been made with a slightly altered formula, and now the altered strand can be traced for up to six months. There're certain anomalies to be resolved, but it's worth the effort to tag every child in the vulnerable group."

"You mean, this side of the river?" Teresa waved at the panorama visible from her tower office, the uptown cluster of beehive, cone, and single-tower Residential buildings clearly visible on this bright morning. "But statistically, it's the illegals in the Linear Residentials who are more at risk."

"If we could catch Linear kids to strand 'em," Boris said, raising his hands palms-up in resignation, "we'd be way ahead. Meanwhile we'll strand as many kids as we can on both sides of the river and hope."

"Hope?" Sascha asked softly.

Rhyssa! She recognized the mental touch of John Greene, the Talented bodyguard of Secretary of Space Vernon Altenbach.

We got problems? she asked.

Girl, you really deserve all the headaches of administration if you can guess that much from just hearing me speak your name.

No precog needed, JG, because you never bother me unless there's political pussyfooting. What is it this time?

A bill to draft the Talented into whatever position the government needs them!

Not again? Rhyssa's response was half-amused, half-irritated.

Concerted attempts had been made in the past by government agencies to circumscribe the freedom of choice originally granted to the Talented. That was prior to the point at which the government began to appreciate the applications of Talent—after the days when Daffyd op Owen, her illustrious grandfather, abetted by Senator Joel Andres, had fought to gain legal immunity for Talents exercising their abilities.

Immunity had been particularly vital for precogs because, when they warned of disasters which were, by those warnings, averted, they had been subjected to expensive and time-consuming lawsuits. There had been attempts since then, from the ridiculous to the deadly serious, to regulate or restrict, all manner of Talents to military, civil service, or mercantile uses.

But the Talented had always managed, quite legally and with no untoward exercise of their particular abilities, to circumvent such attempts. Many Talents had willingly sacrificed personal freedoms to serve in the public sectors, some on a lifelong basis, to preserve the right for their peers to choose. Rhyssa's parents had done that, to give her the opportunity to achieve the position she now held.

Again, and this isn't funny, Rhyssa, Johnny Greene went on, *space is in a bind. The platform has to be finished on schedule before the sheer weight of numbers on Earth becomes more unmanageable than it already is.*

So Ludmilla's been lobbying?

She's got some hefty help, and Vernon's got tremendous pressure on him. I'm the loudest of the Washington/Luxembourg voices, so I'm making the contact with you for the rest of the minders. We've been excluded from far more sessions than we ought to be—sessions that have been attended by some of the most antagonistic Right Mutes that have ever been lined up against Talents. And when you think that I helped him develop his shields against unauthorized peeking, I could spit! The nerve of him closing me out!

One of the more sensitive professions open to empathic Talents was that of "minding" vulnerable top-ranking officials. Terrorism was still a fact of political life, and although the problem of the displaced and the minorities had been somewhat eased by the mass resettlements and the institution of the Linear developments near every major urban area, and the incidence of assassinations had been drastically reduced, empaths were still employed to "mind" those officials who might be targets for the fanatics who still occasionally emerged.

Rhyssa could hear the hurt in Johnny's voice that Vernon Altenbach had been shielding his thoughts from his minder, especially since Johnny was also Vernon's best friend, as well as his brother-in-law. In his official capacity, Johnny served as under secretary in the Space Secretariat. Prior to that he had been a trained etop—earth-to-platform—pilot with twenty successful launches . . . until the twenty-first had grounded him forever. His Talent had saved his crew from death but not himself from losing both left leg and arm. Despite state-of-the-art prostheses, a new career had seemed advisable. So far Johnny had already prevented four attempts to kill or kidnap Secretary of Space Altenbach.

Johnny: *I shoulda been included in these latest talks, but I wasn't.*

Rhyssa: *Which means that Talent was being discussed. Barchenka and Duoml want more kinetics on the platform in the worst way. I'm doing my best to help . . .*

Johnny, in an uncompromising tone: *Anyone thought of telling Barchenka that she's the reason why Talents won't work up there?*

Rhyssa: *Lance Baden did. He thinks she has selective amnesia. Can't even get her replaced, not with the performance record she's got!*

Vernon's tried! She's so bloody good at what she does—it's only how she does it. I'll keep in touch, but we felt you ought to be forewarned. There was a hint of criticism in his voice.

Nothing has come up with any precog, Johnny.

I know, I know. That worries me as much. This thing could be very very big, and not even Mallie's got a whiff!

Rhyssa: *Then obviously the matter is solved before it reaches critical.* She tried to sound firmly optimistic even as a little shudder rippled down her backbone. Someone should have been sensing something! Mallie Vaden was one of the most sensitive precogs the Center had ever produced, and her lack of foresight—if Johnny's reading of the situation was correct—was surprising.

I'll be in touch, Johnny assured her. *I'll even see what the ghosts think. You know how they'd like to see our Talented noses out of joint.*

I think I'll try a frontal attack, Rhyssa said. *Might jog a few brain cells loose.*

When'll I see you then? Johnny asked, his tone brightening.

If possible, today. Run me through Vernon's schedule. When Johnny did, Rhyssa stopped him at the lunchtime engagement. *I like the food there. I'll just drop in!*

Rhyssa always experienced a mild shock when she encountered Johnny in the flesh, for the light tenor of his mental voice was at variance with his strong physical appearance. Medium tall, he kept himself physically trim, and one would never guess his serious injuries from seeing him walk or manage eating utensils. Some latent kinetic ability had proved to be an asset with his prosthetic limbs. He rose as he spotted Rhyssa approaching the table where he, Secretary of Space Vernon Altenbach, Exalted Engineer Ludmilla Barchenka, and Padrugoi Personnel Manager Per Duoml

were seated. Johnny's broad smile welcomed her, and they exchanged touch and a kiss.

*Would you have dared look so stunning if the amorous Phanibal had
come, too?* Johnny's green-flecked amber eyes twinkled with devilment.

Rhyssa: *Why doesn't that odious man go back to the Pacific island that
spawned him and attend to the family's plantations?*

Johnny: *All you need is a strong handsome man who'll scare him off.
Right now you've got this lot embarrassed by your appearance, and yet they
haven't said a thing out of line,* he added, all in the split seconds of the
greeting.

Rhyssa gave Altenbach a genuinely glad smile, then nodded politely to the fiercely scowling Barchenka and the bland-faced Per
Duoml. "Just the people I hoped to see. When I saw you were to be
in Washington, Madame Barchenka, I realized that I should put in
an appearance before matters get out of hand."

"Now, Rhyssa," Altenbach said, signaling a waiter to bring a
chair and set up another place for his unexpected guest, "you can't
disrupt the established procedure of lobbying. That's not the way
to play the game."

"Nor is going behind my back," Rhyssa said, smiling to take the
sting out of her criticism. She turned to Barchenka. "You have a
schedule to keep. What you will not appreciate is that one cannot
schedule Talent or lobby it. The kinetics you so desperately need
cannot materialize to help you meet your schedule. That many
kinetics don't exist. Talent is a random and highly individual trait,
not an imposed one. No one can dictate to a Talent and expect the
person to perform to the best of her or his ability. That dictation
inhibits the Talent as surely as seasickness inhibits appetite. There
is no legislation in the world that may chain the mind."

"There is legislation that will recruit those needed to do the job
that the entire world has decided must be done." Barchenka's
stolid words complimented her uncompromising expression. "The
platform *will* be finished as scheduled. The kinetics *will* partici-
pate."

Rhyssa caught another strong emanation, this time from Per
Duoml, who nodded solemnly to support Barchenka's statement.

"There are ways," Barchenka added, her cold eyes scanning
Rhyssa's whole appearance from the elegantly coiffed hair and subtle makeup to the couture outfit.

"Legal?" Rhyssa asked with a slight smile.

The secretary cleared his throat and handed Rhyssa a menu. "I'm still of the opinion that this—impasse—can be negotiated to the satisfaction of all concerned."

Barchenka made a monosyllabic noise of disbelief and resumed her perusal of the menu. After only seconds, she tossed it negligently to the table. "I would prefer nutritious food to this . . ."

Johnny Greene beckoned to the maitre d', who was famous for his poise under the most trying situations that Washington could produce. "D'Amato, Manager Barchenka requires the *other* menu."

At a snap of D'Amato's fingers, an underling appeared and handed him a slim folder, which he presented to Barchenka with a flourish. She gave him, then Johnny, a sardonic look that turned to agreeable surprise as she scanned a menu composed of the foodstuffs available on the platform.

"Five, twelve, and twenty, taken with tea," she said in a voice that still vibrated with controlled anger.

Watch it, Rhyssa! Johnny cautioned. *Did you catch that flash? She's poison-sure she's got us where she wants us.*

Simultaneously three other minders, dining with their charges in the same room, sent Rhyssa similar warnings. She was particularly glad to feel the mental touch of Gordon Havers, the youngest Supreme Court justice ever appointed, whose expertise might be extremely useful.

Fine! Now discover what? Rhyssa said mentally as vocally she chose her luncheon of cold fruit, soup, and salad. *Gordie, are you available for some quick scans of obsolete statutes that could cover such a contingency?*

Been driving myself and my clerks all hours trying to find one, Rhyssa, replied Gordon Havers. *There's nothing in our constitution, but since the Russians won the contract for Padrugoi, there may be something in the Russian section that does! Their legal system is as convoluted as their grammar!*

"You can, of course, invoke some forgotten but still active statute," Rhyssa remarked all too blandly, waiting for reactions, "to conscript Talents . . ." Both Barchenka and Duoml looked startled.

Bingo! Gordie cried. *I'll concentrate on the Russian end of space law.*

"But," Rhyssa continued soothingly, "it has always proved unwise to force Talent to perform in an area that is either personally or professionally distasteful to them, and under punitive conditions."

"We have been too lenient with your temperamental tricks and traits," Barchenka said, leaning across the table in anger. "You will do this, you won't do that!" She affected a child's petulant tone. "Many concessions were made to cater to the whims and fads of your Talents, and still no significant numbers will volunteer for the most important world project of all history. Your attitude is unacceptable."

"I am protecting my colleagues, not being obstructive. I must repeat," Rhyssa continued smoothly, "it has always proved unwise to force Talent to perform duties unacceptable to them and under punitive living conditions."

"That will change! Will be changed! The platform will be finished on schedule!" Barchenka's voice had risen with each sentence until it stopped conversation throughout the opulent dining room. She pushed herself from her chair, wobbling slightly as her movements, more suited to half grav, brought her stocky body ponderously to an upright position. She kicked the chair away from her. "I do not tolerate insubordination!" And she clumped away from the table.

"I was doing my best for you," Vernon Altenbach said to Rhyssa, his face and manner resigned as he rose, his chair pulled back by a hovering waiter.

"You do not understand our position, Director Owen," Per Duoml added, but he made no move to leave the table. "We are forced to use unpleasant alternatives to avert far more serious disasters overtaking the world!"

"I'll see if I can calm her down, make her see reason," Vernon said with a gesture for Johnny to remain. "D'Amato, send my meal and hers to the private room. I'll be there."

"Do you believe, in your own heart, Per Duoml," Rhyssa asked, leaning across the table to the man, "that we are *evading* our duty to the world?"

He shrugged, his mind, with its metal shield, as impervious, Rhyssa thought, as his unwillingness to understand the nature of Talent. "It is the opinion that this—reluctance—puts the whole platform project in jeopardy."

"It is Ludmilla Barchenka who puts it in jeopardy," Rhyssa said with more heat than she had intended. She smiled quickly, hoping to repair the damage of her candor. Per Duoml might not be Talented, but he was scarcely stupid.

"Ah! My esteemed colleague was correct," he said.

"I am *not* standing in her way. I am protecting my professionals even as she is protecting her project."

Well, she is why Talents won't work for her, Johnny said in swift reassurance. *And we all know it!*

Gordie: *Yeah, but she stays! This will be an interesting power struggle, speaking from a purely legalistic viewpoint.*

"I admire Barchenka's unquestionable abilities as a spatial engineer. I would prefer that she return the professional compliment," Rhyssa said amiably. "This soup is excellent, Per Duoml. Let us enjoy it."

B *ingo!* Gordie Havers told Rhyssa the next day. There was absolutely no joy to his tone.

You mean Barchenka can *conscript Talents?* Rhyssa felt a cold paralysis grip her.

You've got it! I've been over the statute—and it is *Russian, from the pre-*glasnost *days, and should have been repealed long ago it's so archaic. In the good old Bolshevik days, it was illegal—get that, illegal—to be unemployed. The State was the only employer—not the employer of last resort—but the only employer. Ergo, everyone worked. Consequently, the only employer in a system that makes it illegal to be unemployed can certainly do whatever is deemed necessary with its work force. Legally, it gives Barchenka the right, under Padrugoi's International Charter, to draft any technicians, professionals, or workers required by the space effort—the space effort in terms of the original law being the Russian one. But the statute is still in effect, and, by legal crook, she can apply it to Talents. We can fight it, of course!*

And? she prompted.

With a glib-tongued attorney like Lester Favelly, we might just win. But the trial would take years, and could be construed by Barchenka to prove her contention—that the Talents are obstructing the Good Work. He paused significantly. *We could just give her enough rope to hang herself?*

The Talents will be miserable, and they won't perform well. That was what rankled Rhyssa's fine sense of integrity. Talents did the best they could no matter what the circumstances. To give the slightest suggestion that they skimped was against the most stringent of tenets for the parapsychic. But, in space, worn down by punishing hours and psychic static they could not avoid, inevitably their performances would suffer.

Exactly, Gordie said. *Ask the other directors. You must appear to be accepting the inevitable.*

The sort of press this could give Talents would undo the work of the last century, Rhyssa said despairingly.

I know. Although to sweeten this very bitter pill, Rhyssa, Mallie Vaden sees nothing going wrong.

Whose side is she on? Rhyssa could not keep the bitterness out of her tone.

Ours, as you well know, was Gordon Havers's crisp reply. *Ergo, it has to work out by our compliance. But I've initiated some investigations that might just give us a lever against Barchenka. Meanwhile, consult, Rhyssa. Quick action might shift public support to us.*

CHAPTER 5

Some of the fourteen other Center directors were not best pleased to be roused by her urgent request for conference in the middle of their nighttimes, and there was some grumbling. Though all Centers were theoretically equal, no director decided issues that would affect all Talents without consulting the others first, and Rhyssa—in charge of negotiations for the Talents because Padrugoi's administrative headquarters was in Jerhattan—deemed a meeting necessary. As soon as all were attending, she explained the situation.

And from what equally critical positions does this Russian think we can draft these essential kinetics? Lance Baden, the Australian director, demanded. Rhyssa always found it odd that his mental voice was devoid of the Aussie accent. *We sent everyone we could bribe or blackmail up there. Sheer bloody-mindedness keeps some of 'em in place, but my staff's down to nubbins or feather-movers.*

I have told Ludmilla Ivanova, said Vsevolod Gebrowski of the Leningrad bureau at his most apologetic, *time and again, that there are few kinetics not already doing double, triple work in order to supply essential services in Russia. Believe me, I have tried to educate her to the practicalities . . .*

We do believe you, Geb, we do, was the mass thought that reassured him.

What's the levy, Rhyssa? Miklos Horvath, the West Coast director, asked.

She's demanding one hundred forty-four kinetics! Rhyssa said grimly, and threw up a buffer against the cries of outrage. The number of registered Talents in every Center was open knowledge to every director, as transfers constantly shifted key Talents at need from one Center to another.

We don't happen to have a handy gross of kinetics, the Brazil director said angrily. *And I spent six months up there, in the most godforsaken barrio I've ever seen. Constant noise! Dreadful food—nutritious food could at least have a distinctive flavor. How she can expect us to function . . .*

If we use the discretionary clause, we can remove the required number from commerce and industry, Max Perigeaux of the large European bureau began in his slow, thoughtful way.

Ignoring the howls . . .

Under the circumstances, at least we're not liable to penalties . . .

That's a real comfort to those forced up to Padrugoi . . .

Well, Commerce and Industry want this station—they'll have to suck lemons along with the rest of us . . .

Max went on, his message weaving inexorably among the asides: *. . . put the trainees where at least they can be overseen, we could just about manage it. But how can we expect our people to endure the conditions up at the platform and still perform creditably? To do less than our best reduces our reputations, but how can anyone operate at his best in that milieu! And the noise!* The tall aesthetic man imaged a shudder of revulsion.

But something *must be done to give those who are conscripted some relief!*

Barchenka believes we set up the conditions of shielded quarters and short hours to be obstructive! Rhyssa said. *I was informed that there is no noise in the vacuum of space, and, because there is also no gravity, there is less physical stress and* longer *hours can be worked, not fewer.*

The woman is utterly without a shred of understanding or empathy, the director of Africa North said.

Has anyone tried *to adjust her thinking?* Hongkong Jimmy asked.

You've never met Barchenka, have you? Shields tighter'n a chastity belt! Baden said in an acid tone.

What's a chastity belt? Hongkong Jimmy flicked back in genuine innocence.

Images from nine helpful telepaths enlightened his ignorance. Rhyssa was grateful to him for easing the growing tension in the linkage with that byplay.

We are compelled to comply, are we not! Perigeaux said, at his most mournful. *And without delay, so that we can bargain on the best possible conditions for those who must sacrifice themselves. A rotation scheme, perhaps . . .*

If she's after the gross, that makes rotation impossible!

I can try to insist on some sort of short-term stretches, Rhyssa said.

Let us also issue some publicity, Miklos Horvath suggested, *about conditions up there.*

Of dubious value when she needs to recruit so many grunts. You know she has to go to the shelters for anyone below Civil Service-8.

But the public must see that Talent's objections to working in space are valid!

The most valid being Barchenka herself . . .

Can no one lean on her?

It's been tried . . .

Who's the best we've got?

What about her associate, Per Duoml? Any chinks in him?

It isn't that we don't want to help with the project, but she is her own worst enemy.

Did she specify kinetics only?

No one's told her that some kinetics are also telepaths!

Don't anyone mention that! Lance Baden said with unusual vehemence.

Wouldn't dream of it!

You mean, she doesn't know?

Ludmilla Ivanova knows what she wants to know, Vsevolod said wearily. *She only hears the explanations she wishes to hear.*

In twelve minutes of rapid-fire exchanges, the Talents arrived at a grim but workable course of action. Max, Baden, and Jimmy would do the actual selection of suitable kinetics. Some Talents could be excused on grounds of infirmity, pregnancy, or unsuitable skills—though two of Baden's "feather-dusters" were well able to handle the fine tunings. Rhyssa, Miklos, and Dolores of the Brazilian Center would attempt to achieve shielded quarters and work shifts of six hours maximum, four for the less experienced kinetics. Barchenka might be running her operation twenty-four hours a day, but eight hours of telekinesis were impossibly draining, even in space and in 0.5-grav conditions.

What we must also organize, for ourselves, Kayankira of the Delhi Center said as the main issues had been resolved, *is an emergency system in a disaster situation.* In her mind churned images of the previous year's catastrophic floods in the northeastern sections of

the Indian subcontinent, mitigated only by the rapid mobilization
of hundreds of kinetics when the precog had come in.

*Kayan, you've had far more experience with that sort of thing than
anyone needs,* Baden said with unexpected humility. *Advise us and we
will comply.*

*You always do! We'll have to strip all nonessential industrial firms and
reduce Port Authority staff to a dangerous minimum. But we shall be very
short of those we most need.*

Weather permitting! was Hongkong Jimmy's droll remark. *When
are we going to find a weatherman?*

If we weather this one, Miklos said, *we can all apply!*

The mindlink was dissolved, and despite the massive task ahead,
the Center directors were much heartened by the contact. When
Rhyssa informed Gordie Havers of the results, he gave a loud
mental cheer for solidarity.

There're going to be some mighty unhappy kinetics! she told him. *Every
Center is going to be stripped, and I'm steeling myself to endure the slings
and arrows of outraged businesses.*

*Machinery predated kinetics, and men used their muscles before that. Let
'em go back to traditional ways. It'll make 'em appreciate us more than
ever.* Gordie imaged an archaic block and tackle to move matériel
usually hoisted by a kinetic. *Who's handling the publicity?*

*We're going to have to be careful about that—don't want Barchenka to
say we're interfering with her ongoing employment drive.*

*The man I have in mind is not a valid Talent, but he's a brilliant
publicist, Rhyssa. Let me get Dave Lehardt to wave the flag for us.*

Dave Lehardt?

He put our honored president in the White House.

And he's not Talented? That's unfair! That campaign was sheer genius!

*We have to allow the Mutes a few prerogatives, you know. Shall I ap-
proach him on this delicate matter?*

Please do. I'll give him all the help I can.

*By the by, did you realize that most of what you do is totally illegal in
Scotland, which still has antiwitchcraft laws on the books?*

Spare me!

*I had, and look what it got us. I'd been working up to the Russkis by way
of the British Isles and Scandinavia. Sorry about that! You never know
where to start in nullifying age-old bigotry, do you!*

When Gordie had broken their mental link, Rhyssa spoke to
Sascha.

You got touched again? he demanded.

In the head, but not by my peeper. She put in his mind all that had happened in the past half hour.

He whistled in a descending scale. *We're going to get a lot of flak from Commerce and Industry!*

They can't have it both ways. They're the group that gave Barchenka such punitive fines if she doesn't deliver on time. That clause is just coming home to roost where they didn't expect it. They'll have to dust off their machinery and toughen up their muscles. We've made it far too easy for them.

What if they like *the old-fashioned ways and don't want to rehire our people?*

Rhyssa snorted derisively. *Just consider how much money kinetics save industry every year in equipment and maintenance costs—the arguments we used to get them to take kinetics in the first place!*

Yeah, but how do we explain it to our kinetics?

Rhyssa projected an image of her on her knees, tearing her hair out, pleading to amorphous faces, offering jewels and ingots of gold. *Enlistment has always been preferable to conscription. And then we can insist on shielding and short shifts. We can't if she implements that blue law. We're over a barrel, and every Talent will realize that!*

Vsevolod can't help us there? Sascha asked.

He was appalled, apologetic, and all, but apopleptic that one of his nationals was doing this to us.

Nothing mentioned about getting the law wiped off the books?

Gordie's working on it! Rhyssa did not bother to lighten the grimness she felt.

Dave Lehardt swung into Rhyssa's tower office at the Henner estate within an hour of the Talents' reluctant acceptance of the inevitable.

"My God, do you have wings?" Rhyssa commented as the energetic Lehardt shook her hand. He was a full two meters tall, athletic in build, and he emanated a competence and geniality that could only come from a secure, well-adjusted personality. He was handsome enough, with mid-brown hair, blue eyes, and regular but not remarkable features, and he dressed with conservative elegance.

"Not wings! Vanes! More reliable," he said with a charming

grin. He began sorting through the papers in his attaché case.
"Gordie said it was urgent, and I watch the news." He stopped
when he noticed her baffled expression. "What's the matter? Did I
break out in spots?"

"No, but you haven't an ounce of Talent, and you ought to."

"Why?" Dave Lehardt shrugged. "I've never needed it. Astute
student of human psychology and keen observer of body language."

He also had an impenetrable natural shield. With all her skill,
she could not read his mind.

"Now," he said, hauling a spare chair up beside hers and spreading out hard copy of advertisements and graphics, "we get in there
before Barchenka even thinks of crowing in triumph, so the public
will see that Talents are graciously mobilizing all available personnel to be sure Padrugoi Platform is finished on schedule—with
phrases that imply she can't make it on her own without Talented
help."

"That's true enough," Rhyssa said grimly.

"Ah, but there are ways and ways of saying the same thing,"
Dave Lehardt said with a truly malicious smile. "I tangled briefly
with the Barchenka Stonewall for another client, and believe me,
I'm on your side!"

Rhyssa smiled to herself. Dave Lehardt did have something like
a Talent—a self-confidence that radiated from him like an aura.
She had never met someone like him before: someone whose men-
tality she could not delve into, however discreetly. It was a new
experience, and she found herself watching his expressive face,
noting the way his hands emphasized points and how he occasionally added a shoulder movement that reinforced what he said. He
also kept glancing at her, meeting her eyes as few non-Talents
would. Clearly he was not the least bit in awe of being in the
presence of one of the top telepathic Talents.

Oblivious to her reactions, he went on. "I've been yearning to
score on our gracious 'Milla." A flicker of some quickly suppressed
emotion shot across his face, but Rhyssa could not decipher it.
"All-out Talent assistance, even at the expense of long-established
links with the public sector, at considerable personal sacrifice—
'Milla doesn't pay the going rates, since hers is a priority contract
and has worldwide backing."

"She will not believe that money is not a consideration . . ."

"Are you aware of the size of her bonus if she gets the station fully operational on time?"

Rhyssa grinned. "One of the best-kept secrets of the Talents. We also know the percentage she has to cough up if she doesn't."

"You are well informed!" He paused with a hopeful expression and then sighed as she merely smiled. "No, I didn't think you'd tell me." He snagged the corner of a graphic sheet from the pile and spread it out. "To address your two points: six-hour shifts and shielding—very alliterative. I'm going to be able to use that as a slogan, you know . . . Have you *demonstrated* the problem?"

"How do you mean 'demonstrated'?"

"Time and motion studies, energy expenditures—that sort of recordable data. Remember, I've seen your kinetics in action, but I doubt that Ludmilla or even Per Duoml have taken the trouble to watch them work. They've been too busy bitching about weightlessness and the silence of space to appreciate the effort kinesis actually takes. I thought you might not have thought of that gimmick. So I had a chat with a Talent I know who was up on the platform, and he gave me some remarkable insights into the actual shift mechanics. *If* the day's matériel was properly organized, the kinetic could put everything in place for the grunts to lock on and weld.

"Then, the noise element. Samjan ran some of the 'noises' past me—" He grimaced and crossed his eyes in sympathy. "—and I think if we did a tape simulation of what a sensitive hears in unshielded quarters and played it back . . ."

"Not to Ludmilla. She insists there is no noise in space."

"She's more of a Mute than I am."

"But I take your point. I hadn't thought of a trick like that."

"No trick, my dear, just presentation—and that's where I'm the expert." His grin was a mixture of impudence and malice.

For the first time in her Talented life, Rhyssa found herself fascinated by a Mute, and half of that fascination was due to the fact that she could not predict what he would do or say next. It was fun matching wits with him during subsequent interviews, giving the onerous task an unexpected exhilaration.

Dave Lehardt was at her side for the initial meeting with a Barchenka who oozed smug satisfaction that she made no attempt to disguise. Rhyssa was hard put to remain civil. Dave Lehardt talked so fast that the engineer had to listen attentively to catch his points. Per Duoml was, as usual, with her, but Rhyssa had been spared another confrontation with Prince Phanibal.

"All we have had is talk, empty talk," Ludmilla Barchenka said when Dave had explained the dual problems of short shifts and shielding. "Even the physically impaired are able to work proper shifts in space: no gravity, no sound!" She shot an accusatory look at Rhyssa.

"Ah, but it is not gravity which is a problem, nor the vacuum. Ludmilla Ivanova, I have arranged a demonstration . . ."

"I have no time for demonstrations," the Exalted Engineer stated dismissively. "I must return to the platform. Already there are delays which must be rectified."

"Understood, Engineer Barchenka," Dave said soothingly, with just the right amount of respect and understanding. "Perhaps Per Duoml will attend. This demonstration is likely to put the basic problems into proper perspective, and thus help us all resolve the main problems with the maximum benefit to your project."

Duoml would be much easier to deal with—his mind was not totally closed, although he was as dedicated to the project as Barchenka. If they could *prove* their points to him, they would be halfway to victory.

"I think she's disappointed she didn't have to invoke that wretched statute," Rhyssa told Sascha later.

"D'you think we gave in too easily?" he asked. "The news quotes Barchenka calling it the 'cowardly capitulation of the effete.'"

"Let her. If we can just swing Duoml to our side." Rhyssa frowned. "I don't see what else we could have done. Dave Lehardt is running public-opinion polls. One point is clear: *Everyone* wants Padrugoi to be finished, *everyone* wants someone else to work up there, and *everyone* thinks people who volunteer for anything are crazy."

The next day, Dave Lehardt and Rhyssa Owen took Personnel Manager Per Duoml to the most prestigious exercise complex in Jerhattan, a facility that occupied the first nine floors of a Residential ziggurat near Central Park. The largest gymnasium was set up with three sets of stress-monitoring paraphernalia and technicians, three pyramids of standard-size packages, a forklift, a bevy of impartial observers, and the Complex director, Menasherat ibn Malik, who had been a multiple Olympic gold medalist for four times running.

Per Duoml was suitably impressed by ibn Malik. So was Rhyssa, for the man exuded physical vitality and competence. He also had no more Talent than Dave Lehardt, who appeared well acquainted with him. Dave stood by, a slight smile on his face, while ibn Malik accepted Per Duoml's homage and conversed amiably with him.

"Now, Manager Duoml," the Complex director said, gesturing to the three men who entered from the side. Stripped down to their shorts, they were all festooned with wires, which were in turn hooked up to the machines. "Let me introduce you to Pavel Korl, bronze medalist in heavyweight boxing; Chas Huntley, a forklift operator with International Canning; and Rick Hobson, the kinetic."

Rhyssa was almost as bemused as Per Duoml as ibn Malik made the introductions. Korl and Huntley were big men, towering over Duoml and certainly making Rick Hobson, who was average in height and build, look insignificant.

"Now, if you would care to check the movables in each pile, Manager Duoml, to assure yourself that they are equal in weight . . ."

Duoml complied, and it was clear that he had to struggle to lift any of them.

"Then once our guinea pigs' wires are double-checked, we can start the test—which is rather simple. By muscle, by machine, and by mind, our subjects will transfer their piles across the floor. The energy levels required, the stress factors, and calories consumed will be displayed on the monitors. Now," ibn Malik said, moving to the big screen set in the wall for use at sporting events, "on Padrugoi, three men will be doing exactly the same in Q hangar." He spoke into his collar mike. "If you're ready up at Padrugoi?" The big screen lit up with a scene not dissimilar to the one around them, except that all the men wore space suits. "In space, our hand shifter is Jesus Manrique, the lifter is operated by Ginny Stanley, and the kinetic is Kevin Clark. Are you all ready? On your marks—" The gold medalist raised his arm. "Get set—*go!*" His arm came down, and the activity on the gym floor and in Q hangar commenced. "This test will last an hour," he informed Per Duoml, gesturing for the observers to take seats to one side.

After the first few minutes, Per Duoml stopped watching the burly figure of Korl manhandling the packages down the floor, or Huntley zipping back and forth on the loader. He kept his eyes either on Rick, who had seated himself at a table and, with no visible effort, kept a steady stream of packages flowing, or on the platform kinetic, who was doing his work while leaning against a stanchion. Occasionally Duoml flicked a look at the monitors chattering out their hard copy.

Both Talents worked their way through their piles in half the time it took the others. The instrumentation proved that they had expended half again as much energy and used up twice as many calories.

When the test had been completed, Dave Lehardt stripped the hard-copy sheets from all six printers. Neatly folding them, he handed the sheaf to Per Duoml, who took it without a word. The test subjects were all thanked and left the gym, Rick Hobson throwing Rhyssa an impudent wink as he walked by.

"You will, of course, wish to analyze the results of this test with your own motion experts, Manager Duoml," Dave Lehardt said, "but I'm sure you recognized the fact that weightlessness grants no bonuses to the kinetic. As to the noise factor . . ." The publicist took a compact recorder from his hip pocket and thumbed it on.

At the babel and squeaks and metallic groans, Per Duoml covered his ears in defense and stared in shock at Rhyssa.

"*That* is what a sensitive 'hears' on the station," Dave said, raising his voice and inserting his words in between the worst of the noise. It was a fair selection, representing the streams of consciousness of eighty mentalities: resentments, complaints, shouts, pains, angers, and myriad metallic noises that some of the kinetics endured. "With ten thousand people living up there already, the mental noise is never-ending. So all that garbage is a constant secondary drain on their nerves, reducing their efficiency if they have no respite from it in shielded quarters."

Having set the decibel rate herself, Rhyssa knew that covering his ears gave Duoml frail protection, but she did not reduce the volume until Dave had finished his little speech.

"I see that you hadn't realized just what we meant by noise," she said finally. "But the cost of shielding personnel quarters for the kinetics is going to be less than the cost of matériel lost or damaged due to tired minds."

"You have made your points," Per Duoml said with a grim expression. "I shall present them to Ludmilla Barchenka."

"Present them and insure their implementation, Per Duoml, and you will have the kinetic assistance you require. Oh, and one other minor point," she added, smiling to take the sting out. "Barchenka is to relay all orders to the kinetics through the regular channels. We will have no more of her rousting Talents out of their quarters at inappropriate hours and insisting on 'extra duty' because her schedule is two minutes out of line! Have I made myself clear on that point?"

He nodded, his expression solemn.

Rhyssa hoped he could convince Barchenka.

CHAPTER 6

N o, *please!*" Peter Reidinger cried as the electrician was
about to disconnect the tri-d in the ward. His cry was
echoed by the other children.

"Look, kids, there's some kind of freaky drain on the hospital's
power supply, and we've finally traced it to this ward. I gotta fix it,
or some of your support systems will go down when they
shouldn't," the electrician said with a hint of exasperation in his
tone.

"No, wait, please," Peter said. "The program's all about the
space platform and the Talents."

"Huh?" The electrician took a better look at the monitor.

"It'll only be a few minutes! Just the newscast!" Peter pleaded.

"Wal, I guess—"

"Shhhh," Peter interrupted, straining to hear the commentator.
Not that he really needed the voice-over to identify the scene as the
estate of the late George Henner, one of the earliest supporters of
the parapsychics. As the camera panned across the trees and lawns,
the boy was startled by the place's eerie familiarity. *This* was the
place he had sought—a place of tranquil greenery and huge old
trees and vine-covered buildings. The place that had scared him
away. And now he knew why. *They* would not want to have their
precinct invaded. *They* needed their privacy to do all the wonderful
things they did. Like help to finish the last three spokes of the
Padrugoi Platform so that mankind could, at last, reach for the
stars.

"It's not only the Talented who are making a sacrifice," the commentator went on, still standing in that marvelous oasis, "for Industry and Commerce have granted leave of absence to their Tal-

ented employees to assist with this final push out to space. Platform Manager Ludmilla Barchenka announces that the most ambitious world project yet undertaken will be completed on schedule. And now to other news in the Jerhattan district . . ."

"Okay, mister," Peter said, relaxing against his frame. "That's what we wanted to see."

"You're not looking for a career in space, are you?" the electrician asked, half-teasing. He was always a little nervous around kids who were so badly injured.

Peter cocked his head at him. "Why not? With no gravity, I wouldn't be stuck in this frame, and a push of my toe or my little finger—" He waggled the two extremities, which were, after months of therapy, all he *could* move. "—I could float about."

"Yeah, I guess you could. Now, nurse, can I start with this frame?" the electrician asked, gesturing to the multiple-tasking device that gave Peter what independence he had in his condition.

"Yes, it's time for Peter's body-brace session anyway," Sue Romero said. "C'mon, Peter."

"Aw, do I have to? Couldn't I watch what he does?"

"No, the moment for positive thinking has come. Let me see that limbic-system smile on your face."

Peter hated the body brace and the morning's "torture session," as he mentally categorized the therapy. He felt heavy in the frame, his body more lifeless than ever. "But see, I can move my big toe and my little finger. Please . . ."

"Hey, what the—?" the electrician exclaimed. The diagnostic reader he had just hooked up had unexpectedly registered a blip.

While Peter gamely concentrated on his body-brace drills, the electrician checked out the bed's wiring, but except for that one brief blip, he could find no short, no dysfunction in any of the circuitry. By the time an exhausted Peter was back in his bed, the electrician had done a thorough test of all the specialized treatment electronics in the ward. Baffled by the continual surges on the ward's circuits, the man left a small monitor attached to the one piece of equipment that had registered an abnormality, slight though it had been, and left.

Peter knew by her face that Sue Romero was disappointed in him. He did try to make his body remember how to move. The frame sent electrical impulses into his atrophied muscles, the theory being that the little jolts would restimulate neural and muscu-

lar activity. He hated that intrusion into his body even muic than
he hated being paralyzed.

"Peter, if you would only stop resisting the mechanism," Sue
said reproachfully. "If you would only go with it, instead of denying the help it could give you. You could, you know, even get to the
platform. Your schoolwork was excellent—there'd be no problem
with the educational end . . ." She trailed off, fighting her own
dispiritedness. Sometimes with the very badly damaged children,
she felt she was pounding at the well-known immovable object—
generally, as in Peter's case, the child itself.

The boy was exhausted, eyes closed, arms and legs sprawled just
as he had been rolled out of the body brace. Sue Romero could not
afford to pity him—it was unprofessional and helped neither of
them in his rehabilitation—but she did. As she turned away, she
thought he was sleeping. She would have been amazed to learn that
he was reviewing that vision of the Center, with its trees and lawns
and . . . Rhyssa Owen.

That night, Rhyssa was wakeful, going over and over that tele-
cast. She had felt good about it during filming. Dave Lehardt
had done his job well. They would, of course, have to wait until
opinions had been sampled, but Rhyssa felt that Barchenka was
coming out a poor second at the moment, despite her apparent
triumph at the cowardly capitulation of the effete Talents. Rhyssa
fretted that she had somehow weakened the consolidated strength
of Talents and wondered how she could rectify what was still, in
the minds of most Talented, an untenable position with Barchenka
getting her way.

She felt then the gossamer touch—envious, yearning, wistful,
and so terribly sad that a sob clogged her throat.

Wait, little friend, she murmured in the softest of tones.

Say what? With the voice came mixed impressions of startlement,
sense of apology-denial-rejection, and an astringent smell. And
then the touch—timorous and reluctant—was gone.

Rhyssa tried to follow, her touch feather soft, but the retreat had
been too swift, like a flicker of shadow across the moonlight outside her window. She made a quick note of the time: 3:43. Then she
lay there savoring that touch, examining it, letting her perception
analyze it.

Such swiftness suggested a young mind—no old thoughts or experiences to slow the instantaneity of action. A boy on a prank . . . A boy? Doing an out-of-body maneuver? A boy in a hospital— yes, a hospital would account for the astringent odor—his movement constrained so that only his mind could travel?

That fit the pieces together so perfectly that Rhyssa got out of bed and paced over to the console.

"Bud, I want a call out to all hospital Talents," she said, unable to keep the elation out of her voice.

"The peeper caught you again?"

"That's right. An adolescent boy, quite likely crippled or paralyzed. I want to see who was awake on the wards at three-forty-three this morning."

"The last thing you need tonight is some pimple-faced nerd rousing you."

"On the contrary, Bud, I think that's exactly what I did need. A youngster able to go out of body? He's got to have fantastic potential."

"For what?" Budworth wanted to know.

"*That,*" Rhyssa said with a surge of hope, "is what we'll have to find out."

As she climbed back into bed, she had a lot to think about before she could compose herself for sleep. How long had it been since a new Talent that strong had been identified? And what sort of a Talent was it? Even strong telepathy did not leave an image, however transparent. A new type of kinesis? Very few kinetics could move themselves! Inanimate objects, yes, but animate ones, no. Most out-of-body experiences were the results of traumas and useless in a commercial sense—and theorists still argued over whether the out-of-body phenomenon was a kinetic manifestation or a strong telepathic projection.

Just remember, she told herself that it was the commercial applications of Talents that provided us with legal immunities, good jobs, and special status for the past four score years . . . and let us get marvelously complacent. Maybe it wasn't really "noise" that even kinetics heard in space but some other form of interstellar communication, a multilingual garble that they were picking up. Open your mind up, gal. Look around you. Look at Dave Lehardt. He has to be Talented, even if it won't register on a Goosegg graph.

Why, Rhyssa Owen, she asked herself, does Dave Lehardt *have* to be Talented?

And that was the quandary she fussed over as she finally slipped into an uneasy sleep.

I discovered some interesting new facets of employment on the platform," Dave Lehardt told Rhyssa in her office two days later. "Came out in further talks with my platform contact, Samjan, and a few judicious inquiries." He gave her a humorless grin. "The casualties."

"Yes, the total is horrific." Rhyssa shuddered. "But working in space there were bound to be some."

"Some?" Dave raised his eyebrows. "Some, yes, but when I checked with Johnny Greene in Altenbach's office, we found several different sets of figures on the casualty rate."

Rhyssa straightened. When Dave had arrived unexpectedly, she had been busy reshuffling the rotas of the Center's kinetics, steeling herself to endure their understandable reproaches and arguments. Any interruption was welcome.

"Then I got JG and Samjan together, and they both did a bit of research," he went on, "and, using their security clearances, they came up with what we think are the real statistics." His expression was bleak, and there was a stillness about his body that forewarned her. "You know how the unemployed are terrified to be conscripted to Padrugoi? They may not be Talented, but they've got an instinct about baaaaaad situations. They have good reason not to want to get conscripted. She loses grunts at a frightening rate, far beyond the allowable. The major reason is because Barchenka's so bloody-minded about keeping her Sacred Schedules, she won't interrupt a shift to retrieve drifters!"

To be sure she understood his meaning, Rhyssa unconsciously tried to read his mind. It was like stubbing her toe on a stair riser, and she blinked. "Run that past me again, please, Dave," she asked, struggling with confusion at her inability to read him the way she was used to reading most of her friends.

"Surely you've seen the promotional footage," he said, "with the grunts suited up and pushing gi-normous sections of a spoke with the tips of their fingers or a spare foot?"

"Yes . . ."

"In the *real* working situation, not that mockup they did for recruitment, a worker'll push too hard, and with every action causing a reaction in space, the poor sod goes spinning off into the dark deeps."

"Yes . . ."

"Well, Barchenka doesn't stop work to rescue them. Oh, no, anyone that stupid has to wait until the shift is over before his buddies are allowed to go after him. That is, *if* a skiff is available, and *if* the bod's been tracked."

Appalled at the vivid scene his words evoked, Rhyssa stared at him. "Is this public knowledge?"

He gave her a cynical look. "Why do you think the grunts never take surface leave? It's not the fact that they're paid so little that they can't afford surface leave, or that there's no available space on shuttles for mere grunts, or that they're unlikely to have any family to visit on Earth. It's that they're plain not allowed back down to tell *anyone* what's happening. The grunts are also segregated so that even the observant among the more elite employees don't know exactly what's going on. It took both JG and Samjan and some long program analyses to piece fact out of the publicly available fictions."

"But all the recruitment films show safety lines and . . ." Part of Rhyssa crowed with delight at discovering Barchenka resorting to very questionable tactics, while another part balked at the enormity of the crime.

"That's *promo* footage, my dear director. The theory is great. In practice, Barchenka dispensed with safety lines—they kept getting tangled in equipment, slowing down her precious work schedule. So safety lines are a space myth.

"And Barchenka has such saving ways." Dave Lehardt perched his lean frame on the edge of her desk. "For instance, we discovered by an analysis of records that a suited grunt is given only enough air in his tanks for that shift and maybe a sniff or two left over. Oh, there's plenty of safety regs for the engineers and supervisors and skilled technicians—but not the grunts. She doesn't care what happens to them. There're plenty more where they came from."

Rhyssa was outraged. "You just validated my instincts about that woman. Law be damned, I won't ask my kinetics to face such risks!"

Dave gave a snort. "*They're* far too valuable to be risked. There'd be too much of a stink kicked up if a drifting Talent wasn't retrieved right then. Overworked, yes. Samjan confirmed the notion that eight-hour shifts are another platform fallacy.

"On top of that conspicuous savings of consumables, I uncovered several other little anomalies: grunt suits have limited-range com units. They can't be heard shrieking for help! Might disturb their fellow workers."

Rhyssa stared at him aghast.

"There's also a high incidence of agoraphobia among the grunts and genuine space cafard. But ailing grunts are never transferred down. They just disappear! Accidental death! Never suicide! Always accidental. After all," he said, taking on a mock Russian accent, "everyone knows how dangerous it is to ignore safety warnings and procedures. And then there appears to be a neat little system which causes unexpected casualties during the routine drills they so conspicuously hold from time to time on Padrugoi." Dave paused again. "Checking through medical records, it becomes apparent that the unfortunate victims of those drill 'accidents' are always either the injured or the headcases."

"Oh, my God, Dave!" Rhyssa propelled herself from her chair to pace agitatedly up and down the tower room. "*Why* haven't any of the precogs caught this?"

"According to your brief summary on Talents' capabilities, precogs usually latch onto large numbers, Rhyssa. There are never enough—"

"Numerics is no excuse!" Rhyssa was surprised by a vehemence that answered the despair in his voice. She wondered if his mind, too, was filled with faceless forms, twisting and turning in space, drifting farther and farther from the network of lights that was the oasis of air and warmth in the blackness, and a violent shudder seized her.

A warm hand cupped her shoulder. "Easy! Talent spreads itself thin enough as it is. You're not God, or gods, to mark each sparrow's fall."

She blinked and looked up at him. Though his mind was as closed to her as ever, the sympathy and understanding in his warm blue eyes was obvious. She would not tell him that Talents generally disliked tactile contact—surprisingly enough, she had discovered that she liked him touching her.

"Armed with this information, however, you can spread Barchenka over a barrel." His voice was soft and teasing. "If you see what I mean. Or, maybe you Talents are too simon-pure to lower yourselves to outright blackmail."

"Not when the lives and safety of my Talents are at risk, I'm not," Rhyssa declared stoutly. "Not to mention those poor sods who've not even been given half a chance to survive. I'll insist on short shifts and shields, and we'll increase that ante to safety lines for everyone working on the platform and the deployment of rescue skiffs. Or do skiffs have limited power and air on them, too, so as to save costs?"

He crossed his arms on his chest, grinning at her. "Your Talents wouldn't be at risk anyway, unless I've misunderstood their capabilities. There's no way Barchenka can pull the same tricks on *them* that she does with the poor grunts. And unless your response is unique among your ilk, I can't see your folk standing by for some of her tricks, once they know what to look for. Some of the kinetics are telepaths, aren't they?"

"Quite a few." Rhyssa gave a sardonic chuckle. "A fact we haven't actually mentioned to Barchenka, whose understanding of Talent is severely limited."

Dave let out a bark of laugh. "Not the whole truth nor even half the truth, huh? Good girl, Rhyssa!" He playfully knuckled her chin. "Is distance a problem? Or the vacuum of space?" When Rhyssa shook her head, he went on. "Well, you guys could sure be popular with the grunts because *you*"—he waggled his finger at her —"could be *their* insurance. A Talent could haul back a drifter, couldn't he? Without asking for permission during his shift, or waiting for a skiff?" He gave her a broad smile. "That'll help a lot of ways. Damned good PR, too. The best, because it proves that the Talents will help the ordinary grunt where Barchenka just simply hasn't!"

Rhyssa suddenly turned away, not wanting Dave to see her expression. *Sascha?* she called. *I've just found the perfect job for Madlyn! Tell you later!*

I can read your evil mind, Sascha said, *and she's not even on the list for the platform.*

She is, as of right now, Rhyssa replied. *How often have you said that Madlyn could be heard at the space platform? We'll just put it to the test!*

She smoothed her expression and looked up at Dave Lehardt, who
was eyeing her keenly.

"Who were you talking to just then? And don't hold out on me.
I'm getting used to your ways, woman!" His voice rippled with an
odd emotion, and the gleam in his eyes intensified.

Rhyssa's grin was half embarrassment at his scrutiny and half
delight with her inspiration. "We've got a telepath with an extraordinarily loud voice. We'll send her up in an administrative capacity. Put her on a radar scope, and she'll locate and reassure any
drifters for the nearest kinetic to haul back to safety."

"Lady, you don't realize what a difference that could make to
morale up at the platform." Dave's grin was so infectious that
Rhyssa had to grin back. "Not only is Barchenka unaware that
she's her own worst enemy, but her ignorance about Talent in
general will prevent her from realizing that she's just hired a bat-
talion of undercover agents."

"*That's* the beauty part!" Rhyssa said, grinning more broadly.
"Does Duoml? Or Prince Phanibal?"

Dave Lehardt considered briefly. "Prince Phanibal might, but
he's not on the platform as much lately—some crisis in Malaysia
that occupies a lot of his time. Besides, I read him as being just
ornery enough not to tell her something as crucial at this time for
the sheer pleasure of watching her squirm. Now what's this emergency clause Lance Baden wants added to the contracts?"

"In case of a major emergency, we must be able to bring Talents
back down. You remember the floods last monsoon on the Indian
continent and that major shake in Azerbaijan? We knew about each
of them ten days before, so we were able to muster help and reduce
the effect of the catastrophe. Sending her a hundred and forty-four
kinetics has wiped out our disaster-squad organization. We want a
twenty-four-hour clause—to bring key personnel back to Earth in
time to cope here."

"Can't you teleport 'em down?"

Rhyssa laughed. "No, more's the pity. Our Talents are finite,
definite, and nowhere near such a fantasy application as instantaneous transmissions. That takes more power than a human brain
can generate."

"I thought the Moral Code on legitimate bio-engineering permitted—"

"Hold it right there, Dave." Rhyssa held up a warding hand.

"Read the Code: congenital defects, yes—manipulations, no. And I doubt any genetic engineer would monkey with the brain yet—even a monkey's brain."

"If you can find one. Though don't you think it's likely that someone has been doing illicit experimentation, the world being what it is these days?"

"That's cynical of you, Dave."

"Sometimes saying no is registering a challenge," he replied with a shrug. "I wouldn't rule out the possibility."

"Meanwhile," Rhyssa said, bringing the discussion firmly back to relevant matters, "I'd very much like to see a full report on what JG and Samjan have been discovering about platform personnel problems."

Dave grinned, taking three diskettes from a breast pocket. "I thought you might. Gives you a stronger bargaining position for shields, short shift—"

"Safety lines and skiffs," Rhyssa finished, taking the diskettes but letting her fingers linger on his a little longer than the transactions required. "I thank you, sir." What on earth was happening to her in Dave Lehardt's presence? She felt as giddy as—as Madlyn could be in Sascha's company.

When Per Duoml, Prince Phanibal Shimaz, and two other minor officials, one of them the accommodations officer, arrived to settle the minor details, Dave Lehardt had another presentation that altered the proceedings. Rhyssa, sitting with Max Perigeaux, Gordie Havers, and Lance Baden, found the meeting eminently satisfying.

Showing the accurate fatality statistics—figures that bleached all color from the faces of Duoml and the prince—Dave Lehardt talked knowledgeably of some of the "minor" problems that the Talents would be willing to undertake, such as the retrieval of any suited workers experiencing "malfunction of suit jets," and telepathic contact "with those using short-range com units," plus monitoring systems; they would also include among the Talents two with broad diagnostic capabilities. Dave pointed out that the savings on skiff fuel and man-hours required for retrieval would more than compensate for the cost of shielding required in Talent accommodations.

Nor was there any discussion about the emergency clause. Lance Baden announced that he was to be Talent liaison with the engineering staff and that was that.

And what were they saying about cowardly capitulations? Lance commented.

R hyssa was so weary from accumulated stresses that she experienced no elation at having forced every single concession out of the Padrugoi officials. She wanted nothing more than a quiet supper and some mental peace. Per Duoml had a natural shield, but the other project representatives at the meeting had not, and when their initial euphoria at coercing Talents onto the work force was burst by hard facts and figures and compromises, their emotional responses of anger, horror, and embarrassment had been hard to deflect.

Sascha: *I've cleared everyone out of the first floor. Relax!*

Rhyssa: *Oh, you are a pet!*

Sascha: *Lot of good it does me!* But she knew he was only teasing.

Rhyssa entered the Henner house, appreciative of the deep silence in the elegantly appointed rooms. Very little had been altered from the days of George Henner, the parapsychics' first benefactor: all had been lovingly preserved in his memory. The subterranean offices, the annexes, and her tower were modern, with state-of-the-art technology, but the main reception rooms were reminders of more leisurely times. The kitchen, where modern appointments were hidden behind old-fashioned cupboards, exuded an aura of comfort—it was spacious, with an archaic but working fireplace, a huge table, and comfortable chairs. The dining portion faced onto the gardens at the rear of the main house, bright with blooms and bushes.

Some thoughtful kinetic had activated the kettle. She made herself a cup of tea, found sandwiches in the crisper, and kicking off her shoes, curled up in one of the wing chairs.

There was something amazingly restorative about looking out onto the garden, watching the flowers move in the light breeze. She set her mind adrift, savoring the quiet, despite the deep-seated nagging presentiment.

"I'm not a precog," she told herself and sipped her tea. "What I am feeling is just reaction to the last few hectic days. A quite natural depression."

Then she felt the touch, once again colored with wistfulness and a deep sadness that pierced her to the heart, making her own malaise seem insignificant.

She dared not reach out for fear of startling the boy. Boy he was, and despairing. Had her transitory unease triggered a response from him midday? Or was it his need seeking consolation? What could so desolate a young person? One could endure detached misery—tragedy happening at a distance to people one had never met —but to *feel* the palpitating misery of another person was an intense experience.

Delicately she impinged on the boy's mind, hoping to gain some clue to his whereabouts. He was dreading something, and the yearning for trees and lawn and flowers and *someplace* that was not hospital had precipitated the nebulous contact. And her mind, less controlled than usual in its weariness, had attracted his. Dreading what? She inserted the question.

The body brace!

Rhyssa had not expected an answer. She tried to keep the lightest of contacts, though, oddly enough, he felt very close at that moment. *Isn't it meant to help?* she asked cautiously.

It doesn't. It hurts. It's artificial, it's awful. It's a cage. The bed is bad enough. I don't want to. I— don't—want—to!

A wail from the depth of a forlorn and comfortless mind reached her—then it was abruptly cut off.

We got another one of those surges this afternoon—usually we get 'em at night," the hospital's maintenance man said as he held up the printout to the consultant engineer whom the concerned hospital administration had finally called in.

The engineer peered at the peak, a sudden sharp deviation lasting seventy-two seconds. He asked for the other anomalies and was presented with further examples. "Shouldn't be any drain on the systems at three-forty-three, three-oh-three, three-fifty-two, or three-thirteen. You've checked all the equipment?"

"I put meters on several floors. Got a blip on PedOrth Ward Twelve when I was installing it. So I took everything apart on that ward and there wasn't nothing malfunctioning. Craziest thing I've ever seen. And you know how Admin is when you got outages and anomalies with all them life-support systems hooked up. Funny though, nothing in the ICUs."

"Okay, screen me your schematics for all the equipment on PedOrth and see what's being used there." The engineer sighed heavily—he could see it was going to be one of those days.

A stir around the beds in the circular ward alerted Peter Reidinger, and he blinked away the screen that blocked his view. A very old lady stood in the doorway, Miz Allen hovering with her "you'd-better-behave" look on her face as she glanced around the ward to be sure everything was in order for the visitor.

Instantly Peter's attention was riveted on the lady. She was different. That became more apparent to him as Miz Allen began to introduce her to the kids in the ward. Cecily even smiled and answered the lady. Cecily was a spina bifida case who "ought" to have been corrected in utero but had not been. Osteomyelitis had caused her to have one leg amputated, and her recovery from that operation was very slow. She rarely opened up to other people— and particularly not to strangers—so her response to the old lady was a minor miracle. Peter was in a sweat of anticipation by the time the lady reached him.

"This is Peter Reidinger, Ms. Horvath." The way Miz Allen cocked her right eyebrow told Peter that he had better behave himself.

Ms. Horvath just smiled down at him, her eyes twinkling, and they were not at all old, or rheumy, or hard. He wondered she let herself look so old.

I promised my husband that I would grow old gracefully, she startled him by saying. *That way I wouldn't surprise people so much when I don't act my age.*

Peter goggled at her. She had not moved her lips—and yet he had heard her voice clearly in his mind.

"Peter . . ." Miz Allen prompted him.

"Pleased ta meetcha!" Peter managed to get out. Miz Allen cleared her throat warningly.

"Thank you, Mrs. Allen, I'll just chat a bit with Peter," Dorotea Horvath said, pulling a chair to Peter's bedside and dismissing Miz Allen in a manner that astounded the boy. *Miz Allen doesn't really believe in telepathy and Talents. And we just haven't had the chance to go around the pediatric wards lately. So we missed you.*

"Missed me?"

Dorotea smiled again, a smile that was magical because it seemed to envelop Peter with warmth and caring. The hard knot of self-pity and resentment that had been building up at the thought of another body-brace session dispersed.

"That is, until you started visiting Rhyssa."

"Rhyssa?"

Into his mind came a new touch. *I'm Rhyssa. I sent Dorotea to you because you run away from me. Dorotea says you can't run away from her right now, Peter Reidinger. Please come live with us where I know you long to be.*

"Now that you've had an official invitation, will you accept?" Dorotea asked, brimming over with amusement at his stunned reaction.

"But I can't. I'm crippled. I can't go anywhere . . ."

Ahahahaha! Dorotea chided him, still smiling. *A boy who can go out of body on tours of Jerhattan at three in the morning is no cripple!*

"But I can't *use* the body brace!" Peter was horrified to hear himself blubbering and to feel tears streaming down his face. He had not cried in months.

Crying's a natural release for emotional pressures, Dorotea said as she blotted his cheeks matter-of-factly. *All that manly repression has also been blocking Talent. I do believe that the brace also posed an inhibition. I think it short-circuited natural ability. We'll sort it out. Of that I'm positive.*

And suddenly Peter had no doubt at all.

"First, of course, we have to get your parents' permission." Dorotea was always practical. "Do you think they'll mind?"

"Mind?" Peter nearly shouted. He knew that the hospital fees, even with the huge compensation the city was forced to pay since he had been injured on city-owned property, had been a terrible financial drain on his parents. His mother came to see him regularly, but his father's visits grew fewer and shorter. His mother always had some plausible explanation for Dad's absence, but Peter had not been fooled.

Suddenly Dorotea's eyes widened in pleased surprise. "I don't think you'll need much training after all," she said, pointing at him.

"What?" And at that moment Peter realized that he was hovering above his bed—and that an alarm just beneath it had gone off.

Rhyssa! Dorotea's mental shout was a very welcome diversion for Rhyssa.

The Eastern director had not been able to make that first contact for several reasons, the foremost one being the Padrugoi priority. The other reason was that Dorotea was still the most accurate Talent diviner in the entire world, with the deftest touch to allay fear and suspicion.

Rhyssa, Peter Reidinger reeks of Talent. I can't imagine why the resident didn't tumble to it a long time ago, despite the fact that Peter's been suppressing his natural feelings to be considered a brave boy. Being in a hospital situation, he'd have to blank out all peripheral static or get wound up in everyone else's pain. Though he's not your garden-variety kinetic or telepath. In fact, I've never touched anyone quite like him. One thing's sure, he no more needed a body brace than you need a videophone.

Can you expedite his release to us? Rhyssa asked.

In my best granny mode! I don't anticipate any trouble with the family —they've been struggling under the medical costs. I gather the father has trouble visiting his "crippled" son. They should regain some perspective now that Peter'll be able to pay his own way.

How medical is he?

Dorotea gave a mental snort. *With a little help from his friends, he won't be medical past the gate of the Center. Whoops! We've just been charged by an irate electrician and a stupefied consultant, and—my God!*

Dorotea broke off contact, startling Rhyssa—Dorotea usually had no trouble double-talking. Rhyssa waited for the old woman to come back and explain her abrupt disappearance. After three minutes with no further word from her, Rhyssa reluctantly resumed her immediate task.

Worried about Dorotea and the boy, it was difficult for her to keep her mind on the reassignment of kinetic Talents, but the matter had to be cleared up as soon as possible. The Eastern Center would be left with just ten to do the work of thirty, along with five trainees who could be slotted into some of the less exacting hoist work. Airshuttle clients, passengers or commercial, were just going to have to wait longer to collect their luggage; all construction firms would lose kinetics, save those on two nearly completed projects where kinesis was the only way to safely install heavy equipment on the uppermost stories.

She and Miklos Horvath, Dorotea's grandson on the West Coast, also had to arrange "fetch and carry" teams, telepaths and kinetics who could work in tandem and at long distance. But such skills were exhausting and would have to be reserved for emergencies.

Dave Lehardt had come up with yet another valid suggestion that might not improve relations with Barchenka and Duoml but would certainly make more effective use of the four-hour shift of each kinetic.

"I looked at some of the motion studies," he had told her, "and some videos of an actual working day. Samjan mentioned that he spent a good portion of every shift on Padrugoi doing nothing—waiting until matériel was organized from the storage yard or bins, or while the engineers sorted out minor discrepancies. So I got Samjan and Bela Rondomanski, who was Space Lab designer, together with Lance Baden, who's a trained engineer. Bela said a lot of the delays on Space Lab were caused by a chronic disorganization in Supply. Lance said that the problems hadn't been completely solved when he did two tours at Padrugoi, but one of Barchenka's strengths is her organizational skills. Take them one more step forward, and, in a four-hour shift, a kinetic can get everything in a spoke section lined up so that all the grunts need to do during the next twenty hours of shift time is give a tiny shove and the elements will fall into place.

"Of course, it'll mean a good deal of reorganization in the stores and matériel already up at Padrugoi, and maybe some shipment rearranging, lighting a fire under the tardy suppliers, but the time spent doing *that* will cut down on the man-hours upstairs."

"Duoml's returned to the station," Rhyssa said.

"We'll just borrow Hangar Q again for another handy little demonstration. I'll work out the details. Hey, you're looking mighty good today. New hairstyle? Sure shows off your skunk streak." Her screen diffused on another of his famous confidence-inspiring grins.

Skunk streak indeed, she thought, her fingers smoothing it back. At least he had noticed. With a sigh, she went back to her analyses, until she realized that she had not heard another squeak from Dorotea.

Then, as abruptly as the contact had been broken, Dorotea returned.

Well, I said I'd come back as soon as I could. It's too soon to be sure what he does do, Rhyssa, but he apparently taps into electrical sources. He's been glitching the hospital circuits fit to drive the electrician and a high-priced consultant barmy. And it also explains why he couldn't cope with the body brace: the impulses which were fed directly into his synapses were short-circuiting inherent abilities, so the poor lad was trying to cope with an overload. Sue Romero is in bits thinking of all she's been doing to Peter, and he's in a state because he had no way of explaining why the body brace was all wrong *for him . . . and the head nurse, Miz Allen, is one of those by-the-bookers and compounded the problem. Oh, his family are delighted, especially to know that Peter will not be "handicapped"—but their heads read "crippled, useless, financial drain." It'll be standard contract until he's eighteen and fully trained. Here's one kinetic Barchenka won't get her space gloves on!*

When can you bring him home?

We're on our way! Dorotea replied triumphantly. *Get Roddy's room in my house ready.* She shot Rhyssa a mental glimpse of Space-Force posters on every wall, models of space shuttles, mass passenger hotels, stealths, space labs, and generation ships depending from the ceiling, and a bunk bed with desk space below. *Nothing could be more distant from the antiseptic environment he's been living in for months.*

The physical meeting between Rhyssa Owen and Peter Reidinger was not quite an anticlimax. Dorotea had warned her that Peter's mother and older sister were accompanying him in the heli-amb, excited but slightly apprehensive at his new circumstances.

Ilsa Reidinger was a pleasant enough woman, terribly concerned for and certainly extremely proud of her Petey. She struggled with a less than congenial job in order to help meet the medical bills. The sixteen-year-old sister, Katya, was what Dorotea called "pushy," trying to figure out how her brother's good fortune might spill over on her and disgruntled that Peter had Talent and she had none. Dorotea said that Katya resented Peter because the cost of his hospitalization had kept her from having many of the things that she, the elder child, ought to have been able to enjoy.

Perfectly understandable reaction, Dorotea told Rhyssa as the women deftly maneuvered Peter's gurney into Dorotea's house and on through into Roddy's room.

Both telepaths could feel Peter's spirit lifting as he saw the un-medical furnishings and artifacts.

"But how'll you do all that has to be done *for* him all the time?" Ilsa Reidinger began in surprise.

"Oh, Peter'll only need a little help in the beginning, Mrs. Rei-dinger," Dorotea said. Her mental *Alley oop* was the signal for Rick Hobson to "lift" Peter up into the bunk bed. "Now, let's all clear out and let him settle himself in. And," Dorotea added as she shooed everyone before her, "the heli-amb is waiting to take you and your daughter home. Here's the vid number. As you saw, Pe-ter has a set in the room. Call him any time. Unlike the hospital, here you can see what mischief he's getting into. All right?"

Dorotea's positive manner made refusal impossible, and soon the heli-amb was thunking its way up out of the Center's grounds.

Rick, hook me up a line from the 4.5-kpm generator in the garden shed and bring it right into the room with Peter, Dorotea requested.

What is *this all about?* Rhyssa demanded.

I told you, Dorotea said, then added aloud since they were now alone, "he seems to tap into the electrical system and use *that* for power. Some sort of a gestalt. I want some of our engineer Talents to link with me when he's rested enough for us to do some testing. But it'll have to be you and me for a while, Rhyssa. He's had such a terrible time."

Dorotea's eyes welled with tears, and automatically Rhyssa gath-ered the older woman into her arms, smothering her with love, affection, and admiration.

"I'm sorry, dear," Dorotea said with a little sniff, pulling herself away. "You've had a lot to cope with now, and you don't need me turning into a watering pot, but—" She poured into Rhyssa's mind the jumble of pain/despondency/anguish/guilt, the self-accusa-tion, and the soul-destroying terror that Peter had been enduring.

Easing Dorotea to the couch, Rhyssa sat beside her, shaken by that accounting despite years of dealing with the bizarre mental states of emergent Talents.

"I think a spot of tea would go down well right now," Dorotea said, and Rhyssa gave a weak little laugh at Dorotea's ever practical mind. *Peter? A cup of tea? Lemon, milk, sugar?*

Yes, please, was Peter's answer, surprising Rhyssa.

You see? He needed only a little help to project his thoughts instead of squashing them down. Dorotea's face wore an exaggeratedly smug smile.

They were all enjoying a cup of tea when Rick Hobson bounced in, festooned with an electrician's belt and heavy-duty cable.

"I don't know what kind of an outlet or receptacle you need, Dorotea," he said, winking at her, nodding to Rhyssa, and then waving a hand at Peter, who was watching it all from his bunk.

"Well, Peter, what do you think you need?" Dorotea asked. "He'd just been sort of hooking in to the electronic gadgets of the bed," she told Rick.

Both women caught Peter's hesitation and concern.

"Oh, well, it's as easy to sort the specifics out later," Rick said easily, catching Rhyssa's warning look. "At any rate, the generator's right outside and powered up. Any time you need it, it's there." With a cheery wave to all, he left.

"It's all a bit much, isn't it, Peter?" Rhyssa said gently.

"I don't know what I did that makes you think I'm any good at all," Peter said in a voice as pale as his complexion just then.

"Dorotea thinks you used available electrical power to assist those dawn visits you made to me," Rhyssa told him. She gave him a mischievous smile to reassure him. "I'm honored that it was my mind you linked with to bring you where you wanted to be."

"You are?" Peter turned his head away from the drinking straw in his teacup so that he could look down at Rhyssa.

"I don't get many men invading my bedroom, I assure you."

Subtly Dorotea was supporting her, increasing for Peter the sense that his intrusion had been clever and original. Both women generated subliminal thoughts to bolster his perception of himself, reversing the low self-esteem that was currently inhibiting any forward progress.

"I didn't *mean* to intrude."

"You will soon understand that among telepaths a midnight knock on the door isn't considered an intrusion."

"But all those lights . . ."

Rhyssa let her thoughts echo the annoyance she had felt at that proprietary supervision. "You didn't hear me chewing them out for scaring you off, either."

"Ooooh, Rhyssa was angry," Dorotea added.

"You were doing what many have tried and failed at miserably," Rhyssa went on.

"I was?"

"It's what we call an out-of-body experience," Rhyssa went on. "Very few people ever achieve that degree of mental control."

"They don't?" Peter was wide-eyed in awe. "But it's not hard."

Dorotea and Rhyssa exchanged amused glances.

"Nothing's hard when you know exactly how to do it, Peter," Rhyssa said, "and you've apparently mastered the art. Dorotea and I are both hoping you can teach us. I don't have much kinetic ability . . ."

Sascha: *And aren't you glad of that right now?* He sent an image of a space-suited Rhyssa whirling about Padrugoi chased by a whip-wielding Barchenka.

Rhyssa: *Don't you dare interfere, Bearman! This is tricky enough as it is without you in my mind! Oh, my God!* And suddenly Rhyssa began to fathom the potential of the boy. Give young Peter Reidinger access to sufficiently powerful electronic sources, and his kinetic Talent might boggle the mind of the most optimistic theorist. Why, his Talent was as far from spoon bending as modern precognition was from priestly auguries divined from ox intestines!

There was an instant response from Sascha, Dorotea, Sirikit, Rick, and Madlyn. *Damp it down, Rhyssa. Have a heart!*

Dorotea: *Well, you've all got the picture now, so leave us alone with the boy. We can't mess this one up.*

Rhyssa had to take a deep breath, hoping that the sudden revelation she had been unable to keep from other strong telepaths in the Center had not also been picked up by Peter Reidinger's still-emerging skill. He was certainly not reacting.

Dorotea: *I blocked him, Rhyssa. Get ahold of yourself.*

"So, Peter," Rhyssa managed to go on, "if I could get the hang of what you're doing with the generators, it could be an extremely valuable added whammy."

Dorotea: *I couldn't have put it more discreetly myself.*

Rhyssa: *Thanks.*

"I don't know what I'm doing," Peter said sadly.

"It's the sort of thing you don't *think* about doing, Peter. You just *do* it—because you want to, because you need to. And Dorotea and I will help." Rhyssa grinned at him. "Communication is where telepathy excels. The spoken word sometimes isn't as clear as it should be: words can be misused, inappropriately assigned muddy meanings. You're accustomed to a word meaning one thing; someone else will think it means something else entirely and misunderstand what you just said. Speaking mind-to-mind clears up a lot of such confusions. Or have I just confused you more?"

Peter began to smile suddenly. "Like how I couldn't explain to Miz Romero just *why* I hated the body brace."

"That's a very apt example, Peter. You just didn't have the words for the concept of that sort of interference."

"But how'll I move without a brace?"

"By the power of your mind alone, which is exactly what you did when you were going out of body. Only we'll teach you how to take your body along with you! *And* manage most of your daily care. You won't be dependent on nurses or orderlies or anyone. In one sense it was what Sue was trying to get you to do—make your mind motivate your body to remember what it once could do. Only you took it one step beyond that, and neither of you knew you had latent kinetic ability. So, of course you couldn't do what she wanted. You were a good jump ahead of her."

He was still skeptical. "I'm kinetic?"

"Do you know what the word means?"

"Sure. But I didn't think I was."

Rhyssa rose. "Well, you are. So think about it."

Dorotea retrieved his cup. "You take a rest now, dear. Then I'll show you about the house so you'll know where everything is when you want it."

CHAPTER 7

Although Sascha usually handled training, the affinity established between Peter and Rhyssa made it sensible for her to guide his initiation.

"I'll help as much as I can," Dorotea told Rhyssa, a look of resigned disappointment on her face, "but I am eighty-four, and I've slowed down a lot." Then she smiled with bright mischief. "Of course, I've always liked cooking for a male appetite. And he'll be able to do most things for himself in short order. I'm sure of it. I know a strong Talent when I bump minds with it."

So Rhyssa, Dorotea, and Sascha made a little ceremony of adding Peter Reidinger's name to the Registry of Talents at the Eastern Center. Peter was still not quite certain of his great good fortune. Rick Hobson, who was empathic as well as kinetic, monitored the kinetic aspects; Don Usenik, the Center's versatile medic, kept a close check on the boy's physical condition; and the boy resided in Dorotea's house.

"I can still handle the mothering bits," the old woman said staunchly, "especially since Rhyssa has enough to administer."

By the end of the first week, Peter was able to handle all his intimate problems, a success of immeasurable proportion for a sensitive boy. The morning he managed to take a shower all by himself was celebrated by his mentors as the achievement it was. The first time he had attempted a shower, he had nearly scalded himself and then overcontrolled and had to be rescued from icy water by Dorotea.

It also took time, and finesse, to descend from his bed without hitting the floor in a heap. Or to keep from colliding with furniture as he reeled around the house. Gradually he achieved a delicate control of the gestalt and managed to imitate walking; only the really observant would notice that his feet never quite touched the ground and that the bend of his knees only approximated a normal walk. He could not grasp things, but he arranged his hands in appropriate positions so that he appeared to be carrying objects. With such accomplishments, he was a different boy altogether, and the change astonished his mother on her next visit.

"There's never been any Talent in our family, on either side," she confided in Dorotea at one point. "I just can't imagine where he got it from."

"Necessity, Mrs. Reidinger," Dorotea said at her most grandmotherly. "The accident has forced him to transfer motor functions to another part of his brain. Even the best of us only utilize about two-fifths of our brain potential."

Ilsa Reidinger did not really understand Dorotea's explanation, but she accepted it because Dorotea spoke with such authority.

"The human body learns to compensate, Mrs. Reidinger," Dorotea went on soothingly. "All Peter needed was a chance to train in new ways. Which, I must say, he has done extraordinarily well. We're very pleased with his progress." She beamed placidly at her guest.

"Yes, but what will he *do?*" Ilsa Reidinger asked plaintively.

"Why, Peter will do very well here at the Center, helping other youngsters—and adults, too—who have to learn to compensate for drastic handicaps." Sensing the woman's reservations on that score, Dorotea added, "Oh, the work pays very well. He's on a training scholarship right now, of course, but his profession pays very well indeed. He's all set for a fine career at the Center. You're going to be very proud of him."

Dorotea chose to ignore Ilsa Reidinger's other dominant thought: that if Peter was Talented, Katya must be, too. The girl was being ever so difficult, wanting to know why Peter got all the luck and she was stuck in a boring school, doing boring studies while Peter was getting everything his way just because he had gotten lucky.

"Can he read minds?" is what Ilsa Reidinger asked out loud. The idea made her uncomfortable.

"Peter has a very limited range," Dorotea replied mendaciously, intimating regret. "He can hear very strong thoughts, but his projections are short-range. His Talent lies in kinetics. Do you understand that word?"

"Yes, it means people can push things about without having to touch them. Like the ones going up to Padrugoi Station to help get it assembled so we can colonize the stars." The glib phrasing came from Dave Lehardt's clever publicity campaign on the tri-d.

Then Ilsa asked more timorously, "Would Petey go into space?" In her very audible public mind, Ilsa decided that whatever the answer, she would not mention that to Katya.

"Quite unlikely. The platform will be finished before Peter's received all his necessary training." The very thought of Barchenka conscripting Peter Reidinger made Dorotea queasy. Ilsa Reidinger was disappointed, however, suffering from the usual maternal syndrome of wanting *her* son to be unique, which he was; famous, which the Center would not wish on him; and perhaps rich, which Peter would also be, in that, as a Talent, he could purchase through the Center anything he really desired. "He shows a truly unique Talent." Let that be a sop to her pride.

"Yes, but what exactly *does* Petey do?"

"Well, you saw him walk and serve us tea quite by himself. That is all accomplished by his kinetic Talent. So you see, he is no longer dependent on mechanical or prosthetic devices to conduct normal activities. When he's surer of his abilities, we'll add more complicated tasks."

"He'll be able to hold down a job?"

Ilsa Reidinger really had not even grasped the basics, Dorotea thought, or comprehended the obvious achievements. She had barely grasped the fact that Peter would no longer be a financial or an emotional burden to his family. She was just a nice woman who had certainly been devoted to Peter during his convalescence, but the strain had taken a toll on her, too. Dorotea ventured to wax more enthusiastic about Peter's potential.

It suddenly occurred to Dorotea to wonder if the testing routines, established by Daffyd op Owen, needed to be updated or made more sensitive. Hospitals were usually well staffed with Talents of all descriptions. Why hadn't someone spotted Peter? She really ought to discuss that notion with Rhyssa—when the mess with Barchenka was smoothed out.

"I shouldn't think there'd be much young Peter can't do if he sets his mind to it."

"Being a kinetic, you mean?"

"A rather special one, at that, since he's had to overcome severe physical limitations."

Still slightly puzzled by the fuss being made over her Peter but immensely relieved by his future prospects, Ilsa Reidinger departed.

It never occurred to Dorotea that her remarks, meant to allay a mother's natural concern, would have unexpected repercussions. Certainly she and Rhyssa were beginning to realize the boy's immense potential, but even to colleagues they had been discreet.

"It's a case of make speed slowly, Lance," Rhyssa told the Australian director, who seemed to spend more time on a spacehotol and in the Jerhattan area than arranging matters in Canberra for his leave of absence on Padrugoi. He had dropped in to see her on his way from yet another long scheming session with Dave Lehardt and Samjan.

"I've seen some fair dinkums, dealing with the Aborigines and the Maoris, Rhyssa," Lance replied in his distinctive drawl as he slouched on a chair in her tower office, "but this lad takes the peach. If he's come on this fast with only a li'l four-point-five kpm generator for him to play with, think what he could do with *real* power."

"All the more reason to make speed slowly. Control is the most vital part of his training." She projected an image of Peter, head first, zipping around Jerhattan on a whirlwind tour, with a tail of detritus, people, small vehicles, and oddments caught up in the wake of his passage.

Lance grinned, his teeth very white against his perpetual tan, his sea green eyes glittering. "Too right, mate. I get the drift. But with a Talent like his and a proper generator, we could bleeding near shift drones all the way to the nearest planet."

Think that in your most private mind, Lance, she told him sharply. *Don't let a whisper of it escape your shield.*

Lance propped his angular body upright, his expression completely serious. *I was funning!*

Rhyssa nodded slowly, and he let out a long whistle.

Yeah, but just imagine the look on Barchenka's face if we could tell her that precious Padrugoi project had just turned obsolete.

"Not quite," Rhyssa said with a vindictive grin. She had entertained a few very satisfying fantasies on that very theme herself! "A facility like Padrugoi is required for any number of valid reasons apart from a jumping-off point to the stars."

How many know *about Petey boy?*

About his potential? Main staff know he's unusual. I was too excited when I realized the possibilities inherent in his gestalt, but they only know I was excited about the boy. There are just three of us—myself, Dorotea, and Sascha—who realize that the boy might be unusual. I don't think Sascha's had the chance to appreciate the potential that Dorotea and I are just beginning to grasp. Rick Hobson thinks the boy is inordinately quick, but we had to have a kinetic in on his initial training. Like you, Rick's got to go to Padrugoi, so we're cramming as much technique in as possible. He and Peter mesh well. You are my choice for his more advanced training, so don't do anything stupid up on Padrugoi, will you?

No way! That's a mean carrot to dangle in front of me for six long months! Lance rose. "Pure shame that Dave Lehardt's not a real Talent. He's wizard at handling the Finn and that slimy little Neester bloke."

Rhyssa gave a little convulsive shudder at the mere mention of Prince Phanibal.

"You don't like him either, do you?" Lance asked.

"No!"

Lance chuckled. "Always knew you were a woman of good sense, ducks."

Rhyssa did worry about Peter—he looked so frail after so long in a hospital bed. So did Dorotea, both keeping their concerns from Peter, whose telempathy was steadily improving along with his kinesis. He was not limited merely to receiving or sending emotions, but was developing a true telepathy, the ability to send and receive both abstract and lingual messages. Nor did Rhyssa or Dorotea call attention to those moments when, in sheer ebullience, Peter did not draw on the generator in kinetic exercises.

Dorotea enjoyed cooking for his eager appetite, and once Peter was able to perform routine tasks, she fine-tuned his kinesis with food-preparation exercises. He could pare apples and potatoes, scrape carrots, and cut up vegetables, all kinetically. He ate anything and everything, and his body began to fill out with good firm flesh; Rick showed him exercises for muscle tone, and hours spent in Dorotea's garden tanned his skin to a healthy glow. Peter no longer looked the wasted paralytic with atrophied muscles. Still, extreme care was needed in all his activities, since he continued to have no feeling in his extremities or lower torso and would be unaware of cutting or burning or bruising himself in some of his perambulations.

When Rick finally had to leave for his tour at Padrugoi, Peter took it hard, moping about the next day.

"Rick will be back, Peter," Rhyssa said when she joined them that evening at dinner. "He's taught you about all he knows. Now, you have to teach yourself, which'll be hard."

"Teach myself?" Peter was so shocked that his good manners briefly deserted him. His fork hovered above his plate. He and Dorotea had an agreement—he could get the food to his mouth however he chose if he was alone, but he was to observe proper etiquette with anyone else.

"Yes, teach yourself," Dorotea replied blandly.

"Rick has given you the basics," Rhyssa added with a warm smile. "Certainly you're now able to do everything for yourself and help out in the house and the garden. Now you begin the next step—testing yourself. Don't worry. Rick left a long list for you to complete by the time his tour of duty is over."

"But he didn't tell me how . . ." Peter was clearly floundering.

"You know how," Rhyssa said, acting surprised at his reaction. "All paranormal Talents come from an instinctive level. Sharpen your instinct." She smiled at him, patting his arm soothingly. "That instinct led you right to the Center, didn't it? Don't worry about the 'how'! Rely on your instinct. Use it by sending different types of inert objects to destinations farther and farther away. First to places you are familiar with. Then by memorizing tri-d visuals and maybe even using mathematical coordinates. For example, that forkful of mashed potato. Where would you like to put it?"

The fork's burden of mashed potato disappeared.

Sascha: *What is going on down there?*

Rhyssa: *Does it concern a portion of mashed potato?*

Sascha, somewhat disgusted: *It does!* He sent her an image of a white glob in the middle of his desk.

"And where did you send it, Peter?" Dorotea asked noncommittally.

"Sascha's desk. But on the wood, not on anything important," Peter assured her.

"I won't require you to eat it, but do bring it back!"

The well-traveled forkful reappeared on the edge of Peter's plate.

Sascha, sarcastically: *Thank you!*

You're welcome! Peter giggled like any youngster succeeding with a practical joke.

Sascha to Rhyssa and Dorotea: *We just get Madlyn house-trained and now we have Peter! Sometimes . . . I suppose, if he's up to tricks, he's adjusting to Rick's departure.*

Peter was also up to work the next day, using the gestalt with the generator to shift various items about the Center. Dorotea started him off moving small objects from one room to another, emphasizing accuracy of placement and picking locations with which Peter was familiar. By the end of the morning he was shifting heavy bales of computer paper from storage to the Control Room, getting his placements from squares crayoned onto the floor until Budworth finally signaled that his aim was perfect.

"Weight seems to be no object," Sascha said, reviewing the achievements at lunch with Rhyssa. "How much did he have to rely on the gestalt?"

"Not much. We've got a graph on its usage," Rhyssa replied. "His need is verging on the psychological."

"Ah, but that doesn't alter the fact that he does use it," Sascha said thoughtfully. "Can and *does*. By damn, Rhyssa, he's extraordinary! Once he can really lean on generator power, there isn't anything he can't shift, is there?" His eyes were shining with excitement. "If only we could figure out just how he achieves the gestalt."

Rhyssa shook her head, with a rueful smile.

"Could Rick?" he asked.

Rhyssa sighed. "Rick did just the basic kinetic training exercises with him. He didn't have more time. Damn Barchenka. Wouldn't you just know that we'd have a promising emergent who'd benefit from training with the very kinetics that she's yanked out of our reach. Why didn't we have an earlier precog of this?"

Sascha leaned back in his chair, regarding his good friend and director with an uncharacteristically solemn expression. "Rhyssa, hon, could you follow his mind?"

She gave a short laugh. "I'm an adept at telepathy, but Peter's going where no man has gone before. Maybe another strong kinetic could follow. I'm going to dragoon Lance Baden as his advanced trainer as soon as that wretched Padrugoi is finished." She blued the mental air with assorted images of her frustration.

Sascha nodded sympathetically. "Then we'll just have to continue doing kindergarten stuff with him until Lance is free. And build him up physically. Does Don Usenik see any chance of exercise restimulating those damaged nerves? Now that—"

"Trouble!" Budworth's voice rang through the special alarm speaker in Rhyssa's office.

What kind? she asked immediately.

"Goddammit, I want to speak to Director Owen *now!*" said a voice on the room address system as Budworth patched the call through.

"You are," Rhyssa replied coolly. "Please identify yourself."

"Dammit, didn't they tell you? Bob Gaskin, Jerhattan Port Authority. You took our kinetic away from us, and now we've a container pinning three men down and no bloody way to lift it quick enough to save their lives. Right now only the safety bar on the forklift is—"

"Do you have the area on video?"

"I do—the whole yard."

"Relay it to this screen immediately," she ordered. *Dorotea, bring Peter to my office. We've got to try to help. They're patching through the image.*

Dorotea: *Dare we?*

Rhyssa: *We'll never know unless we do. Lives are at stake. He's got the potential, and he's done well enough already with bulky, heavy things.*

Dorotea: *That's halfway across the city. But . . . all right. I'll have Peter there in a dash.*

Sascha and Rhyssa kept their eyes on the screen, which was showing the container, the hoist cables at one end of it still whipping in backlash. It had come down askew across a small forklift, the sturdy frame of which was keeping it from crushing the driver and two men who had been working near him. The Talents could see the dangling arm of one man pinned at one side, the feet of a second protruding under one corner—and nothing at all of the driver.

"Why did that hoist cable part, Mr. Gaskin?" Rhyssa asked calmly. "Surely you checked all your equipment before you put it in use again." She deliberately made herself sound censorious.

The office door opened and Dorotea and Peter entered; Peter's eyes went immediately to the screen.

"If your goddamned Center hadn't pulled our kinetic," Gaskin exploded, "this wouldn't have—Holy hell! How'd you get someone here this quick?"

Rhyssa, Dorotea, and Sascha held their breath as they watched the long unwieldy mass of the container slowly rise off the crumbled forklift, revealing the driver slumped across his controls and another man sprawled flat on the ground while the third staggered to his feet, holding his injured arm. They were also aware of a humming that they could feel through the floorboards of Rhyssa's office. The hum peaked off as the container was lowered carefully to the waiting truck loadbed.

"Bravo, Peter, beautifully done! Magnificent!" Rhyssa said—and then she saw him crumpled on the floor. "Oh, Lord! Did you strain yourself, love?"

Sascha reached the boy before she did, lifting him gently and depositing him on Rhyssa's conformable chair, which instantly altered to fit the boy's limp body.

"Will the men be all right?" Peter wanted to know, his white face contorted with anguish. *They were hurting bad.*

"More to the point, young man," Sascha said, frowning, "are you all right?" *Don, get up here on the double!*

"By God, ma'am, how'd you do that?" Bob Gaskin cried. The Port Authority manager was mopping his face with shaking hands.

"You haven't been completely abandoned by Talent, Mr. Gaskin. We have a skeleton crew"—Sascha's image of Peter's frail form, bony structure emphasized, made it very hard for Rhyssa to keep her features composed—"which we can throw into gear for emergencies of this nature. Do please now overhaul your equipment. We don't have the manpower for unnecessary accidents, you know." She ignored Sascha's exaggerated grimace as she saw medics rushing to assist the injured men as a Southside heli-amb landed nearby. "Good morning, Mr. Gaskin.

"We'll check in with Southside General Hospital later, Peter," Rhyssa assured the boy.

"After Don's checked you out, young man," Dorotea added, "though your concern for the men does you credit."

I know we had to, Rhyssa, Sascha said on a tight band to Rhyssa, *but should we have?*

Rhyssa made a face. *Hobson's choice, Sascha. We maintain an official position of the skeleton crew. By the way,* don't *do that to me again real soon, huh?*

Sascha rolled his eyes, expressing remorse but no reassurance. *I'm not sure how long we'll be able to hang that lie, so would you get all uptight if I tried to follow his mind's thrust when he's lifting? I didn't realize how quickly he's emerging to full use of his Talent.*

No, after this exhibition of Peter's ability, I was about to ask you if you could spare some time to work with him. I need your insight, since you're more expert at training. If we could duplicate the gestalt, even our featherweights could move containers.

"Okay, who's done what to whom now?" Don Usenik demanded as he entered the room. He looked around, then spotted the wan Peter on Rhyssa's chair. "What have you been doing? Moving mountains?"

W hich do you want first? The good news, or the bad news?" Dave Lehardt asked Rhyssa a week later.

She could tell nothing from his expression—the look of his eyes was curiously intent on her face. He might not be a Talent, but he was unusually astute at picking up minute body-language signs. She was so glad to see him that she really did not care what news he brought, but she followed his cue.

"The bad!"

"Barchenka is certain you've been holding out on her. She's heard that you have a team of kinetic Talents that are not on your official register. She's about to create a stink. And I have to tell you that I've heard some mighty peculiar rumors circulating."

Rhyssa laughed. "We're not holding out on her—Talents can't. Telempaths can always detect a lie. She has Russian telempaths on her payroll. Tell her to ask them. What's the good news?"

Dave Lehardt raised one eyebrow in a skeptical arch. "The polls are again favorable to the Talented. When businesses employing

them had to cope with old-fashioned ways, Talent popularity hit a
fifty-year low—worse even than after the Hawaiian volcano disaster—even though everyone was pro-Padrugoi and everyone, meaning the Talents, was doing their share. Seems that this nonexistent
team of yours has provided emergency services. Only no Talent
has been observed on the scene."

"It's a remote technique that we've been developing for emergency situations," Rhyssa said, schooling her face to reveal nothing. It was not that she did not trust Dave Lehardt, but she wanted
to protect Peter. "And it's the one reason we felt we could strip all
our Centers of kinetics to help Padrugoi."

"A remote technique?"

"That's what I said."

"No Talent I've spoken to knows anything about it."

"I said it was remote," Rhyssa repeated, struggling to keep
amusement out of her voice. "Not something we want to go public
on just yet. I'm sure you can appreciate *that!*"

"So Ludmilla can't get her hands on it?"

"She's coerced almost every kinetic we have onto Padrugoi.
She's got sufficient numbers and skills right now to finish her work
on schedule. She shouldn't get greedier!"

"She wants to come in under schedule, and the way your Talents are working, she could."

"Is a bonus involved in early completion?" Rhyssa was annoyed.
Damn the woman to a disintegrating orbit!

"Didn't you know?" Dave Lehardt seemed surprised.

"I heard a great deal about penalties and a completion bonus, but
strangely enough, nothing was said, or even hinted, that *early* completion was her goal."

"I'll do what I can to squash the rumors—and, if I may be so
bold, you should keep that new team out of operation if at all
possible. No more cavalry charges to the rescue without warning
me, huh? Please?"

That was very sound advice, which Rhyssa intended to follow.
Since the emergency lift, she had been chary of using Peter's skill.
It just took too much out of his not-so-sturdy body. He was
strengthening himself daily—exercising was becoming almost an
obsession with him. But she was still rigorously restricting the use
of his Talent to life-threatening situations in the Jerhattan area,
which, fortunately, were few. Meanwhile, in the ongoing training

sessions, he was using fax placement photos to send items to other Centers.

"I can follow his thoughts all the way," Sascha told Rhyssa after a week of linking minds with Peter during those exercises. "I can even feel the vibrations of the generator in his cerebrum, but *how* he effects the gestalt is still beyond me. And, as nearly as I can tell, he's relying less and less on the power. At least for light stuff."

"If he keeps on this way, maybe Lance is right," Rhyssa remarked. "Plug him into a powerful enough source and he could probably obviate the need for Padrugoi."

Sascha blinked, then projected a series of images depicting Barchenka's expression, the consternation on the egg-splattered faces of the space station's major supporters, and one small boy sending out starships the way children his age launched paper planes. The last and largest image was of Sascha himself, elongated mouth wide open, chin to his chest. "Could he?"

Rhyssa laughed, rolling her eyes. "I won't say he couldn't. But you know as well as I do that all Talent has limitations. Now is not the time to put any sort of pressure on Peter. He's such a happy boy now."

"We can thank God he is!" His mental picture was of himself, patiently controlling the lovelorn Madlyn Luvaro, huge wads of cotton wool in his ears.

Rhyssa retorted with an image of stray forkfuls of potato festooning his office. "A kinetic has far more options than a telepath!"

"He's easier to keep happy than Madlyn ever was, too," Sascha said, stretching his long legs. "The odd traffic snarl or two a day, and he feels he's worth his keep. Which reminds me, I've had some pretty pointed remarks from industrial VIPs lately about this remote team of ours. My answer is that we've managed to combine the trainees with an experienced featherweight to achieve the necessary heft, but the application is limited due to the extreme youth of the participants."

Rhyssa sighed. "That old tangled-web routine, huh?"

Sascha quirked an eyebrow. "Favoring Shakespeare? Thought your family ran to Popery."

Rhyssa laughed, envisioning her illustrious grandsire, Daffyd op Owen, as she remembered him, tall, silver-haired, slender, with the face of a poet and the chin of an Italian prince. "Sometimes the Bard fits better. Which industrialists have asked?"

"Nail on the head, girl. Every one of them supplies something to Padrugoi! And, as you know, there've been delays in getting matériel up to the station, weather problems mainly, with all those freak storms messing up launch windows."

Rhyssa frowned and, in an uncharacteristic show of nervousness, flipped a stylus end over end. "Lifesaving, yes; and with the technique he's been showing over distances, I think he probably could launch a drone up to Padrugoi through any sort of weather. But there's no way Peter's going to help secure her bonus or prevent her fines."

Sascha grinned. "I won't mention the possibility of such fun and games to him, you spoilsport." He threw her an image of him hastily raising a solid barrier against the barbs emerging from her eyes. "She couldn't hire him anyway. He's only fourteen. Underage, even under existing Russian law!"

Rhyssa let out a low whistle, then grinned. "Yes, he is a minor, isn't he? And Dorotea reminded me that he's been working pretty hard with you. Tomorrow he has a day off. And I've got all these files—" She gestured resignedly at the stacks on the edge of her desk. "Testing reports to go through."

"Why don't you take a night off?" Sascha suggested, grinning drolly. "With Dave."

Rhyssa sat bolt upright, closing her mind.

"Honey, I don't have to peek," he told her.

Rhyssa groaned. "He's not a Talent."

"There's no law in the Charter that says you have to marry Talent, you know."

"But that's the way to increase . . ."

"Yeah, and where did Peter Reidinger come from? I think sometimes, my dear friend," he said, leaning over the desk toward her, "we have to look with our eyes instead of our heads. Just thought I ought to mention it. Dave's the best friend Talent's got."

"It's not up to me, Sascha," Rhyssa added, feeling uncomfortable for the first time in her old friend's presence.

"Could be. Maybe not. Lehardt's clever enough to do his own promo work." With that Sascha left her.

As Tirla entered the Main Concourse of Linear G, she sensed an aura of excitement, telling her that something was about to happen to relieve the tedium of Linear living. As always, there were some general workers scurrying to the Plaza to see if the WorkBoard was scrolling out any jobs for able-bodieds, concerned with getting enough day work to keep out of Conscriptive Work Services. No self-respecting Linearite wanted to be sent on a hard-labor tour or, worse, spaced out to the shipyards around the Big Wheel. Few CWS ever earned a return ticket. And now even the Talents were not exempt. So most of the little knots of excited people were composed of women.

Tirla edged close enough to a group of Hispanics to pick up the drift.

"He lay hands on . . ."

"Church is always *lo mismo* . . . The singing is bad."

"My Juan now . . . when he is reminded of the purity of the Virgin, he doesn't beat me for a day or two . . ."

"The true man of God provides food for the soul . . ."

Tirla snorted to herself. Food for the soul was not high on her priorities when her belly was empty.

"I have heard," Consuela Laguna was saying earnestly, "that if he lays hands on the lame, he cures." Consuela's son was handicapped beyond remedy or repair, but she remained positive that somehow, sometime, her Manuelito would be restored to health by some new miracle treatment, and she was always asking Tirla to translate the medical bulletins for her.

So, Tirla thought, a Religious Event had been unexpectedly scheduled for Linear G. That was odd. The Public Health meeting had been only four weeks earlier. It was true that there had not been an RE in a long time, but still she was suspicious. *Two* specials within four weeks?

She moved on to the next group, all Neesters from the Levant, and they were babbling about how they could get their men to attend that night instead of adjourning to Mahmoud's squat to see his new belly dancer. Then she slipped around to an Asian gaggle who were chattering excitedly about cures and whether the RE would be bad for business. Asians provided ancient remedies for the many minor ailments that beset those in the warreny Residentials.

"He has come as promised . . ." she heard as she slid up to

Mama Bobchik. The old woman's black eyes were wide; her cheeks
a mottled glowing red of excitement. "You come, too, *dushka*," she
said, catching Tirla's arm. "You must tell us his words, exactly.
The last time I could not hear what was said, and my soul is black
with sin."

"*Nakonetz*," Tirla agreed easily. Most Religious Interpreter
Groups generally said nothing, in the most ornamented phraseology. She could amuse herself by anticipating the trite phrases and
flowery words. "So the Assembly extension was granted after all?"
she asked, eager to maintain her reputation of knowing all that
went on in the Linear.

"*Da, eto tak!*" Mama Bobchik happily reassured her. "My man
was sent word to prepare late last night." Argol Bobchik was one
of the Linear's sanitary engineers. "The word is that this Religious
is all-seeing," Mama babbled on, "with an excellent backup group.
They were well received at Linear P. Early as it is, already this
morning many traders have booked space. It will be an occasion.
We have not had religion here in G for some months. We are all in
need of guidance. The souls of many are dark with sin and must be
purged."

Tirla nodded solemnly. Mama Bobchik was certainly old enough
to be facing a mystic accounting of the sins on her soul. Too bad no
LEO man would be there to hear it.

But how had Tirla missed such a juicy rumor? Maybe it had
been decided very late the previous night. At any rate, the presence
of traders would make it easier for her to wash the tied credits for
the Yassim man. She shuddered at the thought of him. She did not
like to hold onto his money too long. Not that he had any reason to
distrust her—she just wanted to make certain he never did. Especially if he suspected she was close to salable age. She was small
and thin enough to pass for the nine years she admitted to. Some-
day someone would count fingers on her. From time to time she
thought about what she would do then—and tried to keep enough
floaters stuck inside her blouse at all times so that she could flee to
another Linear if she had to. She had even managed to get her
hands on a highly illegal copy of the cargo-train schedules and had
found her way to the nearest access points to the subterranean
concourse to eyeball escape routes.

Deftly disengaging herself from Mama Bobchik's fat fingers, she
moved on to the Pakis, who were chattering about bringing in

some relatives from Linear E and arguing over the advisability of such a move. Some insisted that, since the extension was legal, there would be no risk. Then Mirda Khan—a person Tirla was always careful to please—came up and quickly dismissed such stupid generosity.

"The blessings of such a Lama would be few," Mirda muttered in an intense and angry tone just audible to those around her, "for he cannot waste his holy strength on the trivial. Such as he would be gracious enough to dispense must be for us, here, in Linear G. For us," she said again, poking her thin breastbone with a broad flat thumb, "the true believers, his faithful in Linear G."

"The Very Revered Ponsit Prosit has been at Linear P," one of the other women murmured reverently. "Pandit heard of the miracles he performed."

Tirla was skeptical of miracles for, on close inspection, there were always alternate explanations for healings and savings and revelations. But they were fun to delve.

"Then we save such for ourselves!" Mirda replied fiercely, defying contradiction. Suddenly she spun around, somehow aware of being the object of scrutiny—but Tirla was quicker, moving to flatten herself against the Concourse pillar. She had heard enough anyhow and left.

So this Religious Interpreter, this RIG, had a reputation? As Tirla was quite aware, it took a real clever talker to keep from violating the variety of complex doctrines in a Linear. This Ponsit Prosit might well be worth listening to—and watching closely. In her precarious situation, Tirla was always open to pointers.

If the whole thing was legit. She mulled over the probables as she ducked into side aisles before coming out again onto the Main Concourse, far enough away from the Pakis to be screened by other groups. Then she glanced up at the nearest publi-text screen. She watched through the usual notices and announcements until it scrolled down to 2200 hours, where a legal extension for use of the Assembly was posted, with trading and drinking permitted.

The full details were being vividly proclaimed, complete with fanfares of brass instruments and snippets of the Respected Venerable Homilifier Ponsit Prosit smiling beatifically at vast audiences. A chorus was promised, and a short blast of five-part harmony and high soprano descant was presented as an enticement to attend the full show. This V R & Holy Religious Interpretation Group purportedly had only recently returned from the Eastern Cities of Faith, where Ponsit Prosit had endured "fasting meditations of great length and illumination." Linear G was fortunate in the extreme that he was able to fit that evening's assembly into his busy tour. So, he had not had a booking in a while, Tirla thought cynically. Well, Religious Interpretations were very popular in Linears, better than fights sometimes and often more showy. Tirla liked shows—and legal extensions.

There had been a Public Health roundup recently, so a second, covert one was unlikely in her experience. And while a Religious Event could be staged to mask more illicit operations than washing tieds in public, there still might not be any undercover LEOs. Crowd Controllers would be around, of course—that was standard procedure—but Tirla knew most of them despite the way they altered their appearances.

The important thing was that she had the Yassim tieds to change. She should never have agreed to do it, but Bulbar had been insistent and the "talker"—a hit man whom she would not willingly offend—had told her that she was being given the opportunity in reward for services already rendered. Having consented to a professional engagement with Mama Bobchik, who was not only another person it was unwise to offend but someone who, having presided over Tirla's birth, would always defend the girl, Tirla was committed on two counts to attend.

Prepared with several contingency plans, Tirla began her usual morning routine—bargaining for the day's meals and getting a bath and a clean issue of clothing. But as she proceeded, she was stopped by various female clients, each wanting her company during this Religious Event because the featured Lama-shaman was reputed to speak in tongues and Tirla was absolutely the only person who would faithfully tell them everything he said. There was a limit, however, to how many people Tirla could adequately represent. Surrounded by very insistent, vocal, and physically active prospective clients, none of whom she cared to antagonize, she attempted to organize them.

"Bilala, you and Pilau must come together. Anna, you team up with Marika. Zaveta, Elpidia comes as well. Chi-shu, Lao Wang with you. Cyoto, Ari-san is your partner." And so she grouped them. Ten pairs was as unmanageable as it was unavoidable. Before she got into any further difficulties, Tirla discreetly removed

herself from public view. She still had to get the tied credits out of
their hidey holes and secreted about her for easy access.

"We have an Incident," Sirikit said, her light, crisp voice carrying easily to Budworth, who was duty officer in the
Parapsych Control Room.

"Who?" Budworth sent his gimballed chair spinning across the
tiled floor to her station. Seeing him maneuver so rapidly around
the Control Room made people forget that his spine had been
crushed in an accident and that he had only minimal movement of
his head and two fingers.

"Auer." Sirikit's surprise was reflected in her voice.

"Really!"

"And Bertha!"

"That's an unusual combination."

"Not if Ponsit Prosit the Great Flimflam is involved. I caught
the p.a. for Linear G."

"It is very true she would have his guts for garters," Budworth
said, grinning wryly. Bertha Zoccola was generally a relaxed and
tolerant individual, but mention of that particular RIG was
enough to enrage her. Budworth set himself for her fury in reporting a precog involving the man.

Whenever precognitive Talents responded to an Incident, they
would flash the Center, alerting Control to receive a verbal description of what they had previewed. Budworth positioned his
chair at the fingerboard next to Sirikit and scratched his chin on
the rim of his head support, feeling the surge of excited anticipation that he always experienced at such moments.

"C'mon, you net-heads, report!" he exclaimed.

Sirikit glanced away from her screen to grin at him. Then a
bleep sounded, startling both of them even though they were expecting an entry.

"Auer here," the emotionless voice announced, and the precog's
face appeared in one of the response screens. "A real messy one.
High panic, screams, mob, kids trampled, the usual thing. Why
don't you grab Ponsit and space him to the shipyards? I'm tired of
protecting that scuzfart."

"You saw Flimflam himself, Auer?" Sirikit asked encouragingly.
At Budworth's nod, she took over the routine questions. She was

one of the most deft at post-Incidental debriefing, and Auer always responded well to her. Budworth busied himself with tapping out a query for scheduled public events. More crowd control would have to be assigned to Linear G.

Auer shrugged with an indifference both observers knew was false. "He's prominent. All colored lights and glittering hands. Then running away. As usual. Never stays to calm the audiences he excites to riot pitch."

"Where?" Sirikit encouraged him.

"Your typical Residential assembly hall. Usual Ponsit backdrops. Nothing unusual . . . except—" Auer paused, frowning down at something. "Except—that's odd!"

"What's odd, Auer?"

"All over a scrawny girl?" When he looked up, his eyes were haunted.

"Yes?"

"I feel . . . and her danger is acute. It doesn't end tonight. She's Talented!" That was said in a surprised voice; then Auer passed a hand across his eyes, scrubbing downward. "It's gone now. It's gone." The screen blackened.

Another screen brightened.

"You shouldn't allow that man a *permit* at *all!*" Bertha Zoccola was bristling with indignation. "You've caught him dealing time and again! Those people don't have the credits to spend on mystical cures and miracle healings. He spouts the most appalling sort of pantheist tripe. *And* in the worst language!"

"What did you see, Bertha?" Budworth asked the plump little woman, who still cherished a worn deck of Tarot cards that her great-grandmother had once read with a high enough degree of accuracy to earn a significant credit balance.

"I keep telling you that man is nothing but trouble." Her double chin quivered, and her expression was concerned. "I don't care if the Domestic Satisfaction Index does rise after he's played a Residential. Why should we Talents protect a quacksalver, a faker, a pharisee, a hoaxer, a gyp! An arrant carnie!"

"We're not protecting him! Now, what did you see, Bertha?"

"Halfway through that—that gibberous effort of his—you never can tell *what* he's saying in that mumbo-jumble of his—there's a movement, to the left of the platform . . ." She jingled her left hand, her many wrist bracelets clacking noisily. "Or do I mean his right?" She raised the other hand, splaying fingers crammed with rings. "There's a commotion. It has to do with a large group of women." She waggled her hand again, frowning. "Then everything goes wild! A name! They're all calling a name! And I can't hear what it is! Oh, wouldn't that cause a saint to swear! The one vital detail! And I *thought* I heard it so clearly . . ." She pursed her lips in concentration and then slowly shook her head, sighing. "No, it's gone. I'm so sorry."

"Thanks, Bertha dear. You've filled in some details."

"Who else?" Bertha asked, as always.

"Auer."

"Him?" Bertha was incredulous. "Well, what'd'ya know about that? Do keep me screened, Buddy."

"You bet." Budworth was punching Sascha's office as her picture dissolved. "Sascha, we got an Incident."

"There's only one crowd controller assigned to the RIG, Budworth," Sirikit murmured to him. "Residential Linear G is listed as blue, calm."

"Well, it's about to change color unless we can neutralize. Sascha, something's going to bust wide at Ponsit's meeting at G tonight."

"Linear G?" The large blue eyes in Sascha's Slavic-cast face widened with surprise. "We'd nothing planned *there,*" he murmured. "Who saw it?"

"Bertha and Auer."

"What?" Sascha raised his eyebrows. "That's a first. I'll be back to you, Buddy. I'll organize our infiltration with the Bro." *Rhyssa, we've got an incipient riot.*

That sort of thing's more your bailiwick than mine, was Rhyssa's reply. *Give my regards to Boris.*

As the contact with Sascha faded, Budworth grunted, absently scratching his jaw. He hoped there would be remote visuals set up so that he could watch what went on, and if Sascha's LEO brother, Boris, was involved, there would be. Whether his experience was vicarious or not, Budworth appreciated being involved in these unexpected spectaculars. One never knew what would happen during an Incident. He was honest enough in the back of his mind —the only safe place to think in the Center—to realize that he had not been a physically brave person even before his accident. Still and all, he found the breathless anticipation and stimulation to be very pleasant sensations for one husked by a mobility chair.

Sirikit was making rapid entries, documenting the Incident. Although the Talented had come to have immense credibility, and the meticulously kept daily files might generally be scanned only by Research, the procedures outlined by the Parapsychic Center's first administrator, Henry Darrow, were scrupulously followed. The full spectrum of Talent was far from being known and certain facets of Talent were not at all fully developed, as in the case of young Peter Reidinger's Talent for an electrical gestalt. And who knew what sort of unusual Talent might yet be discovered among emergents? Budworth sighed as he turned back to tasks which once would have seemed far from mundane.

CHAPTER 8

Tirla did not dare be late to the meeting, but she also did not want to arrive too soon and risk being hassled by even more people demanding her particular services. No matter what baksheesh was offered, she could translate for only so many at a time, especially with the other, more pressing, matter to complete. *That* had to be managed. She chose to arrive with enough time to do a quick survey and identify the best vendors, as well as any undercover LEOs or PHOs. The fortuitous scheduling of the Religious Event still bothered her.

Unless . . . It occurred to Tirla that maybe there would be some Treasury persons in the crowd, checking up on vendors, that money laundering itself was the target of this occasion. But the Ts were easy to spot. They were always so obvious about blending into the crowd.

Having arranged to meet the women at the main southeast entrance, Tirla entered the Assembly atrium from one of the side northwest gates. Someone else had already disabled the entrance eye that read IDs and counted attendance, saving her the trouble. The petty vendors had their booths up and merchandise displayed: mainly trinkets and synth clothes, goods that could be quickly shifted. But there were air-cushion carts being angled through the wider doorways, proving that some serious trading would be done. She felt somewhat easier in her mind. The big traders would not risk themselves or their merchandise at a risky-disky.

She took note of prices as she wended her way through the gathering crowd. She hoped there would be some fresh produce—well, fresh in that it had been recently nicked from the underground warehouses that supplied Jerhattan's markets. She would treat herself to a nice crisp pepper, carrot, or apple from the day's earnings, something to sink her teeth into instead of the subsistence mush or compound protein loaf. She wanted to get a stick of real chewing gum, too, to keep her mouth moist when she started translating. She spared only a glance for the activity on the platform, where hands were rushing about, draping curtains and swags and hauling lighting and sound equipment about. She was never impressed by packaging—just the quality of the contents. She found gum at Felter's stall and made him launder one of the smaller tied notes.

She was just savoring the minty flavor of her gum when she caught sight of an all too familiar profile in totally unfamiliar synth-issue clothing. Yassim was actually here? She ducked behind a large man in a stained robe that had once been the height of fashion. He was holding up both arms, wigwagging at someone on the stage. The smell of him nearly made her swallow her gum, but his outline completely obscured her.

What was Yassim doing here? Tirla wondered. Didn't he trust her? As her camouflage dropped one arm to cup his hand to his mouth to shout a direction, Tirla chanced a second look.

Yes, it was him. He was unmistakable. He had done something subtle to his face, altering its shape—probably pads in his cheeks and lower lip—but he had not, could not, alter that long thin hooked nose and the sloping forehead. He walked, as always, as if he owned the place, strutting about in a loose over-robe that had not suffered much cleaning in its long life. His headgear was also appropriately worn, torn, and stained. It was a creditable attempt to blend in, but Tirla *knew* the man was Yassim. There he was, sauntering about, inspecting trinkets, pausing to ask questions of vendors, appearing to go from one group of friends to another, friends she quickly identified as some of his multitude of ladrones, hitters, and sassins. Well and discreetly guarded though he was, why was he there?

Her odorous blocker moved and she moved with him, keeping him as cover. When he stopped, roaring out instructions, she, too, did—and saw Yassim talking to three Neester mothers who had young children with them. Suddenly Tirla knew what he was doing there. With equal certainty, Tirla did not want to be anywhere in his vicinity while child buying was on his mind. She did, however, make a mental note of which ladrones and sassins she knew among his followers. There had to be one she could trust to give his boss the tieds she had exchanged into floaters. There was no way she could avoid that chore.

Subliminal music had started, and the lighting in the Assembly Hall began to alter subtly, heralding the beginning of the Religious Interpretation. Tirla ducked behind the nearest vendor's shill-board and slipped to the southeast entrance.

An agitated Mirda Khan seemed to have eyes in the back of her mirror-adorned headdress, for she swung around, her face as sharp as a predatory bird's, as Tirla approached. She hooked her fingers painfully into Tirla's grasp and hauled the girl to her.

"Where were you? Where were you?" Mirda shook her angrily, showering her with spittle and sour breath so that Tirla pulled back as far as she could. The other women who had commissioned her to translate the RIG's words formed a close circle around her. But since their bodies also shielded her from Yassim's notice, she did not resist.

"I was pricing the merch," she said, unrepentantly.

Bilala and Pilau were trying to edge around Mirda and pull Tirla to their segment of the circle. Mirda jammed Tirla tight against her angular body while Mama Bobchik somehow got ahold of Tirla's free arm, effectively pinning her between the two formidably large women.

"He's here," Tirla said to Mirda, squirming to give herself a little space. She repeated the phrase until all her customers knew.

"He?" Mirda stretched to peer over the heads of their little knot. She gave a snort. "Yassim'll roast in hell before I sell him another child." Her fingers tightened convulsively on Tirla's shoulder. "You stay away from him. You hear me good?"

Tirla nodded enthusiastically. If Mirda knew Yassim, was there a chance she could inveigle the woman to pass on the laundry? Not with any sure knowledge that all of it would reach him.

"He gives a good price," Elpidia whined. She had a girl child old enough to spin off. She also had a drug habit to keep, for which she exchanged the yearly fruits of her womb once they were of an age to be sold off profitably. She fretted whether or not to go back to her squat and bring down the child for him.

"I would not sell to such as him!" Mirda snapped in her own language, black eyes flashing scornfully. "Price or not. Even selling to the station is better."

"What did she say?" Elpidia demanded of Tirla.

Tirla shrugged. "I am hired to translate the speaker, not settle disputes between clients, and she is not one to annoy."

Elpidia scowled at Mirda Khan, who hauled Tirla around, nearly wrenching her left arm out of Mama Bobchik's hand.

"Come," Mirda said. Her outer robe billowing its musty folds across Tirla's face, she led the group forward, acting as a spearhead through the still thinly scattered gathering. She halted right under the stage, where no one could thrust in front of them to block their view. She was about to push Tirla forward when the girl wriggled free.

"I must be able to see him. I will stand here, where I can see, and where all of you can hear." She repeated this until it was clearly understood by all her clients.

Within the circle she felt safe from Yassim. She began to relax and even to enjoy the music despite the patchy sound of the shrill replay as it ground through a multi-ethnic repertoire. Where were the famous live backup performers? This had been publicly billed as an occasion! Tirla took note of activity on the stage, the draperies billowing suddenly here and there from movement behind them. She could just catch a glimpse of the right-hand wings and people milling about, waiting to go on. So, there was a chorus. She much preferred live singing.

Out of the corner of her eye she caught a glimpse of a big man to her right, wandering with all too apparent indifference. She sensed a penetrating assessment of her companions going on under the brim of a battered peak cap, and she leaned surreptitiously into Mama Bobchik. She felt something else then, a soothing brush across her mind which caused the high, sharp chatter of the women to fall off into a less excited pitch. She was not sure what *that* was all about.

The man was not Treasury. She followed his progress, aware that he was in contact somehow with two women who gave every evidence of being oblivious to him as they chattered and laughed together, jostling through the early comers to find a good position near the stage. She peered suspiciously at the two, their faces painted with careless hands, one of them obviously pregnant, though she wore the gear of a prostitute. Their faces were unfamiliar, and Tirla was beginning to wonder if the meeting really had been staged by an authority like Treasury or PH when a third woman, well known to Tirla, greeted them effusively and stayed to

gossip. Reading from their lips the commonplace remarks they exchanged soothed the girl. It was seeing Yassim here that made her
so nervous. She certainly did not owe him so much that he would
come after her. She was not even overdue with the laundered credits. What had happened to his stock? He was not often caught short
enough to brave a public affair. She touched the little pouches of
tieds in the clever vest she wore for the purpose under her issue
suit and reassured herself that all were in place.

A fanfare blasted for attention, and the excited babble died down
to eager anticipation. Not a bad flourish, Tirla thought, quite willing to be carried along by a good show.

Then the choir stalked out self-consciously and arranged themselves with some poking and pulling on one side of stage center. As
close as she was, Tirla could see that their costumes were neither
clean nor new. Not all of them managed to find the right pitch
from the final note of the recorded blurt of brass. Tirla knew the
song they were singing, a really old good one, so the fact that they
were singing it badly was inexcusable. She only had to translate it
for Cyoto and Ari—everyone else mumbled along in their own
languages.

Then the emcee came out, falsely bright, and started the pitch,
waffling on about the training and merits of the Revered Venerable
Ponsit Prosit. As he was merely repeating all the claptrap about
mystical training in Far Asia from the public announcement, Tirla
did not start to translate it until Bilala hissed at her to earn her fee.

There was another song, one which slipped from one musical
ethic to another with no respect for tonality or rhythm. Perversely,
the singers managed to perform the travesty competently. Tirla
identified six who were spaced out on something. That they could
sing at all might indeed be a minor miracle of this RIG.

There were flourishes of recorded instruments and rolls of
drums, which stirred even Tirla's cynical pulses. Drums could be
so exciting! A great crashing of cymbals, a painfully glaring display of assorted lights and narrow beams, an ear-blasting crescendo
of bugle synths accompanied by fragrant smoke bombs, and the
Revered Venerable Religious Interpreter arrived, his robes artfully
gleaming.

Her clients were suitably impressed by his "magical" appearance, but Tirla had caught a glimpse of the square aperture in the
floor before he shot up through the densest veil of smoke to hover

on his column above the stage and the awed spectators. She preferred something more dramatic; she had seen that sort of entrance so frequently that it had lost any impact. But clearly she was a minority. Even Mirda pretended to be afraid, covering her face with a fold of her head cloth.

The Religious Interpreter went into his act immediately, face upturned so Tirla's best view was of a waggling chin and dark holes of nostrils. The light show dazzled as taped music supported his mouthings—for that was what they were, syllables meaning absolutely nothing, with random words from every language she had ever heard tossed in to confuse.

"What does he say, the holy man?" Mirda demanded.

"Tell me what he say?" Mama Bobchik pulled Tirla to her. Bilala and Pilau were equally insistent: one kicked Tirla's shin, while the other transferred a substantial amount of her weight onto Tirla's undefended toes.

"Nothing," Tirla replied, disgusted. "He says nothing!"

She was poked, pushed, and pulled.

"He's saying something." "He speaks mystically." "Tell *us* what he says." "Ah, I understand that word for myself! I will pay you nothing, bitch."

Tirla was furious at that threat. Furious at the RIG. She would translate when he said something translatable. She was pinched and tweaked and slapped. In self-defense she caught the pattern of his babble and, involuntarily mimicking his stance and delivery, rattled off the nonsensical sounds in an undertone, translating the occasional real word into as many languages as she could before picking up the gibberish again.

Then the man stopped talking and spread his arms, his beatific smile radiant in the flood of light picking him out, seemingly afloat in the air above the stage. Then Tirla realized that he was staring in her direction.

In a gesture that startled her as well as her clients, he lunged forward, eyes flashing, face contorted, his accusing finger pointing straight at her.

"Unbelievers, profaning a sacred moment with chatter. Hear, learn, obey, repent your evil uncaring ways. Be taken into the light of the world. Be admitted into the holy sepulcher. Be one with humanity and all loving, caring creatures. Be purified. Be saved!

Be!" His accusing hand lifted and spread open as a beam of light caught his fingers and spilled down his raised arm.

Tirla, translating as rapidly as possible in the dramatic pause, was thankful for some coherent phrases. Her clients might be listening to her, but their eyes were on him. He had the crowd's rapt attention now. Tirla was fairly sure that no one outside the circle could see her, but dared not stop talking. She kept spewing out the gibberish, worrying that such nonsense would not be worth the money promised her. They might not pay her at all. She was already regretting that she would miss the taste of the crisp green pepper she had hoped to purchase with her fee.

The Lama-shaman assumed another dramatic pose, arms out, palms upturned in entreaty.

"Bring me your sick, your weary, your wretched souls. Let me heal them. A touch will ease the tortured mind, the fevered body, the twisted limb, the blurred sight. Approach! Be not afeared. All things come to those who deserve. All creatures deserve Love. For it is Love, Love, Love that heals!"

Tirla rattled it all off easily, trying to peer through the shielding bodies to see who would be working the scam. Barney with his lizard eyelids—one blink, and his eyes were milky white blind; another, and he could "see clear once again, hallelujah!" Maybe Mahmoud with his double joints all twisted out of shape—one touch of the Lama-shaman's healing touch and they would straighten. Or would it be Maria with her weeping sores?

The Lama-shaman threw back his head, his hands turned gold in the narrow spot-beams, glittering from some sort of paint he must have used. Her clients inhaled with awe at the sight, their faces rapt as he made mystic passes with his magical hands. Glistening strands and bits whirled from his fingertips, disappearing in brief sparks as they left the light beams. That was a new trick, Tirla thought. Not bad. Pilau tried to catch a strand, but it disintegrated, leaving no trace in her grubby fingers.

Just then another strand, stronger, shot from the stage and fell on the head of a bemused man. He was less bemused when, with another grand flourish, the Lama-shaman began to reel him in.

"You have been chosen, brother. Come to me! Embrace me!" A ramp extruded from the stage, straight toward the chosen one, who glanced about with apprehension as he was pushed onto the ramp by those behind him and propelled forward by those on either side.

"Kneel, brother," the Lama-shaman intoned, and appeared to glide down the air.

Tirla could feel the faint vibration of the stage mechanism that supplied the effect, but she did not pause in her translations. It was a pretty good gimmick. She wondered where the control was. The mark appeared genuinely stunned at being chosen. He knelt obediently, a dazed expression on his face.

"Rallamadamothuriasticalligomahnozimithioapodociamoturialis tashadioalisymquepodial—Omathurtodispasionatusimperadomusi gena lliszweigenpolastonuchevaliskyrielisonandia. Moss pirialistusquandoruulabetodomoarigatoimustendiationallamegrachiatus . . ." the Revered Venerable intoned, holding his hand above the mark's head.

More syllables and almost-words that Tirla could not anticipate enough to mimic. She could appreciate and admire the Venerable's truly respectable breath control. Why, he sounded as if he could go on forever!

"What does he say?" Mirda pinched her sharply.

"How can I hear when you babble at me?" Tirla replied and made up suitable phrases, which she then translated. "Woops!"

Strange things were happening above the chosen one's head. How did the Lama-shaman *do* that with sleeves so tight at his wrists? Tirla wondered. Hair, face, and throat of the mark were shimmering with gold; the man's expression was first ludicrous and then ecstatic. Tirla wondered what the Venerable Prayman could be using. She was beginning to enjoy the spectacle.

The Revered slowly turned back to the audience, his face also golden-hued, the whites of his eyes visible. "The power is with me. Whom else will it touch?"

Raising his arms again and extending his hands forward, he gave the audience sufficient time to see the effect the "power" had had on the first "chosen." With a twist of his wrists, his palms turned over and strands shot out in all directions. Before Tirla could duck, one of the filaments landed on her head. Whatever it was stuck tightly in her hair despite quick efforts on her part to get rid of it. Her hands were caught by the adhesive, bound to her head now. She began to panic. There was no way she wished to be hauled up in public. Not with Yassim in the hall. Not with tieds on her, credits she had no right to possess under any circumstances.

The choir began to chant for the chosen to come forward, to

receive power. The audience caught up the refrain, and Tirla could hear the ominous overtone of envy from those who felt themselves more worthy of such an honor.

"She's been chosen!" Bilala and Pilau shrieked, bursting into an ululation that shot panic through Tirla's heart as they tried to push her forward toward the ramp nearest them.

"No, she's got to stay. She's got to tell us!" Mama Bobchik and Mirda Khan were not to be cheated. They pulled Tirla back.

"Break it, Cyoto. Help me, Lao Wang. Elpidia! Zaveta!" Tirla began struggling in earnest, terror starting to chill her guts.

All the other newly chosen were making their way up to the stage. The strand tightened, pulling at her hair. She twisted. Then suddenly she was snapped free. She caught the glint of a knife blade as she fell back against the solid Mama Bobchik. Zaveta and Mirda locked with the screaming Bilala and Pilau, who were attempting to regain control of Tirla.

As she had done before in such situations, Tirla dropped to the floor and plunged to one side, tripping someone, who fell heavily on her left foot. She ignored the stab of pain and crawled on, her breath coming in sobs. She rolled free of her encircling clients and scrambled to her feet, plowing through the chanters. Someone saw the dangling golden strand and grabbed it, nearly jerking her off her feet. To free herself she wrenched the tangled hair from her head, leaving the bit of scalp dangling in the man's hand.

"Grab her!" The chant was interrupted to set up the cry. She squeezed past several grasping hands, frantic to get to the lobby and the nearest emergency exit.

"Here, I gotcha!" She was encircled by massive forearms. She lifted her arms and slithered down; a kick was aimed at her belly, but despite being winded, she rolled, too accustomed to such dirty tactics not to have self-preserving instincts. She had a glimpse of one of Yassim's sassins, face wreathed in a witless grin of success, before she landed against the far wall, and suddenly two pairs of trousered legs shielded her.

She was helped to her feet by kind hands and made conscious of soothing thoughts of assistance, understanding, and sympathy. She recognized the aura just as her splayed fingers felt the doorframe. Managing to elude the hands, she whipped out the door and sped across the foyer, paying no heed to pleas to stop. An incredible multi-toned bellow rose behind her, an angry frustrated noise that gave impetus to her pumping legs. As she pounded down the access aisle, she heard a familiar thumping thud in the air above.

LEOs! Had they been on hand? Or had they been called? But it took time for LEO ships to assemble. She found the small square duct she needed, whipped off the cover, crawled inside, and, with some difficulty in the restricted space, snapped it back into place. She crouched in the dirt and grime, tilting her face away from the light as her lungs fought to repay her heart for the strain.

She heard people racing by, heard their exclamations as they reached the dead end, heard them turn and come back, and heard their steps continue on past her refuge. Despite the noise, Tirla fell asleep.

R*hyssa!*" The alarmed voice of the duty officer was accompanied by an impulse through her headnet that roused her instantly. "Yes?"

"Major disaster precog," Budworth said.

Great! Rhyssa thought sleepily. Two major trouble precogs in not quite two days and not a tremble about matters which urgently concerned all Talents.

"Recorded all across Asia," Budworth went on. "Looks like Kayankira's going to get another monsoon overload. They haven't repaired the restraining dams from the last one. How're we going to cope, with all the strong kinetics on the station?"

"Is there time to bring any down?"

"That's the panic! There's time enough, but weather conditions all across the world are freaky. Even if a Padrugoi shuttle launched, the nearest clear landing site is Woomera. The kinetics have to be on site to be effective." What Budworth did not say—"if Barchenka would allow 'em to leave the station"—flashed like a neon sign in Rhyssa's mind.

"Get Sascha up for me, will you, Buddy?"

He did, Sascha assured her. *Are you considering Peter?* His mental tone mixed eagerness to try and awareness of the multiple risks involved.

I must consider Peter's unique capabilities in a situation as critical as this, she told him.

How? Without compromising Peter's security?

They both slapped up internal shields as they felt the arrival of other thoughts.

Kayankira: *Rhyssa, I've got to have all the kinetics you have left. I understand there's no chance of getting any of them down from Padrugoi?*

Rhyssa: *That's my understanding.*

Vsevolod Gebrowski: *I shall insist! I shall take this to the World Council. They have deplored the situation in India. Let them put words into action. Reducing the density of population in that area of Bangladesh also diminished the available work force, and the necessary work has not been completed on time. Now we pay for that.*

Miklos Horvath: *Not if we draft the kinetics on Padrugoi down to help. And the cleanup effort will be reduced by kinesis now!*

Rhyssa: *If we can force the weather to give us a break!*

Bessie Dundall at Canberra: *The precogs all indicate the worst flooding ever in Bangladesh. The new levees haven't been completely restored, so floodwaters will drown this year's harvest. The barriers won't work for some reason—I suspect their erection will prove that once again corruption and bribery have been widespread. We have to do something!*

Alparacin: *Rhyssa, what about that team of yours I hear about?*

Rhyssa: *They're not well-enough trained for a disaster of this magnitude, dear friend. They'd be burned out.*

Peter: *No, I wouldn't.*

Quiet! Sascha, Rhyssa, and Dorotea ordered as one.

Peter: *I was, that was just to you.*

Rhyssa held her breath. But no Talent queried the unknown voice. *Naturally Eastern will do whatever we can,* she told the others. *May we have copies of the precogs? But I assure you that highly skilled kinetics are going to have trouble coping with this sort of thing, and all I have are a handful of fourteen-year-old trainee kinetics.*

Madlyn here . . .

Sascha: *Honey, you're one voice that never has to identify. What have you heard?* He imaged to Rhyssa a vision of Madlyn Luvaro, hands to her mouth to make a megaphone, leaning out of an airlock and shouting down to a wincing Earth.

Madlyn: *Lance has been arguing with Barchenka since he got the precog. She absolutely refuses to risk a shuttle or a pilot. You gotta admit the weather's pretty freaky all over right now. I can see it clear as day: lots of turbulence, and not just over the Indian continent. Lance says there has to be one safe place on Earth they can land, and they've got to help. He's citing her for contractual violation. She says it's too dangerous to risk so many*

Talents—now she's doing the matriarchal, protecting-you-against-your-own-altruism. Ha!

And there isn't a pilot we've talked to who'll risk a drop into the soup kettle down there, she went on. *Wait! Lance says*—Madlyn's mental tone altered to a rote-recital level—*now's the time to try. He says you'll know what he means. He accepts that it could be a risk, but if ever to put it to the test, now's the time. Have you got all that?* She sounded mystified.

Sascha: *You've come through loud and clear, Madlyn, and we copy.*

Lance says that the precog indicates even more horrendous damage than the last monsoon flood caused, so Talent has got to give kinetic support. He's dragooned a pilot into coming, but the guy's scared of attempting to land anywhere. Lance has assured him that all the kinetics on board will do the landing okay. Is Lance gone space-crazy? All right, I'm telling them. He says he, and a contingent of the heavy-duty kinetics—enough to effect flood control—will be on the shuttle Erasmus *in Hangar G at 0800. They're okay in space, but they'll need the help landing. That doesn't make sense to me, but that's what I'm supposed to tell you.*

Sascha came storming into Rhyssa's room. He had pulled his pants on but was carrying his shirt in his hand. He really did have a superb body, Rhyssa thought privately. Why isn't there the necessary chemistry between us? We'd make beautiful children. He looked so magnificent angry.

"Lance is out of his wig if he thinks Peter's up to a controlled landing in Dacca weather," he announced. "Landing pallets in a warehouse is a considerably different can of worms to a shuttle full of live folk we can't afford to smear across a gale-struck concrete runway."

Rhyssa fed a direct repeat of Lance's earlier conversation on Peter's potential and a similar situation into Sascha's mind. "He was only joking at the time," she said ruefully. "Quite a legitimate extrapolation."

"We just can't risk it," Sascha said, pacing up and down the room while Rhyssa untangled herself from her pastel-covered duvet and started dressing. "As neat a solution to the lack of kinetics as it is."

Rhyssa, with ineffable sadness: *Sascha-bear, you're halfway to figuring out just how he can do it!*

They were both startled by a timorous tap on her door.

"Yes?" She and Sascha exchanged glances.

"It's Peter. Can I come in?"

Sascha threw his arms up dramatically.

"Yes, yes," Rhyssa said, shooting a comprehensive warning at Sascha.

In his distress, Peter floated rather than walked into the room.

"No one bothered to channel their thoughts," he said, both apprehensive and defensive. "I couldn't help hearing."

"No, of course you couldn't, Peter," Rhyssa said.

Is Peter there? Dorotea's anxious tone startled them.

I'm here!

Young man, if you ever leave me again in that abrupt fashion, I'll tan your bottom!

Rhyssa and Sascha had never heard that particular note in the telepath's voice before.

I was trying to explain the problem to him when he zipped out of here so fast I thought he'd actually teleported himself.

I know the problem, Dorotea, Peter said in a very patient tone. *To land the shuttle safely at Dacca. And, with enough power, it'd be no more difficult than that container was, or the steel I sent to San Francisco.*

"The turbulence of a monsoon is totally unpredictable," Sascha began.

Peter's expression was one of abused patience. "It'd be the same principle in spite of turbulence. And better, because the shuttle won't be powered, so that won't throw off the snatch and grab of my gestalt."

"Simple when explained in that fashion," Sascha said at his driest. Then he flung up his hands in exasperation and turned to Rhyssa.

She took a reasonable stance. "The distance, the mass involved, even the turbulence are not factors you've dealt with before. We can't, and won't, risk burning you out."

Peter grinned. "You wouldn't. Though I'd need much more than four-point-five kpm. To be safe, I'd need some real power—like the city's turbos. They might seize up—but I wouldn't."

"We don't *know* that, Peter," Rhyssa said gently, permitting him to sense her anxiety.

"But *I* know that about me," Peter said, and levitated to the bed, where he perched beside her, upright enough, but with his arms and legs draped in unnatural positions. He made adjustments when he caught Rhyssa's look. "Instinctively!"

Then she hugged him, feeling tears of pride for the shining self-confidence that had emerged in the past few weeks. She held his lax narrow body for a long moment; then, sensing his embarrassment, she ruffled his hair and released him.

"Peter," Sascha said, hunkering down by the boy, "this *is* different from the exercises we've had you do. And this gestalt ability of yours is unique! We just can't risk it."

"Dorotea said I should trust my instincts," Peter said so firmly that both Sascha and Rhyssa regarded him for a long moment. "I also read the precog report. If there aren't enough kinetics, many people will lose their lives, as well as everything they've been struggling to build over the past two years. There'll be massive ecological damage, more plague, starvation. You keep feeding me all this stuff about the responsibility we Talents have to the rest of the world, how we're supposed to reduce death and damage. If I'm willing to take a little risk, I'd be a real Talent.

"I also heard what Madlyn said to you." Peter grinned ingenuously, wincing as if avoiding a loud noise. "Mr. Baden means me, doesn't he? That it's time to really try me."

Sascha sat down on the bed on Peter's other side and looked helplessly at Rhyssa.

"As I see it," Peter went on, clearly more in charge of the situation than his adult mentors, "we Talents don't have any option. We need the ones with Mr. Baden in the *Erasmus*. Sascha, when I shifted that steel the other day, you said I had graduated into a really useful category of kinesis. With enough power in the gestalt, I *know* I can land the shuttle."

Sascha slowly shook his head. "There's another major consideration, son . . ."

"I've been studying schematics on power generation," Peter continued blithely. "Turbos in particular, as they're more reliable."

"You have?" Rhyssa was constantly being surprised by the turns of Peter's avid studying.

"Well, I thought I ought to get some sort of basic concepts from which to work . . ." He saw their expressions and gave them a little smile. "I used to watch a lot of college-level vid courses. They were a lot more interesting than most of the late-night recreational garbage. Having to think hard took my mind off myself for a while. Engineering was a good think."

Sascha and Rhyssa were reduced to nodding in belated comprehension.

"Especially," Peter added, his eyes twinkling, "as no one really seemed to *know* what to make of my gestalting. And that's the other consideration, isn't it, Sascha? Keeping gestalt kinesis under wraps?"

"He's got us there, Rhyssa," Sascha said with a chagrined expression.

"That's what you're *really* worried about, but look, if the pilot brings the shuttle down far enough, I know I can get it safely through the turbulence and land it. And even the pilot doesn't need to know it wasn't Mr. Baden and the other kinetics who steadied the shuttle." When he saw that they were seriously considering his suggestion, he added, "It isn't as if I'd be bringing the shuttle all the way down from Padrugoi by myself, you know."

"And you think the city's power system will supply the necessary gestalt for you?" Sascha asked in a wry tone.

"The East Side Jerhattan power station's turbos should be enough." Peter's eyes glowed at the prospect of all that power at his disposal.

Rhyssa and Sascha began to laugh at the sheer impudence.

"You know, I really think that'll work," Dorotea said, entering the room. She was still in her nightclothes, a fetching pale lilac that set off her lovely white hair and porcelain complexion. "Since eavesdropping is in general order today, I've been following the conversations with great interest. There won't be time to talk that idiot of a power resources commissioner into agreeing to anything of such an experimental, and highly confidential, nature. The fewer people who know what we're doing the better." Her face took on an exceedingly sly look, totally uncharacteristic. "Let's invoke a G and H!" She chortled, looking exceedingly pleased with herself. "All we have to do then is call Boris—get him to clear the power station and use his official capacity to get us in."

"Invoke a G and H?" Rhyssa stared at the elderly telepath as if she had never seen her before.

"What's a G and H?" Peter asked just as Sascha began to guffaw.

"Why didn't I think of that?" Rhyssa exclaimed in exasperation. To the mystified Peter, she explained, "That's our mayday code, for George—that's George Henner, who once owned this house—and Henry—meaning Henry Darrow, who established Talent as a verifiable paranormal skill. If a Talent invokes a G and H, he gets immediate and unquestioned cooperation from every other Talent."

Sascha rubbed his hands together. "You know, I've always wanted the excuse to invoke that mayday code." *Brother,* he called. *It's a G and H: we need escort to the East Side power station, and it's to be cleared! Shouldn't be difficult with only a minimal night crew on call.*

Boris: *A G and H? Fascinating. I'm cleaning up after a major riot and you elect this moment in time to call a George and Henry?*

Sascha: *All we need is you and a LEO heli.*

Just me? Boris responded sarcastically.

Sascha agreeably: *You to get us the cooperation we need.*

And I can expect return cooperation from you? Boris, slyly.

Sascha: *It's a George Henry mayday, Bro. You can't refuse.*

Boris: *Quid pro quo, Bro. I was about to request your presence!*

Sascha: *For a riot?*

Boris: *I could certainly use your help on this one, Bro. Some oddities have cropped up that require your particularly acute telepathic Talent.*

Sascha raised his eyebrows inquiringly at Rhyssa, who reluctantly gave an assenting nod.

"Did you follow that, Peter?" Rhyssa asked, noticing that the boy's face was still registering surprise.

"Yes," he said tentatively.

"You don't really need me, Peter," Sascha said encouragingly. "You've got Rhyssa . . ."

"And Dorotea," the lady added stoutly.

"To buffer your mind," Sascha continued. *Don, as well, I think,* he added to Rhyssa. *Why does Boris have to need me at this moment in time?*

Dorotea: *Boris always did have an awkward streak in him. Comes from being a LEO by temperament.*

Rhyssa turned briskly to Peter. "Now, you'd better get dressed. Fetch your clothes here. And what should he get for you, Dorotea? You can change in my bathroom."

"I'll get down to Budworth for the vital statistics we need," Sascha said. "The weight of the shuttle, a radar link with the shuttle, repros of Dacca—in good weather—weather reports." *If I really think about this in any detail, I'll go crackers!* he added on a very fine thread to the two women.

Rhyssa and Dorotea replied with equal fervor: *You'll have company!*

If Peter thinks he can do it, I prefer to think he can, Rhyssa added. *After all, it's the thought that counts.*

Dorotea: *That's what does the trick.*

The necessary equations, based on Peter's established use of the gestalt plus distance, weight, and optimum speed of the shuttle, atmospheric conditions, and turbulence at the landing site, were all completed by the time the LEO heli arrived to transport them.

"I thought you were having a riot of a time and we'd get a deputy," Sascha said, but he was exceedingly relieved to have his brother's support.

"I am, but I'm the best authority you have for whatever's going on." Boris smiled with white-toothed malice. "You'll want to be in on this one, Bro. We've got a lead on the kidnappings."

Sascha swore with great ingenuity.

That's as important as this, Sascha, Rhyssa conceded. *With Dorotea and Don to help me buffer him, he'll be fine.*

I wouldn't interfere with a mayday if I didn't have to, the LEO commissioner said, even as he reached down to assist Dorotea into the heli.

Sascha, the kidnappers must be stopped, Dorotea said so sternly that her tone startled all the telepaths. *There! That's settled!*

"And this is Peter Reidinger?" Boris asked, as Peter reached the steps in his treading-water gait. "Hi!"

From the stunned look on Peter's face, Rhyssa suddenly realized that no one had thought to mention to the boy that the LEO commissioner was Sascha's twin brother.

"No, you're not seeing double. I'm older by five minutes," Boris went on amiably, deftly taking Peter under the arms and hoisting him aboard. *We'll both see them safely there before I abduct you, Bro, for my less nefarious purposes. The boy's the G and H?*

Sascha waggled his finger at his brother. *Naughty, naughty!* He swung aboard and started stowing the medical equipment Don Usenik handed up, ignoring Boris's grumbling. When Don climbed in, Sascha slid the door shut, and the big heli-bus glided upward and southeast.

Boris had strapped Peter into a window seat, and utterly entranced, the boy gazed down the black canyon of the Hudson to the mass of lights that glowed from every ziggurat and ribbonway of Jerhattan.

"Rather breathtaking no matter how often you see it," Rhyssa said to Peter, who nodded without taking his eyes from the view. By the time they landed on the roof of the facility, all the Talents were subtly aware of the emptiness of the massive structure.

"Well done, Boris," Dorotea said. "This way, Peter!"

"I hope you know what you're doing," Boris remarked wryly. "My office is on the line in this!"

"Thanks, Boris," Rhyssa said. "Can you retrieve us when we shout?"

"If I can't spare Sascha, I'll send someone you can trust," the LEO commissioner said as he handed Don his monitors. Then the big heli lifted away from the helipad.

Rhyssa took one equipment case from Don as he hauled open the roof door. As soon as Peter glided inside, he began to emanate excitement, his eyes sparkling with anticipation while he maneuvered down the stairs. They entered above the huge turbines, which were humming slightly as they served the needs of the great metropolis. They turned into the control room that overlooked the turbine floor, a room lined with the equipment that registered the flow of electricity to the various substations. With an ineffable air, Peter assumed the conformable chair of the duty engineer, swinging it idly from side to side until the adults organized the monitors and started hooking him up.

Above the windows overlooking the turbines were sufficient vid screens to display what Peter needed to see. Rhyssa began entering the appropriate programs, bringing up on one screen a high-resolution fax print of the *Erasmus;* on another, a display of its specifications; then weather simulations; and finally linking the station's communications grid to the main NASA board to follow the shuttle's descent. The *Erasmus* was already in flight, having begun its descent promptly at 0800 station time, 0130 Earth time. The power-station clock read 0550 as the deep radar net began to show the shuttle's spiraling descent. The final screen pictured the Dacca airport, lashed with rain and whipped by fierce gusts of winds that shifted tree trunks, parts of cars, crates, and all sorts of debris across the concrete runway where Peter was to bring the *Erasmus* safely down.

When Don Usenik had completed his check of the equipment monitoring Peter, Rhyssa and Dorotea took seats behind them, the mind of each lightly touching the boy's. He seemed not to notice, so intent was he on the *Erasmus*'s course. Just as it hit the atmosphere, the generators began to whine.

Rhyssa shook her head, as unable as the others to reach that part of Peter's mind that had linked with the enormous power of the turbines below them. The whine built, the decibels increasing to an almost unbearable pitch. Dorotea scrunched her features up, unashamedly covering her ears with her hands. Rhyssa was staring in disbelief at the wildly altered readings on the control console. Don Usenik kept his eyes on his medical monitors. Peter remained outwardly composed. Rhyssa noticed the slightly condescending smile on his face and just hoped he was not about to overreach himself.

Simultaneously both she and Don noticed the perspiration on the boy's forehead, but the smile remained in place. The generators reached a frenzied peak and maintained it. And the touch of Peter's mind altered! It became hard as stone. Peter had not locked mental contact out, but he had suddenly restricted the contact area, indicating intense concentration. Rhyssa caught Dorotea's eyes, but the older woman merely pointed to Don's patient and unalarmed watch of the monitors. The descent of the *Erasmus* visibly steadied and slowed.

He's done it! Rhyssa, Dorotea, and Don exclaimed in muted congratulatory tones.

Rhyssa hoped someone was recording for posterity what was unquestionably the most dramatic moment for Talent since a Goosegg registered Henry Darrow's delta-wave pattern during that first recorded precognitive Incident. Her mind still in contact with that part of Peter's which was accessible to herself and Dorotea, she watched the *Erasmus* landing, coming to a gentle stop at the passenger terminal, seemingly untouched by the battering wind. Peter gave a little chuckle, and suddenly the turbulence between shuttle and terminal abated, an eerie storm eye of absolute calm. Passengers hastily disembarked, pausing in astonishment as they became aware of the surrounding lull. One, his face indistinct on the small screen, lifted clasped hands above his head in a victory sign and then hurried into the dubious safety of the wind-battered terminal.

"Where should I send the shuttle, Rhyssa? Once I let go, that turbulence will just flip-flop it all over the place."

I hadn't thought that far ahead, Rhyssa admitted on the quiet to Dorotea.

"The weather charts suggest that Woomera would be the safest place, Peter, but . . ." Dorotea quickly scanned the worldwide meteorological report.

Only a slight increase in the generators indicated the effort involved as the *Erasmus* slowly turned and started back to the main runway.

"I think we'd better warn the pilot where he's going," Rhyssa said, and spoke urgently to Sirikit at the Control Center.

We've had the most unusual brownout here, Sirikit told her.

Get Main Air Control to warn the Erasmus *pilot ASAP that he's being diverted to Woomera.*

Erasmus? Diverted? For once the Thai woman's tranquillity slipped into astonishment. *Of course! Immediately!*

Preferably before he wets his britches, Don added as an aside, making both Rhyssa and Dorotea grin.

None of the three adults could feel any stress in the mind of the boy, who was totally wrapped in the curious process of gestalt. Physically he looked more frail than ever, and the bones of his skull seemed to expand under the thin skin of his head. They could all feel the tremendous power surging through him, but they could not deduce how he effected the control.

Slowly, against all the tenets of aerodynamics and in spite of the prevailing turbulence, the *Erasmus* sped down the runway and achieved a perfect takeoff.

"I don't believe this," Rhyssa muttered softly. "Who taught him to fly planes?"

"Every boy in this generation understands shuttle craft," Don remarked, but his expression was no less bemused than theirs. He watched as the *Erasmus* climbed slowly up into the swirling rain and clouds and out of sight. They followed it up to the supersonic level.

The generators wound down from their busy pitch.

"There!" Peter said suddenly with a note of complete satisfaction in his voice. "He's firing his engines, and he should know what to do now. I told him to land in Woomera. That was fun!" he added with less vigor. He was extremely pale and still perspiring heavily. "That was a lot of fun!" His eyes gleamed, and he grinned at Don Usenik, who shook his head with incredulity as he pointed to an almost normal pattern on the bioscan screen.

"Fun? You called that fun, Peter?" Rhyssa exclaimed almost angrily, realizing that she had been under a tremendous strain of worry even if Peter had not.

"With power like this, I could loft the shuttle much easier than the pilot could," Peter said in a voice that was suddenly hoarse with fatigue.

Dorotea, very privately to Rhyssa: *"How're you goin' keep 'em down on the farm, after they've seen Paree?"* She rolled her eyes expressively.

"Marked fatigue, low energy level, but even that's within what I'd call the normal range for a Talent," Don announced in a baffled tone. "You did great, Peter," he added proudly.

Clearing her throat, Rhyssa said wearily, "I don't think Ludmilla's going to believe that onboard Talents *also* 'ported the shuttle out again."

"Well, I couldn't leave it on the runway, Rhyssa, now could I?" Peter asked with weary irritation. "Those shuttles cost billions."

Suddenly all the telepaths were aware of other touches, vying to reach their minds.

Kayankira: *Oh, thank you, thank you. How did you manage?*

Rhyssa, Dorotea, and Don exchanged glances.

No, Rhyssa, Dorotea said on a very thin thread to the other two, *we didn't think this whole thing through very carefully.*

Rhyssa gulped and replied with an evenness in her mental tone that Dorotea applauded, *Lance is right there. It was all his idea. A real G and H. Wasn't it, Lance?*

Lance: *I'll tell her. I'd rather shout "Eureka" but accept the caveat.* He sent an image of a large crocodile, jaws wide in amazement, followed by a kangaroo bouncing from a pictorial map of Australia to the moon. *You never know till you try, do you, cobber?*

"Enough!" Dorotea said suddenly. "Let's get Peter home to bed. Don't you try to move a muscle, young man."

For one brief moment, Peter looked as if he was going to disobey. Then his expressions turned woeful. "I don't think I could right now."

"Nothing a good night's sleep and a hearty breakfast won't put right in next to no time," Dorotea said briskly, but the fierce glance she gave Rhyssa suggested that a lot more recuperation time might be required in spite of Don's optimistic interpretation of the monitors. "Now, how do we get him back to the Center? Boris and Sascha are apparently up to their eyeballs in their riot control."

The Center vehicle's coming, Sirikit said, a ripple of amusement in her voice. *Just stay put!*

Even through the heavy roof sheeting of the power station, they could hear the vibrations of the approaching heli. Then the roof door opened and a figure charged through.

"You all right down there? I was told to come pick up pieces!" Dave Lehardt cried, descending three steps at a time.

Rhyssa nearly wept with relief. What had Boris, the sly mutt, said? "Someone you could trust!"

"Hi, Peter," Dave said. "What have you all been up to that your PR man gets called out of his bed in the wee small hours of the morning?" Then he knelt down by the boy, his expression very gentle. "You look done in. Tell me later, huh?" With tender solicitude, he gathered up the exhausted boy and, moving with exquisite care, started up the stairs with him. Rhyssa followed, immensely grateful for his unexpected presence.

CHAPTER 9

Within minutes of the Event, an Incident Room was in place on the wide mall in front of the Assembly atrium. Crowd-control Talents and LEO specialists had quickly defused the volatile temper of the incipient mob. Although a number of attendees had managed to evade the LEO backup, the rest were being systematically ID'd.

The focus of the Incident, some twenty women of various ethnic groups, had been immediately sequestered in one of the rehearsal rooms behind the atrium and, despite their loud lamentations and protestations of innocence, were being adroitly questioned by a special Talent team.

By then Boris and Sascha had arrived in the big heli. Already the tapes from the hi-eyes, discreetly set in the high ceiling of the hall by two industrious electricians who had come with the RIG setup team, were being viewed in the Incident Room by the original precogs, Auer and Bertha Zoccola. Boris and Sascha took up observation positions. The portable's walls were packed with analyzers keyed in to the LEO mainframe. Debriefing reports by crowd-control Talents were being made at the various stations, while LEO personnel avidly read rap sheets spewed out by churning printers as the wrist-ID scans were processed. Frequently the LEO commissioner was interrupted in his viewing to initial warrants, but the main meat of the Incident eluded all. Revered Venerable Ponsit Prosit had once again flitted off in time.

"So my precog centered on the women," Bertha was saying, studiously avoiding eye contact with Auer. The dour man was pulling at his lower lip, oblivious to her as the replay continued. "While his was for Flimflam. When are you going to bust that guy?

He's obscene, a miserable maggot of a man, leeching off emotions —you know that's all he is! An emotion leech, growing fat whenever he has a mob to suck! The bigger the bunch he manipulates, the bigger his hit." She waved her arms in exaggerated circles.

"As I've explained before, Bertha, he inadvertently serves a purpose," Boris explained patiently. "He works them up, yes. He may get a vicarious pleasure holding a crowd in the palm of his hand, but his histrionics defuse a lot of pent-up garbage in a catharsis not generated by passive watching of the tri-d fare. Occasionally he runs pretty close to dogmatic insult, but usually he's innocuous and says nothing."

" 'Says nothing' is right!" Bertha muttered indignantly.

Boris went on. "He had registered sponsors for tonight, some East Indian Mystical Concept Group which is properly registered and screens as legit. We had no grounds to deny them, or him, the right of religious assembly."

"Religious assembly!" Bertha was outraged. "Religion he ain't got. And religious assemblies are supposed to be uplifting, not downtrodding. He's a rouser, a leech, a spewer of blasphemy. He's dangerous." She waggled a finger violently under Boris's nose. "There're laws against inciting to riot, and he caused one tonight."

"Unfortunately, Bertha, your precog absolves him of primary blame." Boris tried to exude pacification. Her voice was getting louder with each denunciatory remark, and she had never been noted for tact.

"Who gave him strands, Commish?" she demanded. "You can't tell me he didn't use 'em with criminal intent!"

Boris's patience snapped, and he sent a crisp summons to Sascha, who was outside helping the telempaths keep control. "On that count, we've a search-and-find warrant out for him right now."

"It was me twigged Flimflam, Bertha Zoccola," Auer said, glaring furiously at the little woman. "He's none of your business."

Sascha arrived and deftly rendered her helpless with a heavy lean on her speech centers just long enough to escort her to a debriefing position at the opposite end of the room.

"We got another wild one manufacturing that strand stuff for Flimflam?" Auer asked Boris in a low voice.

"Could be, Auer," Boris replied unhappily. "That's the only way fringe fanatics like Ponsit Prosit could obtain strands." The tangling substance was a recent LEO invention, produced from an aberrant chemical compound to provide a fast-drying midrange restraint. Top secret, its formula and processing were of a complexity that ought not to be easily duplicatable. "There's a real smart head out there somewhere. Forensic says the stuff is pretty damned close to our formula. More toxic, which is bad, and less durable, which is fortunate. You've a good feel for technical matters, Auer. Keep your mind open for us, will you? Report even the slightest twinge. We've got to find this bozo as soon as possible. I don't care what sort of Talent emerges from Residential genes but, whatever it is, it should be registered with *us.*"

"I can't imagine Flimflam having enough credit to hire that sort of smarts. Ah, and I see Yassim's got himself a new ladrone?" Auer asked cynically, pointing at the replay.

Boris regarded him with approval. "You caught that one frame of Yassim?"

Auer shook his head but pointed to the tape being played over and over on the screen. "I keep up-to-date on the LEO visitors' list. Every ladrone, hitter, and sassin known to be connected with Yassim was here tonight. He had to be, too. Didja get many?"

"A good crop but no one of particular importance," Boris said, and then grimaced. "You know those new indestructible door-eyes we've been installing? It could have been Yassim's people, or maybe the new Talent who supplied Flimflam with strands, but every one of them was disabled. Very cleverly, with a bit of wire, a hairpin, even a twisted length of foil—nothing irreparable but enough to cloud the count. We're ID'ing everyone who didn't have a chance to leave after the Incident, but we're shy counts on exactly who, and how many, came to the party."

Auer nodded again, sympathetic in his own sour way to the commissioner's frustration. "I'll keep it all in mind, Commissioner. Leave you to it."

Boris turned his attention to the head of the team questioning the focus group. *Norma, any luck?*

No, sir, they're still on the boil. We're getting anger, frustration, envy, some anxiety and worry over being detained, mainly maternal, but really, sir, we can only get the dominant emotions. They're angry at being 'done.' And not by old Ponsit Prosit Flimflam. Trouble is, none of 'em speak much Basic. Could we have a linguist down here? Someone who's got Neerest, Paki, and Asian languages? Ranjit, maybe?

I'll send him along presently. Anything else?

Yes, sir. Nine of them are involved in some kind of feud. We've had to
separate them twice already to keep them from scratching each other or
pulling hair. Something about being chosen and it wasn't right to intervene.
Doesn't make any sense.

"Being chosen?" Boris spoke aloud as well as mentally.

Sir?

Thank you, Sergeant, you've just triggered a thought! Boris turned to
the screen as yet another replay of the Incident began. He forwarded it quickly and then reduced the speed, his eyes on the
screen.

You've got something? Sascha was at his shoulder.

If my theory is correct that Flimflam was fingering people for someone—
Yassim probably, since his men were there in force—I want to know what
the common denominator of choice was, Boris told his twin. *Most of them*
were males except our focus group, which were—ah, here we are!

The two brothers watched as the reduced speed clearly showed
the strand falling in the center of the focus group.

It didn't hit a woman! Unless she was a midget, Sascha said, pointing
to the thin hands clawing up out of the mass. Boris tapped out an
enlarge, sharpening the definition in the center of activity. *A child?*

No child in the group being held. Twenty women. I can count that many
heads.

Sascha: *Are some tugging?*

Yes, and some resisting. Norma said the women are contentious. In an
overlay of thought, Boris repeated Norma's exact words.

Sascha: *And feeling cheated. Look! Knife severing the strand. Now all*
hell breaks loose.

"Okay, who were the nearest crowd controllers?" Boris asked.

Cass Cutler and Suzanne Nbembi were summoned, still wearing
their undercover gear, although Cass had wiped off the heavy
makeup and discarded the tangle of cheap jewelry. Boris spun the
tape back to the relevant scene.

"Cass, Suzanne, good strong damper work today."

"It was very close, Commissioner," Cass said, rolling her eyes.
"Could have been a bad one without that precog."

"Either of you two see a child with our focus group?"

"No," Cass replied quickly, and then frowned. "At least, I don't
think she was with *them.* We first noticed her trying to get away
from Bulbar."

"We would have intervened—no girl child should be caught by

that scuz—but she freed herself," Suz added. "Knew well enough how."

"She dodged behind us for a moment, on her way to an exit. Just then the Incident erupted. Funny about that . . ." Cass faltered, frowning. "I felt *something*, Commissioner, when I touched her. A shield solid as a wall, and that's odd enough for a Linear kid. She might even have some latent Talent."

"We still haven't found the reason for the riot. Could she have something to do with it if she's a possible latent Talent?" Boris mused, tapping the monitor.

Cass gave a diffident shrug, but both she and Suz watched the replay closely. Boris speeded it up, stopping at the moment when the hands appeared, looking more balletic in slow motion than frantic as the slender fingers splayed in panic; then the sequence went on, showing fingers clutching at the strand, the flash of the knife, and the scrimmage of the women.

"Can you get the perimeter of the scene just before they started to boil?" Cass asked.

Boris tried every combination of review, but the hi-eye had been fixed on the precogged site of the Incident, and although the definition was sharp, the angle obscured what Cass wanted to see.

"Ranjit Youssef reporting as requested, sir." The young LEO officer presented himself a respectful distance from the absorbed cluster around the screen.

"And what did the search of the assigned quarters reveal, Lieutenant?" Boris asked formally.

"Commissioner, the count of illegal children under the age of ten is eight hundred and three, including five newborns. In fact, all the children apprehended are under ten."

Although the LEO commissioner was not actually surprised, the total was considerably higher than estimated. He propped himself against the desk edge and folded his hands over his chest, rubbing his jaw pensively. *Eight hundred?* he repeated.

And three, Sascha added, his mental tone equally grim.

Boris: *And all to be sacrificed to produce more underfed disposable kids to be abused one way or another. How can the traffic be stopped when people blindly follow an archaic ethnic imperative?*

"Any with legal wrist IDs?" Boris asked Ranjit aloud.

"The nine-year-olds, sir, but so far no IDs match the genetic print registered for the number. There are also far fewer preteens and teens than a Residential population should generate."

"As usual. How many of the illegals under ten were found in the quarters of the focus women?"

"Thirty-two, some too young to run for it. The older ones had some warning—they always do. But a clamp is already initiated. No one without a wristband will move out of this Linear," Ranjit said, "even through disposal chutes."

"Ah, yes, disposal chutes," Boris added with a further sigh of resignation. "And, I trust, the cargo lines? Good." He tapped a sequence and the screen showed the architectural schematic of Linear G, slowly rotating to display every angle of the immense ziggurat. "Norma Banfield needs your linguistic abilities, Lieutenant. She's in the rehearsal hall to the left of the stage. She's got a mess of ethnics with little Basic, and there are two factions at least willing to pull hair."

"Pull hair?" Cass sat upright, a wisp of a memory surfacing from the recent explosion.

"Got something, Cass?" Boris asked.

"I'll work on it." She sagged into as much of a relaxed state as the activity in the room permitted. Suz began a soothing massage of her neck muscles to encourage recall.

"I'll do what I can to help Lieutenant Banfield." Ranjit saluted and left.

Cass stood. "I wanna check something in the hall, sir, unless some officious moron has sent the cleaners in already."

"Go to it." Boris gestured broadly and turned back to the schematic to try and figure out where refugees might hide in the maze of corridors, closets, and conduits. *Sascha, get your teams to start searching ducts. Scared kids can squeeze into the damnedest places. I don't want a single illegal to get caught by Yassim's slimy hooks.*

Done. Sascha's eyes blanked briefly as he gave the orders.

"I got it," Cass cried, reentering the room. She gave an eerie yodel and held the trophy up. "Her scalp, by all that's holy!"

With two fastidious fingers, Boris took the hank of hair, the dull severed strand tangled right to the bloody patch of skull skin. *Loufan! Find out all you can about the person who grew this!*

The technician hurried to the commissioner's side, received the tress without expression, and went back to his cubicle.

Commissioner, Ranjit said. After a polite pause to be sure he was not interrupting, he went on. *They're hiding something.*

Norma: *Someone. I concur. Someone important to them.*

Ranjit: *I think that's the reason for the dissension, sir.*

Norma: *I would go along with that. May I nudge them, sir?*

Boris: *By any fair means, Lieutenant,* Boris told them. He grinned to himself, knowing Ranjit's scrupulous sense of honor, and then felt the mental touch that meant Sascha had overheard the exchange.

Dealing with the unTalented took heroic efforts, Boris thought. On the other hand, did he really want everyone to have paranormal abilities? Or at least some minor paranormal quirk, so that there would be less hassle? But that gave rise to envy—envy of someone more Talented than oneself, which only increased dissension and prejudice. No, far better to have a small minority, dedicated—and disciplined—to perform functions that the mind-numb could not. And all of the peculiar and unusual quirks *registered!*

Sir? Loufan paused. *I removed the strand from the scalp, as it interfered with the reading and is certainly irrelevant. The subject is a Eurasian ethnic mix, preadolescent female. Good strong genoprint, good immune factors, healthy, unusually so.* The technician sounded surprised. Linear G subsistence fare was nutritionally adequate, of course, but if the child was illegal, as Boris suspected, how had she managed to be healthy? *And there's no match of birth ID.*

Boris: *Did you really expect to find one?*

Loufan: *Yes, sir.*

It was Boris's turn to be surprised.

Loufan: *She could have been a runaway or a kidnap.*

Boris: *Okay. File the data, Loufan, and give the hair to Bertha. Ask her —in your ineffably polite style—if this artifact sparks anything off in her mind?*

Moments later Bertha came storming back to him. "Oh, the poor thing! Hair torn right out of her scalp! Commish, who did it?"

"Possibly Bulbar. Sense anything?"

Bertha pressed the lock against her ample bosom, closed her eyes, and concentrated. "Not a thing, but it's there in my mind now." She grimaced in sudden revulsion and thrust it back to him. "Take it away!"

Sascha intercepted the lock. "Black, good length," he murmured. "Some of those women never cut their hair. Healthy, and much *people be so irresponsible as to produce countless unwanted children and waste them?*

Even illegal kids have rights, Sascha responded, gently quoting his brother his own words. *See that even the least of them get that much.*

Illegals go to the space station. Boris sounded defeated.

They don't go as grunts. They're trained to do something a lot more constructive than their parents ever did. Leave it, brother.

I scratch your back, Bro, not your nose, Boris said wryly. *Now, I'm putting in an appearance to scare some sense out of those flipping focus females!*

No one better. By the way, when you have a spare moment, listen to a news update. Then you'll know why we twisted your arm with a G and H.

I congratulate the triumph I sense in your mind, but I'll have to wait on a replay of the event, Boris said as he entered the rehearsal hall, thinking what a scarce commodity time was right then.

He crossed the threshold, assuming his most awe-inspiring official manner. Tall, handsome, the strength in his powerful frame shown off even by the bulky action uniform, he succeeded in scaring the gaggle of women silent, a silence that did not last too long, though the renewed bursts of argumentative crosstalk were considerably subdued.

I just got something, Commissioner, Ranjit told him. *A flash from the woman fourth on the left, the plump young one with the caste mark. "It's all Tirla's fault." Tirla is, I think, a feminine name.*

"Translate for me, Lieutenant," Boris said, striding imperiously in front of the women, his tone haughty. "I am LEO Commissioner Boris Roznine. Where is the girl child you had with you this evening?"

Boris had no trouble picking up the reactions of resentment, envy, anger, dismay, and fear as he gave Ranjit time enough to repeat his words in the various languages. The women had had time to realize that they were in deep trouble with Authority. Several had vivid worries about their children, left too long alone in their squats. Others concentrated on nursing their sense of grievance. He caught occasional variations on the phrase Ranjit had twigged, but no one else volunteered a name. "It was all *her* fault." They contented themselves with impersonal malice.

"Let me reassure you that the children in your homes are being cared for until you can return to them," he said, smiling kindly.

As the import of his sentence was understood by each group, the

cleaner than you'd expect. Shouldn't be too hard to find a juven
with a hunk torn out of her scalp."

"I'd rather you give it to Carmen," Boris told him. *Ranjit thin*
quite a few of the older illegal kids eluded the search teams, he adde
Could she be one of them? She might lead us to the rest.

Carmen Stein laid the lock across her thighs and stroked it flat,
using her long fingernails to separate the tangled hairs. For
several more minutes she fingered them, softly coaxing a sense of
their grower's whereabouts. Carmen always looked so placid and
imperturbable when she was evoking her Talent as finder. Better
than most, Sascha knew just how much activity her brain was generating at such moments. She was one of the best searchers he had
ever encountered and, because her Talent was intense and exhausting, he protected her as much as he could, limiting her assignments.

"The incident occurred how long ago?" she asked without taking
her eyes from the hair.

"Approximately sixty-two minutes."

"Ah, she is hiding. That accounts for the darkness. I cannot see
where. There is no light. A constricted space."

"A conduit?"

"That's possible." Carmen sounded dubious. "I think she
sleeps."

"That's a cool one."

"No," Carmen said, taking him literally. "Not cool. Tired." She
offered him the hair.

"No, keep it, Carmen, for now. We'll need to know if she
moves."

Calmly Carmen leaned forward, took a clip from the brightly
enameled jar on the table, and fastened the tress, the scalp end now
coated with a protective film, high on the right side of her head.

Sascha had relayed Carmen's comments to Boris.

A conduit, huh? There's so few of those in a Linear. The LEO Commissioner's mental tone was facetious. *We're flushing kids out of every*
available space. I hate this, Sascha, I hate it. Sascha sent quick soothing thoughts to ease the turmoil in his brother's mind, but Boris
went on. *The miracle of life should be a blessing, not a curse. How can*

wailing, breast-beating, and pulling of hair began, and more recriminations were spewed. Boris was well aware of fury, loss, resignation, and relief in one case, but he could not understand any
actual linguistics used in the varied emotional reactions.

Ranjit: *This Bilala says that it is all* her *fault for resisting the Lama's
choosing.* Ranjit was restraining the plump caste-marked virago
from rushing at the haughty, hawk-nosed older woman on the
other side of the room. *She says Mirda Khan brought all this on herself.
Mirda Khan replies that—ah, the name again, Tirla—would not have been
able to translate for any of them up on the stage. She had done little enough
to earn baksheesh, a tip.*

Boris: *Lieutenant, ask them who is Tirla's mother.*

The question shut the women up and briefly closed down their
mental perturbations. Then they all launched into personal lamentations again. The answer was also quick. None of them was
Tirla's mother, and without exception, just as Boris had hoped,
every one of them flashed a quick mental image of the girl in question.

Got it, Ranjit and Norma told him in unison.

As I did. With a gesture to signify that the women could be processed or released as their condition warranted, the LEO commissioner hurried back to the Incident Room.

Loufan awaited him there in front of the graphics pad, stylus
ready. For this sort of transference, Boris grasped the technician's
thin shoulder and concentrated on the vivid image of the Tirla
child. Loufan sketched quickly, capturing in a few clever lines the
intense face—remembered by most in its panic at being stranded—
the wide-set, slightly tilted huge dark eyes above prominent cheekbones, the abundant waving dark hair framing it, the fine straight
nose, the small cautious mouth, the long sweep of a determined
jawline, the odd cleft in the chin. A charming face, if one dis-
counted the fright, intelligent despite the fear. Tirla looked no
more than eight or nine, but some wisp of thought—from the fat
old woman—suggested that she was older. The woman's memory
of her went back quite a few years.

"Is that her?" Loufan asked, transferring the sketch to the
screen.

The LEO commissioner allowed himself a good long look,
matching the image on the screen to the consensus in the minds of
twenty women. "Yes, that's it. Print it, circulate it to all officers

and Talents. I think we should find that child. Cass might be right about latent Talent. And if Flimflam was after her, there may be more to her than we realize. I also need to file an intelligent reason why a RIG damned near turned into a full-scale riot, and she just might provide the answer," he concluded. *Sascha, could someone be an instantaneous translator?*

Sascha considered that. *I'd say that she displayed more than a mere language facility—quite possibly Talent. Anyone who could translate ten different languages as she apparently could would be valuable to either or both of us.* He grinned at his brother. *First we'll have to find her. Then we can evaluate her abilities.*

T irla!

Tirla woke suddenly, jolted out of her exhausted sleep by someone calling her name softly and appealingly. Tirla did not move, or so much as open her eyes.

Clever little trinket, isn't she? Call her again.

Won't work, Boris. She's alert now.

It had to have been part of a dream. She often dreamed that she heard her mother calling her name. It had to be a dream, because no one could know where she was, despite LEOs searching the main conduits and sending drone units down the smaller ones. On her way home from the debacle of the meeting, she had escaped all types of earnest hunters. She had seen the numbers of children being flushed from hidey-holes.

Her hunch about the meeting had been correct. It had served as an excuse to sweep down on the pads, collect illegal children, and check all IDs. No one, absolutely no one, had ever known where she squatted. She did not even think to herself where she was. And no one was likely to discover her even in this intensive search.

Somewhat reassured, Tirla nestled back into the warmth of her sleep sack. Suddenly she heard noises nearby and froze. She heard the doors into the closed section being opened. This search was unusually thorough. Not even she had been able to get into the engineering space, and yet it was being checked.

Not even Yassim's men could find her, and they knew all the ducks and dodges that any subbie had ever figured out. She had been so lucky not to be caught by Bulbar. He was wicked dangerous. Her head still throbbed where the hair had been torn away.

She had dabbed on some dis-wipe. Bulbar could have been carrying any kind of 'mune to infect her, scabby old scuz.

Her problem with Yassim remained. She had not washed the tieds. How would he expect her to when he, and every trader, had been lucky to escape the bust? Not that he took excuses. What awful luck to be singled out by the Lama-shaman! Which of the women had he really been after? And why? It made no sense to Tirla. None of them was pretty or young, or even on the lay—not with *their* husbands!

The noise of search was diminishing, and carefully Tirla reached unerringly for the water jug and food that she kept for such emergencies. Chewing the dry-eat made terrible noises in her head. She had heard about the wide-range ultrasensitive gear that was said to pick up breathing in a radius of five klicks, but there should be enough minor noises from the generators and air-conditioning units to mask her chewing, and she was terribly hungry. Finally, thirst and hunger assuaged, Tirla snuggled deeper into her sack and went to sleep again.

T ake a break, Carmen," Sascha told the finder. "She won't venture out until night. If then."

Carmen rubbed delicately at her temples and sighed. "You're right. I'll rest. She's unusual, isn't she, Sascha?"

"We believe so, even if we don't know specifically why."

Carmen regarded him with some surprise. "It's a lovely clear mind. Like a bell—when she's asleep. She's wary and cautious awake, that one. I can touch her but not read her. And with her in the darkness, I can't even help you home in on her."

"She'll come out in good time."

Carmen shot a look that suggested that Sascha Roznine might— this once—be wrong. He grinned and winked as he turned to leave her quarters.

F rankly, Sascha, we've run everything we got on the people Flimflam fingered for Yassim," Boris Roznine said, tossing a sheaf of hard copy onto the desktop, "and we can't find a common denominator. They're mostly able-bodies, doing enough work to

keep away from Conscriptive Work Services, only minor misde-
meanors on their sheets, none of 'em known to gamble or dip."

Sascha smiled knowingly and felt his brother poke at his mind,
but he kept his shield in place. He could do that to Boris, whereas
Boris could not keep him out at all. "You've had a hard thirty
hours, so I'll tell you. They were all fathers."

"What?" Blood suffused Boris's face.

"Flimflam had accessed ordinary info on residents of the Linear.
Mind you, it was so simple we didn't see it at first. Bertha's sensitive to females and children, Auer to the blacker side of life."

Boris scrubbed at his head. "Sometimes it is the simple things we
miss. So Flimflam was fingering fathers with likely youngsters,
and the girl was a bonus?"

"I guess, and we're still in the dark about her," Sascha added,
aware of his brother's next query. "Carmen's latched, but the girl's
cautious and hasn't moved since she went to ground."

"Scared?"

"Strangely enough, no. I'd hazard that she's had to keep a low
profile before. She's a preteen and illegal."

"That will sharpen the senses."

"How're you doing with Yassim's operation?"

"We figure he picked up at least nineteen children, maybe a few
more." Boris grimaced. "We collected eight hundred and three illegal kids from Linear G. If what Harv believes is possible—that
every one of the related mothers has been having a kid a year—
we're minus a possible forty. We located eighteen of that forty in a
storage basement, but they've got the entry jammed. We're working on it." Boris shook his head. "They really will be better off in
hostels."

"And in space?" Sascha asked wryly.

"Even in space they have a better chance than stalemated in a
Linear."

"But they won't be able to reproduce themselves." Sascha had
never approved of the law that required the sterilization of illegal
offspring.

Boris raised his hands in resignation. "I don't make the laws,
Sascha. I only enforce them." Then he leaned forward and tapped
up a new program on his big screen. "All right. Now, we have to
find Yassim in *his* warren and save nineteen kids or more from
him."

S he's moved, Sascha," Carmen said, her tone half-triumphant, half-anxious.

Sascha consulted his watch. "This time of day?"

"Linear will be crowded with those coming off work."

"Keep as close as you can to her."

"It's very difficult, Sascha. It's almost as if she isn't *seeing* the things she's looking at. I can't get a real fix, except that there are people all around her. Wait! She's stopped. No, that's no good. All I get is a mass of standard-issue clothing. She's still in a crowd."

"I'm in touch with our teams on the main levels of G. Just give us a direction, Carmen. Any direction." *Alert to our quarry!* he added in a mental call to Cass and Suz.

T irla was relieved that it had been Mirda Khan she first came across. Mirda was full of the whole affair, her black eyes snapping with indignation and a certain sly malice that she had not suffered at the hands of the Public Health—it had been a long time since her womb had borne fruit. But she had the grace to mourn her friends' losses, of both their existing children and their hope of more.

"They will see how hard it is for those of us who have no children to sell."

"Was that why Yassim was there? To buy children?"

"Why else?" Mirda lifted her shoulders in an eloquent shrug. "He would have no interest in spiritual things."

"Did he get them all?" Tirla was aghast. Yet if a big score put Yassim in a very good mood, he would be easier for her to deal with over the matter of the tieds she had been unable to wash.

"No, *they* got most of them. Yassim cannot have many, but those he got he got for nothing!" Mirda was indignant. "No price was paid to their grieving mothers and fathers. They ran into his arms to escape the LEOs. Ran! And no credits exchanged, not even a bargain made. Oh, he will not dare to enter G again." Then suddenly Mirda latched steely fingers into Tirla's shoulder. "*What* was the Lama-shaman saying? You didn't tell us. Aiiiye, and to increase insult, you did not even have the grace to accept the strand that chose you. You have earned the undying hatred of Bilala and Pilau for not accepting his choice."

Tirla wrenched herself free. "Choice? I am nothing—why would he choose me? I think he missed. Tell Bilala that I think he was aiming for her and missed. But, as for what he said, you missed nothing. That Lama-shaman spewed stupid syllables only. Not a proper word in any language. Even in his head he wasn't using real words. He didn't mean to. He is a sham man, not a shaman. It was all set up for the Public Health to raid Linear G."

"How could that be?" Mirda was startled. "No, it could not be. Not with traders there with all their goods and some of it not things the LEOs should discover on them. And certainly not when Yassim, and every ladrone, hitter, and sassin he employs, were also present. *They* would have known. Perhaps the strand was meant for Bilala, as you said. She felt that was proper for her, too, you understand, for she has been worthy. A woman who has borne a child every year for her husband. Aiyyee, and they have taken that from her now, and his pride from him. He will reproach her until the day of her death." Mirda began to beat herself across her breasts, and Tirla used the distraction to slip away.

So, Yassim had children from G and had not paid for them. And she had tieds that she could not deal for him, which she had better return. If he had enough children, then with luck he would not take her.

It was wrong of Bilala to hate her. Tirla wished that she had asked Mirda if any more of her clients did. It was essential for Tirla to stay on good terms with everyone in Linear G. She was just as illegal. Bilala or Pilau could be spiteful enough to turn her in, as a token revenge for the loss of their own children. Unless . . .

Unless Tirla could get a price for the children who had run into Yassim's clutches. She knew where he kept such merchandise. It would depend on who he had taken.

She skipped down a side aisle where, looking around to be sure she was not observed, she yanked at a conduit grille. It resisted, and she saw that the screws had been replaced. She felt inside the grille to be sure there were no wires or eyes, but this was a small opening, one only a very small or thin child could have used, and had not been staked out. She got out the vibro-blade she had earned for some long-forgotten favor and sheered off two screws. Then she climbed into the dark conduit.

C armen was exasperated. *Just when I had a good placement—or thought I did—she's gone into the dark again. No, wait, Sascha, there's light around her now. She's in some sort of a cramped tunnel.*

Sascha: *Uses the bloody conduits like a subway. I'll have the schematic of G on my screen for the next year at this rate.*

Carmen: *Think how well you'll know the innards of a Residential by then.*

Sascha: *Thanks. Keep track of our mole.*

Carmen: *Wait a minute, Sascha, I think she's moving out of G.*

Sascha, startled: *How can she?*

Carmen: *She's in the underground. Red light. The freight subways are the only tunnels illuminated in red, aren't they?*

Sascha: *Omigod, which direction has she gone?*

Sascha, Cass here. Mirda Khan was just seen talking with our quarry. Khan insists that the girl escaped from her. I'll believe that when pigs fly.

Sascha: *What were they talking about?*

The meeting, Flimflam, Yassim. Khan has gone into panic and isn't making much sense. She's afraid—there's suddenly a real big dollop of guilt, anxiety, mainly fear. For herself and just a little for Tirla.

Sascha: *Boris! Our quarry may be venturing into one of Yassim's industrial territories. Alert your surveillance.*

At his desk in the Parapsychic Tower, Sascha Roznine experienced the sort of frustration that plagued few Talents. Hardened criminals were easier to apprehend than one preadolescent child who looked nearly half her actual age. And what on earth was the child doing in Yassim's territory? She would have done better to crawl back into her very secret hidey-hole. He was tormented with memories of the pix of vivisected child bodies.

CHAPTER 10

Barchenka was furious when informed that she would be deprived of her strongest kinetics for the week it would take to mitigate the monsoon flooding. She first cried mutiny, then grand larceny, but was brought up short by her own Station Authority, who pointed out that the Talents had a legal right to attend major disasters such as the one that undeniably existed in the Bangladesh flooding. Also, the pilot was an off-duty volunteer, and there had been no damage to the *Erasmus*, which he had returned to Padrugoi as soon as Woomera cleared him for a launch.

Massive efforts in shoring up the levees and careful manipulation of the barriers and dams prevented the Ganges from turning the lower portion of Bangladesh into a vast lagoon from Bogra to the sea. Still, whole towns had to be evacuated and necessary supplies shifted, difficult even kinetically in the appalling conditions. The force of the channeled flood did inundate Chittagong and coastal towns below it, but not as disastrously as the precog had predicted. Talent once again had reduced the impact of a major natural catastrophe.

Peter Reidinger, on the other hand, slept late into the next morning, but when Don Usenik checked him over, he seemed none the worse for his major gestalt effort. But there was no doubt that his achievement had altered him: he neither floated nor essayed to walk—he strutted, chin high, with a slightly superior smirk on his face.

"What was the saying? 'Power tends to corrupt, and absolute power corrupts absolutely'?" Sascha asked Rhyssa, peevish in his frustration over the lost girl. "He's insufferably smug this morning."

Dorotea gave a snort. "Don't overreact, Sascha! He's got a right to crow. Perfectly natural in anyone, especially a fourteen-year-old boy whose only available movement until recently was tonguing a switch or blinking his eyes at tri-d to change channels. Pretty heady stuff to save a country. I scanned him pretty deeply at brunch while he was still sleepy, and there's nothing in his mind that smacks of corruption." She grinned. "A bigger generator, more derring-do, and plenty of self-satisfaction."

"Lighten up, Sascha-bear," Rhyssa said, smiling encouragingly. "Or don't you remember some of the tricks you and Boris pulled at that age?"

"A telepath can't get into quite the same sort of trouble a kinetic can," Sascha said, grimly thinking of a girl fumbling in red-lit freightways. What was her Talent?

"Peter's got a fine sense of integrity, Sascha," Rhyssa said. "He's sensitive and sensible. We have to think *how* to bring him back to cruel reality after his minor miracle."

"A diversion usually helps," Dorotea remarked with a gleam in her eyes. "I used that ploy often with my lads." She wrinkled her nose and sighed. "All too often."

"It's going to have to be pretty good to distract him from the *Erasmus* stunt," Sascha said with uncharacteristic gloom.

Rhyssa was distracted from the conversation by the mental hail of Johnny Greene. *Rhyssa, you guys called a G and H. Did it have something to do with the spectacular landing and takeoff of the* Erasmus?

One of the phones on Rhyssa's desk rang, and being nearest, Sascha picked it up.

"Yes, Dave? No, Rhyssa's got a call on her mind. Can I help?" He listened for a moment and then replaced the handset, his face grimmer than ever.

Johnny, Rhyssa was saying, *it's very complicated.*

Sascha: *You haven't heard the half yet, dear. Dave's got bad news for us, too. Ludmilla's claiming that we've perjured our immortal souls and deliberately falsified our Register.*

Johnny: *Vernon's had all kinds of flak from NASA, the Space Authorities, the Padrugoi Authority . . .*

Rhyssa, fiercely: *Remind Vernon what kinetics are doing on the Indian continent. Sascha, tell Dave that his public pitch is that, despite all odds,*

Talent has kept its covenant of disaster assistance. And I want Johnny and Dave up here as fast as they can make it. Particularly you, Greene. To Dorotea, she said, "I think Peter's immediate illusions of grandeur are going to be heavily dampened."

Boris entered the telepathic conference. *The Power Resources commissioner is also demanding an explanation for a G and H that caused last night's brownout and wiped out all his power reserves,* he said plaintively. *The city commish wants a lot of answers. Sascha, you heard anything?*

Sascha, savagely: *No!*

Vsevolod Gebrowski, urgently: *Rhyssa, Barchenka is out to get you! And there's nothing I can do to distract her. I told her G and H. Her telempaths have explained that this is a Talent emergency code which needs no elaboration. She does not accept that.*

Rhyssa: *You tell Ludmilla from me that she's had plenty of secrets she doesn't share, like early-completion bonuses, as well as fines on delays. I don't question her; she doesn't question me.*

Vsevolod: *She does. I warn you.*

Dorotea, helpfully: *Amalda Vaden sees nothing untoward.*

Rhyssa: *Why did you bring her in on this?*

Dorotea: *I think we need all the reassurance we can get.*

Sascha: *Dave Lehardt, Gordie Havers, and two top NASA generals are on the same heli with Johnny.*

Rhyssa remembered how satisfied Peter had looked after dealing so beautifully with the *Erasmus* crisis. She groaned. "He's only fourteen."

Carmen: *Sascha, I've got a fix on her.*

Sascha was out the door in a flash. *Good luck!*

Rhyssa: *Right back at you!*

"Peter's far more mature than most fourteen-year-olds I've dealt with," Dorotea mused. "Including you," she added, favoring Rhyssa with an admonitory glance. "And he's got all the right instincts for being Talented."

T irla did *not* like using the freight subways. The red light was off-putting. However, a cargo train servicing the automatic industrial complexes all along the riverside was the only way to get to the secreted holding place Yassim used to stash his merchandise, a train going into the J industrial. Then she would have to walk to the correct shunt. There were emergency alcoves set at intervals all along the right-hand side, so she could avoid being crushed by any passing cars. Dead unthinking things like tram trains did not frighten her. Live unthinking things like some of Yassim's sassins and hitters did.

She waited a hundred meters from the yawning red-and-black mouth of the G shunt for nearly an hour before a J train arrived. It would have to slow as it reached the junction, so it was no problem for an agile person to drop onto the first segment, catch a good hold of the flange, and settle down for the trip. Flattened on the top, she was small enough to have several centimeters' clearance from the curved ceiling of the tunnel. She reset her grip as the train picked up speed again, vibrating under her. The fetid wind, a noxious combination of overheating metal, grease, and the acrid stink of electricity, roared down across her body, and she angled her face down.

When the J train finally slowed with screeching brakes and made the left-hand turn into the cargo docks of its destination, she readied herself to jump off. She had to land clear of the coding machinery that opened and sorted out the goods to be delivered from the load. But she had done it with no problem before and did it again, dropping lightly down and running up the narrow ledge by the various chutes and moving ramps that began the unloading.

When she came to the first curve in the narrow tunnel and the last of the red light was gone, she used her handlight, glad that she had filched a fresh charge for it only the previous week. With the dim beam to light her way, she trotted along in a half crouch until the muscles in her legs and back ached. She dropped to her knees then and rested a moment before continuing on.

Motivated by her keen sense of self-preservation, Tirla had once taken the precaution of investigating his holding cell, a room hidden behind a false wall of barrels at the back of an automated factory, where the noise of the ill-tuned machinery would drown any screaming. But he did keep the children reasonably well cared for, since purchasers could view them on a closed-circuit system he provided. Disabling the archaic scanner would be no problem for Tirla, and she knew the precise location of the ventilator hatch in the room's ceiling.

The kids had been in there nearly two days. They would be rested, she knew, and possibly feeling pretty good about their new conditions, which were, after all, a considerable improvement over squats. They might not want to leave. She wished she knew whom Yassim had grabbed—then she could figure out how to stir them to leave Yassim's hospitality long enough to force him to pay their parents proper compensation.

She loosened the appropriate wires on the ancient scanner so that the static would snow the visual. Then, gaining entrance through the ventilator hatch, she dangled from the ceiling to the excited clamor of young voices.

"Hey there, cool it way down!" she ordered in Basic, repeating the message for those who might be slow to translate or need to be reassured. "Yushi, pull a mattress down so I can land soft. It's a drop."

While Yushi and his younger brother complied, she did a quick estimate. Yassim must have been quite pleased at his catch: twenty-four prime kids to sell. The remains of a recent meal relieved her of one obstacle—the guards were not likely to check soon again—but it meant that the kids would have one less reason to *want* to leave such a cushy setup. Why, there were only two kids per bunk. They all had new gear on, and the girls were tarted up like their mothers.

"Yassim take any of you yet?" Tirla asked, imbuing her voice with trembling urgency and widening her eyes with real fear. "I got here as quick as I could!" she added, implying that maybe she had not been quick enough.

"Huh?" Yushi was good at taking orders but not at thinking.

"They took my sister!" Suddenly little Mirmalar's painted face screwed up into tears. "They took her an hour ago. And she had on the prettiest things—orange and brown with gold, and new earrings . . ."

"Oh, I'm so sorry, Mirmalar. I did everything I could to get here in time." As Tirla lavished sympathy on the weeping seven-year-old, she could see panic beginning to spread to the others. She got madder than ever at Yassim. It was one thing to take ten-year-olds, but not seven- and eight-year-old *babies!* What kind of pervs did he supply?

"Whaddya mean?" Tombi, Bilala's eldest son, asked, his manner slightly aggressive. He was nibbling at a sweetbar; judging from the smears on his face, it was one of a series.

"We gotta git out of here," Tirla said, releasing Mirmalar with a reassuring pat. "This place has a baaaad stink."

"It ain't got any at all," Tombi replied, though he turned his head immediately to the rudimentary sanitary unit in the corner.

"They take Raina already, you all are in biiiiig trouble. I'm gonna get you all out. Now. Before more bad men come. You girls know what I mean," she added, waggling a stern finger at them. Tombi and Dik snickered. "Same thing happens you guys, too, and you know you too small for that carry-on yet."

Tombi stopped nibbling the sweet and looked apprehensively at the door.

"Sure they feed you up good. Sweet stuff coming out your ass, giving you a bellyache," she said, dismissing the remains of the recent meal. "This place's good to keep you from crying much. You cry plenty soon and no one hear you ever. Stick it up you good, every which way, and that's the best of it. You know what your mothers tol' you. You know what to watch out for." She was succeeding in scaring them—the younger ones were beginning to weep. She did not want them so scared that they could not move. "Yushi, Dik, Tombi, help me move the bunks. We make a stepstair. There's room up there to stand."

"I ain't goin'," Tombi said, glaring defiance at her. He was heavier and taller than Tirla, but she kicked him so hard that he doubled up.

"You're going 'cause your mother sent me to get you," Tirla knew how scared Tombi was of Bilala. "So you're coming. Now, move! And crying won't do no good, so stop. You need your breath for climbing and walking."

Just then the enormity of moving twenty-four scared and perhaps unwilling kids sank in. Tirla allowed herself only a moment to reflect on it. She had to do it, somehow, because otherwise she would have to leave G, and she did not want to. Linear G was home. She had made herself a place there, she had a business—she was safe there. Well, safe enough, if she laid low for a while.

She chivvied and bullied all the kids up into the ventilation shaft, kicked the telltale bunk over, and replaced the grille. Someone might think that the kids were small enough to escape through it, but where would twenty-four of them *go*?

She led the way, grouping the kids so that there were bigger ones holding the hands of the smallest. She made Tombi rear guard to give him some responsibility and put Yushi in the middle. He would always follow orders.

The unloading platform with its eerie red light gave her no comfort—she knew that some of the kids would not be able to manage the acrobatics needed to get on one of the drones. They could, of course, straddle tracks all the way back to G, but it was a long, long walk, and there would be danger every time one of the speeding trains went by.

Well, maybe they could all make it back one station to I and get lost in that industrial complex. It was safer than staying in J. Or was it? Maybe she would just take the older ones, who would be in more danger? No, they were all in danger, because whoever was left could be made to tell who had rescued the others. Maybe if she put the younger ones in a safe place and went back for help . . . Mirmalar's father adored his daughters and would do anything to save the remaining one. And Yushi's father was one of the strongest men in G.

The vibrations that told her a train was on the tracks beyond the shunt alerted her. How much time did they have before they would know if its destination was J?

"Hide in the tunnels! Quickly! Stand on the ledges!" She took Mirmalar herself, for the little girl was puckering up to cry again.

"Ah, there's never anyone on goods trains," Tombi said.

"Yeah, and how d'you think Yassim's people get back and forth? Dumper cars are big enough to hold a dozen people."

That shut Tombi silent and lost him more face in the eyes of the other boys. Tirla shoved him toward a tunnel as she pulled Mirmalar after her.

The screech of distressed metal announced another goods train being shunted into J from the north. She had not counted on one arriving quite so soon. She would never get the kids on this one even if it *was* going in the right direction for them to get home—unless there was a dumper car.

But there was something odd here: Tirla realized with a sinking feeling that there was no cargo waiting on the platform to be loaded onto the arriving train. If a goods train was coming in here, what was it coming *for?* Could Yassim have someone in the main Dispatch office? Could he know that she had emptied his cage?

There were five cars on the double-ended train. Two looked like empty dumpers. Without waiting to question such great good fortune, Tirla hauled Mirmalar out onto the platform.

"Quickly. It won't stop long. We must all get in."

They were, therefore, all on the platform when the train stopped. So none of them escaped the sleep gas that suddenly spewed out, catching them all in its mist. They fell like wilted flowers onto the plastic-coated loading surface.

S he's some kid," Sascha said as he and Carmen carefully placed the object of their intensive search on a blanket pad and covered her. "Christ, but she's a bit of nothing."

Carmen smiled slowly and turned the sleeping child's head to one side to see where the lock of hair had been wrenched out. Her other hand reached halfway to touch it but then stopped. "She's nothing but skin and bones, Sascha. We'll have to improve her."

Sascha frowned a bit, looking around to see the rest of the team attending the other children. "We may not want to, Carmen. Boris and I have a feeling about this one."

"So do I." Carmen smiled at him with her most mysterious smile.

Boris: *Did you catch her?*

Yes, Brother dear, her and them. She'd sprung the lot of 'em. She must have known exactly where to go. Sascha spoke aloud. "I'm wondering how."

What the hell possessed her? Boris swore with frustration. He and Sascha had followed Carmen's lead, and while Tirla was haranguing the kids, a team had been cautiously organized, aware that Yassim had interests in Industrial J.

How about we find out where they were kept? Sascha asked.

What good will that do now? He's not likely to reuse a holding area that's been breached.

He might if he thought the kids had escaped on their own.

Can you manage that? Boris's tone leaped to hopefulness.

I can try.

If you could, and rigged it, we'd have one more bolthole filed on Yassim. Why did she do it?

"Let's wake Tirla up," Sascha said to Carmen, reaching for the oxygen. "If she can show us where, we can get some good out of this operation."

"We already have. We've found more than we hoped, haven't we?"

"Yes, and no. Bear with me, Carmen. There's a lot more than this valuable young girl at stake."

Revived, Tirla went immediately on the defensive, wary and contained, her dark eyes darting around, taking in the unconscious bodies and noticing the medic, who was daubing scrapes and bruises with nu-skin. Carmen offered a restorative drink, deliberately taking a long swallow of it before handing the cup to Tirla.

Sascha, lightly trying to get inside the girl's mind, could sense only her fierce thirst. With great restraint, she took a very small sip, rolling it around in her mouth before drinking more deeply. Her bright dark eyes challenged him. He sat down beside her in a relaxed position, hooking his hands around his knees and leaning back against the wall.

"Tirla," he began. He saw her start of surprise. "Oh, you're well known in G. And your bravery in releasing the children will be appreciated, and not just by their grieving families."

"How could you find me here, with them?" She glanced inquiringly from him to Carmen and then saw the lock of her hair, which Carmen still wore as talisman. Involuntarily her hand started to the scabby patch on her head. Her shoulders sagged around her narrow chest, but any emotional reaction was carefully guarded in her mind. "I've heard of people like you. You found me because you had my hair."

"It's not witchcraft, Tirla," Carmen said gently. She handed the strand back to the girl. "I have a Talent which allows me to find lost people and things."

"I wasn't lost."

"No," Sascha said conversationally, with an approving grin, "but you found what was missing from Linear G."

"He hadn't paid for them."

Carmen gasped. "You mean, once he's paid for them, he can have them again?"

"Sure. The parents live on subsistence. They need the money for extras only floaters can buy."

Sascha was well aware that the girl's seeming callousness distressed Carmen, who had seen the child in a much different light. "Also puts you in well with your clients, who were rather upset with your abrupt departure from the meeting," he said amiably.

Eyes never leaving his, Tirla nodded once.

"They're all illegal, aren't they?"

Tirla's thin shoulders lifted in an indifferent shrug. "Sure, so it's no credit out of your stash what happens to them."

"Oh, no," Carmen said, pained. "They're alive. They have rights!"

Tirla gave her a quick look before resuming her scrutiny of Sascha. "Illegals don't have rights."

"Only their births are illegal, Tirla," Sascha said. "They're alive. They *have* the right to shelter, food, clothing, training, and useful occupation. They do not have the right to reproduce themselves." Sascha was about to explain the legal anomaly in simple terms when he realized that she understood perfectly. She was mature far in excess of her chronological age, and well conditioned to the realities of Residential life. She was not a romantic like Carmen. "But they do not deserve the occupations Yassim had in mind for them." Sascha caught that instant spurt of fear, followed by the hardening of the young eyes and the flick of hatred. "You don't like Yassim either."

Again one of her indifferent shrugs.

"Would you by any chance help us disable him?"

She had been wary before, but now she appeared to Sascha to coil in on herself. "You're not LEO. Why do you want to queer Yassim?"

"No, I'm not LEO myself, but we have a connection. Especially against someone like Yassim."

Tirla gave a snort. "Someone like Yassim buys himself off every time LEO collars him. He has powerful friends. LEO can never make it stick."

"You wish that LEO could?"

She hesitated briefly, then gave him a candid look. "There will always be men like Yassim, but I could do without *him* very much, thank you."

Sascha would have given a great deal then to have been able to read her mind, to delve that reply. Tirla was far deeper than they'd had any reason to suspect. She sat there in front of him, cross-legged, completely composed, alert—and bargaining just as if she could get up and leave the scene at any moment.

"I want to get rid of Yassim, too, Tirla. Will you help me?"

A glimmer of a smile touched her eyes and mouth. "What's in it for me?"

Carmen inhaled in surprise. Sascha sent the finder soothing thoughts, urging her to let him handle the situation his way. He flicked his fingers, fanning out crisp new floater notes.

"How did you manage that?" Her eyes widened in surprise and indignation.

Sascha did not often employ his kinetic ability, but this trick was always effective. "You help me now—and we must be quick about it before Yassim discovers his birds have flown—and these are yours."

She eyed the notes. Casually she scratched about her ribs. Sascha kept his grin to himself, knowing that she was checking on the tied notes hidden there. She considered his offer with all the solemnity of a computer analyst.

"There's the little matter of your legality, Tirla," he added gently.

Boris nudged him mentally. *C'mon, Brother, we don't have time for amiable lipflap.*

On the contrary, we have all the time we need, Brother. This is a strong personality and a deep one. I'm not rushing her.

Get on with it then.

Tirla gave him a wide-eyed bright smile. "I am the only child of my mother."

"But not her legally registered issue."

"How would you know?"

Sascha touched her hair. "That told us. But it is a small matter that can be quickly remedied."

She regarded him from narrowed eyes. "A small matter?" The twist of her lips was cynical. "You must be in real good with LEO." She considered, obliquely watching Carmen's expression. "And I get to keep the floaters, as well?" Her tone was ingenuous.

Sascha suppressed a grin. Legality would be the most valuable reward he could offer, and still her fingers itched to relieve him of the money. Not that he had offered a large sum, but the amount would keep her in extras for several months.

"If we get a move on—now!" he said, drawing out his acceptance.

She spat in her right palm and held it out to him. Without a second thought, he accepted the deal in archaic ritual. Her grip was unusually strong for the delicacy of her bones. Physical contact with the conscious and vibrant personality startled Sascha with an odd jolt—a sense of precognition that was gone too fast for him to pin it down.

Boris caught the edge of it. *What did she do to you, Sascha?*

I'm not sure, Brother, but this one we handle very, very carefully. I want a special ID for Tirla when we get back. Hear me?

To hear is to obey! Boris might sound facetious, but Sascha was relieved by his compliance. *Keep the bargain, but I want this wild one under control.*

The deal struck, Tirla rose with lithe grace to her feet and tilted her head back to look appraisingly up at Sascha. "So how do we disable Yassim?"

"Can you lead me to where he kept the children?" When she nodded, he went on. "We want to fix it so that he will think the children escaped by themselves."

Tirla snorted contemptuously. "I had to frighten them to make them leave at all. Such things I had to tell them. Though it was all very true."

"How would Yassim know that they were all docile? It need only look as if they had broken out. That one of the guards had been careless locking them in."

She considered that. "Yes, that could have happened. They had only just brought food." She gave him a shrewdly appraising glance. "You will have to crawl." That seemed to amuse her.

"Up this tunnel?"

She nodded, then looked over her shoulder, for the first time betraying some apprehension. "What happens to them?"

"They can sleep on until we get back," he replied. "We've got to move now."

She led him into the tunnel, and he did have to crawl, wondering how she had managed her initial trip until he saw the small circle of light that guided her steps. She had the courtesy not to go faster than he could follow, and he had time to reflect: she might not have an ounce of telempathy, or was perhaps too wary to let down the shield that had protected her so long in her young life, but there was no question that she possessed considerable Talent.

She halted at the end of the tunnel and turned to him. "You wouldn't fit down the hatch I used, but if you know how to open that inspection door, that's an easier way to get to where he held the kids."

Sascha took the scrambler from his belt and decoded the door. He opened it cautiously, aware of the hissing intake of her breath, and listened—on another level than Tirla, who was kneeling at the lower half of the opening. The level and complexity of noise in the main industrial complex was appropriate for an automated factory. He sensed nothing human, but it was Tirla who first slid through the door. He opened it enough for his larger frame and closed it carefully behind them.

Though the industrial space was lit only by occasional green lights of operational machinery, Tirla moved confidently forward. Sascha would have passed right by the false wall, but she went unerringly to the double drum and pinpointed the lock mechanism with her pencil light. She glanced questioningly at him.

"Electronic, I hope?" he murmured, and she nodded.

He scrambled the circuit, and the door swung back to reveal the deserted room, the overturned bunk bed, and the table with the empty food packages. She pulled the door shut behind them, shooting him a disapproving look for his careless entry.

"How did you get them out?" he asked.

She pointed to the darker square of the grille in the ceiling.

"Good work." He righted the bunk bed and pushed it back into its former position, managing to stick a minuscule device on the wall behind it. Then he looked about the place. It stank of many things, not all tangible. "I think you'd better mastermind this escape, Tirla. Make it look like a kid had done it."

Tirla's upper lip curled in derision. "None of them would have!"

"Point taken, but for Yassim's benefit it should *seem* so."

With her eyes half-veiled, Tirla considered the problem. Sascha waited patiently, wishing he could have been in her head, noting her thought processes.

"Okay," she said finally, leading across the room to the corner where pieces of clothing had been discarded. Deliberately she tore strips from several garments, her hands clever in finding the break in a hem or seam that would rip. "There'll be a fight . . ." She hauled mattress pads off two of the lower bunks, and the soiled blankets off the upper ones. She went back to the corner and, using a shirt, gathered up some of the containers and the remaining food before she knocked over the makeshift table. "Now, we open the door just enough to let kids out, and start leaving trails. Come out, I'll just close the door over a bit. Now, you drop stuff halfway to that wall. Then circle around. I'm going this way. I'll meet you at the maintenance door."

He did as she directed, and they met again in the chucking, clanking dark of the automated manufactory.

"Lock it?" Sascha held the door ajar.

"Yes."

"But how will Yassim know how they got out?"

"They're not there, are they? The cage door is open." Sascha saw her shrug and felt, rather than saw, her malicious smile. "Why should I make it easy for him?"

By the time they reached the loading dock, Sascha's muscles were protesting their abuse. The team had loaded the children into the cars, and the dock was full of cargo to be transshipped.

"You cut that fine, Sascha," the team leader told him. "There'll be a goods train through here in two minutes. We're not supposed to disrupt the service."

Tirla tugged imperiously at Sascha's sleeve. "My floaters."

With one hand he passed them to her, with the other he grabbed her wrist. "No tricks now. There's more business we can do together. We'll discuss it back in G."

Sascha did not know whether it was her surprise that allowed him to capture her or if she was willingly cooperating with him. But she entered the car ahead of him as he tried to keep his grip from breaking fragile bones.

Go! he told the driver, and the starting pressure of the special train pushed him against the padded end of his car.

"Are you taking us all to G?" Her tone was casual.

"That's what you wanted, wasn't it? To get the kids back to G?"

"I kept our bargain." Her voice held an element of antagonism.

"So will I. Back at G. Then we deal again."

She was silent for a long time, thinking that over.

CHAPTER 11

Peter tried to follow the tri-d meteorologist's report on the latest freak weather conditions that seemed worldwide, Bangladesh being the worst example. It was difficult to concentrate when he felt "problem" hovering in the air. He *knew* he had done nothing wrong; in fact, he knew that he had done something most extraordinary, about which he felt very good indeed. But it was hard not to be worried. He could sense the nebulous anxiety emanating from Rhyssa, Dorotea, and Sascha. He should not have asked Dorotea about a bigger generator. The moment the words were out of his mouth, he knew it was the wrong time. But he had *proved* what he could do with enough power to increase the gestalt, and that 4.5 felt like puny kid stuff now.

Kid stuff! Peter grinned to himself and gave the 4.5 a little shove; it whined obediently. Like a dog. And who was he kidding? He was still only a fourteen-year-old boy. He had already absorbed enough Talent discipline and seen enough examples of the sort of people Talents were to realize that he had rushed the gate. One did not climb mountains when one could not walk. Rhyssa, Sascha, and Dorotea had supported him throughout the entire *Erasmus* incident, ready to help him, ready to keep him from burning himself out. And he hadn't. But had it been *because* they had been right there to protect him? Think about *that*, Petey boy, and get your swelled head back to normal. There are a lot of things you *can't* do just yet.

He poured himself another glass of orange juice and brought it to the living room as the broadcaster announced that once again supply shuttles for Padrugoi had been grounded by weather conditions. The screen depicted the rank of four perpendicular space vehicles, locked into their gantries, waiting for lift-off conditions with urgently needed matériel so that the First World Project would be finished in time.

Talents were helping to do that, Peter thought with a little thrill of corporate pride. He had just started wondering how big a generator he would need to send a shuttle safely through the foul weather when the program switched to coverage of the flooding in Bangladesh. There were no scenes actually showing the Talents at work; teams of doctors and rescue workers were filmed rushing about. There was also no mention of exactly how the *Erasmus* had landed so safely at Dacca. He had not really expected to be mentioned publicly. But one would think that there would have been some comment that Talents were risking their lives in the appalling monsoon conditions. The results of their work was shown, all right enough, but somehow that did not seem to be enough.

Rhyssa and Dorotea were always subtly mentioning how important it was not to rub Talent into people's noses. People resented differences. Talent had always to be discreet. The way his mother looked at him had demonstrated *that!* Peter grimaced. His own mother was scared of him now. When he had been totally helpless, she had been so good about coming to see him, hugging him, kissing him, always bringing him something: a fax clip about his favorite ball team, a couple of her special cookies, a few flowers. Now when she visited she would not hug him; she sat bolt upright in the chair and tried not to look at him when he wanted so much to show her what Talent allowed him to do.

When Mum was there he redoubled his efforts to appear to walk normally and carry things properly so it would not freak her out. How often had she said she prayed every night to see Petey on his feet and walking around? And she never *looked* at him now. She never once mentioned his ball team. Not that he would ever play sandlot baseball again . . . Then Peter grinned, thinking what homers he could whack and how fast he could run the bases. Maybe now he could be the pitcher he had always wanted to be . . . His fastball would be *something else!* Even if he only used the 4.5!

But he had gone past that sort of *ordinary* thing, hadn't he? When one could zap shuttles about like gameboard pieces, *ordinary* accomplishments no longer satisfied.

He drank his orange juice. Not *all* ordinary things, though.

Some very ordinary and extremely homely actions—like getting himself an orange juice when he felt thirsty for it—were, in a special way, far more important than what he had done with the *Erasmus*.

He sent the empty glass back to the kitchen, rinsed it out, and put it upside-down on the drainboard.

He had to keep things in perspective. It was more important to have the freedom to do little things and the *option* to do bigger ones. But, jeez, it had been a wonderful feeling to have all that power and do something no one else could have done with it—just when help was needed.

The tri-d was showing floodwater flowing obediently away from a small town and its surrounding fields. The sandbags and barriers along its torrent seemed to be containing it, but Peter could recognize the subtle signs of kinetic force. He wondered which Talent was at work. Rick Hobson? Mr. Baden? Now, if he'd had access to a generator, he would have been able to do that. He settled down to learn what he could about flood control from the program. Next time he would be ready to help. The 4.5-kpm was portable, wasn't it?

His thoughts were interrupted by Rhyssa's mental call. *Peter, would you come up to my office, please?*

Sure! He leaned briefly into the generator and sped out to Rhyssa's building and in through the front door, slowing to maneuver the staircase; he got his feet to the ground as he reached the carpeted hallway leading to Rhyssa's office. No effort!

Show-off. Rhyssa was standing by her office door, but she was smiling. "We don't have any mountains for you to move today, but there's trouble in the wind, dear boy, there's trouble in the wind."

Peter stumbled in his forward motion and corrected himself. *Trouble? Why? We didn't do anything* wrong!

Her touch reassured him, as it always did. Dorotea was great: she treated him casually, as she would any of her grandchildren, and that relaxed attitude made many things easier for him. But Rhyssa was different: her mind had so much depth—not that he had disobeyed the prime rule of mental privacy, but he could not help but sense the depth and purity that was there. She was also the most beautiful woman Peter had ever seen, on or off the tri-d. And she was so *good!* Everything about her was shining and brilliant. She made him feel whole and strong.

"We did something a shade too right," Rhyssa said. "And we were not quite as discreet as we should have been."

Momentarily afraid, he reached out to see exactly what they had done wrong.

Peter!

"Sorry."

Rhyssa, more fiercely than Peter had ever heard her: *Damn that Barchenka woman!*

"Was I *supposed* to hear that?" Peter was confused.

"Yes, and double-damn Barchenka!" Rhyssa said aloud, and waved him on through to her office, closing the door behind them.

He halted, sensing the aura of crisis. Dorotea, who was rarely perturbed, was brushing imaginary threads from her slacks. Things must really be bad. He zigged sideways, aware that Rhyssa just missed bumping into him.

Dorotea: *Well done, Peter!*

"This is a strategy council, Peter," Rhyssa said, gesturing for him to sit as she resumed her chair in the tower bay window.

Peter floated over to the conformable seat, grateful for its automatically adjusted support.

"Don't ever forget just how proud we all are of you," Rhyssa said, her gesture including the entire Center. "You've added a brand new dimension to Talent." She gave him an impish smile. "And reminded this Center's manager not to get too complacent."

Without violating etiquette, Peter could hear what she was not saying aloud: Talent was very happy; the unTalented were not.

Dorotea: *The unTalented always resist a new Talent which we haven't carefully led them to expect. In this instance, you!*

Rhyssa: *We don't do something right, Peter, without doing something wrong!* Peter sensed a second qualification behind the thought and, remembering his manners, broke the contact.

Dorotea: And *we've got to figure out how to improve our testing methods!* She cleared her throat in a businesslike manner, then winked at Peter.

He thought, very privately to himself, that something bad was definitely about to happen, but he was assured of their love and approval and that was all that really mattered to him.

"If your main desire right now," Rhyssa said, smiling with that special twinkle in her eye which she saved for Peter, "is to have the biggest generator on the planet at your disposal"—Peter flushed, looking hard at his bony knees—"then the main desire of half the industries on Earth *and* in space is to have you using theirs, and theirs alone."

Space? He could get into space? He looked up in surprise, staring at her. Clearly she did not mean *his* way.

"How do they know about me?" He felt suddenly very defenseless. His father was always talking about the managers working a man to death with no consideration for him as a human being, only how productive he was, a cipher in a gigantic program.

"They don't know it's *you,*" Dorotea said.

"That's the problem," Rhyssa went on.

"Why?" Peter asked, thinking of *big* generators.

"Candidly," Dorotea said, "you're fourteen, you're only just beginning to understand your Talent, and premature exposure could—"

"Burn me out," Peter finished for her, though privately he did not think he *could* burn out—if he had the right power source for anything he wanted to shift. "But I didn't burn out . . ."

"Without in the least diminishing your achievement, Peter, we were closely monitoring you the other night," Rhyssa went on. "What *they* have in mind for you is another can of worms altogether. Speaking as a Center director, I must tell you that it has never been the policy of the Centers to assign trainees even part-time work until they're at least eighteen."

"Even I," Dorotea put in, her hand gracefully sweeping her chest, "wasn't permitted to do much until I was eighteen!" She made a face. "As a child, I thought I was just playing a game, guessing which ones in the room could hear me—people who *thought* they might be Talented." She shot Peter an image of herself as a five-year-old, prettily dressed—and her early beauty was still apparent in her face and manner—walking through the Center's crowded reception area.

"But I've *proved* what I can do," Peter said. "And I was the only one who could land the *Erasmus.*"

"The situation is not about right or wrong, Peter," Rhyssa said, leaning toward him, a sad expression in her eyes and face, "or even a moral obligation to reduce suffering and mitigate disaster." Then she opened her mind to him so he could directly assess the current problem.

Peter had known, of course, that the Parapsychic Centers had

had to send the best kinetics to Padrugoi to help complete the station on time. He had not realized all the undercurrents beneath the carefully contrived public image of Padrugoi, much less the machinations of Ludmilla Barchenka, who had forced the capitulation of Centers, ruthlessly stripping them of kinetics in what was basically a face-saving operation. He fumed when he saw that this Barchenka woman was threatening *his* Rhyssa with all kinds of offenses when it was now patently clear to him that Barchenka was at fault. And he was part of the problem. No, at the moment, he was *all* of the problem, because Barchenka was out to add him to her force of Talent.

"And I used to think working on the station would be the most special thing you could do," he said slowly. It just was not fair!

"No, not fair, Peter," Rhyssa replied, "but Talent recognizes that completing the station is far more important than individual personal considerations. Completing it on time is obviously Ludmilla's personal goal. I can't deny her that, only her means of achieving it, since by her achievement, mankind has made another giant step to the stars. Don't be deflected too much by the skeletons in the space lockers. There's been no major forward progress in all of human history that has not been accompanied by some problems."

"Like letting people float out into space and die because rescue would put her behind schedule?" Peter was aghast.

"That's been taken care of," Dorotea reminded him.

"By Talents, and now she thinks she can conscript me?" Peter was so agitated that he floated above the chair.

Dorotea, prosaically: *You're drifting, dear.*

Peter settled down. *Well, I just won't work for a person like her. And you're not going to ask me to!*

"Indeed and we're not," Rhyssa assured him. "But first," she said with a grin, her eyes twinkling, "we have to prove to *them* that you're *you!* We've been trying very hard to keep you sheltered until you've more control . . ."

How much control do I need if I can move a shuttle about the world?

"Peter!" Despite the sharpness in her voice, Peter knew that Rhyssa was amused by his outrage, proud of his achievement, and concerned for his future all at once. He subsided. "Thank you. Now, we were warned to expect visitors of high rank and great prestige. We wanted to brief you, since you are the cat we are about to let out of the bag."

"I rather think he's the cat among the pigeons," Dorotea said with a sarcastic snort.

"Pigeons? War hawks, Dorotea," Rhyssa corrected, settling into her chair. Then they all heard the unmistakable thunking of a big helicopter landing on the X outside Henner House. "Peter, don't let the fuss get to you. There's bound to be some bruised feelings and outraged sensibilities. You just pay them no heed!"

But he could not help but heed the fine but controlled aura of apprehension. They were worried. About him! *For* him.

Ragnar's voice came through on the intercom. He was duty officer, and twenty years in the Center had made him impervious to rank and prestige. "Rhyssa, there's a bunch here to see you. Do I send 'em up?"

"Yes, I'm expecting them, Ragnar."

His "humph" came over the speaker, and Peter noticed Rhyssa's little smile. He also noticed that she was nervously running the stylus through her fingers. Dorotea sat even straighter in her chair and managed to look not only larger and more imposing but very, very queenly.

There was a polite knock on the door, and Rhyssa pressed the release button. The first man in the room was a telepath, Peter realized, and he was directing tight private warnings at Rhyssa. The second man, very tall, thin, and wise-looking, gazed directly at Peter and nodded. He *knew* who Peter was even if Peter did not know him, and he was also a telepath. He courteously identified himself to Peter as Justice Gordon Havers.

Peter knew the third man, Dave Lehardt, who immediately moved to stand by Rhyssa's desk, facing the others as they filed in. He made his partisanship very clear. He exchanged a glance with Rhyssa and gave an almost imperceptible nod of his head. She had a slight smile on her face, and Peter sensed that she was very glad to have Dave Lehardt so close by. But knowing that Dave was not a Talent, Peter was surprised by the intimate exchange. He felt a flair of jealousy.

The next six men to enter were obviously important people; four were in uniform and only one of them was Talented. That one appeared very nervous and kept looking from Rhyssa to Dorotea. The last man to enter gaped at Rhyssa in a fashion that made

Peter very uneasy—his eyes and his manner made Peter wonder if he was one of those perverts his mother used to warn him about.

As Rhyssa asked them all to be seated, Peter picked up names: Vernon Altenbach, who was secretary of space; the Russian officer was General Shevchenko, Padrugoi liaison official, and even with the shield he wore, he was bristling with aggression. The telempath was Andrei Grushkov, and Peter felt sorry for him—he had to be truthful to his employer, the general, but he felt obscurely that he was betraying Talent in doing so. There were two NASA officers, a general and a colonel, and that pervert was the world-famous Josephson-junction specialist, and a Malaysian prince besides, who did such fantastic programming of air and space traffic. Peter did not like the man any better once he knew he was a genius, not when the man kept sloppily ogling Rhyssa. The man who had come in first was Colonel John Greene, and Peter watched in some awe as the most successful etop pilot of the early days of the Padrugoi Project placed a chair next to him, Peter Reidinger, and smiled quite pleasantly at him. Colonel Greene seemed to be the only one who was smiling. Even Justice Havers looked solemn.

"It would be pointless for me to deny that I am aware of the reason for your visit," Rhyssa said calmly. "Shall I call up the Eastern Center Register for you to check on our memberships?" She placed her fingers over the keyboard.

Peter regarded her with pride. She even had a little smile on her face. And that pervert kept smarming at her.

The Russian liaison general cleared his throat. "We have already seen it, Madame. But we believe that you have not honestly declared your full kinetic strength." He crooked his head to see his telempath's face.

"Andrei can certainly assure you that our declaration is honest and complete. We have nothing to hide. No Talent does."

"Andrei has also assured me, Madame Owen," the general continued ponderously, "that no kinetic anywhere could have successfully landed the *Erasmus,* not even the twenty-two on board her, *or* —" He paused dramatically. "—assisted its takeoff from the Dacca field in the weather conditions prevailing that day." His chest seemed to deflate slightly once he had delivered his accusation.

"It was me," Peter said. He wanted to get it all over with, and get that smarmy-faced man out of the room and away from Rhyssa. "I mean, it was I."

The stunned silence was worse than noisy disclaimers. Then Colonel Greene started to chuckle and Dave Lehardt began to laugh. He also winked approvingly at Peter. Not one of the other visitors appeared to be the least bit amused.

"And tell me just how, young man," Vernon Altenbach asked, skeptically, "you accomplished such a feat?"

Stick to the facts, man, the facts, Rhyssa said, mental laughter rippling her tone.

"Well, the *Erasmus* needed help landing at Dacca because the kinetics *had* to be there to reduce the disaster potential. So Rhyssa called a G and H—that's a Talent mayday—and I got to use the generators at the East Side power station," Peter replied. He kept his face straight, but he was enjoying the incredulity of the non-Talented in his audience; even the Russian telempath was admiring, and Peter sat himself even straighter in the chair.

Dorotea: *Well said, Peter!*

Gordon Havers: *In times of doubt, honesty is the best policy.*

Johnny Greene: *You better believe it, because they're not!* Unobtrusively, he patted Peter's knee.

"You have, I must assume, a kinetic Talent?" Vernon continued.

"Yes, sir. I'm in training as a kinetic, but I can't do as much as I'd like because the people who should be training me are all up on the station."

Rhyssa: *Don't spread it on too thick, Peter.*

Johnny: *Nonsense. They deserve that kick in the shins.*

"How much training have you had then?" the general asked.

"Well, Rhyssa and Dorotea do the best they can, but they're telepaths . . ."

Rhyssa, dryly: *Thank you!*

Gordon: *He's sticking to the truth.*

"Initially Rick Hobson was helping me," Peter went on, "but we'd only just gotten past the necessary stuff when he got conscripted to the station."

"Talents were *not* conscripted," General Shevchenko objected forcefully. "They volunteered to assist in the completion of the first Great World Project."

Peter gave a contemptuous little snort. "If you're not given a choice, you've been conscripted."

"And you expect us to believe that a frail boy manipulated the *Erasmus?*" Prince Phanibal Shimaz shot out of his chair and stood belligerently in front of Peter, shaking his finger at him. "I, Phanibal Shimaz, prince of Malaysia West, know that this would have been impossible from such a source! Tell us the truth, little boy!" he demanded, making the adjective pejorative.

"He *is* telling the truth," Johnny Greene said, rising to his feet to look down at the much shorter prince. Dave Lehardt and Rhyssa jumped to their feet angrily, ready to leap into the fray if need be.

"As Andrei confirms to me," General Shevchenko said in a hard voice. "You exceed your authority, Your Highness."

"And I shall prove it," Peter added, glaring back at the prince. Just because he could do games with Josephson junctions and traffic-flow patterns that no one else could do did not make him an authority on Talent. "Look!" And Peter raised his right arm, wishing he had enough small motor control to point a finger, but he had not quite mastered that yet.

Actually, it was easy enough with power diverted from the Center's equipment to raise and hold the big helicopter just outside Rhyssa's bay window so that all could see it—and see that the huge rotor blades moved idly in the breeze of its ascent.

"Do be careful with it, Peter," Johnny Greene said amiably, one of the few in the room enjoying the moment. "It's government property."

"I'm always careful, Colonel Greene," Peter replied, feeling the euphoria of potency. He was almost sorry that he could not think of an even more convincing demonstration of his kinetic Talent. Dorotea was glaring at him significantly in her enough-is-enough look. He returned the vehicle gently to the ground.

"How old are you, Peter?" Colonel Greene asked, just as if he and Peter were the only ones in the room.

"I was fourteen on the eighth of September."

"And you get about now yourself under your own power?" the colonel inquired.

Peter could see in his eyes that the man knew the true extent of his handicap.

"I was that much"—his fingers measured a two-centimeter gap—"away from paraplegia myself after Mission Number 21," Greene continued.

Peter realized that Colonel Greene was very much on their side

and making it very clear to everyone else that Peter's Talent was
off limits. "I've learned how to compensate just fine," he replied,
and a glance at the colonel told him that that was the right answer
to make. "Rick Hobson really helped me. We were just beginning
to go on to tougher things when he had to go to Padrugoi."

"So you've been Rhyssa's skeleton crew? All by yourself?" Colonel Greene chuckled and looked across at the secretary of space.

"I'm not nearly as much of a skeleton as I used to be." Peter
extended his arms and legs and regarded them dispassionately. "I'll
get some muscle on them yet. I've got to build slowly, you see, and
it takes time."

Colonel Greene rose. "I think that's the answer, gentlemen. It
takes time to build muscle, any kind of muscle, and you build
slowly to last longer."

"Now wait just a moment here," Prince Phanibal said, recovering from his initial surprise. "That is not the answer I came to find.
You have indeed concealed from the world a kinetic Talent of demonstrated ability. He can take the place of those at Bangladesh . . ." He leaned across Rhyssa's desk, and Peter saw her
flinch back from such a menacing posture.

Peter could not stand it. Kinetically he dragged Prince Phanibal
backward from Rhyssa, the prince's face set in a paralyzed rictus of
amazement. The door that opened to allow his exit closed firmly
behind him.

"Peter!" Rhyssa could not quite disguise her relief or her consternation at his breach of courtesy.

"He's got no right to threaten you, Rhyssa! No right at all!"

Dorotea: *Bravo, Peter, though I shouldn't encourage you!*

"Now see here, young man—" Shevchenko took one step toward
Peter and stopped, blinking in astonishment when some invisible
force prevented him from moving farther forward.

"That's enough, Peter," Rhyssa said with appropriate severity.
That was rather clever of you, dear, even if you wouldn't realize it. The
mental image in her mind showed suppressed laughter. "The general will not intimidate you any further. General, I think Peter has
inadvertently displayed another cogent reason why the Center is
unwilling to utilize his unique abilities except in a crisis. At fourteen, he does not always abide by the courtesies that a more mature
personality has learned."

"I demand that the boy apologize to His Highness Prince Phanibal immediately."

"You may demand all you wish, General," Rhyssa said sharply, "but I don't even know why a traffic manager, royal or not, was included in this gathering."

"Engineer Barchenka insisted on his inclusion," Vernon Altenbach remarked, attempting some diplomacy.

"I insist that he be *excluded* from any future meetings involving the Center or myself."

Peter: *He's a slimeball!*

Johnny Greene and Gordon Havers, simultaneously: *Where did you stash him?*

Peter: *He's in the helicopter, and he can't seem to get the seat buckle undone.* He could not help grinning. *I won't let him.*

Johnny: *Buckle down, Winsockie, buckle down!*

Dorotea: *I didn't think anyone in your generation knew that old song.*

"Now, gentlemen, you have, I trust, seen to your own satisfaction that we have only been protecting young Peter, not deliberately denying the platform his Talent. I'm sorry that you had a long trip for nothing," Rhyssa said, coming around her desk to shake hands with Andrei Grushkov. "However, when Peter is fully trained and we have a better understanding of the parameters of his potential, we will, of course, be obliged to let prospective employers bid for his contractual services."

Vernon Altenbach eased the disgruntled Russian general out the door, the NASA colonel and the telempath assisting. But the others lingered until the first group had entered the elevator.

"Ms. Owen," the NASA general began. "Is it possible, given the boy's display of incredible ability, that he could—from time to time, that is . . . Well, we do have a serious crisis right now . . ."

"What kind?" Rhyssa asked in an unencouraging tone.

"NASA's supply schedule is at a standstill with the current worldwide weather conditions . . ."

Peter zoomed out of his chair, hovering between Rhyssa and the general. *Please consider it, Rhyssa. Working for NASA wouldn't be the same as working for Barchenka, would it? But it would be almost as good as being in space.* He exerted all his mind's pressure against hers, begging her consideration. He felt her stern resolve not to exploit him.

Johnny: *It's something to consider, Rhyssa, though we won't be pushy about it. If you say no, we'll go quietly. But it would gall me personally, and professionally, to have Barchenka saying that the Americans couldn't meet their contractual obligations.* He cocked his head at Rhyssa, grinning wryly.

Peter could feel Rhyssa beginning to relent.

Dorotea: *Consider it a training diversion, Rhyssa.*

Rhyssa: *But that's it! He's had hardly any training!*

Johnny: *Repetition hones skills, gal, and it sure reduces the glamour quotient.*

Peter did not understand that but felt Dorotea's approval become more urgent. He sensed that at last Rhyssa was seriously considering the suggestion.

"Look," Johnny said aloud, "this is so important that Vernon would actually get himself another minder for a few weeks. I know all the technical data that Peter needs to understand if he's flinging shuttles about the stratosphere. Hell, I'd get a vicarious thrill out of it myself, getting back into space by proxy. And if Peter's working for NASA, Barchenka can't say Talent has been obstructing Padrugoi's timely completion."

"I know it appears that it's always we who compromise," Gordon Havers said, entering the discussion, "but we put a wedge in her works if suddenly we insure delivery of the matériel she needs."

"You'd have to go with Peter, Rhyssa. I'm no longer up to that sort of sustained effort," Dorotea said. "Sascha's too involved in the present crisis at Linear G to leave that. And frankly, my dear, you *are* the stronger telepath and, I think, more tuned in to Peter's mind than Sascha is. Someone has to monitor him during the gestalts. I can see you squirming to go, Peter Reidinger. Is it what you really want? Will you behave like a mature Talent?"

Peter managed to curl his fingers around Rhyssa's. "I'll behave. I'll do just as I'm told. I promise! And I'd learn a lot."

"You'd call the moves, Rhyssa," Johnny Greene said.

"I don't think we have any choice in this either," Rhyssa said, and Peter leaned against her, wishing for her not to sound so defeated. She looked down at him and cupped his head with one hand, smiling tenderly at him. "I'm not defeated, Peter dear, but I intensely dislike being left with no options."

"Think of the options that you've canceled," Johnny Greene said with a malicious note in his voice as he lifted his middle finger skyward.

"Put like that," Gordie said, grinning, "we're one up on Barchenka."

Rhyssa turned to Dave Lehardt, her expression severe. "And you keep Peter's name out of the 'casts and the fax."

"Your skeleton crew at work again?" Dave asked, pretending to ward off an attack.

" 'Dem bones, dem bones, dem dry bones, and hear the word of the Lord!' " Johnny Greene sang, doing an intricate breakdance step.

CHAPTER 12

The blond man had an air about him that fascinated Tirla. She had never had much to do with Talents, and she surreptitiously crossed her wrists. She had heard such folk discussed in the Residential often enough, in fearful, awed whispers, but she had not believed half of the powers alleged to them: finders of persons and things, seers of souls, readers of secrets, prophets of future things, and movers of mountains.

She stole a look at him where he sat with his head leaned back against the padded wall and his eyes closed; daring to observe him more closely, she noticed the quick flow of facial muscles, as if he were having an argument in his head. His jaw tightened in anger, and his lips thinned. He should have been pleased with his day's work, Tirla thought. She was startled then, when his mouth relaxed into a half smile, a clever sort of smile, and his eyebrows twitched. Had he won his internal argument? He was a strange man, she thought, even though outwardly he appeared no different from others.

He was not LEO, and yet he was, and she could not figure out where he fit in, or how he and his teams had appeared so conveniently at the J shunt—especially when she had just realized the difficulty of cajoling scared whiney brats like Tombi into riding cargo pods back to G. Without that unexpected rescue, Yassim's ladrones would surely have recaptured them, herself included. She shuddered.

So they had been rescued from Yassim. But not from Authority. She wanted no part of Authority: too many conflicting rules and regulations and silly restrictions that only begged to be ignored or evaded. The prospect of a new ID briefly dazzled her, to the point where she could feel the narrow plastic strip knocking against her wrist bone. But she did not—quite—believe that the man would be able to produce any such ID, no matter how well he seemed in with the LEOs.

No matter! She had clean floaters—more than she needed for the tieds she had been supposed to launder for Yassim—so she was well ahead in the game. The matter of the hot tieds bothered her, but she was loath to face Yassim as long as he was in the market for kids. And it was very likely that the LEOs could not collar Yassim, and that he would go into deep hiding somewhere to wait out the furor. So, morally, she could hide the tieds for a while and discreetly exchange them, especially if Yassim was out of circulation, over the next several months. This was the biggest hit she had ever made.

But still she was uneasy. She was trapped in the closed cargo pod and did not really know where they were going, though she had been keeping mental count of the rail junctions. The blond man could just as easily leave her off at the hostel with the others. Who would believe that she had an arrangement with him? The train began to decelerate, and Tirla, with a spurt of dread anticipation, waited for the shunt connect. They were going to the G platform. She was both comforted and concerned.

"Where are we now?" she asked.

Sascha opened his eyes, and she saw that they were an unusual shade of light blue. He looked amused. "You know we're at G. So now we return the lost children to their grieving parents. That is important to you, isn't it, Tirla? That Bilala, Zaveta, Pilau, and especially Mirda Khan and Mama Bobchik know that you helped retrieve their lost ones?"

Now how could he know that? How much did he know about her? Why was he playing her along this way? He was a sharp one indeed. What sort of a scam was he running? Not all of this action had to do with that perv Yassim.

She refused to be drawn by what could just be a shrewd guess on his part. LEOs were not above putting surveillance on Meetings, even a silly RIG with that Lama-shaman. Perhaps there had been eyes on her clients, although why such a gaggle of silly women would be the object of LEO interest she did not know—unless it had to do with selling kids. But none of them had been there to deal kids—most of theirs were too young yet. They had all been

looking for "messages" and "salvations." Yet Sascha had identified
her clients, and he had even known that Mirda Khan and Mama
Bobchik were especially important.

"It just pays to be a good neighbor," she answered diffidently.

"Oh, you have definitely been a good neighbor today, Tirla. And
a very good citizen!" He laughed softly, throwing his head back
and showing large white even teeth. It would be a very nice laugh,
Tirla thought, if it had not worried her that he was laughing at all.
Perversely she liked him, for his strong grip and his droll words,
but she did not trust him any further than she could have thrown
Bulbar.

She gave him a quick stare for calling her "citizen." Citizens
lived across the river in the beautiful hives, luxury cones, platforms, and complexes, not in Linears.

"Trust me, Tirla?" His eyes were not laughing, nor was his
mouth, and his voice was gentle and entreating.

"I have no reason to."

"If I give you one?"

She snorted scornfully. Just then the train braked to an easy
stop, and the lids of the pods opened to reveal a group of adults,
waiting to lift out the unconscious children. A slim woman in a
LEO uniform standing at the edge of the platform spotted Sascha
and thrust a narrow plastic case at him.

"Here's a reason, Tirla." Sascha showed her the ID bracelet in
the case. He took advantage of her surprise to clasp it around her
wrist.

She stared at it, holding her arms away from her, trying to absorb the significance of having a legal identity and then the slowly
dawning knowledge that the bracelet was not banded in the usual
Residential colors. Green banding meant that one could travel between Linears, but what did the gold and black stripes mean?

"You are now legal, Tirla."

Just then the four freight elevators reached the cargo level. A
mass of women flowed out onto the platform, raising loud lamentations when they saw limp bodies on medipads. Sascha drew Tirla
to one side as Public Health personnel circulated, establishing the
parentage of those Tirla had rescued.

"What happens to them?" Tirla asked. This was not what she
had had in mind when she set out on her mad venture. Parents
would not be pleased that their children were in the hands of Au-

thority. Nor would they profit as she had intended. She had an ID bracelet and more credit than she had ever possessed in her life—but what good would it do her if the tenuous position she had carved for herself, her clients, her means of supporting herself, were gone? Suddenly her future seemed as bleak as that of the children she had saved from Yassim.

A tall, slender, very handsome young man in a LEO uniform planted himself squarely in front of the Sascha person and saluted. "What do you wish me to tell the women, sir?" he asked.

"That Tirla here," Sascha said, moving her to stand in front of him, his hands lightly—and, she felt, kindly—on her shoulders, "found where Yassim had hidden their children. She was leading them back home, to their mothers and fathers, when we, also searching, came upon them."

In a voice that penetrated the tumult of wailing women, the young man rattled off the announcement in the required languages —a task that made Tirla restless under Sascha's hands. As each of the linguistic groups understood, they fell to whispering among themselves. When the translator had finished, Mirda Khan and Mama Bobchik waded forward, their expressions grim. Under Sascha's hands, Tirla's narrow shoulders tensed, and surreptitiously she shielded her brand-new ID bracelet by moving her arm slightly behind her.

"And the children?" Mirda Khan demanded in Basic, jutting her chin out. She stared pointedly at Tirla.

"The records have been checked," Sascha said, his voice diplomatically apologetic. "Their births were illegal."

When Mirda Khan frowned, Sascha signaled for Ranjit to translate. The wave of hysterical weeping was punctuated as mothers of now officially illegal children threw themselves across the unconscious bodies, obviously determined to resist attempts to remove them. Sascha ordered the crowd-control partners to neutralize the incipient hysterics. He dampened his own reception, but he could not remain immune to the intense emotional agitation that battered his senses. He was perplexed. These same women would have sold their sons and daughters in a few years.

Boris, he said, *it's going to be a lot easier to buy these women off with something.*

How about the truth? Isn't a hostel a better fate than the future Yassim planned for them?

I would think so, Sascha replied, *but I do not think they'll see it in the same light. I'll tap our slush fund if you won't ante up.* Anything, Sascha thought, to shut up the spine-crawling ululations. He was not used to having to deal on this level.

Getting soft, Brother?

You're not here and listening. And there's Tirla to think of.

You're taking charge of her, aren't you? Boris asked.

I'd rather she wasn't jeopardized. Her Talent could be very useful in multilanguage groups.

The noise was fearful, the aura exceedingly unpleasant for any Talents with the least modicum of empathy. Tears were streaming down Carmen's face.

"How much, Tirla?" Sascha asked.

Startled, she twisted in his hands to see his expression.

"How much will stop their tears and relieve their loss?" he went on.

"You'd pay?"

He saw the leap of astonishment in her velvety brown eyes before a canny veil settled over her expression. *Brother, this one's going to deal for the hairs on our chests.*

"For the youngest, you don't have to give much." She named a figure. "Add ten percent for each year they have, and that should be enough."

"I'd say five percent for each year."

"Seven!" she retorted. "The bigger they are the more it takes to fill their bellies."

He spit in his hand and held it out. She closed the deal and then stepped four paces nearer to Mirda Khan.

Ranjit, monitor this for me! Sascha ordered.

She's speaking Arabic, Ranjit said. *She's saying that she has been arguing hard for the grieving mothers ever since they were caught in the tunnel. Only because she has spoken out so forcefully has a way been made to ease the sorrow of the mothers. Illegal children have rights, the big man says, and she believes him. They will be much safer than with Yassim, for which every mother should be thankful, knowing perfectly well the fate which awaited the children, despite the grief it causes. For how else can people survive on mere subsistence alone? A price has been agreed, as they must have seen, and she has acted in good faith. Sascha,* Ranjit added as Tirla turned to face another section of the women, *this child is amazing. She's speaking Urdu now as glibly as she did Arabic. Oho!*

There was a commotion, and a plump little woman, her face contorted with conflicting emotions until her beady eyes were hidden in the folds of her cheeks, pushed through. Sascha recognized her from her caste mark and the vindictiveness of her roiling thoughts. She would have leaped upon Tirla if Mirda Khan and Mama Bobchik had not intervened. Sascha sprang forward to protect Tirla, berating himself for not anticipating an attack.

"Unwanted bitch," the woman shrieked in Basic. "Illegal, you! The bint is illegal! She is illegal!" She struggled against the restraining hands. "Take her. You take her if you take my Tombi. You take her!"

"Of course I am illegal, wasted barren woman whose husband will beat her morning, noon, and evening for refusing a fair price that will feed him for many days to come on lamb and papadums." Tirla leaned with fervor into the task of returning verbal abuse. She had, Sascha noted, managed to run her bracelet up under her sleeve, out of sight.

Sascha restrained Tirla by her shoulders. "She is illegal, woman. She comes with us. Tell them, Ranjit!" When the message had been translated, he added, "The deal she spoke of will be good for only three more minutes." He looked pointedly at his digital watch. "Then there is no more to talk about. Let each mother who accepts the offer stand by her child."

Then, to shut up the renewal of Bilala's caterwauling, Sascha shot a strong silencing command compulsion on the hysterical woman. She fell back in the arms of the women who held her, her mouth working soundlessly. An awed hush fell over the platform.

The business was quickly concluded then, and Tirla watched solemnly as crisp floaters changed hands. She had never seen so much money in circulation at one time and in front of everyone. It was better so. No one could claim afterward that one had received more than another. Some of the women lingered, displaying real distress as their children were loaded back into the front four cars. Sascha propelled Tirla towards the last car, which the search group was boarding.

Tirla held up her braceleted arm. "You keep the bargain in fact but not in spirit?" she demanded as the drone cover slid shut. She tugged at the coveted wristband.

"The bargain is kept in fact and in spirit, Tirla, but you can't go back to G, not with Bilala your enemy."

"Huh! That one!" Tirla snorted derisively. "She wouldn't find me if I didn't want her to. I'm not afraid of that stupid woman."

"Frankly, I would be, were I you," Sascha said. "She'll certainly make sure Yassim knows what part you had in clearing out his hide."

That caused her to reflect, although Sascha still could not nudge his way past her shields.

"Then what was the point of making it seem as if they'd escaped?" she demanded with some exasperation.

"That seemed a sensible safeguard at the time. Up until you'd wanted to be such a good neighbor. C'mon . . ." Sascha held out his hand. "I think I can find you a safe squat for a few days with a friend of mine." *Dorotea?* he called. *Can you spare a moment for this waif?*

Tirla looked at his hand as if it were covered in acid. "At the hostel? With *them?*"

"You're legal, remember?" he reassured her with a little smile. "Technically, you're free to move anywhere you want to now. You've got a wad of floaters, but—" He raised his hand in a cautionary gesture. "—you know as well as I do that an unattached kid in a Linear right now is in jeopardy. Yassim has got to find replacements, and Mirda Khan and Mama Bobchik wouldn't be there to defend you."

"Defend me?" Tirla was both indignant and astonished.

"Oh, they did, in their own ways. And if a ladrone didn't snap you up, the Public Health would, as you're underage and should be in school." *Wow!* he exclaimed to Dorotea as he sensed Tirla's sudden reaction. *That opened up an excited crack.*

Dorotea: *Keep working it then!*

"Frankly, I would be wary, were I you," Sascha said.

Tirla fingered her precious ID. "School? I could access Teacher?"

"You've the right to all the education you can stuff into your head—that is, once you overcome the little problem of being an unattached minor. C'mon, get into the pod. It's ready to go, and I want you out of this hostile environment."

Tirla cast a look over her shoulder at the knot of women around Bilala and said "Stupid cunt" under her breath, but she did not resist Sascha's guiding hand.

"Once you've caught up with the grade level, you could even go to a regular school."

"Me? In a school?" Tirla was skeptical as well as contemptuous.

"I suspect you've got a lot more talent than you realize, Tirla."

Dorotea, acidly: *You were never one to understate a cause.*

Tirla hunkered down beside him, balancing her torso between spread knees, hands dangling limply between her legs, her butt against the padded end of the cargo pod. She cocked her head up at him, hauling the strands of dark hair off her face, her dark eyes sparkling with, it seemed to Sascha, a private amusement that, for all his telepathic skill, he could not penetrate.

"Talent?" she repeated.

"Yes," he said. "Talent." He settled down beside her just as the train began to ease forward.

"I'm nothing like *you,*" Tirla said warily, swaying a little.

"No, you're not. I cannot talk to everyone in their own language as glibly as you do."

Tirla thought for a moment and then shrugged. "That's not hard to do."

"Not for you. Ranjit, who's quite a linguist, was making heavy weather of the translations just now."

Tirla shrugged again, dismissively.

"In a few years, you could earn a big wage just translating." He could feel her attention. "Enough to live at the top of any Linear and never have to worry about the Yassims of this world."

"Working for LEO?" She was plainly unwilling.

"For someone with your gift of languages, there are far better opportunities than LEO. You do need some schooling."

"I got schooling." Her tone was both rebellious and indignant. At Sascha's prompting, she added, "I used my brother's ID—as long as I had it. I got schooling."

Dorotea, would you check that out? The brother's name and ID are on the Incident report.

I caught a glimpse again, Sascha, Dorotea said. *I'm going to need personal contact with her to get past that shield. I gather you plan to bring her to my place and I'm to play sweet frail harmless grandmama? Boy, this has been a day! In for a penny, in for a pound. Did you get any of the high-level interview?*

Caught most of it! Sascha sent an image of him cheering like a mad soccer supporter.

When all the excitement dies down, Sascha, we are going through the testing procedures with the proverbial fine-tooth comb.

Just then Sascha felt the jar as the four forward cars were detached to go on to the western hostel that would accommodate the illegal children. He caught the look of apprehension on Tirla's face and her quick glance at him.

I'll take her to my spare room if you'd rather, he told Dorotea.

Nonsense. I may hate typecasting but I'm far more suitable. Though you're doing rather well, Dorotea allowed somewhat grudgingly.

Sascha smiled and resettled himself. "It'll be smoother from now on," he said to Tirla. "We're being shunted to the commuter track."

"Where are you taking me?"

"To my grandmother."

I'm not sure I care to be related to a glib philanderer like you, Sascha Roznine. No morals.

"If she'll have you for a few days until I can find the right Residential school for you," he amended. "That would solve the problem of nosy Public Health officials and keep you out of Yassim's notice." The mention of school briefly opened her shield and he saw a fearful startlement—a hunger and a withdrawal—before it lowered. He went on casually. "But, as I said, you've a legal ID, floaters enough for months, and you can suit yourself."

Their car had been shunted several times, and the progress became smoother and faster. Tirla noticed it, and she also noticed how the other people in the car were relaxing, smiling and chatting comfortably with one another.

Residential school, my ass! Boris's disgusted tone echoed in Sascha's mind. *I can just see Fairmont or Holyoke taking in that subbie.*

Tolerance, Bro, tolerance. She's clean and healthy, and that tight mind might conceal a genius.

Boris: *For scams!*

Dorotea, steel in her tone: *You just let us handle one of our own.*

Since when am I disowned? Boris asked.

Dorotea: *When you're wearing nothing but your LEO hat!*

Sascha had a mental image of his brother withdrawing quietly, offending hat in hand. No one took on Dorotea in a crusading mood. He glanced down at Tirla, who was deep in thought, staring down at the floor, though her body appeared relaxed. When the cargo-pod door opened as they reached the vehicle park in the quiet grounds of the Eastern Center for Parapsychics, she reacted with amazement and disbelief. As the other members of Sascha's team piled out, laughing and chatting over the successful assignment, Tirla just stood, her large eyes wide and white as she stared around her. Sascha did not hurry her. The old Henner estate, with its big old beeches, maples, and oaks, the wide lawns and the attractive two-story residential units, was unusual enough in modern Jerhattan and had to be a revelation to a Linear resident. Tirla looked appalled.

"My grandmother lives over there," Sascha said, pointing to the dwelling that had once been the gardener's lodge. "There she is, weeding the border." *You are the most complete ham, Dorotea. Weeding?*

True enough, but I wasn't going to swathe myself in black subsistence and bedeck myself with bracelets and nose rings to make her feel at ease. And the border does need weeding.

What about your arthritis?

I always suffer for my art, m'dear. I've recruited Peter, too. He needs to climb down from rarefied atmospheres, and something homely will help. Also, he may be older than she is, but he looks young. He's to appear with eats. Refreshments are always a good way to start off a conversation, particularly for someone with a Near East background. "Why, Sascha, what a pleasant surprise!" Dorotea hoisted herself to her feet and held out her arms to him. *Kiss me, you lout. Even grandmothers need a ration of passion now and again!*

"Grandmother, this is Tirla . . . Tunnelle."

Inventive boy! Dorotea commented.

"She needs a place to stay for a few days. Would it be too much of an imposition?"

Dorotea extracted herself from Sascha's enthusiastic embrace and extended a mud-daubed hand to Tirla. Since Dorotea had been accepted and acceptable from the moment of her birth, she had about her an aura that made rejection from anyone impossible; Tirla delayed only a moment before grasping the extended hand. *She's got bones like a bird's, Sascha. How could she possibly do all she's just done?*

"Tirla, this is Dorotea Horvath." *There's nothing frail about Tirla's mind, Dorotea.*

"Actually, I was just about to quit and have something to eat and drink. The sun's warm today. Peter, is the juice ready?" she called, and gestured for her guests to precede her into the little house.

Sascha was glad that he had thought of Dorotea, instead of taking Tirla to the far more daunting manor house and its formality. Judging by the girl's stunned expression, even this homey room was far outside her experience.

"I expect you'll want to wash up, and I need to," Dorotea said gently, touching Tirla's arm and pointing to the little hall. "Lavatory's second door on the left, dear, plenty of towels. Peter," she said as she made for the small kitchen, "we have two more guests."

Peter: *What's she like?*

Sascha: *Scared.*

Peter, wryly: *Know the feeling!*

Dorotea: *Tight shield.*

Peter, earnestly: *I'll be careful.*

Dorotea: *And don't show off. You'll terrify her.*

Peter: *I did all the showing off I'm going to do this morning.*

An apprehensive Tirla reentered the room, surreptitiously trailing fingers along wooden surfaces and across the sofa backs. Sascha noticed that she had washed hands, arms, neck, face, and that portion of her chest that was visible above the round neck of her rather worn clothing. She had brushed her long hair neatly back over her shoulders. Sascha thought of the cheerless functionality of subsistence living quarters and gave Tirla another full mark for nonchalance.

"Here we are," Dorotea said, arriving with a large tray laden with all sorts of fingerfoods: savories, small open-faced sandwiches, wedges of fruit, and strips of fresh vegetables. "Peter, don't drop the glasses!" Fortunately, Tirla's back was to the boy who, with both hands on the huge pitcher of orange juice, was allowing four large tumblers to float along beside him.

"Hold it while I pour," Peter said, handing Tirla a glass, a diversion that kept her from noticing the other glasses sliding to positions on the low table near Dorotea and Sascha.

Dorotea: *Peter!*

Peter: *She didn't see it.*

When all had been served with juice, Peter bounced into the chair beside Tirla and took a long drink of the juice, wiping his mouth and exclaiming with satisfaction at the taste.

"Don't inhale the juice, Peter," Dorotea said as she offered Tirla the tray of snacks. *An uncommon fondness for green pepper,* she noted when she saw Tirla's eyes brighten at the sight of the slices. Closely watching Dorotea, the girl had closed her fingers about three, then increased her haul to six when there was no reaction. "The cheese puffs are hot and fresh," Dorotea said, pushing them toward Tirla. "You'd better get them now before Sascha or Peter hog them all."

Tirla let the pepper strips fall into her lap and obediently took a cheese puff.

I couldn't make myself some coffee, could I, Doro? Sascha asked plaintively.

Drink! Anything. She won't until we all do. "Peter, this is just what I needed. I must have dehydrated in the sun. Sascha, there're asparagus in the breadrolls. I know you like them! And Peter, you are not to eat all the chicken sandwiches. He would, you know," Dorotea rattled on, nibbling at a cheese puff which she then put to one side to take a bite of a pâtéd cracker. *Well, we've all sampled everything to prove there's no poison or drugs. Ah, good! Oh, my word! She's starved!*

Tirla had started to drink and eat with quick sharp bites and snatched swallows, as if she was torn between eating and drinking and afraid that the food would suddenly disappear. All three telepaths were aware of a sudden lightening of her carefully guarded thoughts as she made inroads on the snacks. The pastry melted in her mouth, releasing tastes that satisfied unknown cravings with textures that titillated her tongue, from the reassuring crisp watery tang of the green peppers to the bite of sharp cheese and savory meat fillings.

Food would be a trigger, Dorotea went on wryly, *when you consider she's probably been hungry all her life.* She took a long drink of the orange juice. "I hope you've more in the kitchen, Peter, because it tastes marvelous. But then, fresh-squeezed orange juice always does, don't you think so, Tirla?"

Sascha! Boris's tone was authoritative. *Your waif's in good hands. Someone just snatched one of the Jerhattan schoolkids we stranded three weeks ago.*

"Well," Sascha said, rising and dusting crumbs off his fingers. "I'll leave you to it, Tirla. You're safe enough here for a few days, and Peter can show you how to log on to Teacher. Right?"

As he strode across the lawn to the main house, Dorotea told him, *She paused in her eating when you left, but I fear the snack tray and the orange juice pitcher are of far greater moment than you, honey.*

Sascha was not certain, in his private mind, if he liked taking second place to a batch of canapés, even with a preadolescent.

CHAPTER 13

"Y ou been here long?" Tirla asked Peter the next morning as they ate breakfast in the pleasant and, to Tirla, amazing kitchen room. Dorotea was preparing eggs—fresh eggs—in a pan at the stove, using, of all things, a naked flame. Tirla did not wish to distract her from the dangerous procedure, so she spoke in a low voice.

"Hmm," Peter said amiably, taking neat spoonfuls of the ripe melon. "Ever since I got out of the hospital."

Tirla watched to see how he dealt with the food—she would have sliced it thin and eaten down to the rind. "Why were you in the hospital?" she asked. Hospitals were fearsome places to Tirla, who had always made a practice of avoiding medics, as well as quacks. She also had a wary distrust of sick people, never having been ill or injured herself.

Peter gave a diffident shrug of one shoulder. "A wall collapsed all over me."

"You must have been hurt bad." In Tirla's experience people did not survive walls coming down on them.

"Couldn't walk for months. Couldn't even feed myself." His eyes took on an unfocused cast.

"And they let you live?" Tirla was stunned at such good fortune.

Peter regarded her with some surprise. "Of course, though for a while there, I really didn't want to live."

Tirla absorbed that remarkable statement as she bent to the task of eating melon. It was really good—not gone off like most of those she scrounged. She flicked careful glances at Dorotea to make sure the fire was under control. Why didn't the woman use the hotter she had right there in the wall? One of the first things one learned

in the Linears was not to mess with naked flames. Fire was a sure
way to bring down the wrath of the LEOs.

"Why did you?" Tirla asked, realizing that Peter was waiting for
her to comment. "Live, I mean."

"Rhyssa taught me how to move again."

"You do move sort of oddly," she said, having noticed the peculiar gliding motion he used. He did not, in fact, seem to take real
steps, though his legs moved.

Peter snickered, his mouth full of melon. He swallowed and
grinned broadly. "That's because I'm not really walking. I impel
myself kinetically." His eyes glinted with mischief at her mystifica-
tion. "I make my body move. It can't."

Tirla stopped eating, staring at him until she recalled that even
in Linears a lengthy stare was impolite. "Your body doesn't move?
But you're eating. You're using your arm and your hand—just like
me." She held her own hand up.

"I'm pretty good at it, aren't I?" Peter was delighted with his
effect on Tirla. "I've done some other stuff, too, moving—" He
broke off, with a slightly rueful grin. "I hear you're pretty good at
your Talent, too. That was larky—getting the kids away from the
pervert."

Tirla slowly shook her head, dismissing her achievement.
"Nothing like what you do. I don't have much Talent at all."

Peter snorted with good-natured contempt. "That's what you
think. It's not what Rhyssa said. I'm good at what I do. But you're
very very good at what you do. Don't knock it."

Slightly embarrassed by the sincerity of Peter's tone, Tirla
changed the subject, eager to pump him on puzzling topics. "You
said Rhyssa helped you? Is she the dark-haired one who was here
last night after Sascha left?"

Peter nodded his head. "She's the director here."

"Not Sascha?"

Peter shook his head, grinning. "Sascha's the deputy chief. He
takes over when Rhyssa's involved with someone. Like me! I'm her
special project—" He broke off, blinking his eyes rapidly, and
flashed a quick, almost apologetic glance at Dorotea before he
grinned. "Rhyssa has lots of special duties, being the director. I'm
not the only one."

Tirla noticed that his cheeks flamed briefly. What could embar-
rass a boy like Peter? Then Dorotea was passing plates with freshly

cooked eggs and bacon and urging Tirla to sample the hot toast. Tirla ate until she was stuffed. She thanked Dorotea profusely for the effort of handcooking.

"I enjoy it," Dorotea replied, smiling gently. "Especially for appreciative appetites. Peter, why don't you take Tirla to the study and log her in? You've got to go through some assessments first, honey, but once your standard's been decided, you'll be expected to be present for all the classes you're assigned."

Tirla nodded briefly, far more interested in the way Peter got down from his chair—indeed he did glide as he conducted her to the study, and the curious fluidity of his movements fascinated her.

"And you aren't really walking?" she asked.

"Nope, it's all kinetic. My spinal cord got severed when the wall fell on me. Medical science can't splice that—yet—but kinetic science gives me movement. Better'n being stuck in a support chair," he assured her blithely. "Here's your terminal, and here're your earplugs. I've got to do my hours with Teacher, too. Can't slip out of that with kinesis!" He made a face as she slid into the chair he indicated. When she had slipped the plugs into her ears, he typed a sequence with an odd finger movement, and suddenly the blank screen cleared.

"Tirla Tunnelle, may I, as your personal Teacher, welcome you to this Educational Program." The screen showed the School Room and a pleasant-faced woman seated at the desk. Tirla knew that the Teacher was a construct, devised to reproduce the old teacher-pupil confrontation, but she had always liked the look of Teacher; someone a person could trust, who would not laugh at questions or honest mistakes, who was there to help one learn. "Sascha Roznine told us that you have had some credits under the name of Kail, Linear G resident, Flat 8732a. Today, if you will bear with me, Tirla, we will just see how much of those early lessons you remember. Now, shall we begin? If you need to be refreshed about the function keys, please type H for help. Or, if you're ready to begin, strike RETURN, and we'll begin the assessment."

With conflicting emotions—awe at realizing a long-held dream and fear that the miracle might be withdrawn for some capricious reason—Tirla touched RETURN.

I think," Dorotea began, drumming her fingers rapidly on the kitchen table, "Tirla is going into an education-overkill phase. She won't leave the terminal, though Peter has been as slyly devious as you, Sascha, in getting her outside. I also think she finds the grounds daunting instead of pleasant. She sticks to the paths and won't use the playground facilities. But all this study and no play is not an improvement."

Don Usenik, who had joined the informal meeting as medical advisor, shook his head, mildly amused by Dorotea's fervor. "According to the medical reports, she's in excellent shape. Amazingly so when you consider the conditions under which she's lived."

"Well, I think it's wrong for a child her age to try and absorb two years' education in four days," Dorotea maintained.

"Any improvement in receptivity?" Rhyssa asked.

"What does Peter say?" Dorotea countered with some heat.

Rhyssa laughed. "Peter thinks she could if she would. When she's involved in her studying, he can hear an ongoing mental commentary. She has amazing retentive powers, visual as well as auditory. She's answered him telepathically once or twice when she didn't realize it."

"We have got to make her aware of her potential," Sascha said, frustrated.

Rhyssa leaned across the table. "It will take time, Sascha. There's no need to force scope to her Talent."

"Boris would like a hundred more like her," Sascha said, frowning.

"But I thought you and Boris had found the Jerhattan child," Rhyssa said, having followed his thought. She did not like what she read: that Boris wanted Tirla to work undercover with Cass.

"Oh, we found and rescued her all right enough," Sascha replied with no sense of achievement, "and two others, but there were no leads whatever of any use. Only a minor ladrone who reports by phone—another of those conveniently illegal connects. So a dead end. The girls could tell us nothing; they had been gassed, blindfolded, stuck in some sort of smooth plastic cocoon. Their trauma went pretty deep."

"The psychological scarring of their incarceration is going to be difficult to neutralize," Don remarked, frowning. "A new wrinkle in rendering the abducted docile—tactile disorientation. Villainous trick." He shook his head. "You and Peter are off today, aren't you?

So that leaves Dorotea and me to come up with some brilliant ideas on sharpening up the Tests, huh?"

"And me," Sascha said, coming out of his gloom. "I am after all, director of training for this Center. The trouble with a unique like Tirla is that she doesn't realize she's got Talent in the first place. And in the second, how can you test children that aren't supposed to exist?"

"What training have you planned for Tirla then?" Rhyssa said.

Sascha shrugged. "Training? She's a natural at what she does—getting into the communication center of anyone's brain and adapting to whatever language they're using." He spread his hands wide. "How can we improve on that? And she can't explain any more than Peter can explain how he does what he does."

"I'd do it myself, but I hate crowds and I can't walk far," Dorotea said suddenly, "but Sascha, why don't you start by hauling her away from Teacher for an afternoon? Those issue shoes are useless, and while she might feel happy in subsistence issue, I would like to see her dressed in something nicer. Several something nicers."

"Me?" Sascha glanced first at Dorotea and then at Rhyssa and pretended not to see Don's amused expression.

"You!" Dorotea pointed a stern finger at him. "She trusts you."

"But I've never bought clothes for a kid."

"No need to panic," Dorotea replied unfeelingly. "I'm sure Tirla knows what she'd be comfortable wearing, and that's all you need to go by. She's still a trifle young to want to bedeck herself alluringly."

Wanna bet? Rhyssa said in a tight aside to Dorotea, who gave her an unfathomable glance without betraying a mental explanation.

"Take her to one of the good malls. Let her see how the other half lives—the one she's inhabiting now," Dorotea went on. "And then treat her to something tooth-rottening and utterly satiating. Spoil her a bit. Show her there's more to life on this level than a square box and a wrist ID."

"She might know of other kids with unusual aptitudes," Rhyssa added. "She doesn't miss much."

"That's for sure," Sascha replied heartily. "Your heli just landed, Rhyssa. I'll just see you all off."

"Peter!" Rhyssa called. "Dave and Johnny are on their way. Are you all packed?"

Dorotea snorted. "He's been ready since before you thought of the—" She paused and grinned wickedly. "—distraction."

"I'm coming," Peter called. He glided to Tirla's room. "I'll see you," he told her. "Keep clocking in the study time."

She hit the HOLD and regarded him in surprise. "You going somewhere?"

Peter grinned mischievously. "Rhyssa's got a job for me." He winked.

"Job? For you?"

"Sure. I'm very useful, I'll have you know."

Tirla gave him a long disbelieving look. "Doing what?"

"More of what I'm good at."

Tirla gave him a look of profound disbelief. "What could you be good at?"

Peter made a clicking sound in his mouth, since he could not snap his fingers. "I just wish I could tell you, Tirla. But it's a professional secret."

"So don't tell me. I got better things to do than guess secrets!" Tirla turned back to the monitor.

"But I'll be gone weeks."

Tirla wriggled her fingers at him over her shoulder. "Have a good time," she said, keeping her eyes on the screen. The Teacher on hold had her mouth open and hand half-raised as she was making a particular point in the lesson. Tirla tried to resume her studying, but the truth of the matter, though she could not let on to Peter, was that she would miss him. Weeks?

He was the first boy she had ever met who had some sense. She knew he was supposed to be a very clever kinetic—he had talked to her about thought transfer and telepathy, which made her a bit nervous—but he had also been good about helping her with some of the harder problems Teacher set her. At least Sascha would be around. She would not like Sascha to be gone for weeks.

She was surprised to have her lesson interrupted a second time— and by Sascha.

"Tirla! Have you stirred out of this room today?"

"No," she said, tapping out the answer to the problem on the screen.

"Tirla! Turn that damned thing off! We've got something better to do with the afternoon."

She rolled over on her side to look up at him. "What?"

"Buy you some new shoes and clothes."

Tirla looked down at the toes that were visible through the latest cracks in her footwear. "I did try to find the issue slot, but Dorotea doesn't have one."

Sascha hunkered down and firmly punched the Off switch.

"Hey!" Tirla regarded him with astonishment that quickly turned to antagonism. She reached for the switch, and he caught her hand.

"You can pick up where you left off when we get back. On your feet!" Sascha gave her hand a warning pull. "We don't have issue slots at the Center. Generally we get ordinary stuff from the Remote Mall, but as I haven't a notion of your shoe size or what colors you like, I think this once, we'll go in the flesh. When we're done, we're going to have a treat."

That got Tirla's interest. She bounced to her feet, her black eyes sparkling. "What kind of treat?"

"That'll be entirely up to you, my dear," he said, leading the way to the transport lot. "In our malls there's a lot to choose from," he added in a provocative tone.

Whatever misgivings Sascha might have entertained about shopping for a child were swiftly compounded. First Tirla had to recover from her initial shock at the size of the mall that Sascha had chosen. Then she led him a dance through every department of the twelve-story complex, eyes and head constantly on the move as she did an initial reconnaissance.

Back on the first floor, she mused at length over the various items that had caught her attention the first time and then began a second tar. On the fourth level, fortunately the one dealing with shoes and apparel for young people, the sole of one shoe disintegrated—"From the heat of the speed at which she was traveling," Sascha told Dorotea later.

When an officious floor walker moved in on Tirla with the obvious intent of removing the waif from the elegant premises, Sascha intercepted him.

"I wouldn't," Sascha said in a low voice, pushing out his sleeve so the special design of his wrist ID was visible. "I'm escorting her. Is she acceptable as a patron now?"

"Yes, sir, I'm sorry, sir, but you must admit . . ."

"That's why we're shopping."

The man walked quickly out of Sascha's vicinity with several anxious backward glances.

"You weren't going to hex him, were you, Sascha?" an amused voice beside him asked.

He turned to see Cass Cutler grinning up at him. "If I could, I'd put a hurry one on Tirla," he said. "We went through all twelve levels of this place like a dose of salts, and now she's settling down for a second tour."

Cass laughed at his discomfort. "And they sent you out on your own with your protégée?" She laughed again. "That's unkind."

"It's supposed to be mutually instructive."

Tirla reappeared and latched onto Sascha's hand, regarding Cass very narrowly from her suddenly inscrutable eyes.

"I remember you," Cass said. "You ricocheted off me and my partner at Linear G. And you messed up Flimflam's scam to a fare-thee-well. My congratulations!"

"You're one of him," Tirla accused, jerking her head toward Sascha.

Cass laughed again, a throaty, genuine laugh. Sascha could feel Tirla's fingers relaxing. "Not quite, chip. We're on the same side, but right now I'm assigned to LEO, crowd control."

Tirla looked about her, slightly contemptuous. "Not much of a crowd here today."

"I'm not on duty today," Cass replied, grinning down at Tirla. "I see you're on a day off, too. What've you found that appeals to you?"

Will you help me, Cass? Please say yes! Sascha pleaded. *I've a hideous presentiment that that child intends to case the entire mall again before she'll even try something on.*

"If you don't mind me saying it, Tirla, you'll be able to walk further with a decent pair of shoes on your feet. There're some good bargains to be had right now. What strikes your fancy?"

With a sense of reprieve, Sascha followed Cass and Tirla to the shoe department. An hour later, after two harried human clerks had replaced the mechanical fitter, Tirla's small, narrow, and very dainty feet ended up in soft purple leather boots, in the only pair that would fit her feet.

Totally unsuitable for a child, of course, Cass said, *but they do fit.*

And she adores them! Sascha saw how Tirla's face glowed as she strutted from mirror to mirror, regarding her feet.

"Mr. Roznine," the head clerk said wearily as the docket spun out of the teller machine, "your young companion has a most delicate and unusual foot to fit. May I recommend this concern? They do very fine custom work."

Sascha read the man easily and caught the unspoken message: "So we won't have to go through this again." But he was just as grateful to take the card, which could be inserted in Dorotea's mall machine for home shopping.

He blessed Cass with every new purchase, for the woman actually seemed to enjoy the looking, the trying, and the endless discussions of fit, style, and color.

"The concept of having unlimited funds to spend is foreign to the child, Sascha," Cass said at one point, "but you must admit that she knows what suits her."

Tirla was modeling a one-piece outfit as different from subsistence issue as diamonds from rhinestones. The main color was a soft blue with purple accents in seamstitching, pocket trim, and fasteners. Once Tirla found that outfit to her taste and Sascha's—it was always Sascha to whom she turned for approval—it took the combined efforts of both Sascha and Cass to get her to buy additional clothing.

"Why do I need more? I've boots, and this material's hard wearing. It'll do for weeks. Even if I had to catch freights again," Tirla added, peering mischievously up at Sascha.

He had to chuckle at her impudence. "It's a fetching outfit, Tirla, there's no question of it. But even Teacher will get tired of seeing you in it."

Tirla gave him a long hard look. "Teacher doesn't *see* me."

"No, but Dorotea and I do, so do Sirikit, Budworth, Don, and Peter, and Rhyssa. You never see *them* wearing the same clothes two days in a row."

"Oh, they have lots of clothes. Dorotea has closets full." Tirla did not sound envious—if anything her tone was slightly censorious, as if she felt it was improper for people to have so many things to wear.

"A few changes are in order," Cass said. "I've got quite a few myself," she added encouragingly while Tirla merely stared back, her hands plunged into the deep pockets and her shoulders hunched under the smooth fabric.

"This isn't coming out of your floaters, Tirla," Sascha began, suddenly realizing what might be causing her hesitation. "Dorotea and Rhyssa want you to be suitably dressed now that you're a Talent. You're not a subbie anymore, you know." He pointed to her wrist ID.

"Oh." There was look of surprised wonderment on the girl's face as she regarded her bracelet with dawning comprehension. "Is that why those salespersons were so nice to me?"

"Quite likely," Cass said in a dry tone of voice. "Everyone in malls like these recognizes the distinctive pattern."

Tirla twirled hers on her fragile wrist. "They do?" She settled the band outside the cuff of her new clothes. "How much can I buy with just this?"

Sascha disguised a choke of dismay with a cough just as Cass caught him in the ribs with her elbow.

"Let's find out, shall we, chip?" Cass asked cheerfully and held out her hand.

Tirla took it readily enough, but her other hand immediately sought Sascha's, and then she was dragging them after her toward a rack of brilliantly colored trousers.

She was not as profligate as Sascha feared, but she ended up with "something different to wear every day of the week." Then Sascha made good his promise of a treat, inviting Cass to join them in the Old-Fashioned Parlor of Gastronomical Confections and Irresistible Desserts.

Tirla managed to get through three immense, rich concoctions that Sascha privately thought revolting.

Cass: *Let her enjoy, Sascha. Ice cream is something she's only heard about.*

Sascha: *What if she comes home sick? Dorotea will skin me alive.*

Cass: *This child has an iron constitution if she's survived subbie slop until now. And look at how much pleasure she's having.*

Sascha, groaning: *I'll be sick!*

It was then that Tirla realized there were other girls and boys enjoying the parlor. Her spoon on automatic, she took full note of the other youngsters.

That blonde ought never to wear bright colors. She'd look better in pastel shades. Boy, what's he wearing such tight pants for? He'll squeeze 'em dry. Now that red outfit might look good on me. Maybe I can get something like that next time Sascha wants to spend money.

Sascha glanced surreptitiously at Cass, who rolled her eyes.

Sascha: *Stream of consciousness and loud and clear. Does she realize she's broadcasting?*

Cass, busily spooning up the last of her treat: *Highly unlikely. That child's had to be on the* qui vive *all her life. Frankly, Sascha, I take it as a high compliment that she's relaxed enough in our presence to do some unguarded thinking.*

Sascha: *Good point.*

As nonchalantly as he could, Sascha observed Tirla, listening to her pithy and acute remarks about physical appearances, style, clothing, manners, and a range of other subjects that flowed across her alert and fascinating mind.

Then Cass, with apparent reluctance, rose and said that she had to get back to the Center, as she had an evening assignment. Tirla even looked disappointed that their threesome had to break up.

"Look, chip, anytime you want to have a gawk round some of the other malls—" Cass started.

"There are *other* ones?" Tirla exclaimed, shooting an accusing glare at Sascha.

"Thousands," Cass told her with an unrepentant grin. "But you can't really do more than one at a time, or it all gets jumbled up in your head as to what you saw where and which price. Believe me, I know!"

Tirla saw the merit of that and, tucking her hand in Sascha's, was content to return to their transport and the Center.

By the time they reached Dorotea's, their purchases had arrived by express package tube and were piled neatly about the room.

"What a charming combination!" Dorotea exclaimed on seeing Tirla's clothes. *Did you buy the mall out, Sascha?*

Give her a little while and she probably will. Cass made the mistake of informing her there are a thousand more just like Grafton's, and we may never be able to pay her bills.

Dorotea laughed. "I'll expect a fashion show after supper, Tirla."

"Show? Why? I can put on something new every day this week. That'll show you," Tirla replied. "What's for supper? It smells good!"

"After all you just finished eating?" Sascha demanded.

"That was the treat. Don't I get supper after a treat?"

"Of course you do," Dorotea assured her, glaring at Sascha. *If you'd seen the three huge, gooey, sickeningly sweet things she consumed*

only a half hour ago, you might not be so quick to stuff her with supper,
Sascha cautioned.

"Wash your hands, Tirla, and I'll serve immediately. Are you
staying, Sascha?"

"No, thanks," he said, managing to sound polite. *Peter was right
about her being telepathic. But she doesn't know she is.*

*Hmmm. You see, you did learn something from her today. What did she
learn from you?*

How to spend money, Sascha replied sourly, and left.

I f the official spectators at the launch even noticed the youngster
seated to one side in the upper control room, they would have
supposed him to be a child on a special tour, his youth according
him a treat. The men certainly noticed the woman who sat beside
him, for she had an arresting beauty and an unusual silver streak in
her dark hair. However, her attention never strayed from the boy.
Equally involved in him was the tall dark-haired man in fatigues
with a colonel's eagle on one collar tab. So few spared the trio more
than a passing glance. The real action was taking place out by the
massive towering gantry, where gale-force winds whipped the
steam from the shuttle's rocket end. All recent launches had been
pretty tricky, the bad weather causing havoc with all air transport
but none more so than the critical first minutes of a shuttle launch.

The countdown echoed through the shielded room—at the count
of eight, the spectators were jockeying for position for an unimpeded view through the treated slit windows, eager for ignition
and takeoff. Fingers were surreptitiously crossed, for this was the
thirteenth successive shuttle flight.

"We have ignition!" As often as that phrase was uttered, it was
always said with a ring of quiet triumph.

As the shuttle engines began their full-throated roar, none of the
spectators would be able to hear another noise, that of power generators pulsing at ever-increasing speed: a subtle whine that built
and then leveled off just as the shuttle, one of the majestic new
Rigel class, began its first imperceptible upward thrust. The final
link to the launch tower fell away. Everyone held his or her breath.
Then, despite the howling wind and the lashing rain, the shuttle
crept upward from the reinforced concrete without deviating a
centimeter from the optimum takeoff trajectory. Lift became obvi-

ous with increasing acceleration, and suddenly the bird was up and running, disappearing, except for the radiance of its rockets, into the lowering ceiling of dark gray swirling clouds.

Immediately all eyes turned to the newly installed infrared monitors that continued to track the shuttle on its unswerving path through the atmosphere and safely above the turbulence, well on its way to Padrugoi Station, where its payload was urgently needed.

"The pilot has the conn," Peter Reidinger said, opening his eyes. He glanced first at Rhyssa and she nodded, smiling reassurance as she removed her hand from his. He liked her to be touching him in these moments, even if he could not feel it.

"You have the conn, Crosbie," the controller said, letting out a small sight of relief. "Good thrust, Pete. You're working like a charm. Got the whole thing down to a science."

"It is," Johnny Greene reminded him, grinning.

"You know what I mean, Colonel," the controller said, flapping his hand.

"He's teasing you," Peter said, turning his attention to the monitor. He did not really need it—he could follow the ascent of the shuttle like a pulse in his vein, a tingle of power running up and down his bones. He could *feel* that.

"Very economical thrust, Peter," Johnny said, perusing the printout on the generator control panel. "That's the third one in a row at that level gestalt. I think we can now establish certain parameters to power usage in bad-weather launches—even if I still can't tell *how* you do it." He made a disgruntled noise in his throat. The ex-etop pilot had been hoping that he could learn Peter's gestalt link by following his mind during a launch. He and Rhyssa had decided that the fact that he had only latent kinetic Talent might be all to the good—for a pure kinetic might be unable to adapt to Peter's ways. But he had had no more luck than Sascha at discerning the boy's method.

"Maybe you're trying too hard, JG," Peter suggested. "I keep as open as I can . . ."

"I know you do, lad. Wide open. I'm just too clumsy to get through the door. I think it's going to *have* to be a trained kinetic."

"Second-stage ignition," the controller said, alerted by his board. "On its way! You do good work, Pete. Good work."

"C'mon, time for your swimming lesson, Pete," Johnny said. "Gotta keep you fit enough to launch these birds."

"Can't I stay? To be sure it docks okay?" Peter would not admit, even deep in his skull where Rhyssa might see, that he did not have enough energy left immediately after a launch to move from the couch. He grasped at any excuse to gain the few necessary moments to reenergize himself.

"The bird's okay," the controller assured him.

"Look all you want," Johnny said, reseating himself. If he had guessed Peter's secret, he never let on.

The spectators below were beginning to file out of the gallery, hunching into wet-weather gear, bracing themselves for the stiff winds. With a wink, the controller turned on the intercom.

"I tell you, Senator, it is a measure of the state of the art in space technology that we're now able to launch *despite* the weather."

"If I had a nickel for every hold I've had to wait through, m'boy, I'd be able to buy drinks for the entire base. Just how much did you say this new technology cost us?"

The figure mentioned by the congressman was three times as much as Peter's contract had actually cost. And nearly one hundred percent more than the generator.

Peter grinned broadly, thoroughly enjoying the eavesdropping. He had been appalled at how much a big generator cost—though Colonel Greene assured him that it was a pittance when compared to other items purchased for Canaveral—and he could not believe the contract figure for his short-term services. Not to mention the bonuses for every successful launch. He had been even more delighted when Rhyssa suggested that the Center increase the pension that was being sent to his parents.

Talents were generally not contracted until they were at least eighteen years old, but the circumstances and his unusual ability had been construed as sufficient to make an exception—a brief exception.

Vernon's advice to the Center had been that if the technology *cost*, it was bound to be considered more efficient than something in the medium range. The difference between fact and fiction went into the Center's research fund.

At that, it had taken some finagling on Altenbach's part to get the Canaveral staff to consider the "new technology," even with the enthusiastic assistance of General Halloway and Colonel

Straub. Peter had not been mentioned; the generators had, plus some very odd "instrumentation." Peter, in fact, had been hidden behind a screen with Rhyssa when the "new technology" had had its first test. He had kinetically flown a drone from Canaveral to Eglin Field despite gale-force winds and a ceiling of 100 meters. He had landed it right on the target painted on the runway—to show the precision of the "new technology." He was then allowed to launch a loaded drone into orbit, where it could be retrieved by a Padrugoi-based craft. His precision again was the deciding factor: so many drones had wandered off course that the drone program had been drastically curtailed.

Two days later a proper shuttle launch was grudgingly permitted. There was no foreseeable change in the terrible weather patterns, and shipments had fallen weeks behind delivery. That first morning, Peter had been a trifle anxious, and the shuttle had ascended at such an astonishing rate that the controllers had thought that a misfire had occurred, and they had been about to abort the mission. Peter, with Johnny telepathically assisting him, had reduced the thrust and the mission had continued. The pilot later was heard to mention that his instrumentation had registered a g-force of 11 for the first few moments—he had been scared shitless thinking he would not even be able to activate the escape-pod control on his armrest.

The "new technology" improved in finesse over the ensuing launches, and NASA breathed a corporate sigh of relief that it could complete all the programmed supply runs to Padrugoi.

Rhyssa and Johnny watched the expression on the boy's rapt face as he followed the current shuttle's progress. The controller handed them coffee as they waited through Peter's absorption.

"Okay," the boy said finally, as the screen showed the shuttle nearing its docking rendezvous and he had recovered sufficiently. "The new technology is ready for its swim." Though still a bit weak, he managed a proper descent from his chair, raising his right hand in a creditable wave to the controller as he maneuvered the steps to the ground exit of the room.

It had taken four launches before the mission launch controller was comfortable with "new technology" and Peter's peculiar part in its schematics, but he had come to like the youngster and had given up trying to figure out how he did what he did—whatever it was.

"Get your slicker on, Pete," Johnny said.

Peter had discovered that he could kinetically keep rain from soaking him, but he tried to resist the temptation to show off unnecessarily. Dutifully he flipped the slicker over him. Exiting the concrete bunker, they all made a dash for their waiting aircar.

Two weeks after Rhyssa and Peter went to Florida, Boris made one of his rare visits to the Center to apprise Sascha of the fact that undercover agents believed more children had been sold. The agents had noticed a lot of floaters being spent in Linears A, B, and C. So Cass and Suz were sent on assignment to Linear E. As the two women frequented all the Jersey Linears, they were known to the inhabitants. Cass's pregnancy made her even less suspicious, and she pretended ill health to account for Suz's company. So far they had nothing to report, not even a ripple of expectation. Whenever contact permitted, they stuck a locating strand in the hair of each child they encountered.

Similar teams were stranding Linear children throughout the Jerhattan area. Scan teams worked around the clock, waiting for a strand to show up in an unlikely area.

Boris made one of his rare visits to the Center. "You know, Bro," he said, "we've got nothing but stopgap techniques. Planting a telempath won't stop kids being abducted." Sascha was in Rhyssa's office, attending to routine administration details as he took a break from formulating new testing procedures. Boris was standing at the window, looking out on the peaceful scene below.

"No, no, no, and no, Bro," Sascha said without looking up from the monitor. He made a rapid motion across the keyboard, then swiveled about to give his brother a hard stare. "There is no way in which I'll permit Tirla to be used as bait!"

"But she's a natural," Boris said. "She knows how to decipher Linear rumors the way no other operative available to us can."

"You think I,"—Sascha jabbed his chest with his fingers—"would risk her?"

"Candidly, I don't think Tirla would be at risk," Boris went on, beginning to pace. "We could put her in with Cass and Suz, set her up with every telltale known to technology. She *knows* Linears, she can speak any lingo, she's clever as can stare, and—"

"She's twelve years old and you're not using her as bait," Sascha roared, not bothering to dampen his outrage and fury.

Boris regarded him with surprise. "That kid was never twelve! And what's the matter with using the one advantage we've found in dealing with Linear abductions? She's got a unique Talent, a natural camouflage, and an ability for this sort of thing. Look how she managed in Linear G."

"Linear G was a once-off. I'm not putting her at risk like that again."

"She was never at risk. Except maybe from you!" Boris glared right back at his brother. "And this was Cass's idea. I think it has potential. One thing sure, Bro—unless we can get at the mastermind behind this despicable traffic, we're going to be losing kids. Kids who might well be Talented, too."

"You step up your search-and-seizes, Boris. Leave Tirla out of your calculations. There are other ways, ethical and technological ways, to solve LEO problems."

"Sascha, if I had the personnel to do it the hard way, I would," Boris replied, his face reddening in an effort to keep his temper in the face of his twin's intransigence.

"Use some of the Linear G kids as bait then. They'd love a chance to get out of the hostel!"

Boris gave his brother one long look. "You know, that's not a bad idea. I'll check 'em out." With that he strode out of the room.

CHAPTER 14

Despite the work, those last three weeks in Florida had been almost vacation time for Rhyssa, John Greene, and Peter. Launching thirteen of the eighteen supply shuttles occupied two or three hours of a day at the most for Peter.

When Johnny Greene started to explain the mechanics of lift, trajectory, orbiting, and other such matters pertaining to the job at hand, he and Rhyssa discovered that there were woeful gaps in Peter's education. He had not even had bedside schooling during his months in the hospital. So a telempathic tutor was immediately hired.

Alan Eton quickly discovered that Peter had the usual boyish disregard for grammar, spelling, and syntax, though his vocabulary skills were, in technical areas, beyond his age group. His mathematics were well into first-year university, and his understanding of certain aspects of physics was curiously advanced. With the colonel as his role model, Peter was eager to progress in those sciences. Taking advantage of the boy's admiration, John Greene suggested that he had better improve his computer and English skills, as well, even if he was kinetically superior. While Peter understood some chemical and biological concepts—particularly those that had a bearing on his accident—he had, naturally, had no laboratory experience. A course of study was initiated and regular school hours kept, with Alan guiding Peter deftly into independent study of whatever the boy wanted to learn while filling in the more obvious lacks. A university degree, bachelor or advanced, was not at issue for Peter Reidinger: his career was well underway, but if he was to develop to his full potential, it was essential for him to have an overall understanding of many disciplines. Occasionally, as he struggled through his lessons, he wondered how Tirla was doing and what sort of training Sascha was giving her.

Physiotherapy was still a necessity, and without the inhibiting body brace Peter had no trouble exercising his limbs, which he did religiously, hoping to acquire some muscle.

"There have been instances," the physiotherapist had told Rhyssa and Johnny, "where even badly damaged neural tissue has been stimulated. That's what we can wish for Peter. To feel and to move normally."

"What's the probability?" Rhyssa asked.

The physiotherapist had shrugged ruefully. "Who knows? It certainly does no harm for him to exercise kinetically. Improves muscle tone and fluidity of movement. I'll be honest, I wouldn't have guessed he was walking kinetically when he entered the gym the first time."

Swimming was Peter's favorite sport. Water supported his body, and with minimal effort he could give the illusion of swimming. He could even do incredible dives off the board, hovering in the air as he made his body twist and then entering the water cleanly. There had not been enough sun in those weeks to produce a tan, but surrogate facilities had given him an excellent color. Rhyssa had benefited, as well.

"You needed this rest," Johnny told her as they lounged on the sunbeds while keeping an eye on Peter, who was splashing happily about in the pool, pretending he was a dolphin.

"You know," she said with a deep sigh, "I think I did. It's been pretty hectic the last few months." She sighed again. "But that's the rigors of being Center director—and I wouldn't be anything else in *spite* of the negatives."

"You ever going to marry, or have kids?" Johnny asked at his most casual.

"Johnny Greene, what are you leading up to?" She cocked an eyebrow, which warned him that, if he was not straight with her, she would probably winkle the information out of his mind.

Johnny gave her a rakish grin. "Nothing—except that Dave Lehardt just arrived." His grin broadened as he saw her reaction. "Ah! So! You're not entirely immune to his charm, after all."

Rhyssa managed a laugh, though she could not hide the sudden flush of pleasure at the news. "How do you know? You can't 'hear' him if I can't."

"I saw him get out of the car. He's coming around through the house." The gleam in Johnny's eyes was intolerable to her.

"We're just working friends," she said, and heard a mental ha-ha from Johnny as Dave Lehardt strode into the pool room. Johnny chuckled again as Dave's glance rested on her just that moment longer before he greeted the others.

"Hi there, Skeleteam," Dave called to Peter, who had an arm looped around the pool stair rail. "Need a hand out?"

"I think you'd better, Pete," Rhyssa said. "Your lips are blue, and your skin's wrinkled. Hi, Dave."

Johnny, on a tight band: *You'd make a good team, you know. His beauty and your intelligence!*

Rhyssa projected an image of herself chasing Johnny with an outsized hunk of wood with the words "blunt instrument" carved on it.

Johnny: *Dorotea thinks so, too.*

Rhyssa: *You guys let me do my own thinking.*

Johnny: *Dave will, because he can't hear you. And that's about the only drawback. He lusts after you, you know.*

"Really impressive launch today, Pete," Dave went on, hauling the boy out of the pool by one arm and deftly covering him with a huge towel.

"He gets better every time," Johnny said, latching onto a spare lounger with his artificial foot and hauling it closer to where he and Rhyssa were sitting.

Rhyssa: *You watch yourself, John Greene. I've my own minder,* she recalled with amusement Peter's handy treatment of the annoying Prince Phanibal, *and I'll tell him to dunk you if you misbehave.*

Johnny sent her an image of wide-eyed innocence. *Me? Step out of line—especially if you threaten to short-circuit my cybernetic limbs in a lousy pool? D'you know what salt water does to my spare parts?* He imaged a violent shudder that sent bits and pieces spinning off his artificial arm and leg.

"Actually, the last three shoots have been within a jog of the same power settings," Rhyssa said to the new arrival.

Dave Lehardt periscoped his lean length to seat himself on a lounger and grinned at Rhyssa. Was she imagining that his eyes were warmer when he looked at her? Damn him for not having a

Talent! Damn him for having such a naturally dense mental shield! She had no real clue—except in blue eyes she wanted to drown in —to go on. No wonder the unTalented regularly bungled relationships. And yet . . .

"NASA is delighted with the effectiveness of its new guidance-and-tracking system," Dave was saying, looking well pleased, "and they're quite happy to leave it in the 'need to know' category. More queries from Padrugoi, requesting details of this top-secret G and T as a possible adjunct to their systems."

"And?" Johnny queried, flipping over on the sunbed, eyes narrowed to slits and his body relaxing in the warmth.

"General Halloway hems and haws with the best of them about a trial model, with a formidable test schedule ahead of it, by no means a totally proven system . . ."

"I am too a proven system," Peter said, looking disgruntled as he floated over, an eerie-looking maneuver since his feet were invisible under the swathing of towel that he was trying to keep out of the puddles around the pool. His teeth chattered.

"Oh here," Rhyssa said, making room for him on the sunbed. She would have fallen off if Dave had not quickly prevented it with hands and knees. She felt warm where he touched her, a warmth that was nothing generated by a sunbed. Then she settled Peter beside her, adjusting his limbs. "You're up to fifteen minutes' sunning today, aren't you?"

"Tell you one thing," Dave went on, still supporting Rhyssa's body. "I'm going to have to change the nickname Skeleteam. You don't look so much like one anymore."

"All this good wholesome Florida sunshine," Peter said, grinning at Dave. He had finally gotten over his jealousy of the PR man: it was difficult to be jealous of a guy he liked so much, who could think up neat treats and found the best places to eat. Johnny often argued to Rhyssa—when Dave was not around—that the man had to have Talent but that it simply wasn't measurable. Then he discussed things like traumatic breakthroughs and psychological reluctances, and Rhyssa replied that sometimes it was nice to know someone who could always surprise you.

"If you see any of that wholesome sunshine, let me know, huh?" Dave remarked, referring to the fact that the rain had lifted only briefly in the past three weeks. "When are you guys going to develop a reliable Weather Talent?"

"Look, we just got one minor miracle up and running," Rhyssa replied. "Give us at least three days!"

"God only rested one day," Dave said, deepening his voice to a bass register and looking pious.

"Three weeks, three months, three years, three decades," Johnny replied in a sepulchral tone. "Can't even figure ol' Petey boy out, and I've been busting my buns for weeks now."

"Pete," Dave began, "how do you see what you do? Might as well ask the source right out straight," he added in a broad aside to Rhyssa.

Peter laughed and pretended to consider the question, knotting his brows and rubbing his chin the way Johnny sometimes did. "It's like I think that's what I want to do—move the shuttle up—and I sort of lean into the generators, revving them up, and then I sort of"—he shrugged his thin shoulders—"let go."

"Like a stone from a slingshot?" Dave asked.

"Yeah, sort of like that."

"You don't sound sure."

"I'm not. It needs doing. I do it."

Rhyssa, sensing Peter's distress about being unable to explain adequately, put a warning hand on Dave's knee. His hand immediately covered hers, keeping her arm in a slightly awkward position. Over Peter's prone body, Johnny grinned at her.

"There are many operations," Rhyssa went on quickly, "that one accomplishes strictly on an involuntary basis. Like breathing. You don't consciously go through the steps of drawing breath in and exhaling it—it's an involuntary procedure. Or take reaching for a glass. You don't consciously tell your hand to extend the required distance, tell your fingers to encircle it and your arm to lift the light weight. The task is accomplished without much conscious effort. Peter is working on such a deeply involuntary basis that he cannot—yet—analyze the requisite steps. Once Lance Baden is released from durance vile on the station, I think we'll see progress in understanding what Skeleteam does as easily as he breathes."

"It's not quite that easy," Peter said.

"Don't hurt Skeleteam's feelings," Johnny said in mock affront. "He'll strike!"

"Not with his contract, he won't," Rhyssa said feelingly.

"You know, Pete," Johnny began in a thoughtful tone, "what

you said about something needing to be done and doing it. You really *don't* stop to think how? You just do it?"

"As you yourself, if I may remind you, landed a badly damaged shuttle on your twenty-first mission," Dave put in. "Experts still haven't figured out how you did that!"

John Greene grinned at him. "Neither have I. Sorry, Pete."

"You were using kinesis?" Peter asked.

"Nothing else would have gotten us down that day with one wing crumpled and the tail assembly blown off. Technically I had what they call a traumatic explosion of Talent necessitated by an intense urge to survive."

"What hit you?" Peter asked then. He had always wanted to ask, but it had never been quite the right moment and he was not sure if the colonel liked to be reminded of how he had lost an arm and a leg.

"Some damned-fool half-trained clowns, doing aerobatics through the flight path," Johnny told him, cursing fluently and inventively on both audible and telepathic levels. Peter's eyes rounded with awe at the flavorful language. "Fortunately they didn't survive to answer to me, or the law, for their antics."

"Oh!" was Peter's reaction to John's uncharacteristic bitterness.

"You're not going to waste the pool, are you, Dave?" Rhyssa asked, to change the subject, and in the hope of regaining control of her hand before her arm fell asleep.

"You're stuck with me for a few days at any rate," Dave replied. "Without benefit of the Skeleteam, the airport's socked in solid." He rose and, whistling a jaunty tune, began to pick his way through the puddles in the direction of the changing room.

Johnny heaved a sigh and resettled himself on the sunbed, hands cushioning his head. The nu-skin sheathing his artificial arm looked real enough except, Rhyssa noticed, that it did not take a tan. Peter, however, was becoming a rich brown that made him appear like any other healthy, if scrawny, boy his age. He was also falling asleep, considerably more tired by the morning's activities than he would ever admit. Smiling tenderly down at the boy, Rhyssa eased herself off the sunbed and onto the lounger that Dave had just vacated. She checked the timer: Peter had ten minutes to go. She relaxed on the soft mattress.

"*Je-* sus *Christ!*"

Dave's sudden expletive roused her, and she watched helplessly as, in midair, he flailed with arms and legs from a slip in a puddle, his long body poised to come down right across the corner of the tiled pool in what would be a serious fall. The sunbed lights went off, and the next instant his abrupt descent was halted and he came to rest gently on the poolside, unharmed, unbruised, but considerably shaken.

"How the hell . . ."

"My God!" Johnny Greene exclaimed. "Did you do that, Pete?" he asked. The very slightest of snores answered him. "My *God!* I did it! I did it! *I did it!*" His voice rose in a crescendo as he stared at Rhyssa in a state of shocked delight and surprise.

Rhyssa began to shake her head, grinning so hard at the breakthrough that she thought her face would split.

"That was all you," she assured him. "Once again Johnny on the spot!"

The moment Dave Lehardt entered the kitchen that evening as Rhyssa was clearing up the debris of their celebratory meal, she knew "a moment" had come. Over the last few months of their close association, she had learned to pick up the subtle hints of his body language and her own responses to him. She felt her heartbeat begin to speed up, and she tried not to crash dishes about or drop things. Worse, she could extract no helpful clues from this man's mind. Perhaps that was why Dave appeared to be so much more romantic than any of her Talented associations.

He came right up to her so that she had to look about, to acknowledge his proximity.

"The hardest thing in dealing with you Talents is to catch you when no one else is listening," he began. His blue eyes held a very intense look. He took the saucepan away from her and returned it to the soapy water, then put both hands on her arms and turned her slightly but decisively toward him. "Pete and Johnny are so involved in a rehash of my pratfall, they couldn't be paying attention to anything else." With a little pressure of his hands, he pulled her against him.

Johnny: *Don't you dare be coy!*

Rhyssa: *Get out of my head, Johnny Greene.*

Peter: *Ah, just when it's getting interesting. How'll I ever learn how it's done!*

Rhyssa: *Break off! Both of you! If I feel so much as a tendril of thought* . . .
Johnny: *I think she means it!*
Peter: *I know she does!*
Her mind was filled with a deafening silence.

"They're not," Rhyssa assured him.

"I've been told and warned, obliquely and right to my face, that I've no right to ask a woman of your obvious Talent, and talents, to marry a man without an ounce of the right stuff in him."

Rhyssa felt a surge of anger flare deep inside. She wondered who had been inhibiting this wonderful, caring man—especially considering all he had done to aid Talents. Then she willed him not to stop talking such marvelously romantic stuff and tilted her head up encouragingly. She shivered with anticipation.

"But I think such a decision is up to you and me," he went on. "And I'm so totally besotted with you that I can't think straight when you're in the same room with me, and I don't think of much else but you when we're apart. Rhyssa Owen, would you even consider marrying me?"

"What took you so many eons to ask?" she replied, folding her arms about his neck and grinning up at him.

With a gladness that seemed to emanate from every pore of him, he clasped her firmly in his arms and kissed her with a great deal of entirely satisfactory expertise, just as if he had read her mind.

CHAPTER 15

S ascha!

He could not ignore Dorotea's call, but it was coming at an awkward moment. He lifted his hand to signal to Budworth and Sirikit for a slight break in their discussion.

Dorotea's mental tone was colored by vexation. *As you showed her how to use her wristband to purchase damned near anything anywhere, you may now teach her thrift and budgeting. And some sense of order in her own room! There's not an inch of space that isn't stacked ceiling-high with "bargains."*

Sascha: *Where is she?*

Dorotea, at the end of her patience: *Trying on clothes while viewing today's lessons!*

"Look, Bud, run those ethnic groupings again," Sascha ordered. "We've at least got a statistical forecast of how many psionic Talents each generation has produced since Darrow and op Owen's time. Now let's break it down into individual Talent manifestations: precogs, finders, affinities, kinetics, telepaths, telempaths."

Budworth shrugged equably and began to formulate the program.

"I still don't know *how,*" Sirikit said in her soft, lilting tones, "that's going to help us discover Talent in the Linears."

"Where there's smoke, there's gotta be a fire or two," Sascha commented cryptically as he exited. But his mind was already on one particular Talent who had come so far from her early years in the Linears.

Since that fateful shopping trip three weeks before, Tirla had discovered a new pastime that almost rivaled her hunger for learning. At first, Dorotea had been amused. "It's hunger of another sort: acquisition. It'll pass."

Cass had accompanied her on two more expeditions, showing her how to use the subway transport, and thought it was fun to watch Tirla slip into the most exclusive shops and boutiques. Then she had started shopping on her own, and scoffed when Dorotea worried that child-stealers would snatch her.

"Snatch me? Not likely," Tirla replied scathingly. "I can smell their sort coming on the streets. I'm safe in the malls."

But the malls were not free from all peril, for she was detained twice by overzealous officials and, to her credit, had waited patiently until someone—usually Sascha—arrived from the Center to verify her right to wear the ID bracelet and make charges against the Center's account.

She was more amused by the detentions than alarmed, and determined to enjoy her new pastime. Certainly she was not deterred from her expeditions, and since Sascha backed Cass's opinion that Tirla was capable of handling herself, Dorotea's apprehension waned. Invariably, Tirla ended her afternoons at the Old-Fashioned Parlor. When Tirla announced that she was going to work her way right through the five pages of confectionery selections, Dorotea had laughed.

"It might put a little weight on those bird bones of hers, and she always eats her dinner," she said. "I wish she would put on weight. What must those shop attendants think when that child looks half-starved all the time?"

Dorotea was standing in the living room when Sascha arrived in answer to her summons, and she pointed sternly toward Tirla's room. Sascha tapped on the door, and Tirla's cheerful hum broke off.

"Who is it?" There was always that note of apprehension when the girl was caught unawares. Once she could break into the telepathic mode that Sascha was certain she possessed, she would rarely be caught off-guard again.

"Sascha!"

"Just a minute."

For just a moment, Sascha thought he caught a stray coy thought, and then the door opened, in stages, because Tirla had to rearrange things to get it wide enough for him to enter. Sascha looked in and groaned.

"Tirla, what happened to the kid who had to be coaxed into buying more than one outfit?" It was the first thing that came into his head, and it was probably not at all the way to handle the situation.

Dorotea, in disgust: *Ham-handed twit!*

Tirla blinked at Sascha. "But you told me I could shop whenever I wanted to. Just look what I found today!" And she held up a pair of stiletto-heeled sandals with jeweled straps. "And they fit. They didn't cost much, because the shopkeeper had had them around for decades and practically gave them to me. Aren't they lovely? D'you want to see them on? They make me much taller."

"I'm sure they do, Tirla, but to be candid, they're not the sort of thing a girl your age should wear."

"They fit!" she repeated as if that were the most important aspect.

"Tirla! Is there no place I can sit down in here? And that's what has Dorotea so upset. You know how neat she keeps everything in the house."

Dorotea: *That's right. Blame me.*

"While Talents may have what they need, and also what they want, *within reason,*" he went on, "that's the operative phrase. This —" He gestured broadly, hooking a hanger and its layers of clothing off the door. The pile tumbled to enlarge a mass of colorful blouses lying beside the door. "This is no longer reasonable!"

Tirla merely looked up at him, her face expressionless, but he sensed so deep a hurt and disappointment that he relented instantly. "I don't think I can send it all back," she said. "I've tried everything on."

"Look, chip," he said, using Cass's affectionate nickname for her, "sending it all back is not the answer."

It's a start! Dorotea put in.

"Learning to buy wisely is. Some of this stuff—" Sascha pointed to items of intimate apparel in lace and gauze that were far too sophisticated for even a twenty-year-old. "—can be packed up and stored . . ."

Dorotea, acidly: *Where?*

"In the vaults." He began picking up other inappropriate garments. "And we'll get the clutter down to manageable proportions." In doing so he exposed a small hill of shoes, of all colors and in a variety of styles that astonished him—and all of them small enough to fit Tirla's dainty feet.

Dorotea: *Cinderella complex?*

Sascha: *Pairs, every single one of them,* he said wryly.

Dorotea: *Then how can they be pairs?*

"Five pairs of shoes, no more, Tirla." He saw her sulky expression. "Five pairs at one time. And ten different outfits in the closet. None of this . . ." He held up an emerald green ball gown with exquisitely detailed beadwork in silver and leaf green. It was exceedingly stylish, and the color was perfect for Tirla—but not until she reached twenty. Eighteen, at least. "I'll have some trunks sent over so you can put everything away. Then we're going to sit down and work out a budget."

"Budget? Like they do for cities and projects?" Surprised, Tirla came out of her sulk.

"Yes. The Center has a budget, I have a budget, Peter has a budget . . ."

Dorotea: *All God's chillun got budgets!*

"Then I won't be able to go shopping again?"

Sascha was not impervious to her broken voice and her sad expression. "Shop all you want. Look in every damned mall on Manhattan, Long Island, and the Jersey Shore. Just don't buy anything. Window shop to your heart's content."

"Never buy anything again?"

La da da, da da da dah! Dorotea sang, mimicking a nostalgic violin air.

All right, Sascha retorted. *And how would you curb a kid who's never had much in her life and suddenly can have anything she wants?*

More or less as you're doing, Dorotea admitted. *Just don't waver at the sight of tears in her big black eyes!*

Sascha caught an undertone in Dorotea's voice that puzzled him. But he ignored it and returned his full attention to Tirla. "No, chip, not never. Just not so much so constantly, things you don't really need right now, because you've got enough—of practically everything, as far as I can see."

She sank to the edge of her barely visible bed. "But it's not fun to window shop unless you've got someone with you. Where's Cass? She loves to shop."

"Cass is out on assignment."

Tirla cocked her head up at him, no longer a disappointed and confused twelve-year-old. "More kids missing?"

"Not yet," he said mendaciously. "We want to keep it that way."

"Is she in a Linear?" Excitement brightened her expression. Sascha nodded.

Dorotea: *For the love of little apples, don't tell her where, or she'll track Cass down.*

"Why don't you let me work undercover with her? I could be her kid and—"

"*No!*"

Tirla rocked back on the bed at the vehemence of his response. She looked hurt and confused again and even younger than her chronological age.

"Sorry, chip." Sascha ruffled her sleek and shining hair in an effort to compensate for his tactlessness. "Give yourself a little break. We didn't catch Yassim, and if he spots you, he'd have you wasted so fast, none of us could help you."

Tirla noticeably paled.

Dorotea: *Well, she's still afraid of Yassim!*

Tirla seemed so afraid that Sascha gathered her up in his arms and rocked her. "Yassim can't get you here in the Center, Tirla. You're safe here. I want to keep you safe so you can grow up and use that rare Talent you have . . . to earn enough money to pay for all you've been buying." He tried to make a joke of it. He felt her stiffen in his arms. "No, not your floaters!" And he had to laugh. The little witch. Her hoard was precious to her, never to be broached. "Just think how little you'd have left if you *had* spent your stash. Think of that the next time you want to buy something. Pretend you're spending *your* money."

"I *wouldn't* spend *my* money," she mumbled against his chest.

With the slender little body curled trustfully in his lap, Sascha permitted himself just a few moments to caress her hair and savor the feel of her in his arms. Why Tirla? Of all the women in the world, how could this little waif, streetwise and precocious, have become so entangled in his emotions and heart? She could not possibly understand how much she meant to him. She was far too young for that aspect of maturing to have touched her. And yet . . . she responded to him as she did to no one else. With a final little hug, he put her from him as gently as he could. One day, eight or nine years in the future . . .

Dorotea had no comment to make. To his surprise, Tirla obediently began to fold up her possessions, neatly and carefully. Sascha
watched for a few more moments and then went to arrange for
trunks.

Peter and Rhyssa returned in quiet triumph the day that Cass
Cutler reported to Boris that three Neesters and two Hispanics in Linear E were suspiciously more affluent than they had any
right to be. Boris decided that he would not darken the happy
return with such news and did not even inform Sascha of the
event.

Dorotea and Tirla both exclaimed over how well Peter looked,
tanned and healthy and moving with more confidence, while
Rhyssa listened, an oddly soft smile on her face. Dave Lehardt had
remained behind in Florida to finalize his PR campaign, setting the
stage for Colonel Johnny Greene to assume the role of Skeleteam.

In his turn, Peter took full notice of Tirla's new elegance and
was amazed that she had shopped the malls herself.

"Well, Sascha took me the first time," she admitted.

Dorotea, privately to Rhyssa: *And said "Open Sesame," and in a
week Tirla's room was as full as a bazaar.*

Sascha: *I heard that. Knock it off!*

Rhyssa: *Did she pick that outfit herself?*

Dorotea: *She picked out everything herself and a lot of things a twelve-
year-old girl has no need of —yet.*

Rhyssa: *She's got good taste—in what she's wearing now.*

Dorotea: *Good taste all round. Just a trifle sophisticated.*

Aware that Sascha was seething, Dorotea changed the subject.

Peter and Tirla slipped out of the room.

"How come you're allowed to go to the mall all the time?" Peter
asked Tirla, envious of her freedom. *He* was never allowed to go
anywhere on his own.

Tirla shrugged. "Oh, they tried to tell me how dangerous it
was." She giggled. "As if I didn't know how to take care of myself
in any old Linear. Particularly one as straight as the ones here in
Jerhattan."

"And you go whenever you want?"

"Nearly every day." She cocked her head at him. "You ever been
to the Old-Fashioned Parlor of Gastronomical Delights?"

"Me?" Peter thumped his hand against his chest, then grimaced. He still didn't have the small-muscle control needed to use just a thumb or a finger. He was feeling aggrieved on several counts. "Oh, I heard about the Parlor." He pretended indifference, but then his pose faltered. "Is it really that good?"

"Good?" Tirla's enthusiasm bubbled out of her. "It's spectacular. You wouldn't believe the concoctions they serve. 'The most,' " she quoted from the menu, " 'scrumptious, delectable monstrosities of confections you'll ever experience.' " Sensing Peter's longing, Tirla deliberately encouraged it. "Any kind of flavor of ice cream, all homemade, every topping known to man . . ."

"And you just go?"

"Sure. Why not? It's only four stops away on the subway." She jerked her thumb at the murmur of adult voices coming from the living room. "Who'd miss us for half an hour, anyway?" When she saw the hesitation on his face, she added almost challengingly, "They're busy. We'd be back before they'd know we'd gone!"

That decided Peter, though he knew perfectly well that his physical circumstances were far different from Tirla's. Nevertheless, she was younger than he was, and if she was allowed, he was, too.

They left the house by the side door, Tirla skipping beside Peter in delight at his company. It was going to be such fun showing him just how well she knew her way around.

P eter could sense how pleased Tirla was to be able to take him someplace familiar to her but new to him. So he just smiled as they took their seats on the subway from the Center platform. Other Talents on the same car grinned at the two, sending telepathic greetings and congratulations to Peter, who had learned to assume a modest demeanor in public, even among other Talents.

Tirla was describing in great detail her favorite gastronomical delight—the one with four kinds of ice cream, four kinds of toppings, four kinds of nuts, and cherries, coconut, and multicolored sprinkles.

"My mother took me to a place like that," Peter said, "oh, a long time ago now. For my tenth birthday. My sister goes a lot; Mother says that's why she has spots so often."

"Spots?"

"Pimples. Zits. Facial eruptions."

"Oh," Tirla replied in a tone that expressed unenlightenment. Peter imaged a pimpled face at her. "Oh! That sort." Surreptitiously she ran her hand over her face.

Peter laughed. "You may never get spots, Tirla," Peter said encouragingly. "They keep us on a healthy diet anyhow. Not subbie food."

"What was Florida like?" Tirla asked.

Peter had learned a lot from watching Dave Lehardt answer difficult questions tactfully. So he told her about the flat land and the palm trees, the sand, the good food, the pool, and the sunbeds, and she seemed quite content at his implication that he and Rhyssa had been taking a holiday.

She assumed leadership as soon as they reached the right station and eagerly started running up the steps ahead of him before she remembered his disability. When she stopped, he was right beside her.

"Your vacation did you a lot of good, didn't it?" she said, and plowed on upward. "See—there's the Parlor, just inside the mall entrance," she added, pointing.

Neither youngster noticed that their progress was being closely observed by two men, just descending from an elegant private hopper parked on the mall's helipad. The shorter man took a small black instrument from his pocket and pointed it at them.

"How exceedingly careless. Neither of them has been stranded! I want them taken! Especially that odious little boy! I want no slipup, no excuses. You won't have too much trouble with the boy, but his companion mustn't be allowed to spread an alarm. Do it as fast as you can assemble a crew. Have I made myself plain?"

"Yes, sir."

Peter was able to shout just once, his cry more indignant than alarmed. Then an ominous silence descended despite Rhyssa's attempts to reestablish communications. She wasted no more time on the silence but broadcast on the widest band possible.

ALERT, ALL TALENTS, ALL LEO PERSONNEL! Peter Reidinger may have been abducted. Presumably in vicinity of Old-Fashioned Parlor. Tirla was with him.

TIRLA! Sascha's blast was nearly as loud as hers.

Complying! came Boris's calming bass tone. *All units in the area are to commence search procedures. Fax photos of the children are being dispatched to all vehicles. I'm proceeding immediately to question any possible witnesses. This is a Top Priority.*

This is a G and H Priority! Sascha added with bitter vehemence. *Sirikit, what does Budworth have on the strand scanner?* There was a long and stunned pause. *Oh, my God. I never stranded Tirla. Rhyssa?*

Peter neither, was Rhyssa's horrified reply. *How could we have been so* stupid?

You weren't, Dorotea said in a bracing tone. *Their ID bracelets can be traced far more accurately than a stranded kid.*

The exchanges had taken bare seconds while Rhyssa, Sascha, and Dorotea sped toward the Control Room, where the monitoring equipment would, they hoped, be able to give them some indication of where the children were.

Budworth was in front of the appropriate screen, his face twisted by anger and distress. "Bracelets were cut off. Scanner has 'em in a sewer drain in the mall heli-lot."

"Oh, my God!" Sascha's exclamation came out in a sob, then he shook himself. *Carmen, get in here. Bertha, Auer, you come, too. Dorotea, any chance that you can reach Tirla?*

If you can't, I'm not likely to. There was a quality of ineffable sorrow in her response. *She's keyed to you like no one else.*

"There's nothing, nothing there at all," Rhyssa murmured, her voice breaking. "I've always been able to hear Peter's mind."

"Not if he's been anesthetized, my dear," Dorotea said. "That's the only time he couldn't hear or answer." Then she spoke to Sirikit on a very tight band. *Phone Dave Lehardt and tell him to get here as fast as he can.*

Sirikit, her own eyes bleak, discreetly complied.

"C'mon, Bro, c'mon! How long does it take your squads to get moving!" Sascha demanded, pacing anxiously.

The Talents had to wait another five agonizing minutes before Boris contacted them.

The kids sat by themselves. Tirla's well known here, and she introduced her friend, Peter, to her usual waitress. She saw them leave the place. She caught a glimpse of them entering a small hopper with the Talent Center emblem. There were four men, but she didn't see their faces. She didn't see anything odd, except that the boy walked funny and then seemed to be assisted by one of the men. And no, she didn't notice the registration. I've an

APB on small hoppers with Talent emblems in Jerhattan, but it'd be helpful if your scanners have picked up their bracelets.

Sascha: *The IDs were cut off. Left in the sewer outside the mall.*

Boris: *That would be the first thing. So, can you pick something up yet on the strand scanners?*

Rhyssa, heavily: *Neither Peter nor Tirla was stranded.*

Boris, exploding: *In the name of all that's holy, why not? The two most important young Talents? You have everyone running about like lunatics, stranding dumb subbie kids and pampered hive children, and you don't strand Peter and Tirla?* The silence following his outburst was more eloquent than anything he could have added.

Rhyssa began to weep, and Dorotea tried to comfort her, tactilely and telepathically.

All right, then, Boris went on in a calmer tone. *We have to assume the abductors are following their latest procedures. That's the only thing that would account for total telepathic silence. The kids were gassed. They're going to be stashed someplace and in those neat little cocoons. Sorry, Rhyssa, but I'm too angry to be diplomatic. Sascha, have you called Carmen in? My finders are all on the case. Somehow, we'll find 'em. Those kids are smart. Once they wake up, they'll be able to help us find them.*

Suz and Cass further dampened the spirits of the Talents by reporting that in excess of thirty children in each Residential had been sold, or just taken. Ranjit, working covertly in Residential W, also confirmed evidence of more activity in the mall markets than could be discreetly ignored. Such scope and audacity was more than LEO or the Center had anticipated. All had happened so smoothly and simultaneously that both the Center and LEO had been caught unawares.

"My sympathies go out to Rhyssa and the other Talents. It's incredible that two valuable young people like that could also be vulnerable to this despicable group," the city manager told Boris, who passed her message on to Sascha and Rhyssa. "This has top priority, and all the resources of the city are at your disposal. No effort will be spared. Is there anything I, personally, can do? Offer a reward? Trade immunity for information?"

"Get your department heads thinking," Boris told City Manager Teresa Aiello, "where such a significant number of children could be detained. I've got every available person on transport surveillance. They can't have been moved out of the Jerhattan area, not in a group or singly. I put a hold on all rail freight and every container is being examined. Any cargo of a suspicious size is being opened. They've got to be somewhere nearby—for a while."

"Everyone on this staff will start examining possibilities—unused warehouses, old buildings, underground stores," Teresa assured Boris grimly.

Boris Roznine did not have quite all his people on transport duty —he had a good third picking up as many ladrones and sassins as his teams found in mall or factory areas. LEO might just luck out and dislodge a clue from an apprehensive subbie.

"Peter is alive, isn't he?" Budworth asked, too concerned to be tactful.

"He's alive. It's not a dead silence," Rhyssa said, wincing at her choice of adjective, her voice low with tension. "But he's not conscious."

"Nothing yet, Carmen?" Sascha asked the finder, whose hands were stroking the lock of Tirla's hair. She could not meet his eyes as she shook her head slowly.

"Christ on a crutch! How could we be so arrogant as to believe we could protect them with an ID bracelet!" Sascha demanded explosively, stalking around what free floor space there was. "*Why* on *Earth* didn't we think to strand them?" He pounded one fist into the other hand. "We've wall-to-wall Talents," he said, gesturing almost scornfully at the various teams clustered about monitors or swiftly feeding programs into the mainframe. "Where could they have got to? That many bodies are too hard to hide. The kids have to be fed. They can't have been whisked off to their—" Sascha could not find the appropriate noun and grimaced. "Wherever. Boris initiated transport surveillance within minutes. Dammit, the subways and cargo routes have been wired since the incident in G."

Sascha, ease up, Dorotea told him, her warning a very narrow quiet thought. *Rhyssa's feeling guilty enough as it is . . .*

Sascha: *And you think I feel none for not stranding Tirla, for encouraging her to go to the bloody mall? To that unmentionable bloody confectionery parlor?* Sascha's response was loaded with derision. *She'd've been bloody safer if I* had *let Boris use her for bait!*

Dorotea: *Stop castigating yourself, Sascha. Tirla's been safely in and out of the mall and the parlor for weeks now.*

Rhyssa, brokenly: *Peter's worked so hard . . . What could have possessed him to take such a risk?*

Dorotea: *He is just a boy, for all his power. Don't worry, we'll hear. The least whisper, and we'll hear them.* Dorotea's mind cast restlessly for a trace of Tirla's. After nearly five weeks of proximity with the girl, she should be able to spot her consciousness.

MAY ALL YOUR ORIFICES BE CLOGGED WITH CAMEL DUNG, YOUR BELLY ETERNALLY FULL OF VOMIT! MAY YOUR TONGUE ROT AND YOUR TEETH FALL OUT AND YOUR GUMS SWELL WITH BOILS! MAY YOUR LIVER ROT AND YOUR BLADDER DRY UP AND YOUR GLANDS SHRIVEL AND PUTREFY!

"Good God!" Dorotea was jolted to her feet. "Did you all hear that? It was loud enough!"

"Peter doesn't know that kind of language!" Rhyssa said, with a slight grin.

"Tirla would," Sascha replied, beaming from ear to ear. "Pungent, isn't she? Damn, where's she got to? I can't hear her anymore."

"Well, I can, and she's still in fine form," Dorotea said. "Neither of you hear her now? She can certainly broadcast when she's of a mind to." She held up her hand, listening, every muscle taut. *Dorotea here, Tirla. Can you hear me?* Dorotea's mental tone was tranquil and reassuring.

Tirla: *Dorotea? Where are you?*

Dorotea: *More to the point, where are you?* "Can you hear her now, Sascha, Rhyssa?" she asked. Two brief headshakes confirmed Dorotea as the primary contact. She felt the light, firm mental touches of Rhyssa and Sascha, listening in.

Tirla, savagely: *You tell me. I can't see a thing. I can't feel a thing. I can smell, and the stench is worse than the bottom level of a factory bilge. Couldn't you guys track me?*

No, we couldn't, Tirla. Your bracelets were discarded right at the mall when you and Peter were taken. Is Peter nearby? Sascha had motioned Carmen over, but Carmen kept shaking her head at her continued inability to find Tirla. *Can you remember what happened?* Dorotea went on.

Tirla's disgust was obvious. *I can't remember anything. Peter and I finished the new spectacular they just added to the menu. He paid for it himself. Said it was his treat this time 'cause he'd just had a vacation. We left the Parlor and were walking toward the subway when something covered my face, and I don't remember a thing more. Awful stuff. Sweet icky smell. How come I can talk to you all of a sudden?*

Sometimes it's a case of need-to, Tirla, Dorotea said, putting a smile of approval into her mental tone.

You needed me to? Tirla asked. *Or I needed you to hear me? Peter? Peter, answer me!* Dorotea caught the conflicting emotions in Tirla's question, but such competitiveness was not a bad sign.

You and Peter were not the only two taken today. Cass and Suz reported that a number must have been taken from E, as well. A very well-organized affair. That's why anything you can tell us will help, Tirla. Anything, no matter how trivial.

Peter's not answering me in here. Maybe he's just not awake yet. My stomach's sour. I shouldn't've had that spectacular. Peter? Peeeeter!

Dorotea spoke gently. *Don't panic, Tirla. Peter will wake up soon enough if he was gassed the same time as you were. We're very relieved to hear from you, believe me.*

Tirla, mildly surprised: *I do believe you. You can't lie in your mind, can you?*

Not to me, you can't, Dorotea replied, gesturing imperiously for Rhyssa and Sascha to stop trying to insinuate questions into her head. Tirla's voice was clear but, after the first burst of psychic outrage, neither as strong nor as loud. She could not risk losing the link. *Now, tell me what you can about your surroundings.*

They stink!

We've already established that. What of? Besides, I assume, the unpleasant bodily discharges of frightened children. What can you hear?

Tirla, disgusted: *A lot of crying.*

Even that tells me something, Tirla. Can you isolate the individual crying enough to estimate how many children are around you?

Dorotea could sense Tirla's concentration and did not interrupt.

Tirla: *I think there's a lot of kids. There's sure a lot of crying and moaning, and someone's hiccuping. All around me, all sides, above, but none below. Why'd they blindfold us and tie us down like this? Most of these kids wouldn't even try to escape.*

Dorotea: *Yassim lost all the G children, didn't he? I think that, unfortunately, that caused him to change his tactics. He's now employing a disorientation technique, sensory deprivation, to reduce the children to compliance when they are released. You're not afraid, are you?*

Tirla, candidly: *I don't like it, but I'm not scared. I'm mad.* Her tone strengthened. *I missed my math class.*

Dorotea broke into relieved laughter. An angry Tirla would be far more useful than a frightened one. Sascha managed a relieved chuckle, and the tension in Rhyssa's stance eased.

Dorotea: *Stay mad, Tirla. Anger can be a valuable asset. Now what I want you to do is try and calm the children. Get them to tell you their names and, if possible, where they came from. E and R were not the only Linears hit. We estimate that upward of a hundred children were taken.*

Including Peter and me?

A hundred and two. Look, Tirla, we're going to have to rely heavily on you to help us find you, Peter, and the others. Dorotea gave Rhyssa a raised eyebrow at her smothered protest. "Candidly, that child is lot better able to take care of herself."

Rely on me? How? I'm blind and strapped in like cargo! Hey, you lot! Shut up! Quit your grizzling, stupid Neesters. Tirla then dropped into languages that Dorotea could not understand. *They prefer crying for their mommies! Mommies who sold 'em!* Tirla said, suddenly dropping into Basic again. *Some half dozen are from E, seven are from W, and two from C. How they bleat! None of 'em's Peter.*

Dorotea: *Ask them their names.*

Tirla could give ten names of the estimated fifteen children in with her. These were instantly forwarded to Boris.

"Where can Peter be?" Rhyssa murmured softly. At some point while she had been concentrating on Dorotea's conversations, Dave Lehardt had joined the anxious group in the Control Room. He linked his fingers in hers, and the physical contact was almost more reassuring than the aura of encouragement that emanated from all the telepaths about her.

"Ask her again about the various smells," Sascha prompted Dorotea. "There may be *something* that'll give us a clue to where."

Well, there's a sort of metal stink, Tirla replied when Dorotea relayed the question. *And there's a moldy mildewing rotten stink that's stronger. There's another smell I can't identify. Oily. I'm stuffed into something—feels like plastic foam. Even my fingers are separated into slots. I'm bound at the wrists, ankles, waist, and across my chest. If I was shorter, I'd be choking. Oh, cut the caterwauling! No one's hurting you!* She roared out repetitions in other dialects, continuing to broadcast mentally as she shouted at the other children.

"Her predicament is beginning to get to her," Dorotea said grimly. *Tirla, I'm with you. Even if you can't hear them, Rhyssa, Sascha, Boris, Sirikit, Budworth, Dave—we're all here. We'll get you out of there, I promise.*

Tirla: *Soon, please. If I have to listen to all this crying and moaning much longer, I'll space out. What about that woman who wore my hair? Why don't you ask her where I am?*

Carmen is right here and reminds you that she needs light to find you! Remember? That's why she couldn't locate you in the Linear—you were in the dark.

Tirla, wryly: *I'm a lot more in the dark now than I was then. What if they don't turn any lights on?* For the first time, her voice was tinged more with fear than with outrage.

Dorotea: *It may be no consolation to you right now, Tirla, but they'll want you to be in good condition. They'll also have to feed you and keep you clean.*

Tirla: *Yeah? When? Next week sometime?*

You were taken at approximately three. It's ten-thirty now. You can't be left without food and water much longer.

Tirla: *You're right. That's not much consolation. Dorotea, don't stop talking to me, will you? I don't care what you say. Just don't stop talking.*

I'm totally at your command, Tirla. Dorotea projected an image of a flourish and a curtsy. She was rewarded by a little chuckle. *Shall we start with the math lesson you missed?*

Tirla, surprised: *In my head?*

Dorotea: *Write it on the board in my mind. I'll remember for you.*

"And also increase her telepathic facility," Rhyssa said with a genuine smile. "You are incorrigible, Dorotea."

"Also very good at what I do," the old woman replied smugly. *Rhyssa? Rhyssa?*

Rhyssa gasped with incredulity, stricken by the faintness of Peter's call. Dave wrapped an arm about her shoulders, supporting her as she held up her hand to stop all noise in the room as the weak voice reached her mind. *Yes, Peter. I've been listening for you.*

Peter: *I can't see anything. They gassed me. I'm going to be sick.*

Rhyssa kept her mental tone calm and firm as she clung to Dave's hands. *Easy, Peter. Remember our drills. Reduce the nausea.*

It's never been this hard before, Rhyssa. There was an edge of despair in his voice. Rhyssa knew so well how he hated anesthetics. He had reactions to most of the common ones. It was going to take time—which she did not think they had—for him to shake off the residual disorientation and nausea in order to bring his kinesis into use.

Rhyssa: *Focus your mind, Peter, just as you used to do in the hospital. Focus your thoughts; ignore the extraneous.*

Peter: *There're other kids in here with me. Some of 'em are pretty scared.*
Rhyssa: *Call out for Tirla. She's somewhere—maybe very nearby.*
Dorotea, urgently: *Tirla, Peter's awake. Call his name.*
Neither heard the other.
"Christ! Fine team of Talents we are when our kids are vulnerable!" Sascha remarked caustically.
Tirla, echoing Sascha's frustration: *Why doesn't Peter just glide out of this contraption, Dorotea?* Tirla asked, unconsciously echoing Sascha's frustration. *He's the kinetic!* When Dorotea explained Peter's problem with the anesthesia, Tirla gave a bark of laughter. *So it's up to me again, I guess. Don't forget the answers to my equations, will you, Dorotea?*
Dorotea: *Tirla, what are you planning to do?*
Tirla: *Get out of this coffin.*
Dorotea: *How?*
Tirla: *They made one mistake when they strapped me in here. They strapped my fingers down, not up where I couldn't reach anything. I should be able to dig out enough plastic to free my hands.*
Dorotea felt the effort in Tirla's mind, effort and fringes of pain. "Could she do that?" she asked Sascha.
"According to the Bro, the kids retrieved in Manhattan had been wrapped in foamed plastic cocoons. She might be able to scratch at it with her fingers."
You have made contact with Tirla and Peter? Boris's voice was excited.
Contact, Bro, but not release. Both kids are cocooned. And Peter's having a bad reaction to whatever gas they used. Sascha made another face, mimicking the aggravation his brother was mentally expressing. *He'll need a little time before he recovers completely.*
Boris: *Is there time? I've got the city manager, and all her deputies on my back for action. Some of the other kids were legal, too.*
Rhyssa was concentrating on strengthening her link with Peter, helping him to dissipate the residue of the anesthetic. Her face mirrored his desperation and sense of failure, and she leaned heavily against Dave.
There! The triumph in Tirla's voice was evident to Dorotea, and she held up her hand, repeating the girl's words for the others. *Camel-gutted tripe! Miserable dung-eaters! Descendants of snake offal. Scuzfarts! Maggots!*

Good heavens! How pungent. Tirla, how have you hurt yourself? Dorotea demanded, sensing pain.

Tirla: *Never you mind. I'm out of this cocoon. There are nineteen other kids stuck in 'em here, some of 'em still knocked out. Peter's not one of 'em. Tell Carmen not to fracture her skull finding me. This place is black as the bottom of an elevator pit. Ugh. I slipped in junk. Ugh! I've reached one wall. Faugh. It's slimy and gritty. Too smooth and cold for metal. Ah, an opening. A window. Plastic-coated. I can't even scratch a sliver off. Look, I'm going to try something,* Tirla went on. *They always forget about ceilings. There's air coming in here from someplace.* She was silent for a long while, though Dorotea was aware of strenuous physical activity. *I am not hurting you. Just using you as a stepladder. And I won't let you go, crybaby. You're no use to me. Quit your grizzling.* Another period of silence followed, and Dorotea reported more physical effort, punctuated by inadvertent grunts of pain.

Tirla: *Well, I was right. There is a ceiling hatch. And I can see, a little. Well, whaddya know? I'm in a shunting yard. There are rows and rows of train cars, old ones. Can't have been moved in years. And someplace down to my right there's light. Sort of around an edge, like of a window or a door. Any idea where I could be?*

From the moment Tirla mentioned a shunting yard, the description was forwarded to everyone concerned.

Tirla: *I'm going along the tops of cars toward the light,* the girl reported. *I can't hear anyone, and no one would be stupid enough to walk around this place without a light.*

Tell us how many cars have children, Tirla, Dorotea urged.

Tirla: *Peter! Peter! Answer me! Peter! It's Tirla! Answer me! Wow! I nearly fell off the edge of the car. Slippery surface, moist. Whole place is damp!*

"Try for yards by the river, by the sea. Along the Sound," Sascha said, prowling up and down the bank of monitors, checking patterns.

Tirla! Peter cried exultantly. His voice echoed from Tirla's mind to Dorotea and lifted the anxieties of every Talent in the room. Rhyssa sank into a chair that Dave pulled over for her. Then he handed her a stimulant drink, gesturing her to toss it down quickly.

Tirla: *So here's where they stashed you, huh? Now, I'll just drop in beside you. There! The tape'll sting coming off—oh, I forgot. Sorry.*

Peter: *I won't feel it anyway—do your worst. Just don't take all the skin off my wrists! Isn't there any light in this place?*

Tirla: *I guess not. There—you're free. Only the tan came off. Here! Don't go faint. Lie back. Stay easy. Get your breath. Now look, you'd better rest some more.* Dorotea could hear the nervous concern in Tirla's voice, a matter she did not impart to Rhyssa. *I'm going to look around this place, Peter,* Tirla went on. *You get your kinetics working again, 'cause there's no way I can haul you up by myself.*

Peter: *I'll be okay, Tirla. I'll be okay. Just—just come back.*

Tirla: *Oho! Aircar! Big bugger. Expensive! No lights!* There was a long moment of silence. *That was too close.*

"Ask her if she saw a number, a description, anything!" Sascha prompted Dorotea.

Tirla: *I'd say that it's a metallic blue jetter, twelve-seater, no lights. But I got a glimpse—a three, a dash, and R-I-G—I think. Could have been a B, but the I and the G were clear enough.*

When Dorotea repeated what Tirla had said, Sascha exploded to his feet. "R-I-G! We couldn't be so lucky!" He slapped his right palm against his forehead. "Budworth, get through to Auer and Bertha and see if they have any tickles about Filmflam."

"Filmflam?" Rhyssa and Dorotea said together, both reaching into Sascha's mind for confirmation, but he was involved in a tight conversation with Boris and would not let them in.

"Boris is doing a search on the registration," Sascha said aloud, holding up one hand, his expression intent and eager. "Dorotea, tell Tirla she's a star!"

Tirla, surprised: *Was that enough for you? Oops. There's another one coming in, from another direction. Also running dark. I'll see if I can get a better reading.*

Tirla, Dorotea replied hastily, *don't risk discovery. And Rhyssa says she'd rather have you stay with Peter.*

Tirla, blithely: *Peter's okay. Working on it. I'm going to find out who the other dark-flier is!*

Tirla! Dorotea was momentarily stunned by the independence. *Tirla!* She turned to Rhyssa, hands outstretched in appeal. "The little witch has cut me off! Oh, just wait till I get my hands on that child! The impudence of her."

Rhyssa was also irritated. *Peter, stop her!*

Peter on his dignity: *I don't need a minder, Rhyssa. I really don't. Just enough time to catch my breath. 'Sides, no one could stop Tirla.*

"Rather admirable of the child, I think," Sascha replied. For a palpable moment he and Rhyssa locked wills. Then he continued in a gentler tone. "I do realize, Rhyssa, that Peter's inhibited by the gassing he took. If Tirla can manage an ID on the second car, too, we'll maybe catch more than just the well-deserving Revered Ponsit Prosit."

"Has Boris confirmed the owner of that jetcar?" Rhyssa asked, only marginally appeased.

"Registered to Ponsit Prosit, a.k.a. Flimflam," Sascha said with a grin. "Complete with vanity plate—VRPP/2403/RIG—at a Riverside address that is more palatial than reverential. Boris is sending out surveillance and standby teams. I'd like the Center to muster Talent as of right now!" Sascha waited long enough for Rhyssa's assent and then pointed a finger at Budworth to punch the Alert button. "We can move once we've got a definite fix."

"Neither Auer or Bertha have anything for us," Sirikit told them.

"That's odd," Rhyssa said with a frown. "There should be something!"

"I find a precog silence reassuring," Sascha remarked, buckling on his utility belt and checking his trank gun. "Flimflam is at least not going to trigger panic in the immediate future, so we have a very good chance of catching him *in flagrante delicto*. Dorotea, is Tirla available again?"

Dorotea shook her head, her lips pursed in an aggrieved moue. "Wretched little snip of a thing!" she said with a certain amount of reluctant admiration in her tone.

"Got it!" Carmen cried suddenly, jumping out of her chair, rushing to the map terminal, and punching coordinates that brought up the South Shore area. "Tirla's come through again. There simply can't be two such similar situations. She's heading toward an old railway switchhouse. I can just make it out. There's a crack of light coming through a window that opens onto a platform. There seem to be hundreds of cars of old rolling stock rusting there. Here we are!" She pointed to the marked area on the map. "Here're tracks. Acres of them. And obsolete railcars waiting to be recycled."

The others all converged to look at the area magnified on the screen.

"It couldn't be better, could it," Dorotea said slowly, "as a place to hide terrified kids!" *Tirla! Answer me! We know where you are now.* When Tirla did not reply, Sascha gave Rhyssa a long look and then, Dave Lehardt at their heels, the telepaths left the Control Room, jogging to the stairs that would take them to the aircars and teams waiting on the landing roof.

CHAPTER 16

Tirla's night vision had adjusted to the gloom—part mist and part lightlessness despite the angry red-orange glow of Jerhattan that lit the rim of the horizon on all sides. The upper levels of distant Linears, majestic in the night, punctuated the halo of the city with their long silhouettes. From top stories, with aerials and stacks, aircraft-warning signals blinked their light patterns. She moved forward carefully along the curved tops of the railcars. If she slipped, there would be nothing for her to catch on to. The surface was gritty with dirt and slippery in the moist air. She headed toward that thin band of light and the dark bulk of the building that framed it.

She had safely traversed five cars, two more with children moaning and weeping inside them, when she felt a pressure in her mind that she recognized as Dorotea trying to contact her.

Go 'way. I've got to concentrate.

She cursed softly as she slithered for a panicky moment between cars, then waited until her heart had stopped thudding, and she was fairly sure that her scrambling had not been heard. Her sharp ears had caught the sound of muted voices from the building. The line of cars continued past a long platform, and she debated slipping down and getting close enough to the building to overhear the conversations.

But conversations were useless tender; the registration number of an aircar was undeniable proof. She crawled forward on her belly, conscious of every noise she made, the dryness of her mouth, and the increasingly painful stiffness of her fingers.

There was a sudden break in the murk and there, parked beside the less distinct blue jetter, was an expensive sports jetcar, its hull a crisp white, its tail ID equally visible. The two cars were balanced on the one junction of rail that was free of rolling stock.

Tirla: *Peter, I got the second one. The number is CD-08-MAL, clear as day. And the other car is right beyond it. Peter?*

Peter: *I heard you, Tirla. I told them. You come back here. They're mad at you for closing Dorotea out. You're going to have to apologize to her.* Peter sounded fierce.

Apologize? Why? Tirla was so surprised that she slipped, banging down on the railcar. *Now you've done it!* She flattened herself on the far side of the car as light flooded out of the building, illuminating the platform and the slightly bulging side of the car on which she lay.

"I tell you I heard something!" said the man silhouetted in the doorway. He peered around the doorframe, and Tirla had a good view of the scene behind him: two men, one of whom idly swung a short stick, clipping it against his boot with an air of indolent diffidence.

"Shut the door, you cretin!" The door abruptly closed and then opened in a much thinner crack. ". . . a good look around. Up, over, under, in. Mess up once more, maggot—you can be eagle-spread, too."

The door closed a second time, but not before Tirla recognized the angry voice. Her guts froze. She heard the ladrone moving, his shoes crunching the grit on the platform. She heard him haul back one of the warped carriage doors, the plastic creaking as he looked in the carriage. He moved on down the platform, cursing softly under his breath as he dropped down to flash his light beneath the car. Tirla could take no chances. Quickly she moved at a crouch and jumped to the next car. She was just in time—the red pinpoint of a filtered handlight shone briefly where she had just been. She held her breath, hoping against hope that the searcher would not notice her outline on the dusty top.

As he cautiously opened the door of the building, she watched. The stick swinger was nearest the door—she got another good look at his haughty face, with its beaked nose and thin-plucked brows. And she saw a table piled with credits which two other men were counting—floaters, by the size of them. One of the counters looked vaguely familiar, but her attention was caught by the face of the other man as he turned his head; he had a cruel face, and a hungry one. He was idly tapping his black boot with the stick; she caught

the gleam of gold around the handle. Only then did the significance of the pile of floaters dawn on her.

Tirla: *Dorotea! The payoff's being made! Floaters. More than I've ever
seen in my life!*

Dorotea, her voice hard-edged: *Tirla, don't you ever dare cut me out
again.* Tirla was momentarily dismayed. Wasn't she doing what
they needed done? How could such a sweet old lady come on so
tough and hard?

Tirla: *Well, if you crazy Talents don't move your asses, you're going to
mess everything up and I'll have nothing more to do with you.*

Peter! Help Peter now! Dorotea did not sound apologetic, but she
did sound anxious.

Tirla knew very well that Peter—not to mention all the other
kids—needed help. As quickly as she could, she moved back along
the line of cars. If the payoff had been made, some of the kids
might be shifted soon. She had to get Peter out and free as many of
the others as she could. If they all scattered and hid, it would take
all night to recapture them—if she could stop them from crying
long enough to help themselves.

Tirla slipped and this time could not recover her balance, sliding
down the dirt-encrusted side of the car and landing painfully on
stones and cinders that bruised and cut her feet. Cursing her clum-
siness and hoping that she had gotten far enough away so that the
noise of her fall had not been heard, she made her way along the
ground, cursing the bastards who had removed the beautiful purple boots that she had bought on her first trip to the mall.

Crying had been reduced to whimpering in the first two cars.
Tirla winced. How much time did she have to get Peter out if the
payoff had been made? Could he make use of that special Talent of
his now?

Yes, I can, Peter said, appearing out of the darkness between two
cars. He touched her hand. *And I know exactly how. C'mon.* He led
her along the track until she nearly stumbled over a big handle
attached to one side of the track. *We're going to do a switcheroo.* He
laughed softly out loud. *Much faster than letting all those kids loose.
There's a hundred of them.*

They heard a muffled thrumming and saw the whiteness of the
aircar lifting slowly from behind the building.

C'mon, Peter urged. *I've got to get to that transformer box or my idea
won't work! I need the gestalt for this. You know how to uncouple cars?*

Suddenly the process was driven into Tirla's mind and she staggered a bit, stunned by the vivid intrusion. *Then go back and uncouple the last car with kids in it. Stay there and warn me if anyone's coming.*

"You mean like, upstairs?" Tirla asked in a hoarse whisper, pointing to the sky.

No, them! Peter pointed at the building.

"When are we getting some help?" Tirla demanded in an acid-whisper, refusing to talk in her mind when she was nose-to-nose with Peter. "My feet hurt!"

"Soon," Peter hissed and then gave her a shove to help her on her way. "Try walking my way!"

She couldn't but wished she could. Her feet hurt and her hands ached. She did not quite understand how he could possibly do what she thought he was going to do. Railcars that had not moved in years were going to make the most awful racket. Peter was stupid! She hurried, hoping that the sound of the aircar might cover some of the noise the railcars were sure to make.

She identified the last car from the moaning inside it and struggled with couplings encrusted with caked oil and dirt. *Peter, it's—* Suddenly the stiff coupling released itself and she was knocked off balance, staggering back into the end of the car. *Well, thanks!* A wail arose from within. *Shut your faces, you stupid gits,* she ordered, forgetting that the other children could not hear her. *I'm doing my best to save your innards and your virtue.* She banged her fist once against the side of the car and felt the pain worth it when the warning achieved an instant drop in the mewling. That did much to soothe her aggravations.

Nervously she glanced up to see the aircar's slow upward progress. Running dark like that, the pilot had to be careful not to get tangled in the wires that festooned the area around the building. If Peter could just get moving . . . He was! She heard the squeal, rattle, and clanking as wheels long locked on rails reluctantly began to turn. She swung up to sit on the tongue of the coupling, watching the building for any sign that someone within had heard the metallic protest. But the building was two hundred meters or so away, and the aircar was whooshing and thrumming.

She peered at the skyline, yearning to see some subtle movement that hinted of the approach of help. Those Talents were so slow. How soon was "soon"? Her car moved all too jerkily with rattlings and clankings, but it was making progress along the track. The dark building with the telltale band of light was slowly receding. She felt the car clack across the junction, veering right, and experienced partial relief. If that ladrone looked outside and saw half the train missing . . .

She saw the white blur of Peter's face as the car inched past the transformer box; there was no disguise in the dark night for the audible hum emanating from it. What was Peter doing?

She jumped down from the coupling, wincing as her cut feet hit the stony, cindery ground. The cars continued to move obliquely away from danger, down an empty track.

"You can't leave just empty track. They'll know . . ." Tirla put an urgent hand on his arm and then could not release it. She could feel him shaking from the effort he had already made, shaking and more—and she was affected by his shaking and whatever else it was that raced through him.

"I'm trying," he said tensely. "A gestalt's hard with all that anesthesia still slowing me down. Help me!"

"Gestalt?" Tirla stuttered over the unfamiliar word, and then Peter put the explanation in her mind. Before she could ask how she could possibly help with that, she was. Her body seemed alive with the current racing through her, like the time she had caught a jolt from an exposed wire. Only this was not as painful as that shock had been. But it was . . . what was it?

The metallic protest was startlingly loud on the still air. The white jet had moved beyond visibility into the swirling mist. Tirla felt both stronger and weaker, clutching at Peter with both hands, wanting to help him make the gestalt and needing his support. Suddenly she was aware of movement behind her as car after car began to slide past them onto the track—*clickety click, clickety click*—far too loudly. Suddenly, with a resounding clank, the new cars bounced against those near the platform, and Tirla's heart clenched when she heard the shouts of alarm as men piled out to investigate.

Tell me! Did you let all those other kids loose?" Flimflam asked, his nose inches from Tirla's face. She wished he would bend just a little closer so she could bite him. But he would probably poison her, the greasy, coarse, evil scuz.

Unfortunately, before Tirla could help Peter to hide, two of the faster ladrones had caught them. They had been roughly hauled back to the building and into the presence of a seething Flimflam, so enraged that flecks of foam had gathered at the corners of his mouth. Screaming with exasperation, Tirla had been shoved in front of the raging man as Peter collapsed on the floor, groaning.

"We didn't see no others," one of the ladrones said anxiously. "There wasn't a sign of them, nor those cocoons in the cars neither."

"Tell me where the children are!" Flimflam repeated in one of the more common Neester dialects, squeezing hard on her swollen fingers. "Did you let them loose?"

Despite herself, Tirla let out a howl of pain, trying to pull her hand out of his grasp. It hurt so much that she could not even think of a suitable malediction to fling at him. He let her go but scooped a stick off the table and began to slash it across her back.

"Hey, boss, the merch! Don't mark the merch!"

"Tell me where the children went!" he demanded in the most common Asian language.

Tirla let tears run down her cheeks as she glanced quickly around the room, as if seeking help. Then in one of the most obscure languages she knew, she answered him in a piteously appealing tone. "Don't beat me. I don't understand you! Don't beat me again!"

"Of all the—" Flimflam roared, swiveling about to the ladrones and hitters in the room. "What did she say? One of you must understand her! Just what I need. A dumb kid! Well?"

There were murmurs and shrugs as no one admitted to understanding.

Dorotea, reassuringly: *We're nearly there, Tirla. We have the yard on the nightscope.*

"Where—" Flimflam was making ludicrously broad, pantomimegestures, so unlike his polished performance as a RIG that Tirla nearly laughed even though he kept poking her painfully with his stick to emphasize his words. "Where—are—the others? Can no one talk to her? Rouse the other one. We can't waste time. That bloody His Highness will be sending the transports. We must have the merchandise ready. Months of planning, everything goes without a hitch, we've got the money—*where are the others?*"

A ladrone poured water over Peter, who did not even moan. Tirla watched him anxiously. He looked terribly pale, crumpled up like that. He had been fine until they had been recaptured. Perhaps the effort of moving those heavy railcars . . . She gasped as the whip sliced her again right over the previous welt. Tirla tried to back away but hands clamped on her shoulders, holding her fast. She kicked backward with her heels, jarring feet already sore, but her captor had heavy boots on and she only achieved more bruises.

"Let's really put some fear into her," Flimflam said, gesturing, and she was flung facedown to the hard surface of the table where she had recently seen piles of floaters. Cruel hard hands grasped her by wrists and ankles. Suddenly pain exploded across her already lacerated feet. She screamed and screamed again at the second horrific stab of pain, then fainted for the first time in her life.

So she missed seeing Flimflam violently propelled backward to crash against the wall. She missed the explosive entrance of Sascha, Rhyssa, Dave Lehardt, and the Talent teams. And she missed the other excitements that would have given her immense satisfaction.

CHAPTER 17

"Commissioner," Ranjit said, "that's a diplomatic registration."

"I wouldn't care if it was God himself, Lieutenant," the LEO commissioner answered. "Law Enforcement and Order means just that from bottom to top, and right on down the line again. Or it's privilege, not law enforcement and order!" He measured the distance on the huge display map, from the South Shore train yard to the Riverside address. "Assign the best driver we've got to shadow that CD. And I want that beehive—not just the penthouse lift or the domestic floors but that entire complex—secured. Whoever is in that car could go to ground anywhere. Pack all entries with sensitives. Tell them to home in on any strong emotion—we may get a lot of wash on this. You know how hivers hate to have their privacy broached." He turned to another aide. "Barry, get me the city manager and tell her this is a sensitive affair. I want her forewarned so she can back us with the Corps. Feed the situation through Judicial and get me four—no, make it five—John Does and a search warrant. And let's hope that Sascha's efficient."

He shrugged on his tunic top, resplendent with the "bravery bars" and braid, then strapped on sidearms and gestured for Ranjit and his other aides to follow him to the rooftop garage. Jet- and aircars were spinning off along usual routes, having been instructed to move circumspectly.

Sascha? Boris linked with his brother as his aircar took off.

Nearly there, Bro. It still takes time to drive a car from there to here. The other bird has not flown—holy hell, what's happening? Back to you later.

Boris felt the abruptness of the mental break and cursed under his breath as his aircar plowed on to his destination. The pause lengthened, causing him some anxiety. Surely Sascha was competent enough . . . Should he have sent men with the Center teams? If the child-dealers at the railyard should get a warning through to his own quarry, the whole operation might be jeopardized.

My God, Boris—Sascha's voice burst in on him like a bellow—*if you let that Shimaz slime ooze out of this, Highness, Prince, manager, or whatever, I promise you that the Talents will handle him* ex officio!

The LEO commissioner had never before heard such vindictiveness in his brother's voice.

Boris: *What happened?*

Sascha: *The Venerable Revered Ponsit Prosit used a bastinado on Tirla's feet. And Peter's collapsed!*

Boris: *Flimflam didn't get a message off, did he?* If the man had, they might lose the most important criminal.

Sascha, livid with rage: *No, not when he had a little girl to interrogate! Make it stick on that other bastard, will you? Or, by all that's holy, I will. Myself with no help from any other agency, dear LEO Bro.*

Boris: *LEO is on the move, Sascha. You hang onto your temper. Have you got the other children? Have we any proof of complicity?*

Sascha, sarcastically: *I don't suppose Tirla's bloody feet count for more than assault and GBH. But we also took possession of a case full of many too many floaters, ready for a night deposit, complete with an account number I'll bet can be traced to the Venerable Revered.*

Boris: *That should be enough to convict Flimflam. But is there enough to catch this—what did you call him?*

Sascha: *Shimaz, Prince Phanibal Shimaz, who seems to be a whiz at more than Josephson junctions. Flimflam's spilling his guts: His Highness has rather an extensive operation—child labor in his rice paddies and mines, child prostitution, and a child farm where the healthiest are kept that way until someone can pay for the organ they need.*

Boris, growling: *Get me something to link him to that yard. Something that will stick!*

They were well on the way when the comlink heralded a connection from Commissioner Aiello. She appeared on the cabin screen dressed in formal attire. Hovering beside her was her protocol officer, Jak, who, for all his empathy, could at times be quite tiresome about details.

"Do you have incontrovertible proof, Roznine?" she asked.

"We have proof of a connection which is incompatible with any diplomatic occupation," Boris replied, setting his jaw.

"Who? Surely not the ambassador!" At that moment, Teresa Aiello was depressed with pessimism.

"We are not after his Excellency, so Jak can relax. Members of his Corps, certainly, and an embassy vehicle has been identified and traced from the abduction site. There's no problem of proving involvement. Is the DA there, too? Well, give the old dog a comforting word in his shell-like ear. The Talents have cracked this abduction ring." The last he admitted ruefully, for despite protests to the contrary, he and his brother were in constant competition.

The massive beehive was aptly nicknamed. Its bottom levels along the block-square bulk, where other buildings obscured views, housed maintenance, storage, and worker accommodations. Where the hive rose above its neighbors, there were great curved plasglas panels that were part solar-heating, part prestigious display of wealth. Each pie-shaped apartment boasted luxurious gardens and views from the outer wall, and where the hive had an atrium core, rare plants and trees festooned the inner walls. Naturally the top apartments were the most exclusive and expensive, with one whole floor given over to private garden and garage facilities, swimming pools, game courts, and whatever other amenities the residents expected, to secure the ultimate of comfort.

Is the surround complete yet, Ranjit? Boris asked on his helmet com unit.

Just now—completely ringed, sir. No one can get in or out without being observed.

"Commissioner," Boris's pilot said, "here comes the suspect vehicle now."

The sleek white jetcar swooped to settle and deposit its passengers on the roof of the hive.

"Three men!"

"I can see that myself," Boris said. "Secure that jetter the moment it's garaged. See what you can get the pilot to say. Grab the log, and any garage records. And now—" He could not keep the satisfaction out of his voice. "Let's get the bastards."

The LEO pilot put them down on the hive roof, and Boris Roznine and his squad made for the ramp down to the entrance level of the penthouse. Seeing the formal and formidable attire of the LEO commissioner and his aide, the door attendant hurried to open it. His bow was respectful and nervous.

"What are you doing, you naga? I'm not expecting guests!" exclaimed the man at the other end of the magnificent white marbled reception hall. A servant was just assisting the removal of his elegant blue suede long coat while a second man was also shrugging, unassisted, out of his own outerwear. "Exclude them immediately."

"I think not, Prince Phanibal," Boris said, stepping forward while sending Ranjit a quick thought about reinforcements.

The prince's companion moved with astonishing speed out the nearest of the many doors leading from the entry hall while the paralyzed doorman gaped.

"Is His Excellency at home?" Boris asked, some glimmer of Jak's protocol lessons seeping through his anger. The doorman fearfully nodded before the prince ordered him not to respond.

"How dare you—whoever you are—enter a diplomatic residence without invitation?" Prince Phanibal demanded, his expression haughty and totally confident. His gaze ignored the lieutenant by Boris's side and the detachment standing just outside the door.

"Boris Roznine, commissioner for Law Enforcement and Order in Jerhattan!" Boris turned to the awed and shaking doorman. "Please beg His Excellency's indulgence and request an immediate interview on a matter of grave urgency."

The attendant, ignoring the prince's countermands and threats, opened a hidden door and disappeared. He had no sooner gone than all the other doors of the entrance hall swung open and a number of large men filed in with military precision. Three, black-robed and turbaned, with silver-mounted belts and daggers which were exactly the legal length permitted display guards, immediately flanked the prince.

Boris did not need to look over his shoulder to know that the LEO officers just outside the doorway, carrying the weaponry legal for them, outnumbered the embassy guards and were quite ready to force an entry. He waited a moment for the prince to absorb that fact.

"I believe that we now await His Excellency's appearance," he said with a grim and ungenial smile and, in studied insult to a royal person, seated himself on the nearest decorative bench.

"Do you not understand the repercussions this unwarranted intrusion—" Prince Phanibal began imperiously. "I am not only a royal prince of my house but a manager of the Padrugoi. I am due back on the platform on the next shuttle."

"That is why I, as LEO commissioner, am here to explain personally to the ambassador," Boris replied. *Is this the guy who's been giving Rhyssa so much grief? Perhaps if we both try, we can probe his mind,* he sent to Sascha. *It's not admissible evidence in court since it's under duress, but it'll give us some clues.*

There was a brief pause as the brothers tried to breach the prince's mind. Then Boris pulled back. *He's got a dense mind shield. He's had careful conditioning, and I'd love to know where. No, we can't break it, not without breaking the law.*

The slightest of smiles tugged at the corner of the prince's mouth and his eyes narrowed, hiding smug pleasure at deflecting the mental intrusion. He raised his left hand briefly, his fingers closing as if on some accustomed possession. Then he threw his fingers open in vexation and raised the arm indolently across his chest, the smile broadening.

"Perhaps you have mislaid your little stick," Boris heard himself saying. Sascha was there! *Saving time and effort, brother?* Boris asked.

The little stick which made raw meat of Tirla's feet, Sascha said savagely.

Prince Phanibal stiffened in surprise. "I—what?"

"The little switch that you are fond of carrying as an affectation, for you don't own any—animals—I believe," the Boris/Sascha link continued. "The one with the ivory handle and the rather unusual filigree design."

"I do not have to account for my possessions to such as you," Prince Phanibal replied as he angled himself obliquely from Boris, tilting his chin arrogantly to display what many probably considered a handsome profile.

At that point the ambassador, clad in a deep purple velvet robe with exquisite gold designs, entered from the central door. He cast one startled look at the prince and his pose, another at the group by the door, then signaled for the guards to withdraw. Boris Roznine rose and walked forward to meet the Malaysian.

"Due to the gravity of this situation, Your Excellency," he said, speaking on his own although he knew that Sascha was listening avidly, "you will permit me to dispense with formalities. This man"—he gestured to the aloof prince—"and another have been involved in activities incompatible with any function in your embassy. I must ask you to instruct His Highness and his companion to accompany me to the LEO headquarters."

"With what could the Prince Phanibal be charged?" the ambassador asked with great dignity.

"The charge is indeed grave, Your Excellency, for there has been traffic in abducting minors and subjecting them to illicit bondage for the purpose of slave labor, unlawful intercourse, and organ removal."

"You have proof of such a heinous crime?" The ambassador drew himself more erect, but he did not appear to be all that surprised.

"Yes, Your Excellency." Boris inclined his head with a nod of regret. The ambassador was too fine an old man to be saddled with such a scandal. "There are witnesses!" the Boris/Sascha link continued, supporting Boris's reply. "Talented witnesses."

The prince snorted his disbelief, his poise undisturbed. "Such a claim tries all patience. You will dismiss these deceivers, Uncle."

Sascha: *This bugger's clever.*

Boris: *He hasn't turned a hair or admitted a thing.*

Sascha: *Does he think all Talents are adults?*

Boris: *Tirla is on the official Register, is she not?*

Sascha: *Didn't you read the ID bracelet you got her six weeks ago? And there are four of the ladrones, spilling their guts to avoid being spaced, confirming what we've got out of Flimflam for turning State's evidence— his mind took very little pressure when he regained consciousness. That was some scam they had going. Furthermore, it was the dear prince who infiltrated LEO programs and filched the strand formula. He had all the special clearance passwords because he was working on Padrugoi and doing all that fine work with the Josephson junctions. He browsed and took what he needed. Got his island laboratory to perfect a variation for Flimflam to use as a special effect in those REs he put on. We have all the details needed to implicate the prince and that secretary of his. Returned from the religious institutions and a period of meditation in the Far East? He was planning the whole thing with Prince Phanibal's backing.* Sascha's snort of contempt was so strong that Boris grunted.

The ambassador turned his head slightly over one shoulder in Prince Phanibal's direction. "I will not dismiss them, Nephew. Talent cannot be forsworn." Then he regarded Boris steadily for a moment and beckoned for the prince to step forward. "You will go with them."

"But I cannot be arrested like a common criminal!"

"Oh, indeed, Nephew, you are an uncommon criminal, for diplomatic immunity does not shield pederasts," the old man said in a voice that was leached of all emotion.

"You cannot permit such insult to our name," the prince said, slapping his fists to his legs in his barely contained frustration and anger. "My father will hear of this. You will hear of this. You will be disgraced! You will never return to your home. Your children and your children's children are dog meat . . ."

Ignoring him, the Malaysian ambassador strode to the nearest door and closed it firmly behind him. The guards moved to cover each of the doorways, subtly removing official protection from the prince.

Commissioner? Ranjit said politely. *The pilot has been arrested, and we have the jetter's logs and the garage log. Also, Prince Shimaz's companion was apprehended, attempting to escape.*

"If you will come with us . . ." Boris began formally, gesturing toward the roof landing steps.

The prince suddenly erupted into action, his face contorted in rage, flinging himself toward the opening Boris had made. Ranjit, with great presence of mind, neatly tripped the man as he passed.

At that, it took three officers to subdue the raving man.

So, despite appeals from his grieving father, and protests from Ludmilla Barchenka that His Highness Manager Phanibal Shimaz *must* be released until the station is completed," Sascha told Tirla, sitting on the edge of her bed in Dorotea's house, "that scuzball will spend the rest of his life at hard labor on the moon."

"And Flimflam?" Tirla's eyes flashed with an anger and hatred that startled Sascha, even though he understood it.

"Oh, turning State's evidence gave him a choice of occupations," he said with a grin. "He elected to take a job as a sanitation engineer on the Big Station. Not exactly spaced out, but near enough."

"How many of the kids *were* illegals?" she asked after relishing Flimflam's future for a long and satisfactory moment. She and Peter had both been in court to give their evidence but had not heard the sentencing. She still was not comfortable walking very far on her tender feet, and despite Peter's patient instruction in kinetics, she had been unable to levitate as he did. Peter was baffled, sure that she had some latent kinetic ability; he maintained that he had been unconscious when Flimflam had been thrown kinetically across the room just as the rescuers arrived.

"Eighty-seven children," Sascha replied brusquely.

"In the hostels, huh?" Tirla gave a long sigh.

"Just think what you and Peter saved them from, Tirla. You had a taste of it."

"And there haven't been any more deals or abductions?"

Sascha shook his head.

The apathy that had settled over Tirla after the trial worried everyone in the Center. Obediently she had worked with the physiotherapist to regain movement in her damaged feet—she had been more severely injured than had first been apparent. She had dutifully tried to improve her telepathic range, but Dorotea and Peter were the only ones she could hear at any distance; even Sascha she could hear only if he was within a hundred meters. She did test to an astounding degree of empathy, the source of her unusual linguistic feats.

She was assiduous in following her education program, opting for a very wide variety of courses, some of which Dorotea was certain she could not yet comprehend. Her reports proved that she was more precocious than anticipated. She took no joy in the freedom of the Center's grounds and played with no other children despite their repeated attempts to interest her. She had even refused to go on shopping trips with either Sascha or Cass. She tended to become more animated in Peter's company, but she saw him only rarely, as he and Rhyssa were deeply involved in his highly specialized training. She was virtually recovered from the abduction, but her morale was extremely low, so Dorotea had insisted that Sascha come for a visit.

"What does it take to strand a kid?" Tirla asked him.

"Look, chip," he said, laying a gentle hand on her knee and noting that she felt no less fragile to him, though she had put on weight since she had first come to the Center. "You can't save all the illegals. And for the moment the danger is over."

"But not the appetites," Tirla said, brooding. "Like that scuzzy prince." In the privacy of her room, her face took on a malicious expression. "*Is* it difficult to strand a kid? Cass and Suz said they

were stranding kids in Linear E. Have they improved the strand
for a long-term use?"

"I know you're biologically twelve years old, Tirla, but you
sound fifty." Sascha was exasperated.

She tilted her head up at him, regarding him through slightly
narrowed eyes, a little smile playing at her lips. "In the Linears I
am. You surely don't want another scam like that RIG, do you?
And like you said, even illegal kids have rights! I know Cass has
had her baby and wouldn't want to go undercover so soon. But I'd
bet my last credit—"

"All of them are the Center's now, remember?" Sascha teased,
and caught a sly gleam in her eyes. So Dorotea was right about her
squirreling some floaters away. Old habits died hard.

"And the Center also has to give me anything I want—"

"Within reason."

"Well, I'll be reasonable. I'm good at languages—anyone's—but I
can't keep sharp if I'm here," she said, gesturing out the window at
the lawn. "And Teacher says I don't know all the languages of the
world—yet. I'll do you a deal, Sascha Roznine." She cocked her
head at him in what he had come to call her "haggling manner."
"I'll strand illegals in every Jerhattan Linear. I'll strand 'em, but I
won't report 'em." She gave a mirthless grin. "If there're sweeps,
and I was blamed for 'em, I'd lose my—what do you call it—credibility? I got ethics, too, you know. But I'd know when trouble was
brewing, and that I would report. That'd help, wouldn't it? I'd be a
better trouble-spotter than any of those LEO plants of your brother's!" The notion seemed to amuse her, and certainly she had become more animated. "I always knew who was LEO—even who
was Talent."

While there was no question of her affection for Sascha, she was
never easy in Boris's presence, though he had tried to be ingratiating. An ingrained distrust of all LEOs was Sascha's diagnosis, not
wishing Tirla to be at odds with his twin.

"You really wouldn't consider staying here with Dorotea and
extending your Talents?"

Tirla wagged her head, grimacing. "It's not that I don't like
Dorotea. She's the best ever. It's just—I don't feel comfortable in
all of this." Her glance swept around the well-appointed room.
"I'm a Linear brat. My Talent, as you call it," she said, wrinkling

her nose in self-deprecation, "works best in a Linear environment." Her eyes twinkled.

"You can't live all your life in a Linear," Dorotea said, entering the room, her expression worried. She radiated affection, reassurance, and support.

"Why not?" Tirla demanded, lifting her hands in a quick gesture of exasperation.

"Indeed, why not?" Sascha echoed.

"Cass and Suz live on the high side of Linears when they're undercover. I'd really like my own squat on, say, Level 19, so I'd have a view and not so much smog." Her grin was sheer impudence. "In case he hasn't been listening in, ask your brother if I wouldn't be more use to him living in a Linear."

Sascha laughed. *Bro? Did you hear that?*

Little bint! You'll never know where you are with that one, will you? It's demonstrable that she's superb as a pulse-keeper. There are far more squabbles and arguments in Linear G than while she was there. I could use a Tirla in all the big Linears. If Rhyssa doesn't mind . . .

Dorotea: *I mind!*

Boris: *Sorry, Dorotea, but Tirla's a Registered Talent and too damned vital to lay about until she's of age. But there's nothing that says she has to live at the Center while she's waiting for her eighteenth birthday to come around. If she'd be much happier in a Linear, she could live in one. With Lessud and his family in Island K? Go to school properly and still keep her ears and eyes open for the general well-being of the community. With the scam dried up in Jerhattan, Long Island is the next logical pool to fish in for illegal kids. We could use a reliable pulse-keeper like Tirla.*

"Did you get any of that, Tirla?" Sascha asked her, grinning. Sitting beside her, he could feel her concentrating on "listening," but her mind echoed nothing but the desire to hear.

She shook her head and gave a sad little sigh, with a look of apology to Dorotea, who had been trying so hard to train her.

"The Bro wants to know if you'd prefer to live in a Long Island Residential while you're waiting to grow up," Sascha explained.

"A Residential in Long Island?" Tirla became animated at once, sitting up in her bed, her big dark eyes glittering, a delicate tinge of color suffusing her cheeks, and a hopeful smile on her lips. "That'd be living in high style!"

EPILOGUE

Three months later.

Rhyssa?

The tone, apologetic but firm, roused Rhyssa from one of those intense sleeps where it is difficult to move the body even when the brain has become alert. She lay heavy in the bed and managed to open one eye to see the clock; then she heard the familiar sound of Dave singing softly to himself in the bathroom. Once again she had overslept. She really did not know what was the matter with her these past few weeks—she simply could not seem to get enough sleep.

Rhyssa! The tone was more urgent, and then recognition came.

Yes, Madlyn? What's the matter?

I didn't wake you, did I? I thought I had Earth times down pat.

I overslept. What's the matter?

It's her! Disgust, frustration, anger, and exasperation packed into that one pronoun forewarned Rhyssa. *She's at it again. Saying we Talents are not doing our job! We have only pulled her out of her midden and yet she has the gall to blame us for anything that goes wrong up here.*

What is it this time? Rhyssa hauled herself up against her pillows and reached for the coffee thermos—another elegant notion of Mr. Lehardt's, and so civilized. She started to pour herself a cup and then stopped. The smell of it turned her stomach.

There's one last very critical shipment due to come up, Madlyn went on, *only it hasn't because Johnny says he won't ship it yet.*

Won't ship it? That blew the last of sleep-fog from Rhyssa's mind. What was Colonel Greene up to now? *And naturally it's essential for her to complete the installation?*

Vital! It's got the last of the internal mechanisms and remotes. Very delicate stuff, I know, and not something you want bounced about. And there's only a week more before the completion date. Then we can all come down to earth! There was heartfelt relief in Madlyn's tone. *So we want to know why it's being held up. Because we are, too, you know.*

I know. I'll sort it out, Madlyn. Indeed, I will.

Dave was whistling louder now that he knew she was awake. He might not have been telepathic, but he displayed a keen sensitivity where she was concerned that more than made up for it in ways she could never have anticipated. She grinned to herself and then recalled the task at hand. Eight-thirty was not too early to rouse Colonel John Greene out of his Floridian sack.

Johnny boy, phone me! He was too far away to link telepathically with her, but her call would reach him easily enough. She looked at the phone, counting down. It rang in exactly ten seconds.

"You wished parlance with me, Madame Lehardt?"

"I do indeed, Colonel Greene. What hanky-panky are you pulling on poor dear Ludmilla?"

Johnny's chuckle was drenched in malice. "Only what she deserves, petal. She conscripted us Talents to be sure she finished on time, and finished on time she will be. Not one moment earlier, not one moment later. Why?"

"Oh, I see." Rhyssa chuckled. "And you have it timed to the final hour?"

"Lance and I worked out the time it would take to install those controls, and we've scheduled the kinetics needed. We know exactly how long it will take. Lance must have forgotten to clue Madlyn. I'm sorry she's getting hassled, but she's well able for it. Soothe her down, will you, Rhys? We're doing it our way!"

"Oh, I quite agree. Not an hour early and not an hour late."

As she hung up, Dave came in the room, a towel draped about his lean hips. "I did try to wake you, Rhys," he said with a rueful expression. "You just don't want to get up in the morning."

"I'm wanton enough to admit that I love being in bed with you, Dave, but preferably awake, not sleeping like the dead." She lifted her arms and began to stretch, then stopped. "And what's wrong with the coffee? The smell makes me nauseous."

Dave grinned as he sat down on the edge of the bed, looking at her. His blue eyes crinkled. "Figured it out yet?" he asked, glancing down at her abdomen.

"I thought—I mean, I haven't been ill," Rhyssa said, with dawning awareness, "just sleepy! Oh, Dave, could I really be pregnant?"

"Think about it a moment, O wise woman!" He got up, shedding his towel as he began to dress. She loved looking at him, no matter what he was doing, and the intimacy of this daily act was something special for her. "After all, I've been doing my best for several months now!"

Awed by the possibility, Rhyssa did start thinking about her body, placing her hands gently on her belly, intuiting the biofeedback.

"Oh, Dave, I am pregnant. I am!"

"I think you're the last one to have copped on, then," he replied, grinning broadly. "Dorotea knows."

"And she said nothing?" Rhyssa sat bolt upright again, startled and somewhat miffed that she had been left in the dark—and by Dorotea!

"Well, there's some things it's more fun to find out by yourself," he said, grinning as he stooped down to kiss her lovingly. "There's a sort of glow about you, too. Everyone's noticed. They've been politely waiting for an official announcement." He stroked her tangled hair, running fingers down her silver streak.

She sighed, then blurted out, "Does Sascha know?"

Dave stopped in the act of pulling on his tunic and ducked his head out of the folds to regard her with some alarm. "Sascha? I know you're close but—"

"Well . . ." Rhyssa paused. There was one of the few drawbacks to Dave's lack of Talent. Sometimes she had to explain with far more detail than a Talent would require. "Well, Sascha's got to wait, that's all, and he doesn't take waiting kindly."

"Wait?" Dave pulled the tunic down. "Wait for what?"

"For Tirla to grow up, of course," she said, gathering herself to rise from the bed. She felt oddly protective of the new life inside her, which was silly, since it was obviously well settled in.

"Tirla?" Dave's eyes nearly popped in astonishment. "He's gone on her? Dirty old man!"

"Not so old and certainly not dirty where Tirla is concerned. Bolt out of the blue on him, all right enough. He's never felt that way about any other female." Rhyssa permitted herself a little knowing smile. "But she's the one for him, and he knows it. He just has to wait a few years."

"That wight's not even—"

"Tirla is twelve now, going on two hundred," Rhyssa replied with some asperity. Tirla was a very interesting personality, and she and Sascha would deal very well together. It was incredible, really, to have found two such diverse Talents during her directorship: one macro who would shift worlds and one whose skill was a micro-Talent, eroding language barriers. "Neesters ripen a lot faster than we Northern and Occidental types. She'll be more than ready in four years to marry Sascha."

"And that's decided?" Dave was skeptical.

Rhyssa smiled. "Sascha precogged it—to his intense astonishment. Next time you see them together, notice how she looks at him. Quite proprietary that young lady is where Sascha is concerned. And she's better for him than Madlyn would ever be."

"And they'll have Talented kids?"

"That's a very high probability." Rhyssa smiled smugly.

Dave paused. In her presence he always allowed his emotions to show. He cleared his throat and asked briskly, "What about us? When will we know?"

To reassure the man she loved, Rhyssa smiled as she nodded. "No problem there."

"You sound so sure."

She put her arms around his neck, letting her gravid belly rest against him as she pulled his head down to kiss him. "I am. He just told me so."

ABOUT THE AUTHOR

Between her frequent appearances in the United States and England as a lecturer and guest-of-honor at science-fiction conventions, Anne McCaffrey lives at Dragonhold, in the hills of County Wicklow, Ireland, with assorted horses, cats, and a dog. Of herself, Ms. McCaffrey says: "I have green eyes, silver hair, and freckles—the rest changes without notice."